The Scorching Wind

Walter Macken, author and dramatist, died in April 1967 in his native Galway at the age of 51. At 17 he began writing plays and also joined the Galway Gaelic Theatre (now the celebrated Taibhdhearc) as an actor. In 1936 he married and moved to London for two years, returning to become actor-manager-director of the Gaelic Theatre for nine years, during which time he produced many successful translations of plays by Ibsen, Shaw, O'Casey, Capek and Shakespeare. To enable him to have more time for play writing, he moved to the Abbey Theatre in Dublin. Macken acted on the London stage, on Broadway and also took a leading part in the film of Brendan Behan's *The Quare Fellow*. Many of his plays have been published, and of his novels the first two, *I Am Alone* (1948) and *Rain on the Wind* (1949), were initially banned in Ireland. Several other novels followed, including *The Bogman*, which first appeared in 1952, and the historical trilogy on Ireland, *Seek the Fair Land*, *The Silent People* and *The Scorching Wind*. *Brown Lord of the Mountain* was published a month before his death.

WALTER MACKEN

The Scorching Wind

Pan Books in association with
Macmillan London

First published 1964 by Macmillan & Co Ltd
First published in paperback 1966 by Pan Books Ltd,
Cavaye Place, London SW10 9PG
This edition published 1988 by Pan Books Ltd,
in association with Macmillan London Ltd
9 8 7 6 5 4
© Walter Macken 1964
ISBN 0 330 30326 0
Set, printed and bound in Great Britain by
Cox & Wyman Ltd, Reading

HISTORICAL NOTE

After the Great Famine (1846), the spirit of nationhood was kept alive in Ireland by the Young Irelanders' abortive revolt in 1848, by the Fenian Rebellion in 1867, and by the Land League, which by 1909 succeeded in winning for thousands of tenants the ownership of their small farms.

Political affairs since the Union (1800) were handled by elected members of The Irish Parliamentary Party, who attended the British Parliament at Westminster. By 1906, when the Sinn Fein movement was founded with the aim 'that national freedom should be sought not in London but at home', these men were out of touch with the thinking of the young men in Ireland. Alarmed at the founding of the Irish Volunteers (1913) they forced their way into this organization and when the Great War broke out in 1914, on a vague promise of Home Rule after the conflict, they advised the Volunteers to join the British Army. A majority of the Volunteers did so, but a hard core stood fast and, led by dedicated men who believed the country could only be awakened from apathy by sacrifice, instigated and fought the Easter Rebellion of 1916.

The majority of the people were aroused by the deliberately spaced execution of fifteen of the leaders of the Rebellion and by the imprisonment in camps and jails of thousands of young men and women. The Irish Parliamentary Party was wiped out at the General Election of 1918, and Dáil Éireann in 1919, with most of its elected members in jail, established a National Government at the Mansion House in Dublin, and the fight for Independence continued.

The signing of the Treaty (1921) establishing the Free State brought the struggle to a close, but its terms, including Partition (dividing the country into Six Counties of the North and Twenty-six Counties of the South) led to a bitter split in the ranks of Sinn Fein. This split erupted into a state of civil war which persisted until 1923.

The scorching wind shall be the portion of their cup.
Psalm 10

1

THEY SAT with their backs against a haycock and looked out at the sea.

Dominic was chewing a wisp of hay. It tasted quite nice. He noticed that his brother's stretched legs were at least twelve inches longer than his own. He wondered if he would ever be as tall as his brother.

The sea was very calm. There were about twenty black-sailed pookauns making towards the fishing grounds near Gregory Sound. They were having a patient sail. Now and again their tarred canvas would bulge and they would advance a few yards. A small warship, spewing dirty black smoke from its two stacks, smudging the blue sky and making white water at the bow, was steaming scornfully and purposefully in towards the harbour at Galway. The Aran Islands were quite clear. He could see the way the cliffs fell steeply to the sea on the Big Island, and he could see the Cliffs of Moher across the bay, buttressing the hills.

He didn't like his knickerbockers or black stockings, or the polished black boots. He would be out of them soon. He thought of the many fights he had been involved in for the wearing of them.

'Nice to see the sailing ships,' his brother Dualta said.

'Yes,' said Dominic.

'Pity to leave them,' said Dualta, 'but we'll have to go. Trains won't wait.'

'Don't go at all,' said Dominic, suddenly feeling sad.

'Not you too,' said Dualta, heaving himself to his feet. 'Isn't it enough to have Father on my back?' He looked once more at the bay, crinkling his eyes against the glare of the July sun.

Dominic looked up at him. Dualta was tall, nearly six feet tall, and well built. He was fair-haired. Dominic was black. Dualta's father often wondered where he came from. All our

7

side were low men, he would say, and dark. It must be from your mother's side.

'I wonder when I will see all this again,' Dualta said, almost to himself.

Dominic got to his feet. He bit back what he was going to say; that he needn't go away from it all, at all. It was his own choice and a foolish one in Dominic's opinion, who was only seventeen to his brother's twenty, so kept his mouth shut. He followed his brother who jumped the stone wall into the lane. It was a narrow lane, very rutted, the flowering briars leaving hardly enough room to walk between them, and decorated with wisps of hay.

'Go and get Saili,' said Dualta.

Dominic plucked some fresh grass from the side of the wall and jumped over it into another field. The pony was grazing at the end of the field. She looked up when she saw Dominic approaching her.

'Come on,' said Dominic, 'nice grass.'

The pony snorted, tossed her head. She was fawn coloured with a grey tail and mane. She is going to thwart me, Dominic thought. 'Nice fresh grass,' he said again. She just started to race around the field. Dualta was leaning on the stones of the wall, laughing. Suddenly he pursed his lips and whistled. The pony stopped racing, looked, saw him and ran towards him. If she was a dog she would be wagging her tail, Dominic thought in disgust.

'You'll never learn how to catch a pony,' said Dualta. He was rubbing her face. She was nuzzling him. If she was a cat she would be purring, Dominic thought. He knocked a few stones and the pony went out. He threw them back again. Dualta was walking up the lane. The pony was walking by his side. Well, Dominic thought as he followed them, people like me better than animals do, I think.

They came to the main road. They waited while a motor car passed in a cloud of dust. Motor cars were so new that they were still curiosities. The hood of this was down. The man driving the car waved cheerfully at them. The car was bumping up and down as it hit the many pot-holes in the dirt

8

road. The man in the back, sitting upright, resting his hands on the handle of a stick, managed to retain his dignity, even if he was bobbing up and down on his seat like a rubber ball. He inclined his head at them. They nodded. He was a Lordeen from way in. On the other side of the road a barefooted woman in a red petticoat was coming from the village shop. She was carrying provisions in a flour sack over her shoulder. She stepped off the road as the car neared her, and as it passed she bent her knee.

Dominic felt his face burning. Why did she do a thing like that? This fellow was nothing to her. Why did she do a thing like that? Then he saw Dualta grinning at him.

'Don't be wild,' said Dualta, 'it takes a long time for the fear of centuries to vanish.'

'She needn't do it,' said Dominic. 'She owes him nothing. Not even courtesy.'

'God be with you, Sinéad,' Dualta shouted to her in Irish.

'With you both, too,' she shouted. 'The day is red hot. Are you leaving us again, I hear?'

'The birds have tongues,' he said.

She laughed shrilly. They were only yards from her, yet she was shouting as if they were the other side of the bay.

'I was with Poric's mother,' she shouted. 'She is settling the dust with her tears. He is off with Dualta below, they said, the son of the Master. So I know.'

They crossed the road.

'The young must travel,' he said.

'May God, and Mary and St Joseph and all the saints be with you in your dangers,' she said.

She called many more blessings after them. Dualta shouted 'You too,' back at her. In ten yards they turned into the gate beside the two-storey slated house.

'Harness the pony,' said Dualta. 'I'm in to the house to collect my things.' Dominic caught the pony by the forelock and led her around the house to the yard at the back. He saw Dualta standing there, biting the nail of his thumb and looking at the house, before he squared his shoulders and went in. Dominic delayed the harnessing of the pony. He had a

9

good excuse. She didn't want to be harnessed. He had a job getting the bit into her mouth, dodging her kicking legs as he tightened the bellyband and finally backing her into the light shafts of the trap. He had no further excuse for delay, so he threw her a gowleog of hay from the barn and went into the house by the back way.

Brid was in the scullery. She was peeling potatoes. She was crying. She was a young girl. Her hair was caught back with coloured slides. She was too fat for her age.

'What are you roaring for now?' he asked.

'Not,' she said. 'I was peeling onions before.'

He knew this was not true. She was fond of Dualta too. He went into the kitchen. His mother was sitting in the wooden chair in front of the fire. She was stitching buttons on a shirt. She looked up at him. She was a tall thin woman with white hair and deep-sunken eyes. Mostly there was a glint of humour in them.

'We won't need salt on the potatoes tonight,' said Dominic.

'Brid is not happy unless she has something to cry about,' his mother said.

It was a big open hearth fire with two stone seats one each side of it. Dominic sat into one of those. He kicked at the turf fire with his boot.

'You don't cry,' he said.

'Dualta is a restless boy,' she said. 'He has been away before, many times.'

'And back again,' said Dominic. 'He tried to be a teacher like my father; he tried to be a doctor. Why doesn't he settle on something?'

'Will you be different?' she asked. She was smiling at him as she bit off a thread with her still good teeth.

He laughed.

'I hope so,' he said.

They heard raised voices from the other room. They looked at one another.

'Maybe I better go back,' said Dominic. She left the decision to himself. So he sighed and rose and went towards the closed door. He didn't knock. He just raised the latch and went

10

in. It was a darkish room. There was a mahogany table his father used for his books and reports. There was a high-backed chair that he used. He was sitting up straight in this. Dominic knew he was angry because his short white beard was jutting and his cheeks were flushed. Dualta was standing. He was dwarfing his father. The muscles were tight at the sides of his jaws.

'It's nearly time to go,' said Dominic diffidently.

'You are betraying your people,' his father said as if he had not spoken. 'You are betraying seven hundred years of the blood of martyrs.' He hit the table with his fist. 'All those.' He was waving his hand at the pictures on the walls. They were all engravings of drawings or framed ballads. Wolfe Tone, Robert Emmet. Meagher of the Sword. Mitchell, Davis, Davitt; the place was like a museum.

'Has all the struggle of the centuries, our own sufferings with the Land League, the crucifixion of the Fenians, meant so little to you that you will join the army of our oppressors to uphold their Empire?'

Dualta was tight lipped. He spoke low. 'I am a Redmond Volunteer,' he said. 'I am going to fight to free a small nation so that we can win freedom for this small nation.'

'Delusions,' his father shouted at him. 'Here is the place to fight, not there. How am I to hold my head up again if you do this thing? How can I live with the shame of it? Redmond is a man who is betraying thousands of your young men to death with a delusion. Not even a carrot for donkeys, just a delusion. How can you be so blind? Has everything I told you over the years meant nothing at all to you? Would I have been better off trying to teach patriotism to the pigs?'

'Too much of it!' Dualta suddenly shouted. 'Too much of it. I'm sick of it! Sick of dead martyrs. It's in the past. It's gone. It's here and now, we want. Here and now. I'm sick of you raising the dead!' His voice had risen to a shout. He seemed to hear this and was appalled. Quickly, he said: 'I'm sorry, Father.'

His father's head dropped. His forehead was creased. Dominic noticed how the hair of his head was thinning. Of course his father was becoming an old man.

11

'It's time for us to go,' said Dominic.

Dualta went to speak, looked at his father's bent head and then said nothing. He went into the kitchen. His mother was putting the shirt into the tapestry bag.

'It's all ready now, Dualta,' she said. She was bending down, closing the lips of the bag. He got down with her.

'He feels bad with me, Mother,' he said. 'I cannot go back all those years with him. After all, this is 1915.'

'You don't know what we went through in Mayo in the old days of the Land League,' she said. 'You have no memory of them. They were days of great sufferings. But he is afraid for you. He is human too. He is just afraid for you.'

He stood up. 'Bring the trap around, Dominic,' he said.

Dominic left them. He stuffed a bag with hay and put it on the floor of the trap. Then he sat in, left the small door at the back swinging open and drove the pony around to the front. Dualta and his mother were at the front door.

'I believe my way is right,' Dualta was saying. 'Redmond is a good man. He said if we fight for them we will get Home Rule. I believe this. So am I wrong in doing what I believe is right?'

'Do what you believe is right,' she said. 'Write to us when you can.'

'I will,' he said. Then he threw the bag in on the hay and got into the trap and took the reins. He waited for a moment, but his father didn't appear, so he clucked at the pony, slapped the reins almost viciously on her rump so that she jumped, and then set off out of the gate at a fast rate and turned on to the road like a racehorse.

Dominic, even as he held on to the side of the trap, saw his father's face at the window of the room and he thought his father looked sad. Then the dust was rising and the wheels of the trap were leaping in the pot-holes. His brother's face was tight.

'Slow down,' Dominic shouted at him, 'or you'll make matchsticks of the wheels.'

His brother grinned suddenly and hauled on the bit. The pony fought the bit but slowed to a more sedate pace.

12

'He is a one-minded man,' said Dualta. 'He doesn't see that times have changed.'

'Times might change,' said Dominic, 'but if you have principles, they don't change. He has principles.'

'Did you do philosophy at school, then?' Dualta asked.

'No,' said Dominic.

'He makes it hard to love him,' said Dualta.

They saw Poric waiting for them half a mile away. He waved a hand at them. It was a long straight road here, running yards from the sea. They pulled up near him. Poric was very big. He was dressed in a navy-blue suit and brown boots. He had curly hair that was coming out from under his new cap.

'Anyone would think it was going to get married you were, Poric,' said Dualta, 'instead of where you are going.'

Poric laughed as he swung his straw trunk tied with a rope at their feet. He had big teeth and very clear sunburned skin. Dominic marvelled at the thickness of his wrists as he held the side of the trap to come in with them. He sat beside Dominic.

'I'd be saying it's safer where I'm going,' he said. They spoke in Irish. Poric's English wasn't very good yet, and embarrassment made him slow and diffident in the speaking of it. 'How did the Master see you off?' he asked. He was anxious about this, his forehead creased.

'How do you think?' Dualta asked.

Poric shook his head.

'He gave myself the rakes yesterday evening,' he said. 'He said nothing of you going off to their army.'

'What are you? An enemy of the people?' Dualta asked.

'More than that,' said Poric. 'He said: What do they call the places where policemen congregate in England? That set me back. What do they call them anyway, tell me?'

'Police stations,' said Dualta.

'Damme, that's it,' said Poric. 'I didn't know. What are they called here? he asked, then. Police barracks, he said. You see the difference: There are centuries of oppression between the meaning of these two words, Station and Barracks.

13

Policemen in this land are not policemen, they are a military force trained to shoot down their own people. You hear that, Dualta. I don't want to shoot down anyone.'

'What do you want?' Dualta asked.

'It's a good job,' said Poric. 'The money is good and at the end you get a pension. Aren't you keeping law and order? Maybe I'd have to quiet a drunken man with me fist if he was throwing rocks. I don't know. He made me feel small. I wanted his goodwill.'

Dominic took hold of Poric's fist which was clenched on his knee. It was a good strong fist, the size of a four-pound ham, he thought laughing. 'Don't hit anyone with that fist,' he said, 'or you'll knock him into eternity.'

They laughed.

Then Poric stood up and waved. They were passing a lane. It led to a row of thatched houses up among the rocks. Out here, they said if the rocks had straw on them they were houses. They could see the people standing in front of the whitewashed wall, man and woman and many young ones. The woman's red petticoat stood out startlingly against the white background.

'I wouldn't let them come to the road,' said Poric. 'They'd make a spectacle of me for all time.' He turned his back on them deliberately then, sat and pulled the peak on his cap down over his eyes and was silent. Dominic thought: That will hurt Dualta. Dualta's father wouldn't be waving farewell after him.

Later Poric said: 'Would you stop at the barracks in the street town? They will give me the travel ticket.'

'What made you desire to be a policeman?' Dominic asked.

Poric thought over it. 'The sergeant in here, I suppose. He said: You have the size for the police and you have the education. I got that from the Master. They didn't care one way or the other at home, but it would be respectable. My eldest brother Sean is there for the landwork and the boat fishing. I don't know. Maybe it will be nice to be a policeman. I don't know. I wish the Master respected my choosing.'

'Did you expect him to?' asked Dualta.

'It didn't trouble me to think,' said Poric. 'All his talk

about the great patriots and that. It all seemed like stories from books. And singing the ballads. My soul, but I didn't think it was real with him.'

'There are only a few of them left,' said Dualta grimly.

They came down the hill and crossed the bridge into the small town. There was no great activity. Mostly people were working in the fields. They stopped near the police barracks. 'I'll put no great delay on you,' said Poric and went down there.

'Don't waste your time in the University,' said Dualta.

'Oh-ho,' said Dominic.

'It's because I did, I'm telling you,' said Dualta. 'Don't imitate me. If they gave degrees for playing cards I would have earned a first-class honours.'

'Are you doing what you want now?' Dominic asked.

'I think so,' said Dualta. 'Ever since we were doing those things in the Volunteers, drilling and such. It appealed to me. So being a soldier will appeal to me.'

'Even a military funeral?' Dominic asked.

'Don't be an old woman,' said Dualta.

They watched Poric come out of the barracks with the sergeant. The sergeant was nearly as tall as Poric. He held himself well. He filled his black uniform. His boots were shining. He wore a moustache with the points of it waxed. He had thick eyebrows which slanted up, making him look like the devil, so the people called him Sergeant Nick. He had small eyes which always seemed to be darting here and there. People didn't love him much. He was too efficient. He came close, put his hand on the side of the trap. There was a thick growth of dark hair on the back of it, Dominic noticed.

'I was saying that I didn't like Patrick travelling with disaffected persons,' he said. He had a harsh sort of voice. He laughed to show this was meant to be humour. 'Your father is still an old Fenian,' he said. They didn't answer him. 'I hear you are joining the colours, Dualta,' he said then.

'I might change my mind,' said Dualta.

'Don't,' he said, 'or someone might give you a white feather.'

'They'd get it back where they wouldn't like it,' said Dualta. 'Right, Poric? Hup, Saili.' The pony took off at once. They left the dust of the road enveloping the sergeant. He stood there looking after them.

'That fellow puts the hair up on the back of my neck,' said Dualta.

'There are worse men,' said Poric doubtfully.

'Hear Poric,' said Dualta laughing. 'He hasn't met a hundred people in his life and he knows the best from the worst. If they ever put you under a one like that he'll make you jump.'

Dominic knew that they weren't an hour from the town now and his heart began to sink.

Dualta had been away before and he had come back. Dominic had been away for five years at a secondary school and he had come back. But Dualta was always there somewhere, sometime. They didn't know much about this war in France. The papers mainly seemed to be full of lists of dead ones. Dominic didn't like to think of Dualta dead. They didn't talk.

They drove through the town slowly. It was fairly filled. There were soldiers in khaki walking the streets, drab ones and Lancers with white strings on them and bandoleers, some of them standing and laughing with linked girls in front of shop windows. It was slow work getting through the horse drays and the horse carts, an occasional Crossley army lorry, or a motor car with officers in it, honking furiously while policemen tried to make the people concede a way for them.

In the open of the Square they saw that a platform was being erected for a recruiting meeting. It was draped with the colours of the Empire, and men were still hammering at it. They got past this and turned right up towards the station. The entrance to the station was so jammed with traffic and people that Dualta said: 'We'll stop here and walk the rest.' He drove the trap to an opening beside a house. 'Now,' he said, 'we go and you go home, Dominic.'

'I'll go with you to the train,' said Dominic.

'What for?' Dualta asked. 'What the hell good will it do? Aren't there enough people for that?'

16

Dominic could see this for himself. Men were moving towards the station with women and children around them. They were all bawling. Young soldiers walked silently with white-faced girls holding to their arms. He tried to imagine what it would be like in the long length of the train.

'Goodbye,' Dualta was saying, holding out his hand.

Dominic took it. Dualta's face was very stern.

'When you get my address,' said Dualta, 'you will write and tell me how things are going at home. Don't forget.'

'I won't forget,' said Dominic.

'Come, Poric,' said Dualta and started to shoulder his way towards the station.

'My blessings on you, Dominic,' said Poric, nearly kittling him with a blow on the shoulder, and then he followed Dualta.

Dominic stood for a few moments holding the reins in his hands. He tried to stop tears in his eyes by clenching his jaws until sweat broke out on his forehead. The leather of the straps hurt his hands as they bit into his palms. He won that way. He decided not to go for home yet. He led the pony up this street where they were wont to buy their provisions and he tied her in the yard here and threw her the hay from the sack. Then he set out to walk and kill the flood of loneliness, at least until he heard the train whistle.

2

WHEN DOMINIC reached the Square, he saw that it was filling. The platform, a solid business raised on porter barrels with a handrail around it, looked very efficient. In the distance he could hear the army band approaching. They had marched through the town and were marching back again, hoping a battalion of recruits would follow the flag and the spine-tingling sound of the brass and the drums.

Farther to the right, near the Bohermore, he saw a smaller crowd. He went towards it. There a man was standing on a

17

horse cart. Below him there stood four men, dressed in Volunteer uniforms of green. He was speaking in low tones. There were few people around him, a lot of children, and more policemen than spectators. The big sergeant with the moustache was writing in a notebook.

This man was slender and was fair-haired. Sometimes the hair was blown over his forehead and he swept it back with an impatient gesture. He had thin lips and his eyes were gleaming.

'You don't die for an empire,' this man was saying. 'You live for your country. Does a man go and put out the fire in a neighbour's house, when his own house is smouldering? Does he go to put food in the mouth of starving ones, when the bellies of his own children are slack?'

'Go and join the army if it's fighting you want,' a woman shouted. She was a woman with a shawl. She had a few drinks taken.

'God help those who help themselves,' the man said. 'How can you pretend to be fighting to raise a small nation from the heel of an oppressor if your own neck is under a boot?'

The sergeant spoke.

'I'm warning you,' he said. 'Don't go over the limits.'

'That is the freedom of speech we possess,' the man said. 'I say to you: Love your country. Is that treason? I say to you: Die for your country. Is that treason? I say to you buy the products of your own country, not bellybacon from America, matches from England, cloth from Birmingham. Is that treason? I say to you buy what we can make, to keep your own people at work and in jobs so that they don't have to die in mud like pigs. Is that treason?'

'Yes, it is treason,' said the sergeant, putting his notebook in his pocket. 'You have said enough now. This meeting is over.'

He signalled with his hand to the other five policemen. They started to move towards the man on the cart. The four young men in uniform who were hatless came forward to meet them. They had no arms.

'No,' the man on the cart said. 'We will obey you. I know

18

how dearly you would love to use batons. Did you ever stop to think that you are Irishmen?'

'Move on now, move on now,' said the sergeant, 'if you don't want to end up down in the jail.'

'Attention,' the man said in Irish. 'Oghlaigh. By the left, quick march.' He came down from the cart and got to the head of his little column. They marched up the Bohermore. Dominic knew the Sinn Fein Club was somewhere up there. The people looking on whistled derisively. There was something very pathetic about the five marching men, something forlorn, like boys playing at soldiers. He knew they were the remnants of the great Irish Volunteer Movement. When the Great War came there was a split in the ranks, and Redmond siphoned off the vast majority of the Volunteers and pledged them to fight for the freedom of a little nation called Belgium. Very few people knew where it was. The five marching men were the tatters that remained of the Volunteers who opposed Redmond. They called themselves Sinn Fein.

He was brought to himself when knuckles rapped quite hardly against his head.

'Here,' a policeman said to him, 'get away from here. This is no place for you. Do you want to become disaffected.'

Dominic felt his face go pale and then red, he supposed. It was all he could do not to hit the red-haired policeman, even though he was twice his size. Then he wanted to spit in his face. He did neither of these things. Just looked murder at him. The policeman put a large hand on his shoulder and pushed and Dominic staggered. 'Off with you now! Off with you!' he said, and then turned away. This was most hurtful to Dominic. That I am only worth knuckles on the head and a push, he thought. He looked at the broad back of the retreating policeman.

'If you had a gun now, would you shoot him?' a voice asked. 'Right in the middle of that broad, bullocky back? Eh?'

Dominic blushed. This young man stood beside him. He was grinning. He was a thin sandy-haired man, deceptively young-looking Dominic now saw. He had deep, sunken eyes. His cheekbones were broad, almost Asiatic. His nose was thin, like his lips, and as he smiled now, Dominic saw he had small teeth, the sort that sloped inwards. He was ashamed that this stranger had seen the naked look on his face. He felt as if he had been seen without some of his clothing.

'I don't suppose you would,' this young-old man said. 'You know that's what's wrong with us,' he went on. 'None of us wants to shoot a policeman.'

'Why would we shoot a policeman?' Dominic asked cautiously.

'I don't know,' he said. 'Just for fun, say, like you would shoot rats. Have you ever shot a rat?'

'Yes,' said Dominic, seeing the body of a running rat he had got, flying fifty feet in the air after getting the full blast from the shotgun.

'What's the difference?' the man asked.

Dominic laughed, imagining the big body of the red-haired policeman flying through the air.

'There's a little,' he said.

'That's the trouble,' the man said. 'You are not from our town?'

'No,' said Dominic, 'I'm from way out. You are a man of the town?'

'Yes,' the other said. 'Call me Sam Browne. I don't know if that's my name or not, but it's short and simple and it sounds good. Have you come to join up and save all those pretty Belgian girls from being raped by the Germans?'

Dominic was a bit shocked. Then he saw the man was trying to shock him, watching his reaction, smiling.

'No,' he said. 'I was seeing my brother away. He joined.'

'One of Redmond's people, eh?' he asked.

'He thinks Redmond is right,' said Dominic.

'Poor fellow,' Sam said. 'So do thousands of others. It's terrible when you think of those Germans killing all those Belgian babies and boiling them down for gun-grease.'

'What are you up to?' Dominic asked.

'Nothing,' said Sam. 'I'm just sad about the babies.'

'Nobody believes that about the babies,' said Dominic.

'Oh, some people do,' said Sam. 'Thousands of noble Irishmen have gone out to battle for those babies. They are the most valuable recruiting babies that were ever invented. You watch it or they'll get you too.'

He had to shout now. The band had come from the narrow street into the Square. It was a grand brass band. The drummer wore a leopard skin over his uniform. He was a tall man and he was sweating, but he was a flamboyant drummer. The band was followed by the Lancers on horseback. They looked very well; the horses were groomed and their coats shone in the sun. Behind the Lancers there were soldiers marching. They were very neat. Then came guns on carriages pulled by six mettlesome horses. It made a brave show. The parade was followed by hundreds of children, shouting and screaming. Dominic felt the tingle running up and down his spine.

'They could do with those guns in France instead of here,' Sam shouted into his ear. 'I didn't hear your name.'

'Dominic,' Dominic shouted, trying hard to keep the glitter out of his eyes, wondering at himself, at the sort of feeling bands and soldiers and banners waving could arouse in him.

The Square was well filled now. There were pictures tied to the railings of the place, posters of Germans with the faces of monsters; Germans behind bayonets, or machine guns, straddling burning churches; leering Uhlans bending from their racing horses to lance children, and in front of the platform there was a great banner with letters two foot high beseeching:

GOD SAVE IRELAND FROM THE HUNS.

The platform was filling up with well-dressed gentlemen with whiskers and high collars, and army officers, and long-dressed ladies in flowered hats, and suddenly Dominic found himself hemmed in from all sides and pressed by the multitude of people. They were separated from the platform by the soldiers who stood all around it in two ranks. The band had wheeled smartly and its martial air came to an end with a great flourish and a tremendous bang-bang on the big drum. And the people there cheered and called shrilly and hand-clapped loudly, and an army man came to the front and held up his hand and said: 'Citizens!'

'God bless you, General,' a lady called shrilly, and everyone hurrooed, although even Dominic, who knew nothing about such things, could see that the officer wasn't a general.

He got some silence, and he said: 'Mister . . . (Dominic couldn't distinguish his name) will address you. He . . .' The rest was lost in cheers and shouting, so the army man retired and a black-suited tall man with a moustache, and side hair brushed over a bald spot, came to the front, and grasped the rail with practised hands and shouted: 'Ladies and gentlemen, but more particularly young men of this patriotic city, I come to address you here on behalf of our great Leader: John Redmond!'

This was the signal for renewed cheering, and shrill cries of the shawled women: 'God bless him! God bless him!'

'If blessings were negotiable,' said Sam in Dominic's ear, 'he would have been canonized years ago.'

'I could talk to you today,' the man said, 'about many things. But there is nothing that speaks louder than example and nothing more true than the sight of reality.' This didn't get a cheer. People boggled at it. Dominic heard Sam chuckling.

'Too many syllables,' he said to Dominic.

'You know, by rumour and report, that this city in its great generosity has opened its gates and arms in a warm-hearted gesture to some of the stricken citizens of that little land, bowed under a load of hate and terror, crying out to the world for the succour that all free men are bound in conscience to give with all they possess. Ladies and gentlemen, I refer to that noble little land of Belgium.'

They answered this one with great cries, and groans and cheers.

'I will not refer to the delicate matter of the religious ladies who are in our midst, so unspeakably treated by those monsters of iniquity; not to cloak their shame, of which they are not guilty. Who is guilty? I will tell you who is guilty. The Nero of Europe, the unspeakable Emperor of the Germans, who loosed his barbarian Huns on a defenceless and peace-loving people.'

22

'That ought to rouse them,' said Sam, just before the thousands of people broke into a roar of hate. A forest of fists seemed to be raised in the air and shaken at the terrible-faced Emperor of the Germans who glared at them from a poster, his helmet gleaming menacingly.

'There is here on this platform,' he went on, 'a citizen of Belgium, who, because he has suffered under this awfulness, can tell you more about it than I; who in his person can be a witness of the terrible things, which you and I, and every citizen of Ireland capable of shedding a tear, must stop with our blood and our very lives.'

'Hear! Hear!' they called, and 'Long Life to You!'

'There'll be none of his blood let,' said Sam. 'He's over the age limit.'

'I will say no more,' said the platform speaker, 'just introduce to you this man.' He turned and went back and came to the front again holding this thin frail-looking gentleman by the arm. He looked a bit bewildered. He had gentle features. His hair was white. He wore a small beard.

He was greeted with the silence of sympathy, and he spoke into this silence.

'Decent people of this town,' he said, slowly and haltingly.

'Ah, the poor man hasn't the English,' a lady said in what she thought was a whisper, but that came out of this silence almost like a shout.

'No, the English well, I do not have,' he said, 'but I have the tongue. You are being what you call, deceived. Out there, those ones that are dressed in the habits of nuns, and that are pregnant, I tell you now, this I say, two are not nuns. You hear this. I tell you. One, she is a prostitute of France, and the other she is of the Belgians, but not good no. I tell you this, she is not what you call ten-shilling prostitute. She would be a two-penny prostitute – of Belgium, but trash, a slut. I tell you. Do not be deceived. Facts are true. This indecency is not necessary. We do not need this. You hear? What I say is true, true, true. No need for lies. No need for lies.'

His face was very pale with red rising in his cheekbones. His eyes were flashing with anger.

There was a terrible silence in the Square, as if everybody had suddenly died.

Two army men came from the back and took the old gentleman by the arms, as if he were a dying lunatic. They had to force him away from the railing. One of them had to unclench his hands from it, and as they went back with him he kept calling out: 'Is true. Do not be deceived!'

That was all Dominic saw or heard. He was pushing his way through the crowds almost in a panic. He could see Dualta, tall fair-haired Dualta, riding a train into a nightmare.

It was easy enough to get through the tightly packed people. They were shocked. They didn't resist his pressure. He broke free of them on the far side of the Square and ran towards the railway station. Just let me be in time, he was thinking, just let me be in time. When Dualta hears this, he will know and he will not go. Something wrong. Something wrong. Can I persuade Dualta? Dualta will listen to me, he said, through clenched teeth. Dualta will listen to me. What have we to do with things like this? What have we to do with things like this?

His heart sank as he met people coming away from the station, some of them with red eyes.

They couldn't wait to say goodbye, he thought, that's what was wrong. They couldn't wait to say goodbye.

He ran up the stone steps and into the station. A man in a uniform tried to stop his passage, but he broke through and stood on the platform and watched the end of the train. He ran along the platform. He even shouted: 'Dualta! Dualta!' but it was no good. The train pulled away and his shout was echoing against the lofty smoke-begrimed panes of the roof.

He was breathing heavily. His hands were clenched.

'He wouldn't have listened anyhow,' said the voice of Sam beside him.

'Leave me alone,' said Dominic. 'You just leave me alone.'

He turned and walked away from him.

'I'll see you again,' he heard Sam calling after him. 'He wouldn't listen anyhow.'

'He wouldn't listen anyhow,' the echo came after him. He thought of getting out the horse and the trap and the long trip home. It would be dark, and his father and mother would be sitting one each side of the fire, and he would have to talk to them and what would he say? You were right, my dear father, Dualta is riding the wrong dream. I don't know why, but if he dies he'll be dying for a Belgian prostitute. Nothing more noble? Oh, nothing more noble, my dear father.

And his father would be terribly sad.

Dominic rubbed his sleeve across his eyes and went down the steps of the station, and from the Square he could hear the band playing a lively tune.

3

DOMINIC LOOKED at his cards. They were useless, so he threw in his hand and leaned back in the chair to watch the others. The room was thick with cigarette-smoke. His own mouth was burned from smoking. Even if he had got good cards, he reflected, he wouldn't have had the money to play them.

The other five students at the table put on their poker faces as they looked at the cards. The actors among them looked very pleased as they asked for one or two. Poker didn't really excite him, but it was a way of passing the hours until it was time to go home to the digs and bed. He thought that young people could never sit in a chair in comfort. They had to be straddling the chair, or half-sitting in it with an arm embracing the back of it, or leaning back like himself, with his thumbs in the band of his trousers, balancing the chair precariously on its two back legs. He thought that the chair didn't have much more life in it. He could waggle it as well as balancing on it. He didn't like Saturday night.

He was facing the door when it opened and this tall fellow came in. He was a handsome one with darting eyes, broad shoulders and tawny-coloured hair. He looked around the crowded room. Dominic thought a look of distaste came over his face. This room in the College Club was like something out of Dante where the first-years or Gibs went through their period of delinquency, sharing their misspent lives with the chronics who never got out of first year until they had exhausted their fathers' purses; condemned for ever and ever to playing poker and billiards and borrowing the price of a cigarette or a pint of porter.

He was smiling at this thought, lazily, when he saw the eyes of the man at the door holding his own. This one was known as Lowry. Dominic didn't know if this was his surname or his Christian name, or just a nickname. Nearly everyone had a nickname. Lowry wasn't the type for the condemned cell in the Club. He was the sort of hero type, Dominic's mind sneered, who effortlessly won races at athletic meetings, threw weights around as if they were feathers, jumped as high as a horse, had all the girls fainting with admiration, and yet who was responsible for many of the Rags that so annoyed the citizens. Trouble was he shouldn't be here looking into Dominic's eyes now, and beckoning him, yes, beckoning him imperiously, to come outside, because senior students rarely consorted with the Gibs. It wasn't considered good form, sort of lesser vermin.

So Dominic pointed to his chest, and soundlessly in amazement formed the word Me with his lips, and the big fellow nodded and just went out, leaving the door open after him. There's an imperious gesture for you, thought Dominic, wondering if he would just leave it like that, but secretly flattered that he had been even beckoned to like this. Still, a man has his pride.

'You better go,' said one of the students at the table who had been watching, 'God has called.'

The rest of them laughed. This annoyed Dominic, so he got up immediately and walked towards the door. The chair fell on the floor behind him. Nobody picked it up.

'Forgive us our trespasses,' said one in a loud voice after him.

He closed the door.

There was no sign of Lowry outside the room, so he went

26

outside the building. He wasn't there either. It was getting dark. It was March and it was cold. Then he looked towards the gateway and saw that Lowry was standing there. He went towards him. Lowry was illuminated faintly by a poor street lamp outside on the roadway. He was looking up at the twenty-foot high walls of the County Jail right opposite.

Dominic pulled the collar of his coat round his neck and stood beside him wordlessly. Lowry was leaning against the arch, one hand on his hip.

'You know most of the citizens of this town think that the positions should be reversed,' he said.

'How?' Dominic asked.

'They think that the inmates of the jail should be in the Club, and the inmates of the Club behind the walls.'

'Maybe they have reason,' said Dominic, thinking of the many forays, hundreds of doorknobs removed from doors, and knockers, and citizens' clothes ruined with bags of flour, and many citizens in pubs, over the weight, who had to defend their powers against younger opponents.

Lowry grunted.

'Many men were in there over the years,' he said, 'who should never have been there. Many died in there who should never have died.'

'You mean it would be better for first-years to die in there?' Dominic asked.

'I served Mass in there,' said Lowry. 'I used to pass notes to the Castlegar men who were in there for the land troubles. Your father was a good man.'

'What do you know about my father?' Dominic asked.

'Come on, walk,' said Lowry, turning right and striding off. Dominic hesitated, and then followed him. They crossed a river bridge and then headed towards the bridge over the canal.

'I know of him well,' said Lowry. 'So do many more. Does your life consist of nothing more than playing poker, sitting around in a room like a zombie?'

'I also cut up frogs,' said Dominic. 'I draw nice pictures of flowers. Ask me something about chemistry.'

27

'What does your country mean to you?' Lowry asked. 'You are not stupid.'

'What proof have you?' asked Dominic facetiously, because he was annoyed.

'Time is running out,' said Lowry. 'Do you know Sam Browne?'

Dominic thought of Sam Browne.

'I know Sam Browne,' he said bitterly.

'Sam Browne likes you,' said Lowry. 'Wake up. The time is getting short.'

'The time for what?' Dominic asked.

'The time for doing,' said Lowry. They were walking now over the canal bridge. The water looked black and smooth, like velvet.

'There's a big meeting tonight. Have you heard of it?'

'Something,' said Dominic.

'Don't you even read posters?' Lowry asked.

'No,' said Dominic.

'A big meeting,' said Lowry. 'A few of us are going to applaud. We want you to join us.'

'Applaud a recruiting meeting?' Dominic asked.

'That's right,' said Lowry. 'Appropriately. Sam Browne said you wouldn't like recruiting meetings. I don't know enough about you. He suggested you. So make up your mind. Now. Go or stay. It's all one to me.'

'Do you treat everybody as if they were dirt?' Dominic asked.

Lowry stopped. They were near the entrance to the University.

'I didn't mean it to sound like that. I do not. I'm impatient perhaps with people who waste time. Time is a precious thing. It's going now, tick-tick-tick, like that, and there is so much to do and few of us live to be eighty.'

'Right,' said Dominic. 'I will applaud with you.'

'Good man,' said Lowry, suddenly smiling. His whole face seemed to light up with the smile. He clapped Dominic on the shoulder. 'Let us run. The others will be waiting.'

Dominic let him run and then followed him into the gate-

28

way, and increased his pace on the wide drive towards where there was a body of young men clustered under a feeble light near the archway. He could recognize some of them. They were in different faculties to his own, just nodding acquaintances, superior nods if they were a year or so ahead, sympathetic if they were not. And he wondered all the time why Lowry had come after him in particular.

'We are ready now,' Lowry was saying. He handed Dominic an old tattered raincoat. 'Put that on, you'll need it,' he said. 'You'll find a glass phial in the pocket. Don't do anything with it until you are told. Right, lads, off we go.' He himself took hold of a broomstick with the College colours tied to it and they set off towards the main gate. They were laughing. They were a very tattered-looking crew, Dominic thought. Students didn't dress very well anyhow. Lots of times their Sunday suits were resting temporarily on the shelves of the pawnshop, but all these ones looked as if they had dispossessed all the tramps in the town. They started singing a marching song:

'Sound the bugle, sound the drum!
Give three cheers for Kruger!
To hell with the queen and the old tambourine,
And Hurrah for Kruger's Army!'

Lowry came back to them.

'Please! Please, fellows,' he said. 'Think of the cause we are here to applaud.'

'Hurrah,' they shouted. There were two dustbin lids which they proceeded to pound as they came out of the gates. They beat them with hurley sticks. Some of them had penny whistles. Some of them had jew's-harps which were surprisingly audible and some of them played on pocket combs. The rest of them sang, hardly in harmony:

'Keep the home fires burning
While your hearts are yearning,
Turn the dark clouds inside out
Till the boys come home.'

'That's better! That's better,' Lowry shouted his approval and as two policemen stood on the road and watched them passing he shouted: 'Three cheers for the Royal Irish Constabulary. Hip-hip!' and they applauded the two policemen right heartily. This didn't seem to reduce the Royal Irish Constabulary to tears, Dominic noticed, because they turned and thoughtfully followed after the marching students.

Once they got around the jail walls and on to the Weir Bridge they got caught up with a great number of people who were making their way to the Town Hall. Lowry would turn and shout: 'Three cheers for the noble Lancers! Three cheers for the Fighting Fusiliers!' whenever he saw one of these soldiers among the crowd.

They broke their way into the Town Hall square with the sheer noise of themselves. The place was crowded. There were two columns of Redmond Volunteers drawn up, with Garibaldi rifles at the slope. They held the people back from the steps of the entrance to the Town Hall where the distinguished visitors would enter. Many police held back the crowds at the other street entrances. The students following Lowry made their way to the far side where they could climb the stairs to the balcony of the hall. Halfway along here there was a woman speaking. She was held up on the shoulders of two men. She was saying: 'Don't send your sons to fight for them! Don't let them go with them! Keep them here, I tell you, because the fight will be at home. Three months is all they last in the mud of Flanders. Three months and they are part of the muck; Irish blood and guts fertilizing the fields of a foreign land.' She was dressed in a green uniform, a long green skirt and tunic with a Sam Browne belt, and a hat caught up at the side with a badge.

About eight policemen converged on her. There was scuffling. He saw her hat being knocked off, the hairpins falling from her long hair. Brown hair she had and it almost enveloped her. The hands caught at her. She kept talking and a large hand was clapped over her mouth.

'Shame! Shame! Shame!' the students shouted. 'Three cheers for the Cumann na mBan!'

'No! No!' Lowry was back shouting at them. 'Away with the woman! Three cheers for the Royal Irish Constabulary. Cheer, ye misbegotten sons, or they'll never let us in.'

30

So they cheered heartily for the police.

Dominic could see the straining people laughing. Them bloody students, he heard people say. Always up to their tricks. He noticed a face. It was the face of Sergeant Nick. Sergeant Nick was looking closely at the faces of the students. Dominic tried to avoid his eyes, but couldn't. He saw the recognition dawning so he shouted louder than any of them for the Royal Irish Constabulary, and then as they turned towards the back parts of the hall he saw his father in the held-up traffic, sitting in the trap with his mother. He was sitting there calmly holding the reins of the pony, who was quiet, as if she was used to these things. And his father saw Dominic. He was smoking his pipe and in astonishment he took the pipe out of his mouth. He caught a quick glance at his mother. He thought her face was sad and that her eyes were red. Maybe he was mistaken. The light was very poor.

Then they were in the hall climbing up the stairs. Here he saw another face he knew. That was Sam Browne, an idle spectator, who nodded at Lowry as he passed. He was looking closely for someone. When he met Dominic's eyes he nodded expansively, like a hypocritical stage parson. He had acquired glasses now, wobbly ones on wire frames, and he was wearing a large cap.

They pushed their way up the stairs, and forced their way through the people and right down to the front of the gallery. Here they banged their dustbin lids, and sang College songs and hurrooed and cheered. All the people in the body of the hall below turned their faces up to them, either laughing at their antics or frowning heavily. The stage was draped with the usual banners and flags; the chairs set, and the table with the jug of water on it.

The audience consisted of the respectable people of the town, the many shopkeepers and traders who drew most of their living from the barracks on the hill since it was a garrison town. They had their wives and daughters with them. Some of the daughters were known to the students, who shouted their names and the girls blushed and when their fathers weren't looking discreetly waved back at them.

Then the trumpets sounded from outside and the swelling

cheers of the onlookers. You didn't have to be out there to
see the cars coming down carrying the Government Officials
from Dublin Castle and the politicians and the big brass. They
could trace them down the street and stopping, and, as a
cinematograph light from behind them brought the dark stage
into a white glare, they all stepped into it and took their places
in front of the chairs. The decent people in the body of the hall
got to their feet and clapped and clapped and the students
clapped and roared and banged their dustbin lids and just then
all the lights in the place went out and, as he had been in-
structed, Dominic reached in his pocket and got out the phial
and flung it in the darkness towards the stage, and then turned
and pushed his way towards the exit. He had marked his
passage before the light went out, where the bunched people
were thin. He thought he would be out in time, but he had
hardly gone four paces before he was enveloped in the most
appalling stench ever concocted by man. It was a choking
stink. It was a combination of all the most vile and terrible
smells that it was possible to devise in a chemist's laboratory.
Choking, he thought of all the nice girls down there. Such a
shame. Now he knew the reason for the old clothes. This
stink would stay, he knew. Clothes would never be the same
again after it. Whoever wore the clothes would smell for ever
like out-offices. It was a terrible plan, but it was successful.
There would never again be a recruiting meeting held in a
hall in the town, from which the authorities thought hecklers
and disaffected people could be excluded.

All he was interested in then was to get to the fresh air. He
heard screams and shouts coming from behind him, and had
reached the air, when the lights went on again. He came out
of the place coughing, feeling like retching. So what must the
people of the stage feel like.

'Get away! Get away!' he heard Lowry saying. 'Let you
all get out of sight for a week.'

And the face of Sam Browne loomed in front of him. Sam
had to bend down to him. Sam didn't smell at all, Dominic
thought. Sam had been wise enough to get out before the
bombs exploded.

'Now you see,' said Sam. 'That makes up for the Belgian.'

'I see nothing,' said Dominic. 'I see nothing.'

'You will,' said Sam. 'You will,' and he was gone and Dominic was running towards his digs.

They weren't far. Up by the market-place and into a street of a row of two-storey houses. He opened the letterbox and reached for the string of the key, pulled it up and inserted it and opened the door and closed it quickly behind him, and stood there looking at his father and mother.

They were sitting at the kitchen table, just sitting, with the lady of the house turning from the range where the kettle was boiling.

'What's that awful smell, Dominic?' his father asked.

Dominic didn't answer. He shed the old coat and ran with it to the back door and heaved it into the yard. Then he stood and sniffed. He didn't smell quite as bad, he thought. Then the face of his mother came into his mind and he turned and looked at her. The kitchen was lighted by two gas brackets with coloured globes jutting from the bricked walls each side of the range, but even in that poor light he could see that his mother was very pale.

'What's wrong?' he asked.

'It's Dualta,' she said. 'We got word. He is missing.'

Her head dropped in her hands. Dominic got on his knees before her and pulled one hand from her face and said, 'It will be all right, I tell you. It will be all right. I feel nothing.' Although he knew he felt as if he had been kicked in the heart.

4

EASTER TUESDAY there was no postman.

This was a sensational occurrence. Dominic's mother was always watching the postman now. She had heard that Dualta was missing, that was, officially, but she also knew from other people that the captain of the company or the chaplain or someone always sat down and painfully composed a scrawl. This was what she was waiting for.

Dominic kept away from the house as much as he could. His father had developed a cold and stayed in bed surrounded by books and hot drinks mainly composed of heated potheen. It was reputed to hunt the germs of a cold in short order, probably burning them to death, Dominic thought; one time it had been forced on himself.

When the postman didn't call on Tuesday he went to the post-office shop to find out the reason.

Nobody could get in or out of the town, he was told. There were no trains, no mail, nothing allowed in or out on account of the rebellion in Dublin. Who? He didn't know. Some young blackguards. They said there was something moving in the county too. Police and military were piling into the town. Didn't he see all the warships puffing into the bay, making white water?

He told this to his father. It nearly cured his father's cold. It couldn't be true, his father said. Tackle the pony and go and see for yourself.

So he tackled the pony and only got two miles when he was turned back by armed policemen, strangers, who searched the trap and himself, asked his name, what was his business, where did he think he was going, and when asked 'What's up?' told him to mind his own business, turn the pony and go back to hell from where he came from. He did so. A rising in Dublin, his father said, just could not be. Who was there among the young men who would have the courage to rise now? Wasn't the patriotism burned out of the lot of them? Well, there's something up, Dominic told him. There are no trains. There are no letters. The shopman below cannot get supplies. Have you ever known this to happen before? No, his father admitted, but it was something to do with the war. All the red-blooded young men of Ireland were spilling it in France under the Union Jack. What about the Sinn Fein Volunteers? Them, said his father. Wet wind most of them. All they were good for was throwing stink bombs in public buildings. He said this looking over his glasses at Dominic. Then he settled back to his book.

Dominic wasn't so sure. He remembered Lowry. He seemed to have an air of dedication about him, and sureness. It wasn't just talk with him. If it wasn't for the Easter vacation, Dominic would have been in there and would know.

One night as they sat with their back to Moran's gable-end, they heard the sound of the ships in the bay and saw the flash of a searchlight sweeping the coast. It brought them all to their feet in amazement. The searchlight played along the rugged coast for nearly an hour as the cruiser worked up and down the bay.

'My soul, but they'll ruin the potheen business, if they keep lighting the land like that all night,' said Peter O'Flaherty.

They laughed. But it was a strange business. One said he had heard a German boat was to land arms at Spiddal. This was scoffed at. Who was there who knew one end of a gun from the other except soldiers?

Finally the searchlight went out, and they could barely see the outline of the cruiser making its way back towards the town. Later, they heard the crump of a ship's gun firing a few rounds. It was distant. They could recognize this sound because they had often heard it before at sea when the warships were practising or whatever they did. The fishermen said they always disturbed the fish.

It was Friday before they came on more perfect knowledge.

Dominic was in the field behind the house helping Poc Murray to plant potatoes. Poc was a big young man who was excellent with a spade. He wore heavy hobnail boots and they said he could split rocks when he drove that spade into the ground with his right foot. The field was small like all the fields within the eyes of man around here. Most of them had been won from bog and rocky soil with great labour, and the cleared rocks built into dry-stone walls to shelter them from the bitter winds of the Atlantic.

As far as your eye could see were those small wall-enclosed fields, sloping down to the sea in front, and at the back towards the bogs and the lakes to the horizon where the mountains reared themselves, mistily blue today, and deceptive with distance.

The road was a few hundred yards below them, and even if a dog moved on it they would lean on the spades and speculate about the dog. If it was a man or a woman they would conduct a shouting match. God Bless the Work, and You Too, and What Story is at You, and Devil a Story that is New and many others and they would spit on their palms and get back to the digging.

It was Poc who drew Dominic's attention to the cyclist.

'See there,' he said, 'there is a stranger on the road.'

Dominic looked. Sure enough about a mile away there was a man pedalling a bicycle on the road. He wore a raincoat that was open and flapping in the wind that he was creating himself. Dominic wondered how Poc knew he was a stranger. Why couldn't it be one of their own? He thought of the number of people with bicycles in the area. They were few, and the ones who owned bicycles he would recognize. So this was a stranger, but he thought that the stranger looked familiar, if that was possible.

'Where would he be going now?' Poc wondered.

'He has a hard time wherever it is,' said Dominic as the cyclist continued a most erratic course, dodging the many pot-holes.

'This won't get the work done,' said Poc, spitting on his hands and digging again, but, as Dominic noticed, keeping one sharp blue eye on the behaviour of the cyclist. 'By the grain,' he said later, stopping work again, 'if he isn't turning into the house!'

They lost sight of him then. He must have propped the bicycle in front of the house, because he didn't pass it. Then they saw him coming around the back of the house and rattling the latch. They saw the door opening and a conversation taking place, Brid appearing and pointing up the hill.

'It's for yourself,' said Poc, 'I'd swear. Don't let the stranger catch us idling,' and the soil flew as he dug with great vigour. Dominic dropped his shovel as he got a clearer view of the man who had jumped the wall below and was coming towards them by the cart-track.

'I know him,' he said to Poc. 'I will go to him.'

'God go with you,' said Poc, disappointed. 'I hope he has favourable news for you.'

'It won't be long until you know all about it, I'm sure,' said Dominic, leaving him and running.

He met the man below the second wall and leaned there until he came near him.

'Sam,' he said, 'you are a long way from home.'

'I am,' said Sam Browne. 'What cursed roads this country possesses. Maybe that's what the rising is all about. Maybe they were just unhappy about the state of the roads.'

He shook Dominic's hand.

'You are well?' he asked. 'You are all well?'

'Yes,' said Dominic. 'Not now. Every time I see you there is trouble around the corner. Have you plenty of stories, new ones?'

'I have,' said Sam grimly. 'I wanted a holiday, just for a few days. It is very hot in the town.'

'There is frost at night everywhere,' said Dominic gravely.

'I wish to see your father,' said Sam. 'Maybe he would ask me to stay with ye for a few days.'

'I am sure he will,' said Dominic. Sam had the ends of his trousers tucked into his socks. The pockets of his suit and the overcoat were bulging with papers. The old raincoat he wore was the worse for wear. Sam saw him looking him up and down. 'If your mother won't object to a tramp,' he said.

Dominic clapped him on the shoulder. Sam stood firm under the blow. He looks frail, Dominic thought, but he is really very wiry. 'Our house is yours,' he said. 'We wouldn't even turn you away if you were a tramp. Do you know a lot of what is happening?'

'I know enough,' said Sam. 'We'll save it for your father. Not that it will sour in the telling. The place is like a hornet's nest. Aren't you lucky to live in the peace and quiet of a place like this?'

'I don't know,' said Dominic. 'Maybe we are. Come on down. You had a hard trip out. A wonder you were not stopped.'

'I went by many by-roads,' said Sam, as they went down. 'Sometimes I shouldered the bicycle and walked through the

37

bogs. Soldiers and police are as thick as horseflies in August. Lowry is taken.'

'What's that?' Dominic asked.

'They took Lowry,' said Sam.

'Where do they have him?' Dominic asked.

'They have himself and many others battened down in a warship,' said Sam.

'Not Lowry,' said Dominic.

'Why not,' said Sam. 'They'd arrest a donkey now if they thought he was braying in Irish.'

'You got away,' said Dominic.

'No,' said Sam. 'They don't know much about me. I'm doubtful. As long as I'm not under their eyes, they'll forget about me.'

They were silent then. Dominic thought about Lowry. All that vast energy and excitement which he generated closed up in a small space. 'Lowry will explode,' he said. Sam grunted.

They went in the back way. Dominic's mother was in the kitchen. She was laying places for the dinner.

'This is Sam, Mother,' said Dominic. 'He is a friend of mine. We want to see Father.'

'You're welcome,' said his mother, shaking hands with Sam. Dominic thought her face was thinner, her hair a little whiter, and he felt sad. But her greeting of Sam was warm.

'Himself is a bit better today,' she said. 'He is not as choked. If I can keep him in bed another few days he will be all right. You will eat with us, Sam?'

'It would be a pleasure, ma'am,' said Sam.

'Sam wants to stay for a few days, Mother,' said Dominic. 'Is that all right?'

'I'll ready a bed,' she said immediately.

Sam followed Dominic up the narrow stair. Here on the landing over the scullery they turned to the right. As he was about to knock Sam placed his hand on Dominic's arm.

'You have heard nothing of Dualta?' he asked in a whisper.

Dominic was shocked. He felt his heart miss a beat. It was always like this when anyone mentioned his name.

'Nothing,' he said. 'We have heard nothing.' He knocked

then and went in. There were two windows looking out at the sea. The head of the bed was against the door wall, facing the windows.

'I have a man wants to see you,' said Dominic to his father. He was sitting up in the bed propped by pillows, wearing a scarf around his neck. The patchwork quilt on the bed was littered with books. There was a small table at the side of the bed where he was making notes with a pen. Dominic always admired his father's calligraphy. He wrote a copper-plate hand. Dominic could still feel the tingling of the stick on his palms when he was corrected for his slovenly writing.

His father looked over his spectacles at Sam.

'I'm Sam Browne,' he said. 'You don't know me, sir, but I know a lot about you.'

'I hope they are good things,' said the old man, taking off his glasses. He loosened the scarf on his neck. Sam could see the red flannel covering his chest. 'Sit down. Can I do something for you?'

'Yes,' said Sam. 'You can get up from your bed and dress yourself and go to a neighbour's house where they won't find you.'

Dominic saw his father's eyes widening, and then he started to laugh. He had always marvelled at how good his father's teeth were.

'Are you trying to cure me with humour?' he asked.

'No,' said Sam. 'I'm serious. There has been a rising in Dublin. A lot of Galwaymen came out too. They are in a panic. They are arresting everyone within reach. I think they will come for you.'

The old man laughed again. He had deep-sunken eyes. They almost vanished. Then he coughed, and had to stop laughing. He leaned on a hand.

'Dominic told me something of the rumours,' he said. 'I wouldn't believe him.'

'Read this,' said Sam, separating one from a bundle of papers he had taken from his pockets. 'It's a copy we got.'

The old man put on his glasses. He looked at the broadsheet. It was well crumpled. He had to sit up and turn it to

39

the light of the window to see it. He read out loud, disbelievingly:

'*Poblacht na hEireann. The Provisional Government of the Irish Republic to the People of Ireland. Irishmen and Irishwomen: In the name of God and the dead generations from which she receives her old tradition of nationhood, Ireland, through us, summons her children to her flag, and strikes for freedom.*

'*Having organized and trained her manhood through her secret revolutionary organization, the Irish Republican Brotherhood, and through her open military organizations, the Irish Volunteers and the Irish Citizen Army, having patiently perfected her discipline, having resolutely waited for the right moment to reveal itself, she now seizes that moment, and supported by her exiled children in America and by gallant allies in Europe, but relying in the first on her own strength, she strikes in full confidence of victory. . . .*'

His voice trailed away. They watched him tensely as he read the rest to himself. They could see him changing as he read it, the disbelief giving way to a wide-eyed awareness, his fingers tightening on the paper.

In five minutes he took his eyes from the paper and looked at them. He hardly saw them, Dominic thought.

He said: 'These men who signed it, I know the man Sean MacDiarmada. He is a handsome man with a limp. I talked to him. He used to be around the province on a bicycle. And this Pearse man. He writes in the language. He is a poet. I have heard of Connolly, and MacDonagh. Listen, these men are dreamers.'

'Dreamers don't die,' said Sam.

'What did you say?' he asked.

'Dreamers sit in corners dreaming dreams,' said Sam. 'They don't fight. These dreamers have the whole of Dublin in flames for the last week. That is the proclamation they put up outside the post office.'

'But Clarke is an old Fenian,' said the old man. 'He is as old as myself.'

'He's not too old to fire a rifle,' said Sam.

'Good God, so it's true,' he said. 'What are we doing here? Where is my son Dualta? Is the whole of Ireland up?'

'No,' said Sam. 'The whole of Ireland is down.'

'They knew?' Dominic's father asked. 'Who rose? Tell me. Who rose? All this activity in the bay?'

'They were to rise on Easter Sunday,' said Sam. 'Others didn't agree. There were countermanding orders. So people were bewildered. There was a German ship to land arms. A man called Roger Casement was captured in Kerry. The ship with the arms was captured. It was scuttled. Now the crabs have it. What were the people to do? No arms. Conflicting orders.'

'But these men went ahead with it anyhow?' the Master asked.

'They did,' said Sam.

'Can they win, then?' he asked.

'No,' said Sam.

'How do you know?' he asked passionately.

'One of us has been there,' said Sam. 'In a few days it will be over. The odds are too great.'

'But how about the people all over the land?' he asked. 'Aren't they on fire?'

Sam took a newspaper from his pocket and opened it.

'Listen to this,' he said. He read from the paper. '*Citizens Meet. Committee of Public Safety Formed. At a great meeting of the citizens of Galway held in the Town Hall at 4 o'clock pm on Wednesday, the Chairman of the Urban Council presiding, the following resolutions were passed with enthusiasm:*

That this public meeting declares ill-advised the actions of persons in the County of Galway, who have, at a time when the valour of Irish troops has done so much to shed glory on the arms of the Empire, chosen to shock and outrage public opinion by bloodshed and civil strife. That we declare our opinion that the advice of Mr John Redmond indicates the course which true political wisdom shows to be right; and we call on the authorities and people of Galway to co-operate to crush by every possible means the efforts of the disaffected fanatics and mischief makers.

41

That a Committee of Public Safety be formed to take any steps that may be deemed to be necessary to deal with the existing situation in co-operation with the authorities.

That we invite the citizens of Galway to offer themselves for enrolment as special constables, or in any way the authorities consider they may be useful in the present crisis.

'Is that enough?' he asked then, 'or do you want more?'

'What was it all about?' the Master asked.

'Some hundreds went when they got the order,' said Sam. 'A few skirmishes here and there. You'd think the Huns had landed. They had no arms. A few ·22 rifles, two or three revolvers, a few shotguns. No good. What was the use of going to Dublin? They had nothing but their hearts. Now they are gone. Here, I will leave you this paper. It won't cure your illness, sir, because it's the same all over.'

'Did they in Dublin know that they could not win? Did they know this? Answer this if you can?' The muscles on his neck were standing out as he glared at Sam.

'I hear they knew they couldn't win,' said Sam. 'I don't know. People have sunk so low. You heard what I read. How much lower can people go than that? Maybe they will fail, and they hope that their failure will be successful. I don't know.'

'By God, they tried!' the old man shouted, hitting a book with his clenched fist. 'I didn't believe it was possible. I thought now they have got their bits and pieces of land, they will forget the rest. Not so, eh? Not so at all. You realize that this is great? You realize that even if this fails, it is great? It is new blood being pumped into old veins. You understand this?'

'No, sir,' said Sam, 'I don't. They are gathering everybody into their nets. The ships and jail are bulging with the only men capable of believing.'

'And my son Dualta, where is he?' the old man asked. 'He was in the wrong war. You hear that. The wrong war. Oh, Dualta, why didn't you wait?'

'Dualta believed he was right,' said Dominic. 'He believed.'

'Listen,' said Sam. 'Listen a moment.'

They listened. Sam suddenly went to the window and looked out cautiously. The others could now hear the sound of the army lorries. He turned back to them.

'You see,' he said. 'I heard they were going to take you.'

'It's ridiculous,' said the old man. 'What danger am I to anyone?'

'You pass on thoughts,' said Sam. 'They know of you. It's schoolteachers like you who inspire dreamers, and now dreamers are dangerous.'

'Don't be ridiculous,' said the old man. 'I don't believe you.'

'They are stopping outside the gate,' said Sam.

Dominic ran to join him. He saw three lorries, and one car with policemen. They were jumping down from the lorries with speed. The policeman was coming in the gate. He wore sergeant's chevrons. Sergeant Nick.

'It's true,' said Dominic, bewildered. 'They are coming here.'

'Get away, Sam,' said the old man. 'Get Sam out of here, Dominic, it's probably him they are after. Go, Sam, go from here.'

'I tell you,' protested Sam.

'Go,' said the old man. 'Go! Dominic, get him away. I order you to get him away!'

'Come on, Sam,' said Dominic. He nearly always obeyed his father. Sam shrugged and followed him, closing the door, getting a view of a coughing old man sitting up in bed with dawning pleasure on his face.

They went down the stairs quickly. There was a heavy knocking on the front door. Dominic's mother stood there, her hand on her heart. Knocks to her could only mean something about Dualta.

'It's too late,' said Sam. 'Here!' He went to the dresser and grabbed a mug from it, scooped milk into the mug from the pail, took a piece of cut cake from the table and ruffling up his scanty hair went to a stool and sat hunched over the fire. He looked like a tramp in real earnest.

'Don't worry, Mother,' said Dominic and went to open the door.

43

5

'I<small>T'S THE</small> most stupid thing I ever heard of,' Dominic shouted at him. 'You are just making bloody fools of yourselves.'

The sergeant remained unmoved.

'We are only doing our duty. We are ordered to take your father into custody as a disaffected person. If you want to complain, complain to the people that matter.'

'You are a liar!' said Dominic. 'How would they ever hear of my father if it wasn't for you? You are the one that gave them the names. Don't try and clear yourself of this stupidity.'

'I'd advise you to mind your tongue,' the sergeant said.

'You'd have more reason to take me,' said Dominic. 'I don't like you. I don't like your methods. Do you think this sort of fool-hawking is going to make me feel any better?'

'Ma'am,' said Nick to his mother. 'Would you tell your husband that we want him?'

Dominic's mother was standing at the table. There was no expression on her face. There were two armed policemen standing behind the sergeant and an army captain with a small fair moustache tapping a light cane against his leg. He was indifferent. He had not spoken.

'If you want my father,' said the furious Dominic, 'you'll have to fight me to take him. I don't give a damn!' It was because he was so helpless that he was so furious.

'Don't make a scene,' said the sergeant coldly.

'I'll make more than that,' said Dominic. 'I'll make more than that!' walking to the bottom of the stairs.

'Hold your peace, Dominic,' his father said then. Dominic looked up in astonishment. His father stood at the head of the stairs. He was dressed. He wore the tweed suit and had even put on his collar and tie. He looked pleased with himself. 'You were looking for me, Sergeant?' he asked.

'Yes,' said the sergeant. 'I have orders to take you into custody.'

'If you only knew,' said the old man, 'how happy you have made me. I couldn't believe me ears. What is the reason for my apprehension?'

'We are not given reasons, sir,' said Nick. 'You ought to know yourself.'

'Do you think I have guns hidden under the rafters?' he asked, coming down the stairs.

'You have always preached disaffection in your school,' said Nick. 'You know that.'

'I have taught history,' said the Master. 'If I have taught disaffection I have failed, signally. How many of my pupils had the courage to rise against oppression? None, as far as I hear. So you can't say I was a successful teacher of disaffection.'

'You have a room in there that is a museum of treason,' said the sergeant angrily. He went over to the door of the room and pushed it open. 'Take a look in there,' said the sergeant to the officer. The officer strolled over and poked in his head.

'Don't be a bloody luderamaun!' shouted Dominic.

'Be quiet, Dominic,' said his father. 'I have always taught one thing,' he said to Nick. 'It's not original. As long as one man, one man in any community, feels that his liberty and freedom is being curtailed, he is entitled to take up arms against tyranny.'

'Where's the tyranny? Where's the tyranny?' the sergeant asked. 'It's people like you who make it.'

'It's people like you who uphold it,' shouted Dominic.

'I wish I was as powerful as you think I am,' said Dominic's father with a smile.

'You can take a small bag with you,' said the sergeant.

'Nora,' said the old man to Dominic's mother. 'Would you pack a little bag?' She nodded silently and went up the stairs. 'If things were different,' Dominic's father went on, 'I would offer you refreshment, but under the circumstances it would hardly be fitting.'

'We'll go now,' said Nick. 'They can bring out your bag.'

'Go and help your mother to put in a few books too, Dominic,' he said to him sharply, looking at his clenched hands, the muscles tight at the side of his jaw. 'Mitchel's *Jail Journal*, for example. Suitable reading like that. Go on, Dominic!'

Dominic glared at Nick. He looked at his father. He didn't seem so old now, for some reason. He was a small man, but he had always been commanding. He didn't have to use a stick in his school as often as he might. His tongue was as good as one. Dominic went up the stairs.

His mother had a small straw case open on the bed and was putting clothes into it.

'Mother,' said Dominic, catching her arm. It wasn't trembling.

'It's all right, Dominic,' she said. 'He's happy about it. You saw him. It makes him feel important. They won't hurt him.'

'Jail hurts everybody,' said Dominic. 'It's a terrible thing. It's not necessary. You know how harmless he is. What age is my father?'

'He is about fifty-eight,' she said.

'Is he that young?' asked Dominic. 'Why do I think he is older?'

'Because you are younger,' she said.

'What makes them so stupid?' he asked. 'What is the good of them taking men like my father? What good will it do them?'

'They feel that they are doing something,' she said. 'Stupid people always strike around them when they are in panic. Your father was in jail before.'

'That was different,' said Dominic.

'It was more serious,' she said.

'Holy God, look at them!' said Dominic at the window. You'd think the soldiers were deploying for a major battle. There must have been twenty of them, facing out from the lorries, all in war equipment. He saw many people coming down the road from both sides, some of the children running, older people scattering the dust of the road with their bare feet. The red petticoats of the women made a brave splash of

46

colour against the grey of the rocks. The soldiers had bayonets fixed to their rifles. 'It's so ridiculous! It's so ridiculous!' said Dominic, snorting exasperation. 'One old man and all that. What do they expect? Do they expect the people to rise up with pitchforks and rescue him from their clutches because he taught them Robert Emmet died for Ireland?'

'I'm ready,' said Dominic's mother. He took the closed case and ran down the stairs.

There was nobody in the kitchen, nobody except the tramp who had hunched himself in on the hob seat beside the fire. That Sam, Dominic thought as he went out the door, you hardly know he's there.

'Dominic!' his mother halted him. She was coming down the stairs. 'Make your father wear this scarf,' she said, holding it out to him. 'He is not better of his cold.'

Dominic took it and left. She sat at the fire opposite Sam. He noticed her hands were joined, the knuckles white.

'They won't hurt him,' said Sam. 'They will just crowd them all into a jail for a few weeks and then let them go.'

'He is not as young as he was,' she said. 'He might forget that.'

'He's the first man I ever saw happy to be arrested,' said Sam.

Oddly, she smiled. 'It makes him feel part of something,' she said. Then she stopped smiling. 'As if it would make up for Dualta going off.'

'Maybe it will too,' said Sam.

His father was sitting in the police car. There were two hefty policemen one on each side of him, their carbines between their knees. Talk about taking a sledge hammer to crack a nut, Dominic thought in exasperation. The sergeant, standing beside the car, took the case.

'You forgot your scarf,' said Dominic. 'Put it on, my mother says. It is not warm weather and you have a cold.'

'Tscha,' said his father, taking it and wrapping it around his neck, impatiently. 'Women.'

Then he looked around him, became conscious of all the people being held back by the soldiers. 'Hey, Master!

Master!' they were calling. Well they might, since he had been the master for most of them at school. The whole village was there and more were coming running.

'All right,' said Nick to the driver. 'We'll be off.' He put the case at his feet and sat in beside the driver. The engine was turning over. The driver moved the lever. The car back-fired and then moved off erratically, stopped and started and then was away in a cloud of dust.

The soldiers started to climb into the lorries which had been turned to face south. Dominic stood there on the road looking after the car. He saw a thin white hand being raised to wave once. He heard the people talking to him. 'Why, Dominic?' and 'What has he done?' 'What did they take the Master for?'

'He's a dangerous man,' said Dominic. 'Didn't ye know?'

They laughed.

'He's dead dangerous with a stick in his hand,' said Peter O'Flaherty, 'and your bottom within reach of the stick.'

'We are sad for you, Dominic,' they said. 'It is indeed a shame. How little they have for doing: God is good, you'll see, they'll let him go in a short time.'

Dominic was barely listening to them. Then he was conscious of the young soldier who stood in front of him. He had no arms, no gear. His black boots were highly polished and his puttees mathematically wound on his legs.

'Are you young Duane?' he was asking, and when Dominic made no reply he caught him by the sleeve of his shirt and shook his arm. 'Hey, are you young Dominic?' he asked. The people were silent. Dominic focused his eyes on him.

'Yes,' he said gruffly. He saw that he was a young soldier. There was a scar on his face.

'I want to talk to you, by yourself,' he said.

'All right,' said Dominic. He moved away from the people and walked inside the gate. Halfway to the house he stopped. 'Well, what do you want?' he asked coldly.

'It's about your brother, Dualta,' the young soldier said. Dominic's heart missed a beat. 'What's there about him?' he asked, thinking: Was he there when Dualta died? The scar on his face was newly healed, he saw now. He had been in the war.

'I got a lift out in a lorry,' the soldier said, 'when I heard they were coming this way. Godamme if I knew what they were coming for. Listen, that was your father they took, Dualta's old man, eh?'

'That's right,' said Dominic. 'What about Dualta?'

'He's in the military hospital in Dublin. I was there with him. This rising thing. There was no way to get word to you. All the trains are stopped, no posting of letters, see. I was sent down to the town inside. I said I'd tell you. Didn't think it would be this way, by jee . . .' stopping himself. 'I didn't know what the bastards were up to.'

'Dualta is alive?' Dominic was asking, gripping his arm.

'That's what I said. A few scratches, he told me to tell you.'

'But he's alive?' Dominic asked again.

'That's what I'm telling you,' said the soldier.

'Please come,' said Dominic almost running him towards the house. 'Please come.'

The soldier followed him. The door was still open. Dominic pushed him inside.

'Listen to this, Mother,' he said. 'Just listen to this. Go on, tell her again.'

The soldier took off his cap.

'I'm sorry, ma'am,' he said. 'At a time like this. Dualta is in the military hospital in Dublin. A few scratches, he said. He'll be out soon and home to see you. I didn't know. Like this. I'm sorry, ma'am, it had to be like this. I didn't know where the lorries were going, just out where you lived. If I had known I would have come another way. But Dualta and me, we were friends, see.'

She was standing on her feet. There was colour coming into her face. He thought she would cry, but she didn't.

'Thank you,' she said. 'Thank you very much. No messenger has ever been so welcome.'

'Well,' he said. 'That's all. I have to be going. They won't wait. Just so that you know. I don't understand this. A man goes to France to fight, and he fights and he is wounded. And

49

while he is wounded, they come along and take his old man away. I don't understand. What is it all about?'

'You came through Dublin?' Sam suddenly asked.

'Yes,' said the soldier. 'Boy, they battered that town. All black rafters sticking up and glass. Why did they do this? What is it all about?'

'Bullock! Private Bullock!' a voice was calling from outside. 'Put a stir in it.'

'I have to go,' he said, putting on his cap, adjusting the angle of it. 'I'm sorry. But Dualta is all right. He will be all right.'

'Thank you,' said Dominic's mother. 'Thank you very much.'

He looked at them, and then turned and went out. Dominic followed him to the doorway. The lorry was impatient. The others had gone. Private Bullock ran and jumped. They hauled him aboard as the lorry moved and he stood and looked back and then waved tentatively.

Dominic waved back at him.

I will not go back into the house now, Dominic thought. I will go back to the fields and I will plant potatoes with Poc Murray. I will take it out of the earth, he thought. I will dig it viciously. It would be fatal if I stayed with my mother now.

Then he shouted to the crowd still gathered on the roadway.

'Poc ! Poc! Stir your lazy bones. Let us get back to the potatoes,' and he set off walking to the field.

6

DOMINIC AND his mother were hemmed in with the crowd facing the jail gate. The wicket was closed, and black-uniformed warders stood outside it. Armed police and some soldiers had pressed the people back on the right-hand side. They were mainly country people and all of them were carrying packages of food and clothing. Most of the women were in beige shawls and heavy homespun skirts. But there were young women there too, and boys.

Dominic felt a sense of distaste, crowded up like that with his brown paper package in his arms, using his elbows to keep a space for his mother, terrified of moving his shoe and standing on a bare foot, because many of the people were in their bare feet. There were many accents. The accents of the town and of East Galway and the soft Irish of the west coast.

'Who have they on you, a stór?' a woman asked his mother.

'My husband,' his mother said.

'God help them,' the woman said. 'I don't know what's wrong at all today. Another day they'd let you in easy. But nobody is going in at all today. What could be wrong, do you think?'

'I don't know,' his mother said.

'I hear they are shifting the lot of them,' a young woman in front said back to them.

'Don't say that, agirl,' the woman said. 'As long as they're here we know where they are, and they're safe.'

They couldn't get out anyhow, Dominic thought, looking at the towering buttressed walls. It was a fine jail. If you could look through the walls you would have a nice view of the river going over the weir and the flowers on the banks, spring flowers growing in profusion. Crossing the bridge you could see nothing except the gate and the walls and the top glass of the hanging-shed. One time they used to throw open the main gate and hang them just inside for the benefit of the public. Judging by reports of all the people they had arrested the walls should be bulging.

'You are calm,' he said to his mother.

'I have visited jails before,' his mother said. 'I know Castlebar jail well. That's where he was the other time.'

'It's all so stupid,' said Dominic.

'Don't say that to your father,' his mother said.

'Hey,' a man was shouting up in front, 'why the hell don't ye let us in? What's wrong with ye?'

They didn't answer him. The soldiers just held their rifles in front of them and kept pushing.

51

'Back there! Back now,' they said.

Dominic wondered what it would be like to go into the jail. Was there a separate room where they could see his father, or would they have to see him in his cell? People said that there were six men in every cell now. They were only built for two. It was a very handsome jail, the authorities said. They were quite proud of it.

Suddenly thére was a lot of activity. An army lorry came from the other side and stood, its engine throbbing, about twenty yards away from the main gate. Then the main gate was thrown open, and more armed policemen came out facing towards the people. And then just as suddenly the head of a column of marching prisoners came out of the jail and as they were marched towards the bridge the lorry started forward to head the column, the soldiers standing up in it facing outwards with the rifles held ready in their hands.

There were screams from the waiting people and a surge forward that was barely held back. He heard women shouting, and girls calling out names, but they were forced back by locked guns.

'We'll never see him now,' he said to his mother. 'I'll try and break through and get to him in the town.'

'All right,' she said. 'I will wait here for you.'

He elbowed his way backwards, and got clear of the pressing throng. Then he went towards the wall bounding the bank of the river, where the numbers of people were not as thick. He got through here to the bridge, sidled his way past a soldier and got on to the footpath. He was near the head of the column. His eyes searched frantically for the figure of his father. He wasn't to be seen in the first lot, so Dominic walked quickly, cleared the police guard, and then outpaced the lorry. He knew their destination must be the station. Some of the prisoners had been taken on the warships. Some of them were transported that way, people said, others of them sent back to the jail. These would be marched to the train, taken to Dublin, and sent on to prisons and internment camps in England. As he hurried up the long street to get into the Square, he thought he might be dreaming all this, or that it was the recurrence of

52

a dream. Always there had to be men marching under armed guards to prison ships or prison trains, a long line of them stretching back over the centuries. You read this in your history books (not the ones in the schools) and it made no impact on your mind. But this made it all real. He could hear the voice of his father, walking him down by the docks, talking of the ships that had departed from there carrying Irishmen and women, as felons to Australia, slaves to the Barbados, dying on Atlantic coffin ships, fleeing from hunger, famine, disease, exploitation. Still it was hard to believe. He stood at the street that entered the Square to wait. Here he would have a good view of them passing. He would be able to dart in and hand the parcel to his father get out again before he could be stopped.

He could hear a roar coming from the march behind him. Looking down into the shop street, he could see people pouring from there coming and thickening the arteries of the town, so that the traffic had to stop and horses reared high and had to be quietened by cursing drivers. More police appeared then and held them back from invading the line of the march and, as the head of the march appeared, their voices rose in a roar of execration.

Dominic felt himself going pale. An empty feeling came into his stomach. They were shouting vile epithets, names, scraping the bottom of the barrels of obscenity, and throwing what they could find there at the marching men who were coming into the Square.

Bewildered-looking men they were. Tall men and short men and young men and old men with grey hair. Some of them had long overcoats that nearly touched the mud of the streets. Some of them wore big caps, and some of them wore beaver hats, and some of the young ones wore no headgear at all, just thick hair of different hues that was blowing in the breeze. Some of the men you could spot had been soldiers, somewhere, sometime. They marched in a sort of step with their shoulders back and pale sun glinting off the brass studheads holding their shirts together. Some of them tried to march in step, but they did it with an awkwardness that seemed to embarrass

53

them. They had an assortment of parcels under their arms, or cases. You could see here and there a strong face, that looked as hard as rock, with eyes fixed to the front, looking neither to left nor right, deaf to the insults that were being hurled at them.

Certainly you felt, if these are rebels, then the rebellion never had a chance. Look at them, for God's sake, a marching slovenly crowd of civilians who wouldn't know one end of a gun from the other. This was the bunch that a Committee of Public Safety had to be formed to preserve us from. The Lord preserve us! He thought it was this feeling that made the people so brutally cruel. As if you were terrified by a tiger and then found out that all the time it was only a mouse.

Boo! A sound that is used by a cow, but when it emerges from hundreds of human mouths it sounds terrible.

And then the bunch of women bent down to the ground and picking up mud and horseshit which abounded they started to pelt the marching men. Men behind Dominic were laughing. 'These are the Separation Allowances,' a man said to some one else. 'Pour it on them, girls! Give it to them, girls.' They were young girls, badly dressed. Some of them were older. They wore shawls. The shawls were trailing in the dirt as they bent and fired and screamed.

'That's it, girls! Give it to them, girls!' If he felt it would have done any good, Dominic would have turned and belted the man in the mouth, but what good would it do? He was watching closely for his father. Some of the mud and the dung landed. He saw it on the side of men's faces. But they didn't rub it off. They just left it there. Like a badge. But some of the police got it on their uniforms, so they moved on the Separation Allowances and stopped them, with threats, and they stopped throwing dirt with their hands and kept throwing it with their mouths, waving their skinny fists. Some of them were very handsome. It was almost obscene to see the way their beauty was transformed by the grimacing of hate. They had husbands and sons and lovers fighting in the Flanders mud. That was their cause. What mixed-up feelings were in their breasts? Who was fighting for Ireland? What was all this about? Would this endanger the lives of their men

54

or their separation allowances from their departed sons or husbands or lovers?

So they screamed and shouted, and as the last of the hundreds of prisoners passed they followed them up towards the station.

Dominic didn't move. He had looked at each face closely and he was sure his father was not there. Then where was he? Could they really be so stupid as to think him so important that he must be transported by warships.

'He's not there, Dominic,' said Sam behind him.

Dominic turned on him.

'Come away from here,' said Sam, taking him by the arm and walking around the corner. Dominic went with him. Sam had his hands in his pockets and a soft hat pulled down over his face. Dominic kept his peace. They walked down another street and another one until they stood under a tree, near where the waters of the great Corrib poured under a railway bridge and surged in a powerful, sleek, velvety flow over the weir.

'They didn't take you, Sam?' he asked.

'No,' said Sam. 'They overlooked me. There were an awful lot of good men in that bunch you saw passing. Dangerous men. It is a mistake to pelt mud at dangerous men. One third of all those men before they were arrested were as innocent of rebellious thoughts as children. How many of them are going to be really rebellious after treatment like that?'

'Do you know anything of my father?' Dominic asked.

'I do,' said Sam. 'He was taken to the Union Hospital two nights ago. I only found out today. I was looking for you. I couldn't go near the jail. It was too conspicuous.'

'What's wrong with him?' Dominic asked, his mouth suddenly dry.

'Bad cold,' said Sam. 'That cold he had when they took him. It didn't get better. A jail is no place for a cold.'

'It might have saved him from worse,' said Dominic. 'I will find my mother. Will we be let in to see him?'

'Yes,' said Sam. 'It's all clear. No police guards. It won't ever be in any book that he was arrested.'

55

'Thanks, Sam,' said Dominic, moving away. Trying not to move too fast.

Sam looked after him. He took a cigarette from a battered packet and lighted it. He watched the figure of Dominic moving away from him with a parcel under his arm, and he felt very sad. He tried to think of something else: of the fury he felt as he watched the marching men and the screaming citizens. Someday, he thought, someday, we'll make some of them *eat* horseshit; then he relaxed, smiled at the absurdity, watched the head of Dominic, now running, passing over the bridge, flicked his cigarette into the water, turned up the collar of his coat and went away.

They were put into this waiting-room, a doctor's room of some kind. They weren't talking. At least, Dominic thought, my father will get his parcel.

This young priest came in to them. He was taller than Dominic. He had fair hair standing in a sort of bush on his head. He had a long thin face and fine broad forehead.

'Mrs Duane?' he asked.

'Yes, Father,' she said.

'I'm afraid your husband is very sick,' he said.

There was a silence.

'What's wrong with him?' she asked then.

'He has a touch of pneumonia,' he said. He tried to keep his face impersonal, Dominic saw, and trembled. 'He should never have been put into that jail,' he said. 'And the way he was. It wasn't good for him.'

'We can see him?' she asked. The priest admired her. She was wearing a straw hat held to her white hair with hatpins. The ends had coloured beads, faceted, that glinted in the light from the window. She had regular features, and a good clear skin, showing wrinkles around her eyes and her mouth. It was a strong, quiet face. There would be no hysterics, he saw, no reproaches, and was glad. The son's face, he saw, was drawn, and his eyes were gleaming, or was it glowering? His forehead was puckered, making the black spiky hair almost stand up on his head. The top part of his face was like his mother's, but the chin was bigger and stronger. May be difficult, he thought.

'Pleurisy, too?' the young man asked.

I wish he hadn't asked that question, the priest thought, now he will know.

'A touch of that too,' he said. 'Will you come with me now?'

They followed him. He held the door for Dominic's mother. Dominic knew his father was doomed. They don't send priests to relatives. He knew enough for that. It would be a nurse or a doctor. He wasn't far advanced in medicine, hadn't tramped the hospital wards yet, but he had instinct. When they went into the ward and saw the screens around his father's bed, he knew, and braced himself.

They sat one each side of the bed. His father's cheeks were sunken. Sweat rolled from his forehead. This nurse then said to him gently: 'There is someone to see you.' And he opened his eyes, and they were not clear, but the pallid hand on the bedspread moved and his mother put her hand into it.

'Hello, Dom,' she said. And his father's hand squeezed her fingers, and his eyes kept looking at her, a strange unconcealed look, revealing, and the pale lips smiled. Dominic looked at them, at this bearded dying man in bed, and for a moment he could strip them of age and see them for a second as they had been long ago.

'Dominic is here,' she said then gently. He turned his head from her and looked to the other side.

'Dominic,' his father said.

'I brought you a parcel,' said Dominic, feeling so awkward, so awkward.

His father smiled again.

'Dualta?' he asked. 'Dualta?'

'He'll be here,' said Dominic bravely. 'We heard from him. They are letting him go from the hospital. He will be home soon.'

'Good,' said his father, turning his head back to watch Dominic's mother again. 'Light head,' he said to her. 'Strange. Sometimes lucid. Other times little men in uniform, small as a thumb, climbing up the glass of the window. Think lots of Irish tales written by men with fevers.' He smiled.

'Could be so,' she said.

57

'Sometimes think I'm young again,' he said. 'Back in those days.'

'Those were good days,' she said.

'Good days. Good days,' he said. He had to close his eyes again. He moved his head from side to side. His beard was soaked with sweat, like his thin hair. 'Don't go away, Nora,' he said. 'Don't go away.'

'No,' she said, 'I won't go away.'

But Dominic did. He couldn't take any more of this. He wasn't geared for it. He crossed the wall and stood looking out a window, blindly. The men in the beds on either side of the window looked at him, then at one another, and then at the screened bed, and they shook their heads.

Dominic looked out the window and saw nothing.

It took his father two days to die.

On that same day three men, Pearse, Clarke, and Mac-Donagh, were taken into the stone-breakers' yard in Kilmainham Jail and killed by the foreigners, and then their corpses were taken to the yard in Arbour Hill where a great mass grave had been dug, with quicklime standing by, enough, men said, for a hundred bodies, and they were the first three to be planted.

But Dualta was not home in time.

7

HE WASN'T home until shortly before the Month's Mind for his father. People were shocked because the man was buried as it were in secret. Times were disturbed, and he was well buried before men were even aware of it, so they made up for their neglect a month after his death, when eleven o'clock Mass was celebrated for the repose of his soul, on a blazing June day in the small church that overlooked the green sea and the graveyard on the lip of the water.

Dominic was surprised at the people who came. All the

local people came, although it was such fine weather and ideal for working, but men also came from across the mountains and from across the big lake beyond, well into the county of Mayo. They came in hired motor cars and horse traps, and riding horses, and in ass carts from the coast road. They travelled through pickets and policemen; nothing stopped them from coming.

He always remembered this, because he discovered relations he didn't know he possessed, and because he also learned something from them, particularly the older ones.

They had to be fed, naturally. That kept his mother busy, which was as well for her. He thought she was preparing excessive amounts of food, but she was right. They had to kill a pig. Poc Murray butchered it and quartered it and separated the parts they would use fresh from the parts which he salted and barrelled. And he killed a sheep and hung it in time in the barn. Eamon of the Shop, as he was called, sent down six bottles of whisky and a half-barrel of porter to honour the finest man that ever handled a quill pen even, as Eamon remarked, if he could never pound any knowledge into his, Eamon's, head, except a few sums which were all he wanted anyhow. He was doing fine with the sums. But it was nice of him.

They had to clear the barn and put a few tables in it, and sweep the yard after they had weeded it. The place looked all right with the sun shining on it and the tables covered with sheets. They fed some of them in the kitchen.

Thinking of it afterwards, Dominic would remember how the old ones treated his father's death, as if it was a triumph rather than a tragedy. Uncle Feilim, who was married to his father's sister who was dead, was a stout man with a bowler hat, flattened on top, wearing a heavy frieze suit cut in an old-fashioned way and a hard collar that was cutting into his double chins.

'Why didn't they take me?' Uncle Feilim asked. 'I did more than 'm. Everyone in Mayo knows that. Didn't I always oppose them? Wasn't I in jail five months more than him? You know that, Nora?' to his mother.

'Yes, Feilim,' she would say, 'yes, Feilim.'

Cousin Tom was a spare man with deep lines between his cheekbones and his chin. His grizzled hair grew in locks by his ears and his cheekbones; his eyebrows were heavily tufted. His face could have been hewn from granite.

'Does it matter, Feilim?' he asked. 'Wasn't he a dangerous man nor you? Look at the things he was spreading among the young ones?'

'Far it got him,' said Feilim. 'How many of his young ones were took? Very few, man. How many did they take from me in the village? Hardly left only the dogs and the women, Tom. You know that.'

These two, and other older men he heard talking, seemed to bridge the centuries. They had never been complacent. Their resistance stretched back into time, away back. They could almost attribute every new outbreak, every new, quickly squashed bid for liberty, to their own hearts and tongues. The fourteen men who had been recently executed were to them, without any quibble, the greatest men who had ever lived in Ireland, and their memory or the memory of their mothers went back to Robert Emmet, Wolfe Tone, Henry Grattan, Isaac Butt, Daniel O'Connell, the Young Irelanders, the Fenians. They saw this bloody failure as the greatest achievement of the centuries. Didn't they hold off the armed forces of an Empire for a solid week against all the odds that adversity could contrive against them, and proved it with the shedding of their blood? There was nothing in it for them but death, man, when the country was crawling on its knees. They had a clear picture. If they were fools, hot-heads, dangerous intellecttuals, disturbers of the peace, traitors, these men weren't apologizing for them. They had the vision of the back years to guide them and they saw through the fog of trouble as clearly as if they always walked in the day.

Dualta disconcerted them.

He was the Master's son, but he was dressed in the uniform of the common foe, his cap and his jacket and his puttees and his badges. He had his right eye heavily bandaged, so that he peered from the left one, and his right arm in a sling, missing the little finger and the next one to it, and this thumb and other two fingers useless on account of the nerves having been blasted away, and he was walking favouring his left leg, using a heavy stick to lean on because he had lost much of the calf of that leg, some of the tendons.

They eyed him a lot in the church, Dominic saw, as he bent with his head resting on his good hand. For Dualta had suffered about his father, Dominic knew. He would hardly ever forget the half hour he had spent with him down at his father's grave. He hadn't thought Dualta capable of such emotion, and it hurt him. Dominic could guess at the deep feelings that moved him, but could only stand there helplessly, finally turning away from him as he pounded his good left fist on the mound, and he looking out at the sea with his eyes half blind.

It was his mother who had to find a way for Dualta. This was why she was such a remarkable woman. She spent over two hours with Dualta in the study before he came out with his face ravaged but a calmer look in his one eye.

So when the old men came out of Mass to wait and shake hands of sympathy with them, they were wary of Dualta, of his wounds and of his uniform.

Not Uncle Feilim.

'A disgraceful thing,' said Uncle Feilim, 'to be at the Mass of a patriot wearing that uniform. Have you no shame in you? Did he fail, then, with the bringing up of you?'

This, with everybody listening!

'Is that the way to speak of the uniform of your King?' Dualta asked, and watched in great amusement as Uncle Feilim's face turned the colour of an autumn sunset, and he started to pound his stick on the ground.

'You said that! You said that!' shouted Uncle Feilim. 'You, you, you —' looking around and seeing there were ladies and the parish priest present, he could do nothing but spit on the ground.

'If anyone gave you a shilling a day to fight for your country,' said Dualta, 'you'd be off like a shot, you old cod. The only thing that stopped you was that you were always in bad physical condition. And you were never a fighter. You wouldn't fight your way out of a paper bag.'

'Hold me!' Uncle Feilim shouted. 'Hold me before I split him!'

But Dualta laughed and put his arm around his shoulder. 'Come on, Feilim,' he said. 'Talk to me and convert me. Let me see are you able to convert me.'

In the house they were stuck in a corner for an hour, Feilim and Tom and some of the others, and Dualta must have impressed them, because here was Feilim digging Dualta in the ribs and chuckling with him, and winking broadly whenever he saw him afterwards.

And Dominic got an impression of something when he walked into his father's study, where Dualta was sitting with Sam Browne and the son of Cousin Tom. He was a slender young man in his early twenties with silky brown hair. He had a thin ascetic-looking countenance. He rarely smiled, but when he did the smile lighted up his face. His name was Morgan.

The three of them looked up when Dominic came in. He saw that their minds weren't on his entrance. Their thoughts were somewhere else.

Morgan was talking.

'You know my father, your Cousin Tom,' he was saying. 'It was the same with me. When a thing is pounded into your head for years you are inclined to dull your intellect to it. You are not alone in this. I have talked to other young men. They agree. Some of them say it is like a planted seed that takes time to come alive, if the ground is fertile.'

'And your ground was fertile?' Dualta asked.

'It must have been,' said Morgan. 'As soon as I heard about the men of Easter, I was in the potato fields and I left them and I went home. I cycled to the town to find out if it was true, and as soon as I knew it was true, I thought, this is what we have been waiting for. So I went out into the highways and the byways and in twenty-four hours I had a hundred men. This was after the executions. There was no arguing about it, you see. I just had to say: We are forming a company of Volun-

teers. None of them had been in before. Young men. Not Redmond Volunteers or Sinn Fein, just when we knew that this
had really happened, we all felt: This is the time. But we
have a long way to go. This is only the start. Not even
wooden guns. Not even able to put one foot in front of another.'

'It's happening all over the place,' said Sam. 'People don't
think of what it means. The majority of the men they took
are farmers and farmers' sons. Some of the places in East
Galway were left with only a woman and a few children to
look after them. So I sent out a call in the town and the
University for volunteers to go and help them. You should
have seen. It would have raised your heart. The number of
them. They walked and they went on bicycles early in the
morning and they came home in the evening singing songs, or
holding hands. They swarmed over the hay fields and the
turnip fields like ants, and they worked. It was wonderful. You
see, when a single torch is lighted, it can set fire to a forest of
torches.'

'I was out in the mud,' said Dualta. 'I didn't know if I
would ever be found. What for? I wondered. I thought of my
father. He was right. Why was I there? I was deceived. Just
two great stones, squeezing thousands of men to death each
time they came together. Bloody massacres, and there will be
more and more. Why didn't I wait? When I saw the burned
city, tattered tricolours, and the executions, how they died, I
thought, out there, I had no cause, just an amateur mercen-
ary. Now there is a cause. You see?'

'I see,' said Morgan. 'I see.'

'It's a great thing,' said Sam, 'that they are so self-right-
eously stupid. They take away thousands of lukewarm, mild
nationalists and clamp them into camps and jails. So they go
in tepid and they come out roaring revolutionaries.'

The three of them laughed at this, Dominic saw, as if it was
a wonderful jest.

'Academies of revolution,' said Dualta.

'Just so,' said Sam.

'And now they will have to let them all go again,' said

63

Morgan. 'They are afraid of America. They want her in their war.'

'And they want thousands of extra bodies to be squeezed between the two stone blocks,' said Dualta grimly. 'They will probably even try conscription to get them, and they will be surprised at the result.'

'They will certainly be surprised,' said Morgan. 'They kill our people and then they are surprised we won't go and fight their favourite war for them.'

'There are going to be fun and games,' said Sam, rubbing his thin hands together.

Dualta and Morgan laughed. They were excited.

Dominic left them.

That brought their attention to him.

'Dominic is not convinced,' he heard Dualta, slightly jeering, as he closed the door after him.

It was the same in the kitchen. They were excited with whisky and politics. They were talking at one another in Irish and English. It was the same out in the barn, and in the yard, which was now filled with them. There was a heady smell of porter from the barn. He saw his mother with the tidy white hair unsettled, and strands of it falling over her face, supervising the distribution of the funeral meats. She caught his eye, brushed back the hair from her face with a long thin hand and smiled at him. There were deep circles under her eyes.

He waved back at her and then he left the yard and went out on the road, making his way through all the vehicles, and took the lane down to the sea. He walked with his hands in his pockets and kicked at the loose stones in his way.

He came to the graveyard. He saw the gate was open. In surprise he saw that somebody was kneeling at the mound of his father's grave, praying. The mound was settling. All the real flower wreaths had withered away. The artificial glass-covered wreaths looked a bit decayed, with moisture inside the round glass covers.

The girl was brown-haired. She wore her hair long, but it was caught at the back of her neck with a slide. There were small glass stones in the slide and they glittered in the sunshine. She was wearing a long white dress caught at the waist with a ribbon. She was a young girl, way off twenty, he thought.

She became conscious of his presence. She looked quickly over her shoulder. Then she calmly blessed herself, rose to her feet and came towards him. She wasn't embarrassed.

'You are the only one of them,' said Dominic.

'The only one of them what?' she asked, puzzled.

'You are the only one of them to think of him,' he said, nodding at the grave.

She considered his words. She walked past him. He closed the gate. They automatically turned towards the sea which wasn't far away.

'They prayed for him at Mass,' she said.

'You should hear them,' he said. 'It isn't that he wouldn't enjoy the day and the conversation. He would be alive with it. But he's dead and they don't think of him as a man, just a symbol.'

She said nothing to this outburst of bitterness.

They walked on. They came to the sea. It was a small narrow beach here, silver in colour from the sand, where a great heap of round stones had been piled up by the waves. Dominic sat down on the stones.

'Who are you?' he asked. 'I saw you at the Mass. I wondered who you were. Are you a cousin too?'

'Yes,' she said. 'I'm Finola Brady.' She sat beside him, her arms wrapped around her knees. 'I'm about your twenty-second blind cousin,' she said.

'Ah,' he said. 'Your father is Boat Brady. You live over the mountains beyond, near the lake.'

'That's right,' she said.

'Your father hasn't the Irish,' he said, smiling as he remembered the tall rangy man roaring at Uncle Feilim. 'For God's sake speak so that I can understand, Feilim.' 'You should be bloody-well ashamed not knowing the language of the land.'

'I'm Dominic,' he said. 'Pleased to meet you.' He held out his hand. She put her own gravely into it. It was a pleasant contact. She was a good-looking girl with regular features and big eyes.

'I know you well,' she said. 'I saw you in College, when you were giving the lectures in Irish.'

'Oh,' he said. 'What are you doing?'

'Arts,' she said.

'On account of all this,' he said, firing a stone at the water, 'I am doing nothing. I won't be able to do an exam this year even.'

'There's always next year,' she said.

'You see,' he went on, 'those up there, they have caught fire. I cannot catch fire. I am not like that at all. How can I force myself to be something that I am not?'

'I don't know,' she said. 'Do you want your country to be free?'

He thought it over.

'Yes,' he said. 'It is necessary.'

'Well?' she asked.

'Has your house been like ours too?' he asked. 'Has freedom been preached from the cradle?'

'Yes,' she said.

'You accept all you have been taught then?'

'Most of it,' she said.

'Are you on fire?' he asked her, but he didn't wait for her to reply. He leaned back on his elbow. 'These men that were executed, they have already become symbols in a short time. Well, I see them as men, standing up, waiting to be shot down. Human beings, you see. I think of the sorrow of their people who must be weeping hopelessly for them, for they were exceptional men, but they were men, and sad people will be crying for them. I am sad for my father. He was a nice man. He found it hard to communicate with his sons, but he was a very nice man. I don't want him to be a symbol. I just think of him as my father, who was witty, and clever, and just, and had his principles. I think it was silly the way he died. That was due to stupidity. He had many more years to give to young people, imparting knowledge and some wisdom. I'm very sorry he is dead, and that has nothing to do with rebellions or oppressions or burning breasts. It's just because he was my father and I don't want to kill anyone because he died like that. It's just what I mean, they are up there talking about symbols when they should be talking about him.'

He put his arm over his eyes and lay back on the stones.

She looked at him. He was very defenceless, she thought, even though he had a strong face and a strong body.

'Somebody has to light the fire,' she said, carefully. 'That is the way it has always been. There have to be fire lighters. If they become symbols, it's not their fault.'

'Yes,' he said, from behind his arm, 'but they burn a lot of people who don't want to be burned.'

'Maybe it's good for them,' she said spiritedly.

He laughed ruefully, and sat up, wiping his eyes with the sleeve of his coat.

'Maybe so,' he said. 'We better go back, Finola. All the same, I'm glad I found you where I did. I'm sorry nobody else got the same idea.'

They stood up, and looked for a moment at the sea. It was glassy calm, and was merely whispering on the sand as it came in. Then they turned and walked up the lane.

'They involve you,' said Dominic. 'They involve you.'

8

I T IS an unnerving experience to fail an examination. Dominic was determined that it wouldn't happen to him again. So he started to work and concentrate, realizing that it also presented him with a good reason for not becoming involved. He kept his eyes on his books and his ears shut.

So it was on an August day, over a year after his father's death, that he was in the room of his digs, when the door opened and Lowry burst in on him. It was a small room. It held an iron bedstead with a white quilt, a basin and ewer on a stand, a cupboard for his clothes, and a small table under the window where he studied. The outlook from the window was not exciting. You could see a portion of sky through the lace curtains, but mainly chimney stacks of all sorts and sizes.

'Man,' said Lowry, 'what a fug!' He came over and opened the window. He placed his hand on Dominic's shoulder and looked at him. 'Your eyes are bugged,' he said. 'Your skin is white. You have a tremble in your hand. Come on into the fresh air.'

Dominic thought how big Lowry was. Parts of his fair hair were bleached white from the sun. He was tanned, very handsome, and had great charm.

So Dominic said: 'You go to hell, Lowry,' and lighted another cigarette.

Lowry sat on the bed.

'What has come over you, Dominic?' he asked sadly. 'You have become a hermit. You might as well be in a monastery for all we have seen of you. Have we offended you?'

'Look, Lowry,' said Dominic. 'I'm not like you. I'm not very bright. I stuck up to my neck in the last two exams, because I let things prey on my mind. You see, I'm a one-track-minded person.'

'Tell me more,' said Lowry, folding his arms.

'I'm not like you,' said Dominic. 'I can't hop off to jails and come back and toss off examinations as if I had been in a rest home.'

'It is unkind of you,' said Lowry, 'to refer to my sinful past.'

'I'm only using it as an example of the difference in our mentality, that's all,' said Dominic. 'Look, I'm a plodder. I have to believe everything they tell me before I assimilate it. I can't accept things without thinking over them. I'm slow-minded. Right?'

'Come over here and have a look at yourself,' said Lowry. He caught him by the arm and forced him over to the mirror. 'Take a look at that face.'

Dominic looked at it. Hair standing up, dark bristle on the jowls, bloodshot eyes, yellow complexion.

'Well,' said Dominic defensively, 'I'm not looking for a beauty prize.'

'I was talking to your mother,' said Lowry. 'For God's sake get him into the sun, she said. Make him take the air.'

'I don't believe that,' said Dominic.

'It's true,' said Lowry, still holding his arm and going down the narrow stairs with him. 'Dualta was home for a while. You didn't see him?'

'I didn't see him,' said Dominic. 'He's home very often for a fellow that's supposed to be studying to be a teacher to take his father's place.' He said this sarcastically.

Lowry tut-tutted.

'You shouldn't talk like that about your crippled brother,' he said.

'Crippled my eye,' said Dominic, thinking of his brother racing him on the strand at home with his game leg and beating him because he had evolved a way of throwing it out and sort of jumping each stride, and making his left hand very strong by constantly squeezing a rubber ball in his palm.

'Mrs Casey,' said Lowry to the landlady, 'we are taking the patient into the fresh air.'

'A good thing,' said Mrs Casey vigorously. 'He'll be dead in a month if he does much more sticking his nose into those books. It's pagan,' she said. 'Horrible things,' she said. She had opened the pages at times, and was shocked at the illustrations of babies in wombs and the drawings of men in all their particulars. 'There should be a law against them,' she said stirring the batter in the yellow bowl.

'You see,' said Lowry, and there they were outside the house and walking on the warm pavements and turning right towards the river.

'I see that I am outside when I should be inside,' said Dominic, 'and I had no intention of being outside. Where are we going?'

'We're going up the river,' said Lowry.

'I'm like a tramp,' said Dominic. He was wearing trousers and a shirt with the sleeves rolled. He felt the bristles on his chin.

Lowry was saying hello here and there. Everybody down

69

here knew him. Dominic saw how people's eyes lighted up as they looked at him. Lowry's eyes were curious, steel-blue with a black edging. Striking eyes. Dominic remembered him the time he was released from jail. It had been raining that evening the prisoners came home. Probably the greatest shock to them during the whole business was the roaring reception they got when they came off the train. The same people who had pelted them away were now gathered in their thousands to welcome them home. They passed through the people on sidecars and drays and horse carts and motor cars, waving and answering the cheering with incredulous eyes. And the rain poured down and everybody was wet and nobody minded, and he remembered the grim-mouthed police with their glistening capes, sour as lemons. He remembered the dominating figure of Lowry, his wet raincoat, the hair plastered to his head, accepting the cheers and the roaring. There were bonfires on the hills too as they went home.

That was the last time he had seen Sam. Sam said: It makes up for the time they went away, but they don't know what they are cheering. They think all these nice men will now sit down in front of the fire and become regular parliamentarians. They might as well be cheering a bunch of tigers.

Not Lowry though, he thought, Lowry told everybody who was willing to listen that he was done with politics. He had been an innocent victim, anyhow. Now he was going to settle down. No more lousy jails for him and British cooking therein. Marriage, when he found the right little woman, security, and a large family, all of whom would be born with little Union Jacks in their mouths. He publicly embraced the sergeant who had arrested him, and thanked him for making him see the error of his ways, and offered to sing 'God Save The King' for him in the middle of Shop Street.

'I hope you kept to your resolution about no more politics,' he said, as he thought of these things.

'Strictly,' said Lowry. 'As far as I am concerned, Dominic, they can take holy Ireland and sink it. Wouldn't that be the best solution? Hello, Mrs Walsh, how is himself. Hey, George, I saw you last night. Never mind, I won't tell.'

Calling like this at people, and laughing, white teeth shining in the warm August sunshine.

There was little wind and the water of the river was calm. But they were not alone. Six or seven of the light rowing boats were already on the water on their slow way up the river, loaded so the gunwales were near the water by young men and girls, about a girl to each boat, he thought. Lowry's boat was waiting, with four young men and a girl, and he was a bit taken aback to see the girl was Finola Brady. The others were students, Red Jack, Speck and Tope.

'I got him, fellows,' said Lowry. 'Let's cast off.'

'Aye, aye, Admiral,' said Red, and they got aboard cautiously. The boat would have been loaded with three in it.

'You know Finola, Dominic,' said Lowry. 'She's out your way.'

'Hello,' said Finola. Dominic was sitting practically nose to nose with her. He had kept away from her. Saw her once or twice in the distance. Somehow, he didn't like to remember the last time he saw her. It made him embarrassed. He was conscious now of his unkempt appearance.

'I wouldn't say exactly that she lives out our way,' he said. 'Maybe the flying birds would think so.'

'Anything outside the town is out your way,' said Lowry airily. 'All those parishes and villages out there should unite. Take it easy, Tope,' he shouted to the young man who was very heavy and shifting his weight in the bow. 'Don't let's get wet. How about singing a song? No, we won't do that, there's a young lady present.'

They laughed.

'How is your mother?' she asked.

'She is well,' said Dominic.

'And your brother?' she asked.

'He's fine,' said Dominic. 'I don't see much of him.'

'Absence makes the heart grow fonder,' said Lowry. 'You and Dualta strike sparks off one another, don't you?'

'Brothers are different,' said Dominic.

'You are in the wrong department,' said Lowry laughing. 'You should be doing philosophy.'

71

There was a nice smell from the river. The rushes were rustling in the faint breeze. Dominic filled his lungs with the clean air.

'You have changed,' he said to her.

'Have I?' she asked smiling.

'You have become a young lady,' he said. Trite remark. But that was the way it had to be, girls gradually becoming young ladies.

Lowry laughed.

'You have a way with girls, Dominic,' he said. Then he and the others started talking football. They were due to play Turloughmore the following Sunday.

'That's what the trip is all about, really,' he told Dominic. 'Limber them up.'

'What do the girls do?' Dominic asked.

'They'll do the cooking,' said Lowry. This amused him so much that he laughed a lot at it, the others joining with him. Dominic was puzzled.

Not for long.

They landed on the long green sward in front of the ruined Menlo Castle and with great speed all the young men lined up and numbered off and formed fours, and they marched and countermarched on the grass under Lowry's eye. Most intricate movements they performed that they couldn't have performed without a lot of practice.

Then the picnic baskets were opened, and from white cloths they removed bits and pieces of guns, so that they ended up with two rifles, and they shared them for arms drill and sighting, while others of them jumped walls and crept up on sentries, and wrestled on the grass; and some of them bared arms or legs while the nice girls opened boxes and proceeded to bandage their limbs or apply splints with great vigour and much laughter, but an underlying seriousness.

Lowry left them and came back to Dominic. He sat with him, watching.

'This is what it's all about,' said Dominic.

'Just training the football team,' said Lowry. 'It's nothing to do with politics.' Suddenly he pulled a ·38 revolver from his coat and pointed it at Dominic and said: 'Bang, you are wounded. Finola,' he called, 'come and bandage Dominic, the poor chap is wounded.'

She came towards them, smiling.

'Where is he wounded?' she asked.

'Pick your own spot, Dominic,' Lowry said.

'We'll say your arm,' she said, getting on her knees. 'It would not be too painful if the bullet went through,' she said. 'But if it didn't you are in trouble.'

'Leave me alone,' said Dominic petulantly, turning away from her. He heard the silence then.

Lowry was lying on his back twirling the chamber of the revolver.

'Before Dualta left the army,' he said. 'He brought out a few bits of equipment. It's a pity they wouldn't keep him in the army. No use to them any more. No trigger finger, can't bash a square with a hobnailed boot. But they fired him too fast. He could have equipped a division if they'd kept him in long enough.'

'So Dualta is a hero,' said Dominic.

'Dominic,' said Lowry, 'they let us all go because they wanted to ameliorate America, and get them into the war. Now they will want more bodies. They will try and conscript all the young men. Do you want all the young men of Ireland to end up clots of blood in the mud of France? Do you?'

'Listen,' said Dominic, pounding the grass with his fist. 'I have to pass my examinations. My mother is not wealthy. She earns a hard living teaching kids. She no longer has my father's salary, just her own. She is expending a lot of it on me. I cannot divide myself.'

'All the young fellows in the country need is a lead,' said Lowry. 'It's people like you who will have to give it to them. They will listen to you. They are not going to conscript us like sheep for the slaughter, I can tell you. We will resist. Will you stand out there on the road and watch all the young men of your parish taken away by the lorry load, just because you want to pass your examination and don't want to be involved?'

'There's Dualta,' said Dominic. 'Let the brave Dualta do it.'

'Dualta is too important,' said Lowry patiently. 'And it's better for him to remain unknown. The less people know about him the better. This is a job you can do, without having to fail your lousy examination.' There was silence then for a while. 'Listen, Dominic, they can't do it, if every single young man says No! It's as easy as that. Just enough people to say no and it can't be done. But it can't be a token resistance. They must have some form of training, so that they are a menace, and not worth the price they would have to pay for conscripting them. You see? Nearly all the young men in the University are organizing their own villages.'

He looked at Dominic's sideface. Not very prepossessing with the black bristle on it and the heavy chin under the clamped mouth.

'It may interest you to know that Finola and myself are engaged. And since she is your umpteenth cousin once removed, you and I will be practically related.'

Dominic thought of this. He turned on his side to look at them. He felt, this is a bit of a shock, as if he should have been consulted. He looked at her sideface. She was looking at Lowry, and smiling. I should have known, he thought, that was the change in her. The girl is in love. Well, she couldn't be in love with a nicer or odder character, he thought. Then he held out his arm.

'So I am wounded in the arm,' he said, and they laughed and he felt the softness of her fingers on his flesh.

It was a February morning. It was very cold. They had to walk very carefully. Away behind them Dominic could see the first streak of dawn in the eastern sky, a faint touch like yellowed whitewash. They had to be careful walking in the puddles of the ground. They were frozen solid. In fact, many an incautious hobnail had landed and sliddered and they would hear the thump of a heavy backside hitting the ground. There would be heard a curse, and suppressed laughter, and Peter O'Flaherty coming back and growling: 'Quiet, I said, quiet! Do ye want to waken the hens?'

They would move on again.

Dominic thought how well Peter O'Flaherty had turned out as an OC. They had wanted to make Dominic the OC. He had pointed out that he would be away in the town most of the time, and they would have to pick one of their own on that account. So they picked Peter, much to people's surprise, because Peter wasn't what you'd call an active man. His mother was a widow woman, and they said she had to do the work of two men; her dead husband and her son Peter. He had a voice like a bull seal out on the rocks of the sea, and oddly enough, he had this something that made men, some of whom thought little of him, listen to him and what was more, obey him.

They moved again after the fall, two small columns of men, five in each. Their destination was the road that ran near the sea. They could almost see the sheen off the sea now, and Dominic thought, if you didn't know better, you'd think that here was a well-armed band of men moving with force and determination.

How wrong you would be only themselves knew. The rifle tips that you might see silhouetted against the dawn light were only the tops of wooden guns, painted brown. Of the ten men: Peter O'Flaherty, Poc Murray, Pierce the son of Eamon of the Shop, Sean Ned who was the brother of Poric the policeman, the two Reardons and three Conroys and himself, only Peter had a revolver with three rounds of probably decayed ammunition, and Pierce had a single-barrelled shotgun.

Dominic himself was the Quartermaster and Intelligence Officer, whatever that meant. He was the one that was supposed to arm them. A rifle cost five pounds, when GHQ in Dublin had one to sell. A handgun cost something less. But five pounds took a lot of collecting in pennies and sixpences and shillings. They were fed up with wooden guns. They had come a long way all the same from what they had been over a year ago, a few men practising drilling on the strand, or in the barn at the back of Dominic's house, much to the amusement of the children who imitated them afterwards in their games. Uniforms would have set them up, Peter thought. You have to give a man a uniform, a nice green Volunteer uniform.

No, said Sam. No uniform. Uniforms any more are for

75

older men who march at funerals and attend meetings. They are marked men, the boyos in the uniforms. Leave them alone. So Dominic left them alone. They would be too expensive for the lads anyhow, who had enough trouble fitting themselves out in their homespun clothes.

Peter was beside him.

'You there, Dominic?' he asked. 'We should be near the Cross now. Will you go ahead and get to the far side. Listen as close as a bat. Note all the movements that you hear and whatever you see. Then we can give them hail holy afterwards.'

'All right,' said Dominic.

'Down now,' Peter told the others. 'Warm the heather.'

Dominic set off on his own.

It was an eerie hour of the morning, this half light. They were on a great plain of rock and small fields and lakes that separated the mountains behind them from the sea. Very tricky ground. Even the sheep broke their legs on it. You had to proceed cautiously. It was very cold, yet he couldn't put his hands in the pockets of his coat because he needed them to balance his body on the bad ground. As a band of light spread around the horizon he could see every breath that came out of his mouth. They were three hours walking from the village. They had gone out of the back of the village and made a great circle towards the Cross. Much grumbling. People in the winter slept later in the mornings, since there wasn't much to do; just rise late and milk the cows and throw a little fodder to the animals.

He could see the gaps in the walls now and didn't have to clamber over the loose stones. Then he came to the wall that shut off the road from the field. He climbed over this and stood on the road. He looked across and saw the low-sized gnarled thorn tree that stretched away startled from the fierceness of the west winds. He walked across the road, jumped the other wall and crouched beside this. He was blended into it and he could see the Cross well, so anything they did would be under his eye.

He blew into his hands and cuddled them under his oxters. Now he wanted to laugh. Since all this started it was like playing games. Times he was sobered. Dualta could sober him, or Sam or Lowry. They weren't playing games. But when he was not with those, he had a notion that he was playing games, and that he was too big for it, too old.

They won the Conscription battle. That was fine. It was reasonable. People outside the church gates on a certain Sunday, listening to the Bishops' Manifesto – *We consider that conscription forced in this way on Ireland is an oppressive and inhuman law which the Irish people have a right to resist by every means that are consonant to the law of God* – which Dominic had to translate and read in Irish.

That's when the Volunteers ceased to be a joke with their wooden guns. They got sixty new volunteers overnight but when the crisis passed they dropped away. They had more excuses than the people who refused to go to the Lord's Supper. They thought they had won the war, when they hadn't even won a skirmish.

He raised himself now and screwed up his eyes to see if he could spot anything of their approach from the opposite side. No sign of them. You would think it was a place no human being had walked for a thousand years. He listened. He could hear nothing. He sat back again.

He thought of the spate of oratory that descended on the country when the foreigners' war was over in Europe and they had to call free elections. Even he had been excited in the town. He thought he would always remember the young men with blazing eyes, the planes of their faces ferociously sincere under the light of the torches. Baton charges held back by hurleys; running men, screaming women; the fights at the election booths. Most of the Sinn Fein leaders in jail in England, and in Ireland wherever there was a jail, yet from their cells winning an overwhelming majority of the Irish people to their cause; nobody could say that was playacting, or the new word that was emerging from the arrests and the drilling and the bonfires and the hunger strikes, with all the shawled women outside the jails saying the rosary while the rain pelted them, this word – Dáil, which meant freedom to govern themselves. If any nation had ever voted for freedom

77

to govern, this was it. Dominic could see the logic of it all, and yet it seemed to him like playing games. He couldn't feel that it was real. It could be a tale of Celtic Twilight told over a turf fire of an evening. Even if the blood chilled at the news of the first policeman shot dead at Soloheadbeg a few weeks ago, it seemed a charade, a sort of shadow-boxing in which you were a performer, not a participant. He wanted to feel, and he couldn't feel.

He raised himself again and looked.

Now he thought he saw a vague humped shadow in the field on the other side. Somebody with his behind too high.

He smiled. This was the epitome of the playacting. A mock attack on a non-existent police force at the Cross outside a village near the bleak shore of the Atlantic. Why would a thing like this have meaning? Wooden guns and frost and sweating men. He liked these men, more than any others. He had grown up with them, gone to school with them, laughed and tricked with them. He couldn't imagine any of them no more than himself pointing a gun at a policeman and shooting him dead. Such a thing could never happen.

He heard a sound then too. Aha! A loud curse as somebody hit his knee on a rock. He heard Peter shushing him. Another black mark and then he heard nothing, so they were presumably crouched behind the wall and Peter was building up the scene for them: the police tender coming down the road from the west, having done the circle of the country from the barracks in Spiddal. A land mine would have been placed at the Cross (if they had a land mine or knew the first thing about making one) that would be exploded and then behind a tree would fall, blocking the escape. There wasn't a tree within fifty miles of them. The wind out here was the master of the landscape and trees were its victims. Then when the vehicle was nicely trapped they would open fire. Shoot straight and shoot to kill, since ammunition was short. Ready? Aim! Fire! Right now, Peter, for God's sake, let's go home and get our breakfast.

But life is a jest. Life does the unbelievable things, as if making a mockery of the mock.

For the blood in Dominic's veins went as cold as the ice in the pools as he saw a lorry come bumping from the west with its lights on. It was bright enough to see the lorry even, and the few dozen policemen who were in the back of it. He could see the tips of their rifles and he knew they weren't wooden.

Who can think of coincidences that never happen, he thought, as he crouched down behind the wall?

What would the other men think of this? What would they do? Why, they would do nothing, just stay hidden there like himself, petrified until the lorry had gone past.

And then the lorry stopped right at the Cross and the lights went out. But he could still see it, and the stiff men getting down from it and stretching their legs, and the driver getting out of the cab, stretching his legs too. He heard their voices. Talking about how cold they were, and stupid bloody patrolling, and the silly inspector home in bed, warm with his wife and what was it all about. Irish voices because these were Irishmen. You had to keep reminding yourself of this, and they had merely alighted to unstiffen themselves and relieve themselves at the Cross.

Dominic thought of the little bunch of men opposite. What were they thinking? He was supposed to be the Intelligence Officer, and he didn't even know there would be a patrol like this. Let them relieve themselves and go!

And suddenly there was the sound of a shotgun going off.

It was as if the earth and the sky and the dawning light suddenly stood still. The policemen were like ungraceful statues. Then after the world seemed to have held its breath for a fraction of time it suddenly came alive again.

The driver ran to his cab and the policemen ran to the back of the lorry. Before you could count them they were aboard and crouching low and the motor was screaming as it revved and the gears caught and it ran away raising clouds of dust bumping and jumping on the bad road, and as Dominic raised himself a little he could see the men behind the wall on their feet, running and running and spreading out. So he got this picture of a racing lorry and running men, and he leaped into the road and leaped over the wall and went after them, running

79

in giant strides trying to catch up with them. Not afraid but bewildered. This had only been practice, and it could have been real and they could have all been dead with their wooden guns, but it was a symbol of the whole thing, of the unreality.

Nobody stopped running for half a mile and then they had to stop since the lot of them were out of breath. They sat on the stones puffing like nearly deflated bagpipes. Peter was on a hill looking along the road. Then he came back.

'The curse of the seven blind bastards on you!' he shouted at Pierce. 'Did you want to get us all killed, did you?'

'My soul from the devil, Peter,' said Pierce. 'I never knew the cartridge was in it. When you whispered: Ready? Aim! Fire! by the holy God I fired, and I nearly died with the shock.'

'We could be dead!' said Peter. 'We could be cold clay on account of you. You know that, if the others hadn't run away, they'd have killed us like rabbits? You understand that?'

'Take my life, Peter,' said Pierce. 'I only put in a cartridge in case we came on a rabbit and I forgot about it.'

'What were you aiming at?' Peter asked.

'Damned if I know,' said Pierce. 'The thing blew up on me. I was shooting at the stars.'

Dominic started to laugh. He couldn't help it.

'It's not for fun, Dominic!' Peter shouted at him now. 'Do not laugh. It is not for fun.'

'I'm sorry, Peter,' said Dominic. 'I saw them go and I saw you go. It was like a play.'

'It is not a play,' said Peter. 'It could be a tragedy, but not a play. Maybe I will laugh too, tomorrow. But I won't laugh now. When are we going to get arms, Dominic? You are the one to say. Let us be able to defend ourselves. Are we to die with wooden guns in our hands and be the laugh of the country?'

He was nearly crying with vexation, Dominic saw.

'I'm sorry, Peter,' he said. 'We have enough money now for two guns. I will try and get them. Your men are good. Do you know that? I watched as you approached the Cross. I only heard two things and saw one behind. I wouldn't know

80

ten men had come on the Cross if I was an enemy. I swear this.'

'They were good,' said Peter. 'They held fine under the shock of seeing the lorry. Why, they even did what I told them. They aimed and they fired. Only for that Pierce. If you weren't a Christian, I'd slaughter you.'

Pierce groaned.

Poc Murray laughed then. He clapped Pierce on the back.

'My soul to you, Pierce,' he said. 'You are one of the earliest men in Ireland to fire at a policeman this year. You'll get a medal.'

'And pin it on his head with a nail,' said Peter. 'All right. Get going. Scatter abroad in case they come back. Get home and lie low. They wouldn't know what part we are from. Ye did well.'

He walked ahead of them. They took their wooden toys and followed after him.

If this had been real, Dominic wondered as he followed them, if this had been real, how would I have felt?

He was to find out soon enough.

9

I N FACT he was to find out the following April.
Dominic was packing his big fibre suitcase in the room. He was getting ready to go home.

He was looking forward to going home. It was a pleasant change from bits of bodies, chemical smells, exuberant youth. He found it easier to study at home anyhow, even if there were distractions like currach fishing with Sean Ned, spending two hours over a pint of porter in the shop of Eamon, flirting with the girls at the gable-end in the evening, dodging the police patrols while they did their bit of harmless drilling; it was a restful life with blue skies and the fresh smell of the sea. Not that he didn't like life in the College, if it wasn't complicated by Lowry and his men, but that too seemed a game, like playing football or handball or the bit of boxing in the gymnasium. He liked this. He wasn't brilliant, but he was strong. He could always take a certain number of blows, weather them and then beat his opponent, lean on him, wear him down dourly.

He had packed and was looking around to see if he had left anything that he should bring home, or leave things which he didn't need, when he smelt the frying bacon from below. It didn't tempt him, since he had had his tea, but it intrigued him.

When he went down with his case he was surprised to see Dualta sitting at the table in the kitchen, eating from a large plate of bacon and eggs, with Mrs Casey at the range frying up more; also black pudding and sausages.

'It does my heart good, Dualta,' she was saying, 'to see a man who can really eat.'

'I'm your man,' said Dualta through a full mouth. 'The wonder to me, Mrs Casey, is how you can have remained a widow so long, and the hand you have with the frying pan.'

She laughed.

'One was enough, Dualta. One of ye is enough in a lifetime.'

'Hello, Dominic,' said he. 'I was passing through and I thought I would call and bring you home.'

'Well,' said Dominic, 'I'm most grateful to you. How do we go? Do you carry me on the bar of a bicycle.'

'Not at all,' said Dualta. 'You are going to ride in state. I am a proud possessor of a motor car, which I got on loan.'

'Well,' said Dominic, 'you have borrowed everything else, why not a motor car.'

Dualta laughed.

Dominic didn't see him often, but whenever he did see him Dualta dispossessed him of the little money or cigarettes he might have.

'Stuff that into you,' said Mrs Casey, putting more on his plate. 'You are like a fellow that didn't eat for a fortnight. Don't they give you anything to eat up in Dublin?'

'Ah,' said Dualta, 'it isn't what they give you but the way they give it to you.'

She poured the tea. She buttered the brown bread which she baked herself. She fussed around Dualta, Dominic saw, like a nun in a parlour. Dualta had this quality of making people light up when he was in their company. Lowry also had it. He wondered what it was. A touch of recklessness, or else the way they devoted themselves to enjoying what they were doing or saying at the moment and the way they made you part of it.

'You are wasted,' Dualta told her as she sat beaming at him. 'You should be running a boarding house with a hundred and sixty-five bedrooms.'

'The Lord save us!' she said laughing. 'One is enough for me, Dominic there, even if he is a quiet one. It's better that way. I'd never be sure of yourself or what you would be doing next.'

'That's the way to live,' said Dualta, mopping up gravy with a piece of bread. 'Isn't life a gamble, Mrs Casey? It's like going to Heaven. You don't know until the last second, but I'll tell you something – they need fryers like you in Heaven.'

'More useful in hell, at that rate,' she laughed.

'If I only had a fag,' said Dualta, searching his pockets, so Dominic had to throw him his packet. He barely lit a cigarette when they were out of the house, the suitcase thrown into the back of the car.

'Oh, my God!' said Dominic as he looked at it, 'what a crock!' It had no hood, the bonnet was loose, the front mud-guards were tied with wire, the steel springs were visible through the reefs in the seats from which bits of coarse horse-hair protruded.

'She's a beauty,' said Dualta, going to the front with the handle and winding it until he was blue in the face before it chugged doubtfully and then took heart and kept going.

'Will she get us home?' Dominic asked.

'After a while,' said Dualta. 'We have to do a bit of a round first.'

'Oh, we have,' said Dominic.

'Won't take long,' said Dualta. 'We should be home to-morrow night.'

'That's bloody fine,' said Dominic.

'Don't be introspective,' said Dualta.

He drove the car down and over the bridge and around by the jail into narrow streets over the Canal Bridge, down another long street and then up a long winding lane with small houses on each side. It was getting dark. There was no wind. It was quite bright. There was a full moon due.

He stopped then in deep shadow at the top of this lane. He waited, peering, and then as a man detached himself from a gateway, he got out. Dominic got out too, because he recognized Sam's slouch, and the combination of Dualta and Sam made his heart drop into his boots.

'One good deed deserves another,' Dualta was saying quietly to Sam.

'Hello, Dominic,' said Sam, 'glad you are in on this.'

'What am I in on?' Dominic asked.

'Did you tell him?' Sam asked.

'Well, you know what Dominic is like,' said Dualta. 'He'd blind us with questions.'

'Isn't his ignorance dangerous?' Sam asked.

'Not at all,' said Dualta airily. 'His ignorance will be convincing.'

Sam chuckled. 'You'll be the death of me,' he said.

'Of me,' said Dominic anxiously, 'what's up?'

'Better light the lamps on that yoke,' said Dualta. 'There's carbide in a tin in the back.'

'Right,' said Sam. 'How long?'

'It's a five-minute job,' said Dualta. 'All your information is right? He's there now?'

'He was a couple of minutes ago. There's a man across the road watching the front. If there's any change he'll tell you.'

'Right,' said Dualta, 'five minutes.' He pulled a cap out of his pocket and pulled it down over his right eye. 'Come on, Dominic.' He walked away. Dominic had to hurry after him.

'Listen, Dualta,' he said. 'You can't do this.'

'Here,' said Dualta, 'put this in your pocket.' He held out his hand. Dominic took it. He felt the cold steel of a small revolver.

'Listen, Dualta,' he said in a panic.

'It's not loaded,' said Dualta. 'Just put it in your pocket. You don't say anything. You just stand there with your pleasant countenance, frowning. You say nothing.'

They walked into the main road, where the houses stretched back with long gardens in front of them. Very respectable houses. Very respectable people. Dualta paused at a low wrought-iron gate. He looked around him. There was the dark figure of a man leaning against the high wall on the opposite side. He made no sign.

'If I nod my head solemnly,' said Dualta, 'take out the gun. Just show it.' He was taking a red-stained bandage from his pocket; wrapping it around his bad hand. It was a long one. He put the tied ends around his neck, so his hand was in a sling.

He went to the white painted door on which highly polished brass was gleaming in the moonlight. He pressed the bell. Dominic was standing behind him, and his stomach was like water.

The door opened. In the light a young girl dressed in a blue dress and a white cap on her head to match a small white apron stood there.

'The doctor is in?' said Dualta. 'We have had an accident.'

He didn't give her time. He held up the red-stained bandage and stepped into the hall. There were three doors in the hall. She looked at the middle one.

'I don't know if he wants to be disturbed,' she said.

'That's all right,' said Dualta. 'Don't go,' he said to Dominic. 'Close the front door.' Dominic did so, stood with his back to it. The little maid was bewildered. If she only knew, so was Dominic.

'How did it happen?' she asked him. 'Is it bad?'

Dualta had gone in the middle door and closed it after him.

'I don't know,' said Dominic. She was looking at him closely. He hoped she wouldn't remember him again. It was a dim light in the hallway. His whole body was bathed in sweat.

Then the centre door opened and a middle-aged man, a bit bent at the shoulders, came out with Dualta behind him. Dominic thought the man looked pale.

'That's all right, Chrissie,' he said. 'You can go.' They waited until she walked down towards the end of the house.

'Which room?' Dualta asked.

'This one,' the man said, nodding at the first door.

'You go first,' said Dualta. He opened the door, put his hand inside and switched on the light. Dualta didn't enter. 'Is the blind down?' he asked.

'Yes,' the man said.

'Come in,' said Dualta and Dominic followed them. It was a sort of library. There was a large case with guns in it.

'You cannot do this,' the man said. 'It is a Greener gun.'

'You'll get a receipt,' said Dualta. 'It will be restored to you.'

'Restored!' the man snorted. 'In what shape? Where do you fellows think all this will get you?'

'Get the guns out of there,' Dualta said to Dominic.

He went over. It was a glass case with a felt-lined back. There were three guns, a double-barrelled shotgun, a single-barrelled and a ·22 rifle. He loosened them from the ratches.

'This is vandalism as well as robbery,' the man said.

'Don't you want to help your country?' Dualta asked.

'The country can get on fine without fellows like you,' the man said. He was getting angry.

'Cartridges?' Dualta asked.

The man shut his lips tightly.

'Try the drawers below,' said Dualta. Dominic opened them. He felt the fine sheen of the wood. He saw the square cardboard boxes. There was a brown canvas shooting bag hanging beside the case. Dominic took this and put the boxes of cartridges into it.

'You won't get away with this,' the man said.

'We will all walk out the back way,' said Dualta. 'If you want to be a hero, there's nothing to stop you.'

'What would you do?' the man asked. 'What would you do?'

'I think at this stage, my life is more important than yours,' said Dualta.

'You wouldn't have the nerve,' the man said. 'I know your kind.'

'Walk out now,' said Dualta. 'Softly past the kitchen. If Chrissie comes out, tell her everything is fine.'

The man went first, Dualta followed him and Dominic came after them carrying the three guns in his arms and the bag over his shoulder. He could smell the gun-oil off them. The hall past the kitchen was flagged. Their feet resounded off the flags. Then the man raised the latch and they were in a back garden. Dominic could smell flowers. He breathed air deep into his lungs. The walk up the back seemed endless.

'Open the small gate,' said Dualta. The man, after hesitation, did so. 'Out,' said Dualta over his shoulder to Dominic.

There were three men in the lane. He felt the guns being taken from him. Then Dualta was beside him as another man slipped in the gate.

'You'll pay for this,' they heard the man's voice.

'We'll hold him here for ten minutes,' he heard Sam whisper. 'The car is ready to go. Many thanks, Dualta.'

'Pleasure,' said Dualta. 'Any time at all. Thanks for the car.'

Then they were in the car and it moved. Dualta drove sedately. Dominic's mouth was bone dry. His tongue seemed swollen. His hand was hurting him, his grip was so tight on the door of the car.

'Very neat,' Dualta was saying. 'Five minutes, like I said.'

Dominic couldn't answer him. Not for ages, until he had moistened his mouth and his tongue could talk.

Then he said: 'But this is not the way home,' because he saw that they were driving on the great long plain on the south side of the river, away from the coast.

'No,' said Dualta. 'We are just going the long way round. I had to help Sam in order to get the loan of the motor car to help Morgan.

'Oh, no,' groaned Dominic. 'Oh, no.'

And Dualta laughed and clapped him on the back.

It's all right for him, Dominic was thinking. It is all right for him. But I'm not made that way.

He didn't sleep that night. They had driven the car in behind a huge garden cock near a farm house and shared a big bed in the room off the kitchen. Dominic just took off his shoes and lay on the bed, listening to the drone of the voices. The old man in the corner with the stick and the beard. He might have been a bigger edition of his own father. The same talk. Ireland for these old men was a beautiful woman with whom they had fallen in love because they heard about her from their own fathers. She was a tangible image as real as the Blessed Virgin before whose statue on the wall were always little jars with flowers. Now the young men like Morgan didn't talk this way, but their eyes shone when the old ones talked, even if they winked behind their backs. Their hospitality was enormous, boiled chicken and bacon, with cabbage and huge pots of potatoes, the lady of the house hurt because he could not eat enough. He couldn't say to them: my stomach is like water. I am afraid.

He dozed off now and again uneasily, to awake startled, staring at the darkness.

He felt Dualta lying on the bed beside him; later, and most galling, he heard him sleeping, the calm breathing which he tried to emulate almost maddening him. Was it lack of sensitivity? He knew it wasn't, because Dualta was far brighter than himself and more quick-minded. But he could put things out of his mind, things like attacking a police barracks in the broad light of day.

Good God, thought Dominic, they're mad! He had a strong temptation to rise from the bed and creep out of the house and walk the long way home. He sweated over this thought. The way they talked about it, they might just as well be going into the village to buy a loaf of bread.

Yet it was Dualta who shook him awake in the morning.

'I don't know how you can sleep so peacefully like that,' said Dualta, 'and what's ahead of us this fine morning.'

Dominic groaned. Dualta was already shaved and was wiping off the soap with a towel. He looked fresh and healthy. His eyes were clear. Dominic rose and doused his face and head in cold water from the ewer, and then shaved himself. He thought his eyes looked hollow in the small mirror. He cut his chin and wet a little piece of newspaper that was lining a drawer of the dressing table and stopped the blood. Then he followed Dualta down to the kitchen.

It was barely dawn, but the old man was there already and the woman was bent over the open fireplace frying bacon and eggs on the triangle. It was a big kitchen, flagged, with a huge dresser taking up one whole wall, loaded with brightly coloured mugs and jugs and flowered plates and delf.

'You slept well, Dominic boy?' the old man asked.

'Oh, yes,' said Dominic.

'Isn't it well for ye to be young?' he asked. 'Wouldn't I give all I possess now to be as young as ye, this moment?'

'You cannot buy youth, sir,' said Dominic. 'And people who have it don't want it.'

'Oh, woe, woe,' said the old man. 'Ye don't know yeer luck.' He pounded his stick on the flags.

'Sit in now to your breakfast,' said John's wife. 'You must have a hole in your stomach, so little you ate last night.'

She had a white table cloth on. Of course it was Sunday, Dominic thought, as he smelt the black polish that had been used on the boots. 'Thank you, ma'am,' he said, sitting at the table. He didn't think he could eat but found that the food tasted nice.

Dualta came in with John and Morgan. Morgan was dressed in his Sunday best, a nice navy-blue suit. He looked very well. Dualta was pulling on a sort of short belted tweed jacket. Then he put on the unshapely tweed hat which had trout flies stuck in it.

'Now,' he asked. 'How do I look?'

'That's it,' said Morgan. 'As long as you keep your mouth shut you could pass for a gentleman.'

'Let ye sit over and eat,' said John. 'Even gentlemen have stomachs.'

'I must go,' said Morgan. 'I have to be at the church well in time. You have it all now, Dualta?'

'Clear as a bell,' said Dualta, sitting at the table. 'I could eat a horse.'

'Leave here when you hear the bell,' said Morgan. 'Then you will be dead on time.' He thought of what he had said, and smiled. Dominic shivered as if it had been an omen. 'You know where to go afterwards?'

'First left, first right, fourth house on the left,' said Dualta. 'Are you listening, Dominic?'

'I'm listening,' said Dominic, not looking up. He had said the directions in his mind so often during that sleepless night that he would never forget them.

'Right,' said Morgan. 'Good luck to ye. I'll see that the lads are in their places. It should be easy. If anything happens out of the ordinary, just let it go. You hear, Dualta? We have to live here. We can live with success but not failure. They'll make life miserable unless they are frightened.'

'Don't worry, Morgan,' said Dualta.

'Right, I'm away,' said Morgan, going out putting on a soft velour hat. Through the window, Dominic could see him getting into the trap, and clicking his tongue at the pony. He waved his hand as if he hadn't a care in the world, just a young man going to Mass of a Sunday morning.

All too soon, Dominic thought, they were ready. Before they left, John's wife sprinkled holy water on them. Dominic thought this was a bit incongruous as he blessed himself. Then he went into the yard and put on a long dustcoat and the dark driver's hat with the peak and pulled the goggles over his eyes.

John had the engine of the motor running over.

'There's only a half pint of water in her,' he said. 'By the time ye reach the barracks, she should be steaming.'

'Right, Dominic,' said Dualta, 'in with you.' Dominic got behind the wheel. Ordinarily he liked driving motor cars. He hadn't driven a lot. He liked the feel of the air on his face, and at fifteen miles an hour it seemed that they could be floating, if it wasn't for all the cursed bumps. He drove her to the gate near the road and waited. John bent to the road and gathered up the fine dry dust and flung it at them. They had to spit some of it out. The old man stood at the door watching this and laughed.

Then they waited for the sound of the bell. The sound of a bell is beautiful in the countryside. On a calm evening in the fields it is as soothing as a cold hand on a hot brow. Dualta was sitting in the back, rustling the road maps. He was impatient.

'Now!' he said, having heard the first faraway peal before any of them. John opened the gate, Dominic depressed the pedal and they were away.

The road was narrow. Each side there were tall hedges of thorn bushes, and pruned sycamores entwined with the vines of the wild woodbine. The newly green shoots were already whitened with dust thrown up from the road.

'Dominic,' said Dualta, leaning on the seat and speaking into his ear. 'I want to say something to you.'

Dominic grunted.

'Police have always been the eyes and ears of the rulers. You agree to this?'

'Yes,' said Dominic.

'With all due respect, there wasn't a man could piss in the whole land without a full account going up to Dublin Castle. The talk of the pubs, the language of the fairs, the whispers in the market-place. You see how quickly they jumped after Easter Week, every single person who had ever said or done anything that was in their eyes wrong, they could lay their hands on him and did so. Right?'

'Yes,' said Dominic.

'So now we put out their eyes,' said Dualta. 'They have been officially ostracized by the new Dáil. That has shaken a lot of them. It has made them think. A lot of them are going to resign. But they must be helped with a few kicks. They are kicking them well down in the south. The idea is to get them to pull in their eyes from the whole countryside, so that the Castle will be blind.'

'Why am I being lectured?' Dominic asked resentfully.

'Damn it, can't you be cheerful?' Dualta asked. 'We're not going to a funeral. Can't you see this as an adventure?'

'I keep thinking of Poric,' said Dominic. 'Suppose it is Poric. Poric wouldn't hurt anyone. Just suppose it is Poric.'

'I wish you'd stop anticipating everything,' said Dualta. 'Cowards die many times before their death, you know,' he added airily.

Dominic stopped the car. He lifted the goggles off his eyes and turned back to him.

'Don't call me a coward!' he shouted. 'Don't call me a coward! It's nothing to do with that. It's just something you fearless types wouldn't understand. Don't say that again!'

Dualta was grinning at him.

'Now we're getting somewhere,' he said. 'Drive on, my man, or we'll be late for our appointment.'

Dominic turned back and got the thing going again. He was seething. He started to think. Why am I seething? Because this is the way Dualta wanted me to be. Then he got mad and put his foot down to the boards. Not that the car went much faster, but it seemed to. Already the steam was coming out from under the bonnet. So he concentrated on that. Would there be enough water to get them to the barracks at all, or would the cursed thing burst into flames?

As it was he was driving into the small street of the village almost before he was aware of it. Five houses this side, and two shops on the other side, and the small church facing them where the road divided. He could see all this clearly. He could even see the overflow of the people at the outside doors of the church, where Morgan would be under the eyes of the five policemen who would also be at Mass, leaving just one man to mind the barracks.

He couldn't miss the barracks. There were sandbags piled around the front door, topped with barbed wire, and a sort of gate of barbed wire that had to be pulled away. It was a solid two-storey stone-built structure that would want a ton of dynamite to make an impression on it. He saw that this was the only chance. He drew to a stop right outside the barracks, gripped the wheel tightly, swallowed his Adam's apple, and watched the steam rising furiously from the radiator.

He heard Dualta getting out of the car and standing there.

'This is ridiculous!' he was saying. 'This is ridiculous and very stupid. I wish you had not come when you didn't know the road.'

He heard him rattling the maps in his hand.

'Where on earth can I get help? Is this village dead?' He

heard him walking to the barracks and shifting the barbed gate and knocking loudly on the door. There was an improvised peep hole in the door. This slid back.

'I wonder if you could help me,' Dualta was saying. 'This dunderhead of a driver has led me astray. I don't know where I am.'

You wouldn't know what nationality he was. He spoke in a very neutral way, Dominic thought. He was looking at his knuckles. They were white with the strain he was putting on them. He relaxed them, and then realized that the muscles of his stomach were the same, so he relaxed those too, and tried to breathe easily, for the policeman was outside now, talking to Dualta, looking at the map; but unfortunately he had closed the door behind him, the cautious man. He wasn't young. He had grizzled hair and a bit of a belly. There were stains on his tunic. If he straightened himself, he would be as tall as Dualta.

'I see. I see. I see,' Dualta was saying. 'The fool!' glaring up at Dominic.

'By the holy,' the policeman said then, 'you'd want some water in that yoke or it'll burst.'

'It's hopeless,' said Dualta, exasperated. 'They shouldn't license these boys to drive motor cars. Where can we get water? Get down from there, you, and go to the village pump and get some water. Don't just sit there. Could you loan us a bucket or some such thing?' he asked.

'It's all right, sir,' said the policeman. 'I'll bring out a jug of water from the tap.'

This was it. He had made the suggestion himself. He turned back to the door, opened it from the bunch of keys hanging to his belt, and as soon as it was opened Dualta got behind him and put the revolver to his back and said, very coldly: 'Put your hands over your head, and don't cry out.' Dominic could see the back of the man stiffening as if he had jerked to attention. He waited a terrible second for the policeman to do something. He wondered if Dualta would kill him. He thought, with a chill, that Dualta would.

Then the six men came from each side of the barracks. They had masks pulled over their faces, and were dressed in very old and ragged clothes, like the Wren boys of St Stephen's Day. Two of them had revolvers and two more had shotguns. As they moved in on the policeman, Dualta backed out and got into the car. The police barracks door closed and Dualta was saying: 'Now. Move now!'

Dominic thought the car would stall. This had been part of his dreams during the night. He was surprised when it moved forward, as if it had been a great miracle. First left, first right, he kept saying to his mind, fourth house on the left. There would be a big barn where the car would be hidden, and a cave where they could hide, and later tonight a boat to take them across the lake.

He was sweating, sweating, sweating. He felt like a chicken that had been cleaned of its intestines.

10

DOMINIC ALWAYS thought of clever things to say to Dualta long afterwards. Unfortunately Dualta was never there when he thought of them. It was so now, very early in the morning, as he leaned over one of the many bridges on the Headford road and waited for Finola. He watched the water being channelled into a deep flow as it went under the arch of the bridge below him. It was clear grey-coloured water, not like the bogwater at home. The rushes on the river banks were inclined to turn. Most of the hay cocks had been carted away from the fields, leaving circles of withered grass amidst the new green where their butts had rested.

He should have said: Yes, but when you put out the eyes of the lion and blind him, isn't he a much more dangerous animal? Won't he strike around him blindly at whoever comes within reach of his claws? A very clever remark that would be. Probably Dualta would say: So much the better. The more innocent people who are hit, or wounded, or inconvenienced, the greater will be the number of the lion's enemies. He thought of last

Easter, when over three hundred abandoned police barracks had been burned to the ground; the great funeral pyres of the old police, the gaping roofs, the blackened gables, the decaying water-butts, left as ugly monuments to the memory of a man named Peel.

'Are you thinking of going for a swim, Dominic?' she asked him.

He turned quickly. What a soldier, he thought, so easily surprised? I want to be more careful.

'I never heard you coming, Finola,' he said. 'You frightened the life out of me.'

She laughed. She was leaning on the bars of her bicycle. It was a new one, a lady's bicycle with coloured threads stretched from the mudguards to the wheel-hubs to protect the skirts.

'You cannot afford to be dreaming,' she said. 'Will we go?'

'All right,' said Dominic, getting his bicycle. His medium-sized case was strapped on to the back of it. 'You look well,' he said to her. 'You are an ornament to the morning.'

'Were you composing poetry,' she asked, laughing, 'while you were leaning on the bridge below the town?' She got on her bicycle and set off.

'No,' said Dominic, mounting and following her. 'I was thinking of my brother Dualta. I always think of very clever things to say to him when he's not here. He takes you over, you see, no matter how much you protest to him. All your arguments seem weak against him until he is no longer there.'

'Ah,' said Finola, 'these are the leader types, Dominic. They leave you to sort it out afterwards. They are in a hurry. They cannot wait while the rest of us are chewing the cud. They have to be prodding us, goading us. They see the end of the road while we are scrutinizing the ditches.'

'I didn't think you gave much thought to it,' he said.

'What do you think I am then, a featherbrain?' she asked.

'No, no,' said Dominic. 'Lowry is the same as Dualta, you know.'

'I know,' she said. 'Lowry is in a hurry too. After all, there is not much time. But Lowry is different.'

He looked at her. Her eyes were glowing.

'Ah,' said Dominic.

'It's not because he and I are – eh —' she said laughing. 'Lowry takes time out sometimes for thinking of the impractical things of life, outside revolution. Only for short whiles, but he does.'

'He takes too many chances, from what I hear,' said Dominic.

'I know,' she said frowning. 'But he says he is indestructible.'

'I sincerely hope so,' said Dominic. 'All the same he would want to watch himself. Sam says the new ones are after him. And they are dangerous.'

'You are making geese walk over my grave,' she said with a slight shiver. They turned right and continued on a smaller road that was lined with bushes. They had to follow one after another, because the ruts were deep and they had to cycle in the middle where the hooves of the horses had made a smooth path.

'You are going teaching soon,' he called. 'Will you like that, do you think?'

'Yes,' she called back over her shoulder, 'I will like that very much. I am looking forward to it. My mother was a teacher, you know, and her father, so it's in the blood.'

'So is my mother and my father was,' said Dominic, 'and others way back, but I don't want it. I think of myself and my fellows when we were young, and I would prefer to die than be trying to teach us.'

She laughed.

'You will be a better doctor so,' she said.

In about fifteen minutes they turned left again. It was a very bad road, so they had to stay silent. In another fifteen minutes they climbed a hill towards where they could see the telegraph poles on the main road above them. They got off the bicycles while Dominic surveyed the road. It was empty in both directions, so they went on to it and cycled along its comparatively smooth surface. They weren't five minutes on this road when they heard the roar of the lorry behind them coming from the town. They stiffened. The sound of the Crossley was becoming familiar now; late at night in the streets during the curfew, and scuttling along the road like a terrified cat in the daytime.

Finola put out her right hand and caught Dominic's tense left hand. He relaxed it, and held her hand. 'Look at me,' she said. He looked at her. His heart was pounding. Not because he was holding the hand of a pretty girl and looking into her eyes, but because this menace was coming from behind them and he wanted to throw down the bicycle and flee. He wouldn't, but this was what he wanted to do.

They heard it coming closer and then it swerved and passed them, slowing down a little as the men in the back watched them. They were carrying rifles and smoking. They were wearing the odd mixture of black and khaki uniforms that was giving them their name. The thing that was frightening about them was that they had foreign faces. Before, a policeman was a man with an Irish face and he spoke with an Irish accent. But these had accents it was hard to understand.

One of them said something as the lorry cruised. The others laughed and he flicked a cigarette butt that fell in the dust in front of the bicycles. Then he pounded at the window and the lorry sped away, turning around a far corner of the road in a cloud of dust.

'Do they make you afraid?' he asked.

'No,' she said. 'Just furious. I just get furious.'

He released his hand from hers, wiped off the sweat on his coat, wondering at her. There were hundreds like her, who did ordinary jobs during the day and spent the rest of it carrying messages in the hollow frames of the bicycles, carrying guns in baskets and handbags, steaming open letters addressed to police barracks or suspected people. Very calmly they did it, taking chances that would drive many men grey.

'Well for you,' said Dominic sighing, and said no more.

Lowry was waiting for them a mile farther on, where they left the main road again and got into the little roads that were lined with bushes and ripening blackberries all draped with the wisps of hay stolen from the loaded carts as they passed by.

'I thought you'd never get here,' he said. 'I'm glad to see

97

you. I heard a lorry. Was it them? They didn't interfere with you?'

'No,' said Dominic. 'Finola was holding my hand. They thought we were lovers meeting in the early morning.'

'A strange time for courting,' Lowry laughed. 'They seem to be fairly active this morning. There was another load of them passed down below. It was as well we didn't go straight to the station. They'll be searching well there this morning. And how are you, Miss Brady? It's you that's looking fine and free and fit this blessed morning.'

He took her hand. They forgot for a few moments that Dominic was with them. The early sun was reflecting on Lowry's fair hair. He was a tall man, so she had to look up at him. She reminded Dominic of ladies he had seen in a chapel looking up at the unmoving face of the statue of a saint, their faces glowing in the waxlight of the candelabra. So he looked away into the sun. He was faintly disturbed.

'Yes,' said Lowry with a sigh, then, 'you brought all the stuff?'

'Yes,' she said, opening the leather satchel she had attached to the handle bars of the bicycle. 'The money, mainly and the papers.' He put them into an inside pocket. 'Sam says to be careful. He has a feeling.'

'Sam and his feelings,' said Lowry laughing.

'Are you being careful?' she asked.

He shrugged. 'I move from house to house,' he said. 'The hospitality of the people is like a bottomless well. When this is all over somebody should erect a monument to just the people.'

'Nobody will,' said Dominic sourly. 'Nobody ever did.'

'We will have to go,' said Lowry. 'I have this timed to seconds. Go back the main way, Finola, openly. You will be safer on the main roads.'

'Couldn't I go farther with you?' she asked. 'I'll have all day to get back. You will look more innocent when there is a girl with you.'

'No,' said Lowry. 'Go back. Dominic will be a good cover. His face is not well known.'

'Once seen, never forgotten,' said Dominic. They laughed.

'Right,' said Lowry, 'off we go.' And he mounted his bicycle. Dominic had to do the same. Lowry cycled away without another glance back, he noticed. He himself nearly fell off the bicycle waving to her where she stood, her arm raised and her face clouded, before they went around a bend and he could see her no more. He wondered if it was emotion that made Lowry part from her so abruptly, or if he had put her out of his mind to get on with the business in hand.

'She's a great girl,' he said.

'Maybe you better take this money and the papers, Dominic,' said Lowry, reaching into his pocket and handing them to him. 'You are less noticeable.'

'All right,' said Dominic, thinking, so it was business. He could envy a man who could empty his mind of one thing and fill it with a fresh thing, almost while he was breathing.

'We won't go into the station together,' said Lowry. 'You go first and I'll get in just when the train is ready to go. We will remain separate on the train.'

'Fine,' said Dominic.

'I have been longing for this,' said Lowry. 'The lads are well trained. There is a hard core of them who will be very good. When we come back with the guns, we will be going into action. They have to be hit. These fellows have to be hit, again and again. It is the nature of the bully to be afraid of being hit. When we get back with the stuff we will make it hot for them.'

I have no doubt you will, Dominic thought, looking at the strong face.

The roads were terrible. Here and there the stonebreakers sat on their piles of stones and broke them methodically with their squat hammers, goggles protecting their eyes, but none of the stones reached the ruts, because in the local elections all Sinn Fein members had been returned and the first thing they didn't do was to repair the roads, since it was mainly police and military who travelled them now, and the worse they were, the better. Several bridges had been blown here and there and remained blown.

'It is good to be alive in these times,' said Lowry.

'How do you make that out?' Dominic asked.

'Do you really feel like that, Dominic, or is it that you can't help making those remarks?' Lowry asked him.

'I don't know,' said Dominic. 'I think I mean them, Dualta says I'm not convinced. I don't know what that means.'

'Don't worry, Dominic,' said Lowry, smiling and putting his hand on his arm. 'Sometimes sincerity is more valuable than conviction.'

'You talk like that,' said Dominic, 'and I don't understand.'

'You will,' said Lowry. 'I'm sorry you can't share the feeling. It is a feeling in the stomach that you are living in great days. You want to be on the run like I have been. Going to different houses every night, meeting the people, often people who have been abused and still bear the bruises. It is like a small stream that is getting deeper and broader every day. It will be a great river by the time it reaches the sea. We are part of something big. You mark me, something that is going to be successful, on account of this feeling among the people. Because out of this feeling will come the confidence to perform great deeds. You know that all you have to do is reach out and you will find backing for glory. You understand?'

'No,' said Dominic, and again Lowry laughed.

'You will,' he said. 'You will. Now listen, when we come near the station, there is a house set back from the road. You just open the gate and leave your bicycle inside. If you see anybody, say nothing. If they see you, they will say nothing. It is all arranged. When we are coming back in a few days we can pick up the bicycles. We will be carrying some of the stuff, but the rest of it will be hidden on the train. There will be a reception committee. All clear?'

'It seems simple,' said Dominic, knowing that it wouldn't work out so simply. It seemed simple to them. 'It will have to work out,' said he. 'I can't go back home without the rifles we promised them. They are getting tired of shooting out of broom handles.'

'Now you are getting enthusiastic,' said Lowry, hitting him on the back. 'You want to be careful. We are near enough now. I'll stay here. You go on. Just leave the bike and walk. If there are passengers at the station get in the middle of them.' He looked up at the clear sky. 'It's a nice morning for adventure.' He took a crumpled cap from his pocket and pulled it on. Covering his fair hair seemed to alter his looks completely. 'Good luck,' he said then, holding out his hand. Dominic took it. A fine firm handclasp, Lowry had, and his eyes were twinkling humorously at Dominic. 'You are a tonic,' he said. 'Like a swimmer going into the sea on a cold day, testing the water with his toe. You know he'll go, because he feels that when he came this far, he has to go the whole hog, but he'll test and shiver and hug himself with his arms. My friend, I don't know what I would do without you.'

'Be careful,' said Dominic, turning to go. This made Lowry laugh again as if it had confirmed his opinion. This was what Dominic had in his ears, the laugh of Lowry, a silvery kind of laugh; the gay laugh of the reckless ones; not reckless really, he thought shrewdly, but seemingly so, because they had assessed all the difficulties and saw their way through them; it was the sense of anticipation that leading men had, having most eventualities covered in their minds; knowing what way they would jump in various circumstances. Lowry was a warm person, he felt. He could leave you glowing.

He came to the house. He got off his bicycle, opened the gate and went inside. A long hedge of fuchsia, heavy with the bell-like suckers, separated the place from the road. He remembered when young wondering why the bees loved the fuchsia flowers. They used to pull one and bite on the green back and, sure enough, when you sucked you tasted on your tongue a faint sweetness. He detached his case from the bicycle, felt for Lowry's papers and money, and his own papers and money and then closed the gate. As he did this, he glanced at the house. A man was standing at the door in his shirt sleeves. He had brown leggings on and was smoking a pipe, and a brown and white collie was standing beside him wagging its tail. The man made no sign and Dominic made no sign. He closed the gate and walked on the dusty road.

He could see the station from here. There was just a shelter and the small office.

He went in. He bought his ticket. There were no houses near the station. It seemed to be built in the middle of nowhere, just a gravel drive outside where some donkeys rested wearily in their carts. On the small platform itself there were only four or five people; two buxom women with red faces, obviously sisters, and one man with a case who would be a commercial traveller, and two farming men, dressed in their best broadcloth, their faces shining from shaving, and a porter in shirt sleeves standing by a loaded truck and looking off to the right from where the train would come.

There was no sign of police or military; nothing more official than a porter's cap. So Lowry had the right idea of cycling to this obscure little station and joining the train there. Dominic relaxed. Even his cautious nature could find little to worry about in the situation.

They saw the train before they heard it; saw the plumes of black smoke rising into the clear sky, the engine, hardly warmed up yet, vulgarly belching into the blue, and they saw it puffing and blowing and coming to a stop with terrible hissing of steam. Nobody put a head out of a carriage.

There were empty ones, and Dominic opened the door and went in. It wasn't a corridor carriage, just two long seats, covered in red upholstery, and if you hit them they would spout white dust at you. He put his case on the rack overhead and sat down by the window. He was near the entrance to the station so he would see Lowry when he came. Lowry intended to buy his ticket on the train from the inspector, cutting his coming as fine as possible.

Now Dominic started to worry, because the train couldn't be long here, five minutes at the most, just to pick up what they had to pick up and get moving.

It had started to move when Lowry came into his sight. It meant that he would get into a place behind Dominic.

He had his hand stretched to open the carriage door, when the whole station seemed to erupt.

From the place outside there came a screeching of brakes and shouting. He saw Lowry turning his head, and then making a move to go to the right. Dominic heard doors opening and

102

slamming and almost in seconds, it seemed, Lowry was surrounded with uniforms and drawn guns. There were six of them came in from the outside, running, with carbines in their hands, and at least six more must have jumped from the train.

Lowry was trapped.

But the train kept moving slowly but surely, puffing its way out of this drama. To Dominic it had all the ingredients of a nightmare. You are in the middle of this dream. It seems to have no beginning and no end, and you wake up sweating, your own shouting in your ears, as you try to force the ending to it.

He was standing up, his arms pressed to the glass. He was tugging at the thick strap, trying to lower the window. He had to hit it hard at the top and nearly broke the strap at the bottom before it would move for him. Then he shoved his head and shoulders out of the window. Immediately he could smell the coal dust in his nostrils; taste the coal grit on his tongue.

Lowry was standing there tall in the midst of them, calm, Dominic saw, his eyes hooded. They were all of the new police, all of the new police except one, Dominic saw as his heart sank. This one was Sergeant Nick with his waxed moustache. He was there. He was face to face with Lowry. He was gesticulating with his finger. Oh God, thought Dominic, and as the train took them around a winding bend that was the last he saw, one of them taking Lowry by the shoulder and pushing and the whole group making their way to the exit of the station.

He sat back on the seat, leaving the window open, the coal-laden air rushing in on him. His collar felt tight, so he opened the stud, to free his breathing. It wasn't much help.

All the precautions. What use were they? Lowry was taken. Unless he could bluff his way out of this. But he was a marked man. He also knew this. He was a valuable leader. He was one of the few men willing to shoot a policeman, as someone said. But maybe they didn't know this, he thought hopefully. Maybe they thought he was just another crazy volunteer student. He hoped they might think this. They were making so many mistakes, thinking all the trouble was caused by a few halfwits of gunmen, not seeing, as he had seen, the careful organizing; the whole land divided into companies, battalions and brigades, some active, some coming alive, some inactive but speculating, and all of them needing leaders like Lowry to direct them.

He'll bluff it out, he thought. He'll bluff it out. And, anyway, all it will mean is going to jail, and if necessary we can get him out of jail. Jails can be broken, and if they put Lowry in, there will be some way of getting him out. Sam will know, he thought, and Sam won't sit on his hands. Lowry will be safe in jail until we can reach him.

But Lowry wasn't in jail. He probably saw that end for himself when he was suddenly surrounded. He made one tentative effort to run, but when he saw it was no use, he put his hands in his pockets, his brain racing.

Then he saw Sergeant Nick coming and he knew that his situation was worse than he had thought. Because, unlike many others, Sergeant Nick had gone over wholeheartedly to the new police.

'All right, Lowry,' he said. 'You will admit who you are, or will you deny it?'

'What's it all about?' Lowry asked, a puzzled look on his face.

'You don't know?' Nick asked him. 'You don't know. Listen to me, you . . .'

'That'll do,' the one with him said. He was a beefy man. 'Let's go. You admit you are Lowry?'

'Yes,' said Lowry.

'Let's go,' said this man. Lowry didn't know him. He was thinking hard as he got into the lorry, crowded with them, silent and unfriendly, of what he would say when they took him to the barracks. If he had to take a beating, which was normal procedure, he would take that too, but mark the men. He was arranging the form the interview would take when the lorry stopped at the side of the road. He was pushed on to the road here.

'Listen,' he began, 'what's . . .' when the beefy man shot him in the back of the head. Lowry dropped in the channel there, a short footpath before a town. The beefy man bent down and shot him again in the temple. There was no need. The front of his face was blown off. His cap had fallen and his fair

104

hair, bloodstained, was touching the dust. His beauty was destroyed.

Dominic didn't know this, of course. Dominic was thinking of Finola and how she would take it, and a coldness was coming over his bones as he wondered: How did they know Lowry was going on the train this way? Who told them?

Clickity-clack, said the wheels of the train, but this was no answer.

11

DUALTA LEFT him outside the Broadstone station, handing him the little case, very heavy in weight. It was then he told him.

'Dominic,' he said flatly. 'Lowry is dead.'

Dominic was looking at him. He didn't understand what he had said.

'What? What?' he asked.

'Lowry is dead,' said Dualta. 'They killed him almost as soon as they took him.'

'No,' said Dominic.

'Yes,' said Dualta. He put his hand on his shoulder. He wore leather gloves. The right-hand glove was filled with wooden fingers for the ones he was missing.

'But they couldn't do that,' said Dominic. 'I mean they couldn't do that.'

'Wake up,' said Dualta. 'He's dead and gone, and dead is dead.'

'You knew,' said Dominic. 'You knew all the time?'

'Almost since it happened,' said Dualta.

'Why didn't you tell me?' Dominic asked.

'I'm telling you now,' said Dualta. 'Shake yourself up. Any of us can go the same way if they lay their hands on us. Remember that.'

'But Lowry was indestructible,' said Dominic.

'Nobody is indestructible,' said Dualta. He was sorry for the shock in Dominic's eyes. He himself hadn't known Lowry well, of course. Just talked with him a few times, and assessed him, which was his job, as a potential leader. He was sorry he was dead. But mainly he was sorry for a gap in a production line of men. Who will follow Lowry? He could see that Dominic was personally involved. His nature was analytical. He would have to work on the whys and the wherefores, and suffer a lot in the process. 'Look, Dominic,' he said. 'The best thing to do is to forget it as quickly as possible. There is no time. There is just no time. You hear me?'

'Do I have to be as inhuman as you?' Dominic asked. 'He was my friend. Do you know what he meant as a person, do you?'

'There is no time,' said Dualta. 'Weeping belongs to afterwards. We find out who did it and we kill him, that's the important thing. And find a man as good as Lowry. These are the thoughts that matter.'

'You have seen a lot of death,' said Dominic bitterly. 'Men to you are just blobs of guts in mud. I won't even be at his funeral.'

'No,' said Dualta. 'He got a great funeral.'

'I want to hit you,' said Dominic.

'Do,' said Dualta, 'if it will relieve you.'

'These other men I saw with you,' said Dominic. 'They are all the same. They sit there and they hear and they say: Ah, poor old Charlie is gone, or Sean is gone, or Lowry is gone. All it means is stroking out a name with a pen.'

'You're wrong,' said Dualta. 'You don't understand. I will have to leave you. We are becoming conspicuous.' He diverted him this way. People were walking towards the station with bags in their hands. Dominic took his eyes from Dualta's face and looked at them. He didn't really see them. He felt a pressure on his arm, and then Dualta was gone. Dualta was thinking: At least it will take his mind off what he is carrying in the case. He paused to look back at him. He was standing bewildered, a bit stricken, a low-sized powerful-looking young man with a hurt frown, holding a case in one hand and the small silver-gilt trophy cup in the other. He was looking at this, not seeing it, just thinking.

When he came to himself, Dualta was gone. There was no sign of him. His mind was filled with Lowry; trying to fit this vibrant, all-alive young man into the pattern of death. He was finding it difficult to do so. His feet felt leaden as he walked into the station. He stood in there thinking, letting all the movement of porters and passengers and trucks pass all around him; the shouting of men, the shrill voices of women. He looked in four carriages before he got into one that was empty. He put his case on the rack and sat on the seat cuddling the little trophy cup in his hands, feeling the cold smoothness of it, thinking of Lowry and Finola in the laneway, saying goodbye, and the sun shining on his fair hair, all of them enveloped in the scent of the meadow-sweet, remember that, a sweet smell, that had nothing to do with death, but life and love in August. The cow parsley was growing in the dykes. He remembered the wisps of hay on the briars, but it was this scent of autumn, which meant fat life, growing fronds, ripening oatfields, burgeoning love, and Lowry wiped out as if he had never existed, a necessary person. There, you see, a necessary person. Himself could have gone, bathed in a sweat of terror and fear, and little loss he would be, but Lowry, Lowry laughing. He groaned and turned his head and put his forehead against the cold window glass.

He was this way when the door was flung open and three of the new police came into the carriage. They were carrying coats which they threw on to the racks. Their loud voices made him open his eyes. He turned and looked at them. One of them was enormous. He had a huge chest, a big face with a double chin, made more apparent by the tightness of his collar. He was all in black and wore a Glengarry bonnet with ribbons at the back of it. He wore a revolver holster that held no gun. Now he put his hand under his tunic and took out a ·45 revolver, which he put into the holster.

'Those effing engine drivers,' he said, in an English voice. 'Why don't they shoot the bastards?'

The other one with him was thin, but he had broad

107

shoulders. There was a cigarette in his mouth. He was coughing through this.

'Not enough of them to go round, Mac,' he said. 'Shoot them and you have no trains at all.' He also took a revolver from under his tunic and put it into the holster.

The big man plopped down in the seat opposite Dominic.

'I presume,' he said, 'that you are not keeping the other seven seats for anyone?'

Dominic shook his head.

Mac laughed.

'That was supposed to be a joke, mate,' he said. 'Don't anyone in Ireland laugh any more? Here, let's see what's going on.' He went back to the door and lowered the window. He had trouble getting his great shoulders out through the opening. 'Think they might be going to move at last. Could that happen at home, Skin, an engine driver refusing to carry the forces of His Majesty if they were armed?'

'Might,' said Skin, putting his feet on the seat opposite him, 'if the Jerries were in Kent, like.'

'Here,' said Mac, turning a bit from the window, 'whose side you on, Skin?'

'Just saying,' said Skin. 'They have courage, these chaps, but they know they are on a good wicket. Refuse to drive the train, right, jail for six months, and then they have to let them out the next day to drive the train to Cork. Not enough train drivers to go round, see.'

'Well, they are going into the cab now,' said Mac, 'the troopers have decided not to travel with their guns. Just as well. Those boys stink up the place.' He closed the window and came back to his seat. He looked at the third member. He was a fair-haired, thin-faced, austere-looking man who had taken the corner seat. He wore coloured ribbons over the left pocket of his uniform. 'You say nothing, friend. Do we know you?'

'No,' this man said. They waited. He said nothing. Mac and Skin looked at one another, and shrugged their shoulders. Then Mac turned his attention to Dominic.

'Now then,' he said. 'what's that you've got there in your hands?'

And Dominic looked down at the cup he was clenching, and realized that he was afraid; that his guts were turning to water with fear. It could be the result of the shock on hearing about Lowry; that his defences were down. It could be a natural fear. After all, he was here with those men; of the same kind who had taken Lowry from boarding a train, brought him a little way and shot him dead. No judge or jury; no rights of the common man. These were the people who had established those rights into their way of life, but it was for themselves really and not the lesser breeds outside the law. He should by right be filled with an all-consuming hatred, a slow-burning fire in which he could contemplate having a gun in his hands and shooting these men dead, and feel that he was wiping out vermin, but it wasn't like this at all. His mouth was dry. He felt like long ago when he was small and woke in the dark, sweating from an unrecollected fear-dream, calling: Mother! my mother, come to me!

He had to clear a frog from his throat, wet his lips with his tongue; wondering if they saw those signs of fear, or if they were so used to them that they would hardly notice them.

'Boxing,' he said. 'Got that for boxing.'

'Is that so?' asked Mac, interest in his eyes. The train was moving well now, clattering in walled caverns, the windows of the brick houses looking blankly down. 'Let's have a look. I used to be a boxer. I was the champion of our regiment. I could have been champion of the whole army if I could have bought bottles of second wind somewhere.'

'More bottles of wind,' said Skin, 'and less bottles of booze.'

'It's not bad,' Mac said, examining the cup. 'How many did you have to beat to get this?'

'Three,' said Dominic, conjuring up the imaginary bouts.

'Did they all go the distance?' Mac asked.

'Oh, yes,' said Dominic. 'I'm not that good. Good at getting out of trouble and hitting while I'm retreating.'

Mac laughed, handing back the cup.

'That's the way to win 'em,' he said. 'I was always walking into haymakers. You a student then?'

'Yes,' said Dominic.

'You a Sinn Feiner?' he asked.

Dominic remembered Sam's advice: If they ask you to say God save the King, say it and God save the Queen too. If they ask you to walk on the tricolour, ask them for two or three to walk on:

'No,' said Dominic. 'I don't like politics,' thinking, this was true anyhow, remembering Dualta's jeer, Dominic is not convinced; the way he introduced him to the men in Dublin: This is my brother Dominic, he is a reluctant revolutionary; thinking of Lowry dead with his hair in the dust; the last thing he remembered of him was his laugh. He had white even teeth and he laughed heartily.

'You mean you wouldn't fight for your country?' Skin asked, coughing.

'What d'you mean, fight?' Mac asked. 'Shooting from behind a wall. Shooting from behind a girl's skirt. Killing and then hiding a gun down the front of her blouse or under her skirt. That fighting?'

'It works,' said Skin. 'They got me frightened. My eyes are turning into periscopes. Did you know the rations of lavatory paper have gone up in the barracks.' He bent forward laughing.

'Funny, funny,' said Mac. 'What's your name?'

'Joe Murphy,' said Dominic.

'The whole country is crawling with Murphy's,' said Mac. 'What are you doing?'

'I'm a medical student,' said Dominic. He was amazed to hear the calmness of his voice, the smoothness of his lies, when all the time he felt like screaming.

'You have a boxing club in the College then?' Mac asked.

'Yes,' said Dominic.

'You the only one to go to the bouts?' he asked.

'There were others,' said Dominic. 'They came down yesterday.'

'Did they do any good?' he asked.

'Oh, yes,' said Dominic. 'We won over all.'

'Good stuff,' said Mac. 'Do you hate us?'

'I don't hate anybody,' said Dominic. 'How can you hate

110

a person until you get to know him and see if he is worth hating?' Skin laughed again.

'You should be a lawyer, Joe,' he said. 'Not a medical man.'

'How long does this frigging train take anyhow?' Mac asked.

'Hours and bloody hours,' said Skin. 'You'd get there quicker walking.'

'I bet they got there quicker when they had coaches,' said Mac.

'No,' said Dominic, to his own surprise. 'It took two days then.'

'It did?' said Mac. 'So this is like two years. Get out the cards, Skin, and we'll play a few games. You play poker, Joe?'

'I'm not very good at it,' said Dominic.

'That's not the point,' said Skin, taking a pack from his tunic pocket. 'It's how much money you've got that's the point. Eh, Mac?'

'Students never have money,' said Mac. 'We'll stake him.' He stood up, looked around. He saw Dominic's case. 'You mind if we use this to play on?' he asked then, taking it down. 'Boy, that's heavy stuff you've got in here, Joe. What were you doing? Hitting your opponents with lead in your gloves?'

Dominic was sure he had gone pale. He could feel the sweat on his brow. The case contained his pyjamas, socks, shirt, handkerchiefs, underwear, a few books, six hand grenades, a ·38 revolver, a mixed assortment of ammunition, small arms – with one box of dum-dum bullets bearing a Union Jack on the lid and titled 'Best British Make'. He didn't think that he would ever be able to answer.

'Books,' he said, 'and a new set of snooker balls for the club.'

'Snooker!' said Mac, sitting down again with the case on his knees. 'Now that's one thing you can't talk to me about. I'm the best snooker player in the business. Eh, Skin?'

'Professional,' said Skin, deftly shuffling the cards.

'So you like snooker, Joe?' Mac asked.

'Love it,' said Dominic, wiping the sweat off his eyebrow with his finger. 'We had only billiards, you see.'

'Balls to billiards,' said Mac. 'You get bloody fed up with

111

billiards. I like snooker. You come over to our hotel and play snooker. There's a good table there.'

'I'd love that,' said Dominic.

'You know the hotel?' Mac asked. Dominic knew the hotel. It was a good place to avoid.

'I do,' he said. 'I'd love to play snooker there with you.'

'I can give you points,' said Mac.

'Would you like to join in our little game, sir?' said Skin to the policeman in the corner. Mac turned his head to look at him too. He had been looking out of the window. He turned to them. He had cold, unblinking blue eyes.

'No, thank you,' he said. 'I don't play cards.'

It was as if he had poured cold water over them. He held their eyes and then turned back to looking out of the window again.

Skin looked at Mac and made words silently with his lips. It was easy to understand what he was saying, obscenely uncomplimentary. Mac laughed. 'All right, Skin,' he said. 'Deal from the top.'

Skin dealt the cards.

They were blurred to Dominic's eyes. They played in pennies and sixpences. It was different playing poker here to playing it in the club, thinking of Lowry and the first time he had come after him, out there in the darkness, under the light of the street lamp, looking up at the walls of the jail. He wanted to cry for Lowry when he thought of that and wanted to cry for himself when he looked at the case on the huge knees of Mac. There was only a tenth of an inch separating Dominic from death, he thought, if the lid of that case was opened. He tried to concentrate on the cards. Most times, if he could, he threw in his cards, leaving Mac and Skin to conduct a loud and hilarious game of bluff between themselves.

He wondered, to take his mind off his predicament, what it would have been like in normal times to meet these men. What they would be like stripped of uniforms; if one could imagine them at home in their houses in England, playing on the lawn with their children. Mostly they were hardbitten men who had risen to the rank of officer in the army in the war. They were called cadets. This implied young men learning to be police-men, when in reality the auxiliaries had no young men. They were all seasoned campaigners, majors, captains, lieutenants, trained soldiers, the leftovers of a war that was gone, holding on to a war that was present. He thought men like them had been present as mercenaries in all the wars of history, and when a country was desperate enough to call in the mercenaries, there was bound to be brutality, and looting, and sudden death for the innocent.

He won one pot with three aces. That relieved him, as it left enough coppers and silver for him to keep going for some time to come if he wasn't reckless.

But all the time he noticed that he was in a sweat of fear. If he raised his leg from the ground, it was inclined to tremble, so he had to put it firmly down again. He could feel the wetness of sweat under his arms, around his waist, under his knees. He wondered at it. I am not a coward, he thought. I can face a situation as bravely as anyone when I know what it is about. He didn't know what this was about. He thought of Finola. How was she feeling now, deprived of Lowry? It would have been terrible to have been in love with him and then to lose him. Such a vital personality. Would any man ever again measure up to him in her eyes. Had she a true picture of him or was she adoring a sort of Greek god?

'We'll go and have a drink,' said Mac. 'Are you coming, Joe?'

He was amazed to see that they were stopped at a station.

'Yes,' he said, getting to his feet. Mac threw the case on the seat. It didn't rattle. The stuff was well wrapped in his clothes. They opened the door and went out on to the platform. Not the man in the corner. Dominic met the cold look of his eyes, and thought of his case left casually on the seat and wondered if this man would investigate it. Then he wondered if it was even locked. Almost in a panic he put his hand in his coat pocket to feel for the key. It was there, but that solved nothing. It could still be there and the case unlocked.

He left the carriage as calmly as he could without a further glance at the case.

The bar at the station was crowded with soldiers and police and civilians, and parents getting bottles of lemonade for their children. He saw Mac ahead of him using his huge shoulders as a lever and clearing a space at the bar. Skin followed him nonchalantly and Dominic followed Skin. They reached the counter and Mac shouted for three whiskies, and got them. Dominic wondered if it was ethical to be drinking with your enemies.

'That corpse in the corner of the carriage,' said Mac, 'who is he, Skin?'

'Don't know,' said Skin. 'One of those secret blokes. Looking things over. Making notes in his little book. One of those. They have them everywhere.'

'We'll chase him out of town if he starts any of that,' said Mac. 'We're not in the army.'

'Thank God for that,' said Skin.

'Here,' said Mac, handing them their glasses. 'Here's to love and loot and death to Sinn Fein.' He laughed.

Dominic sipped the whisky. He didn't drink much whisky. He wasn't used to the burning taste of it.

'Will you drink that toast, Joe?' Mac asked, leering at him.

'Sure,' said Dominic, 'here's to it,' drinking to the death of Lowry, thinking of how little these men knew of what they were up against. They were believing their own propaganda, a few scattered skulking gunmen just having to be flushed out and killed like rabbits. He thought of the place where he had been in Dublin, the tall brick building where business was conducted as if it was a merchant company. Typewriters and files, and the two Micks, Cork men, arguing about two machine guns. The heavy Mick, like a wrestler, with great shoulders and long arms, with clenched fists waving. The other Mick, handsome, with thick hair and a smile behind his eyes. He shouldn't have bought machine guns. That was for the purchasing committee. The language of the heavy Mick about the purchasing committee. He walked the streets of London and bought two machine guns in a shop. Down in Soho. Where were the asterisk purchasing men then? More arguments and flailing arms, and the leader Mick saying: You can keep them anyhow, because

114

at least you bastards will use them. Laughter and embraces. It was the businesslike efficiency that made you confident, this aura of casual leadership they possessed, the seemingly careless conservation of their lives, just because they were useful; men who would do anything that would get results, absolutely ruthless in the pursuit and killing of the informer, the type who had always made an easy living in Irish history. Dominic got some idea of the threads stretching all over the country; the careful undermining of the law as it had been known and its replacement by a new law that was being obeyed and each day fortified, so that it would never be uprooted. All intangible it seemed, but real. In every walk of life there were guided people who were willing to die, but who would regard death as being failure in the sense of usefulness.

How could Mac and Skin know what they were up against?

They returned to the train. Mac brought a bottle of whisky back with him. He was fed up with cards. He caught the case and threw it up on the rack carelessly. He loosened the collar of his tunic and put his feet up on the seat and he started to sing songs. Skin sang in seconds and had a thin sweet voice. Mac had a voice like a bull frog, and rarely hit the right notes. They sang war songs, and army ballads. They laughed inordinately at the songs. The face of the man in the corner remained as cold as ice. They didn't give a damn.

Dominic was thinking of coming into the station and going out of the station. He thought Sam would have something arranged. Somebody there to take the case from his hand before the exit where he was sure the police would be searching. Maybe they wouldn't. Sometimes they searched and sometimes they didn't search. But Sam would arrange something. He knew that there were at least half a dozen rifles somewhere on the train. He didn't know where. He had enough to worry about.

He was weary. He closed his eyes, the bawdy words of the ballads dinning into his ears. He looked at the sprawling Mac. What a big man he was, his fists like hams, like Poric's fists. He thought of Poric and wondered what happened to him.

He wondered where he was when he was suddenly jerked

115

awake. The train was stationary. Doors were opening. Loud voices. How could he have slept. Why hadn't he remained awake?

Mac was asleep too. Skin was shaking him to waken him. The door was open. The cold-eyed policeman was gone.

'Rise and shine, Mac,' Skin was calling.

Mac opened his eyes, raised his huge hand to wipe spittle from the side of his mouth, shook his head and got himself awake. He stood and yawned, rubbed his chest. 'I feel good,' he declared then, starting to button his tunic collar. 'You come with us, Joe. We'll get you a lift.'

'No, thanks,' said Dominic in a panic. 'There's somebody to meet me with a car.'

'Good,' said Mac. 'Don't forget to come to the hotel. We'll play some snooker. I'll show you a few shots you didn't even know were in the bag.'

'I will,' said Dominic, getting his case. 'Thanks for the company.'

'Come again,' said Skin. 'We'll be seeing you. If we don't, no skin off your nose.' He laughed. He had a very bad cigarette cough.

Dominic stood on the platform and felt as if he had just got off a ship and his legs were unseaworthy. He looked around him and could see nobody he knew. Then he pushed his way into the crowd making its way to the exit. Perhaps, he thought, somebody will just come and take the case out of my hand. He waited expectantly to feel a hand on his own hand relieving him of this case which might have been a hot poker, so sensitive he was now about its contents.

They were making people open their cases, he saw, his heart sinking. What would he do with the case? There were many armed police around and soldiers. The normally noisy Irish travellers were subdued as they approached for the searching. There was a table, a long wooden table resting on iron stanchions, where they had to put their cases as the police went through their contents.

What am I going to do, he wondered as he came closer? Would he just drop the case and walk out with his hands free?

116

Or would he let them search the case and as they searched make a run for it? It was getting dark outside. He noticed that the lights had been on in the carriage. He decided to let them search and run.

He looked almost frantically into the hall outside where people were waiting for their friends and relations, striving to see a familiar face. He would have given all he possessed at that moment to have seen the face of Sam.

He saw no one.

'Open it up!' said the policeman. He was filled with despair. Because I am not suited for things like this, he thought. My reactions are too slow. I will never get away with it.

'Listen, copper,' said the voice of Mac then. 'You just leave my friend alone. I won money from him playing poker. He drank my whisky.'

Dominic felt his hand on his arm, pushing him forward. The policeman who spoke was going to protest, then he grinned and said, 'All right, away with you!' and Dominic walked out into the hall devoid of feeling, thinking: imagine having a guardian angel named Mac, turning to him and smiling and saying, 'Thanks, Mac.' 'It's a pleasure, Joe,' said Mac, clapping him on the back, 'any time at all. Sure we can't give you a lift?'

'No; thanks all the same,' said Dominic, standing there on the steps, a feeling of fog in his brain, hardly able to see, finally focusing on the driver of the sidecar who was waving a stick at him. 'Two bob!' he was shouting. 'One seat left. Two bob.'

Dominic looked more closely and saw Sam sitting up on the sidecar, and two girls on the far side, leaving the one seat near him.

'I'll give you one and six,' Dominic shouted.

'Two bob,' said the driver, shaking his head.

'One and six,' said Dominic.

'All right, to hell with it,' said the driver. 'One and six.'

Dominic stepped from the steps to the precarious perch, sitting beside Sam, the case on his knees, having to raise his face to get air. The driver clicked at the horse and it moved on slowly and turned the corner below, going at a good pace left of the hotel.

'Go like hell now,' said Sam to the driver, 'towards the Docks.'

'Oh, Sam,' said Dominic. 'You will never know how glad I am to see you.'

'We couldn't get anyone inside,' said Sam. 'We sweated. Faster,' he said then to the driver. 'Hell is going to break out there.'

'Why?' Dominic asked.

'A diversion to get the guns off the train,' said Sam. 'And also to get the one that shot Lowry.'

'He's there?' Dominic asked.

'He's there,' said Sam grimly. 'We better get under cover fast. They won't be pleased.'

Dominic felt bleak. Lowry and the man that killed Lowry. He thought of Mac. If circumstances were different. If he met him under different circumstances.

He was due to do so, and he would hardly like it.

12

THIS DAY in September began very peacefully, he remembered.

He was down helping at Poric's place. Not indeed that his help was really necessary, but from the way Poric's father, Ned, talked, you'd think he was the reincarnation of Cuchullainn.

For Poric was home. He had come back about three weeks ago. He didn't say much, since he didn't have a lot of talk in him anyhow. Dominic was glad to see him back. Reading and hearing of all the police barracks' raids, he had often thought of Poric down there in the South where they were very active. Poric just said: Himself was right about the police barracks. This crazy new policeman had lined them up, and told them to shoot every Irishman they saw with his hands in his pockets, since that was a sure sign that he would be concealing a gun.

This request solved the problem for some of them, who threw in their arms, suddenly discovering that they too were Irishmen.

'Certain men wanted me to stay on as a policeman, that I would be of more use inside than outside,' said Poric, forking up a sheaf of oats to Dominic who was going around on his knees building up the stack in the small garden behind the house.

'What did you say to that?' Dominic asked.

Poric leaned on the fork, his broad forehead creased with thought. 'How could I?' he asked. 'Can't the whole world read my face?'

Dominic laughed, looking into the broad open countenance. 'You'd find it hard to be two-faced all right, Poric,' he said.

Poric threw him another sheaf. He leaned on the fork again. 'I liked being a policeman,' he said. 'Is that a sin? Not all the bits with guns and things, just being a policeman.'

'What's wrong with that?' Dominic asked. 'Wait'll this is all over and we have our own police. Can't you be a policeman again?'

'Will it ever be over?' asked Poric wistfully.

'Everything must have an end,' said Dominic, pausing from tying the sheaves under his knees, and thinking. Peter O'Flaherty was in jail. Poc Murray was taken up too, and Poric's brother Sean was on the run somewhere over near the big mountains. So they never got around to having a real ambush.

'Wouldn't the two girls bringing the turf do more work than the pair of you?' Poric's father asked, coming in with more sheaves tied to his back.

Dominic laughed.

'Only this morning,' he said, 'you told me I was a better man than Cuchullainn.'

'Ah, that was this morning,' said Ned. 'And look at Poric. Didn't the police ruin him? Now he's a gentleman afeared of hurting his hands.'

Poric grinned and threw more sheaves.

'Sean, that's away,' said Ned, 'is a great loss to me. He'd

eat less and do more. Isn't it always a man's best that is taken from him?'

Ned was a tall, thin man. He affected a drooping moustache that was brown in the middle from his pipe-smoking. He threw down the sheaves now and sat with his back against the rising stack and proceeded to fill his pipe. He was always fond of whatever son was away, extolling his value to the detriment of the one that was at home. He was always loud with his talk of punishment, and what he was going to do with one or other of the eight of his children, as soon as he got his pipe filled, or his boots off, or his meal eaten. Bottled wind was all he was, his wife Mairéad said, clouting a head, or smacking a bottom or slapping a hand. Then there would be roaring and screaming and they searching out their father, showing him what my Mhaimi did to me, and of course this ferocious tyrant would comfort them and rub the raw places, completely spoiling his wife's necessary work.

Dominic loved being with them.

They had a three-roomed thatched cottage, the thatch tied down with wide-mesh nets to pegs driven in under the eaves, for the winds out here were sometimes incredibly strong. It was always well whitewashed outside, with a bit of blue dye in the wash. Mairéad was a tall rawboned woman with big teeth. Poric got his bulk from her; rarely she wore anything but the red petticoat and she worked in her bare feet, as most of the women did. Sundays they had laced boots and new petticoats and the beige shawl going to Mass. The house inside was as tidy as a large family would permit it to be. Dominic loved having his meal with them in the evening after the work. The oil-lamp hanging on the wall would be lighted after the wick was trimmed. The large white scrubbed table under the window would be pulled into the centre of the flag-stoned kitchen, and the four wooden kitchen chairs occupied by Ned, Mairéad, Poric and himself, while the six children, two boys and four girls, would fight for the wooden form or the two converted apple barrels, until Mairéad put an end to the row with threats to get down the sally from where it was hanging over the great open fireplace.

The man of the house would say the Grace, carefully taking off his black-brimmed Connemara hat to show his balding head and the place where he was sunburned up to his forehead, and would carefully put it back on again before he stretched for the huge pile of steaming potatoes with splitting jackets that would be piled from the three-legged pot in the centre of the table. Potatoes and butter and a little boiled fish, with great mugs of buttermilk. Dominic always remembered those meals.

When he left them that evening, he looked back at the house. It was dark outside, no moon, just a vast array of glittering stars. He saw the open door, the half-door shut to keep out the chickens, the great chattering of the children, the sight of Mairéad going around knuckling heads, the noise dying down, and they getting down on their knees saying the Rosary. He waited outside, watching to see if Ned took off his hat for the Rosary, smiled when he saw he did, laughed and went his road, having a picture in his mind of this packed house and the light shining into the night from the small four-paned window and the top half of the doorway. He was glad that Poric was back and safe. He was to think of this later.

About two o'clock in the morning the lorries came roaring into their own yard with their lights blazing, one in the front and one in the back.

Dominic was in his father's study bending over *Anatomy*. It was his weak subject. He had failed it once and he would be back again with it in a few weeks. There was a tall paraffin lamp on the table. It was made of brass, a slender elegant stand, and had a pink glass bowl around it.

They came so suddenly that he hardly had time to think. But when he did, the name that came into his head straight away was Dualta. Dualta was asleep upstairs. He didn't come often, but this was one of the times. He was on his way into Mayo.

He no sooner thought of the name than he was out of the room with the tall lamp in his hand. The blinds were down on the windows so he couldn't be seen. He went halfway up the stairs calling: 'Dualta! Dualta!' He thought his voice was a little hysterical. After all the care, they were caught flatfooted. The sound of his calling was drowned by the hammering on the doors, front and back, and the voices. Dualta came to the landing. He was just wearing his shirt, his clothes and an army rucksack piled in his arms. He bent and loosened the boards at the landing, put them aside, threw down his gear and then lowered himself with his hands. Dominic left the lamp on the landing and put back the boards; then still sitting there he took off his boots and socks and threw them from him. He was just wearing a shirt and trousers, so he took the braces off his shoulders and went down the stairs again, calling as loudly as he could, 'All right! All right!' thinking about Dualta, and how little he left to chance. The scullery was under the landing. In the scullery he had made a false wall that left about two foot of space. It was boarded like the rest of the scullery wall and painted the same colour. Dominic had jeered at him about his priest's hole, but he wasn't jeering now. Here once again his brother had proved himself to be right.

The gun butts were pounding on the door. There were heavy boards on the door but already one of them was splintering near a joint, he could see.

He pulled the bolts. He was pushed back violently into the centre of the kitchen. He was backed up against the table. The lamp rocked where he had left it, and he put out a hand to save it. He was surrounded by them, enveloped by them, small men and tall men and medium-sized ones, all police, no army uniforms among them at all. He picked out the face of Sergeant Nick.

'You're welcome, Sergeant Nick,' he said. 'You always bring us pleasure on your visits.'

He shouldn't have said this. Sergeant Nick hit him across the mouth with the back of his hand. His eyes blazed and he was going to react when two others suddenly caught his arms.

'Where is your brother?' the sergeant asked. His face had changed, Dominic noticed. It wasn't the face of the old sergeant they had known, say the day Poric was going off to be a policeman. He remembered him the day Lowry was caught at the station.

'Do you want him for the same reason you wanted Lowry?' Dominic asked through bruised lips. He was glad he said this when he saw the flash of apprehension in his eyes, and then he lost track of him when Mac pushed his way in and stood in front of him, his hands on his hips.

'If it isn't Joe Murphy? How are you, Joe?'

'Fine, thanks, Mac,' said Dominic, 'and how are you?'

'You bastard,' said Mac, poking him in the chest with a big forefinger. 'You fooled me properly, didn't you, Joe?'

'Upstairs,' he heard Sergeant Nick saying, 'search the whole place.' Dominic didn't know how they all fitted in the house. He heard them running up the stairs.

'No, Mac,' said Dominic. 'You said yourself nearly everyone in Ireland is named Murphy.'

'And you have this dangerous brother,' said Mac. 'You didn't tell me that, Joe. And you didn't tell me what was in the case we played cards on, did you, Joe?'

'Yes, I did,' said Dominic. 'Snooker balls I told you.'

'Snooker balls to you, Joe,' said Mac and hit him with his open hand on the side of the face. Dominic felt his head ringing. He relaxed his body, felt the hands loosen on his arms, shook himself free and hit out at Mac. He didn't reach him. He was chopped down from behind by the butt of a gun.

He was dazed. He fell to his knees, but they hauled him up again. Then he heard his mother saying, 'Stop it! Stop it!' He turned his head. She was on the stairs. Her hair was in long plaits. She was wearing a white nightdress with a black shawl over her shoulders. At the same time he heard a scream from Brid, who had come out of her room opposite the scullery. 'Shut her up,' he heard Mac say, and heard a slap.

'Now, Joe,' said Mac, 'you are going to talk. Here, Skin. You remember Skin, don't you, Joe?'

'Hello, Skin,' said Dominic.

'Glad to see you, Joe,' said Skin. 'Since you didn't come to play snooker, we came to play it with you. Mac, get the women out of here.'

'Get the women out of here,' said Mac.

123

'No,' said his mother, 'leave him alone. He has done nothing. He knows nothing.'

It didn't do her any good. They caught her and pushed her into the room which Dominic had left before they came. He heard them doing the same thing to Brid. He was pleased. He didn't want his mother there. Brid would have been a better proposition for them, if they only knew. He was very pleased Brid was out of the way.

'Nothing up there,' he heard a fellow say from the stairs. 'But a bed is still warm. Someone was in it.'

'I was in it,' said Dominic.

'You're a liar, Joe,' said Mac, hitting him again with his open hand. It was as good as another man's fist, Dominic thought.

'Tear the place apart,' he heard Sergeant Nick say. Why had Sergeant Nick turned out like this? Someone had said he had gone over completely to them. He was a Northerner. Had someone belonging to him been killed in the pogroms against the Catholics? He found himself thinking like this. Summing up things. To his surprise he found he wasn't afraid. He thought, it is fear of being afraid that makes a man afraid.

'Your boys killed one of ours that evening at the station. Did you know that, Joe? And what do I do, Joe? I see you out of the station with the snooker balls. You think I can forgive you for that, Joe?' His face was pushed up close to Dominic's. It was a very angry face, Dominic saw. It could even be honest anger, that he had been deluded by a boy. 'Joe, you are going to tell us all about your brother.'

'Mac,' said Dominic, 'I know nothing at all about my brother.'

He tried to gird himself for what he knew was coming. Now that it was here, he thought that he would be able to survive it. The way he felt, there was no way they could get him to speak. He was surprised at this feeling. He was feeling angry and outraged instead of being afraid.

Dualta heard everything on his knees inside his hole. He had managed to pull on his trousers in the restricted space, his

124

shoes; to get himself ready, in case. Then he knelt, listened. He had a Luger pistol in his hand.

He had to bow his head between his knees and cover his ears with his arms. Because he was afraid of his going out on top of them and killing as many of them as he could. It wasn't that it was easy to stay there. It was just that it was hard to stay there. He knew too much, that was his trouble, and if he was caught and made to speak, it would be terrible. As he tried to block out the sounds coming to him now in his cramped hole he thought of the Corkman, the leader he had met in Dublin. They were talking about this very thing. He had said, he remembered, I don't blame a Volunteer for breaking under torture. We are all only human. I would have to shoot him afterwards, of course, but that doesn't say that I blame him.

He couldn't block out all the sounds. There was no way. He heard him groaning, bad when it was forced from him like that, for he knew Dominic better than he knew himself. He knew Dominic wouldn't talk. He would have felt better if he thought he would. It would end this terror. He was holding his face against the wall, stretching himself in agony. The sweat poured from him in streams, just holding on there; not going out. Not going out. He couldn't think of Dominic as anything other than his little brother, a semi-nuisance, spoiling things for bigger brothers. He only hoped that his mother didn't know, couldn't hear.

Dominic thought he shouldn't have taken off his boots. It had been an unnecessary camouflage. If he hadn't taken off his boots he couldn't now have this almost unbearable pain in his insteps and the soles of his feet.

Sometimes he knew he must have blacked out.

Then he would feel the water that was thrown on him from the bucket on the floor near the sideboard, precious well-water that had to be carted painfully for several hundred yards, so it was precious.

He would be on his feet then again.

There always seemed to be a new face that he said no to. If he could have, he would have spit in some of the faces, but he had no spittle.

'Where is your brother?' became almost like a misty refrain, sung in the evening over a bog where a low fog was creeping, blotting out the Jack o' Lanterns.

He thought this then: Dualta said I was not convinced.

I am convinced now. Man, I am convinced now. Laughing weakly. All his father's history was knitted into place like the gansey his mother put together on the big needles, tumbled wool pouring into her busy hands and a pattern coming out below, each thread fitted into place, having design and meaning.

For this was what it was about, what the few hundreds and the few thousands had always resisted. This. Just what he was getting now. The rule of non-law. It had always been so. Why, they had said, enough is enough and taken their swords or their pikes or their long guns or their bare hands and gone out to fight it. And he saw now that they were happy at dying, because it was better to die with a purpose than to live with unreason. Sneer at their ineffectives, 'down the hill twining, their blessed steel shining', or twenty men in Dublin town, ill planned, ill engaged, riddled with informers, doomed to death in the coffin ships or the West Indies or Australia, or fetid prisons, or on the gallows, their bodies laid out like fish waiting to be boxed. You said: What was the use? Why didn't they do this? Why didn't they do that? Why were they so bloody stupid? Now he had an inkling of what had moved them. This. To be free of this and all that it implied. So that their children might never have to go through this. That they might have life and law and the pursuit of happiness, and if they couldn't have it, then they were better dead. Death would be honour and surcease from the blazing contradictions of feelings, the ballads and the flags and the poor uniforms. The whole of history seemed to culminate for him at this moment.

Then he must have gone away a long way. But he remembered these thoughts. He was never to forget them. They gave him food for thought for a long time to come. As if he had made a great discovery that had been hovering on the brink of his mind since he was born.

He was wet again. He knew this. But his head was resting

126

on softness. And the wetness was a hand with a cool wet cloth dabbing at his forehead. And he felt drops falling on his face. He was most surprised when he got his eyes open to see that these were coming from the face of his brother Dualta, who was bending over him, holding his hand tightly. Dominic wanted to cry out and say: No, no, Dualta, you are hurting my hand.

Dualta was saying: 'Dominic, I swear by Jesus Christ that I had to force myself not to come out. Dominic, it was the hardest thing in my life not to come out. You hear me, Dominic? You hear me?'

Dominic said: 'Dualta, listen, I am convinced now. You hear this? I am convinced now. You were right. I wasn't convinced. It was just that I didn't know, didn't see, Dualta.'

This seemed to make Dualta feel worse, he saw.

'Easy, Dualta, easy,' he heard his mother's voice. He looked up at her. She it was who was bathing his forehead. 'How do you feel now, Dominic?' she asked, her face close to his own. Like it always was when something sensational happened to you. That was good.

'Let me up,' he said. He was on the floor of the kitchen. He felt cold. He knew all his shirt was wet. He could see the blood that had dripped from his face seeping in the wetness. He didn't feel too bad. Some parts of him had no sensation at the moment. He felt a looseness in his mouth with his tongue, put up his hand and two teeth came away in his fingers. He looked at them on the palm of his hand. 'My beauty is altogether spoiled,' he said, trying to make them laugh, knowing that he wasn't at all beautiful anyhow. His mother took them from him, her face tight, and then she and Dualta helped him to his feet. Dualta had his face turned away from him. He was relieved to sit in the chair. His feet were painfully sore.

Then he heard the voice of Brid from behind him.

'Ora, Dualta,' she said. 'Out the back. There is a house on fire. I think it is the house of Ned.'

'Oh, no,' said Dominic. 'They went after Poric too. Go on, Dualta. Go and see. They don't like ex-policemen.'

127

'Are you sure you are all right?' Dualta, his broken hand on the side of Dominic's face, tenderly, like the touch of a woman.

'Go and see,' said Dominic, and then he was gone.

He closed his eyes, his head back. This way he could assess himself. He could move his arms and legs, so none of these were broken as he had thought at times. His face and jaws and his head were very painful. He knew this when he spoke. His mother and Brid were at his head. His mother said: 'It will be painful now, Dominic.' She always said this before the iodine went in. He braced himself, and sucked in his breath, but that didn't save him. His whole head and face seemed to be a vast jagged pain.

He wasn't quite aware of the passage of time.

Then he saw Poric standing in front of him.

Poric was saying: 'Are you all right, Dominic?' terrible anxiety in his broad face. Dominic wanted to laugh, because Poric himself wasn't all right. His face was a mass of cuts and bruises. His shirt was torn and bloodstained and the great arm he placed gently on Dominic's shoulder was pitted with three-inch cuts. He hadn't to be told. They had given Poric the belt, the one with the steel buckles.

'I must go back,' said Poric. 'They burned the house.'

'Oh, no,' said Dominic, thinking back to the light shining from the window and the family inside saying the Rosary. Only a while ago, he remembered.

Then Poric was gone. His mother made him lean his head on the table, while she got at the back of his skull. He must have fallen into a doze. He heard Dualta's voice from a great distance, and felt him shaking his shoulder.

'Dominic! Dominic!'

He raised himself. He thought he could see more clearly.

'You'll have to go,' said Dualta. 'You hear, Dominic. They will be back. I'm getting yourself and Poric to the other side of the hills. Try and stand up, Dominic.'

Dominic tried, with the help of his hand on the back of the chair. They stood back to let him do so. He managed with the help of his chairback. He didn't feel too bad, just that his feet were hurting him.

'I'm all right,' he said. 'But I have to get back to College.'

'You can whistle College goodbye until this is over,' said Dualta. 'Here, I have a clean shirt and trousers for you. You will have to get dressed.'

So he got dressed, the three of them helping him. The most painful part was his socks and boots. He thought he would never get into them, and that he would never walk in them, but it was amazing how he managed to do so, walking carefully on the kitchen floor.

He remembered that, and saying goodbye to his mother. She was a wonderful woman, but then, of course, he knew that she never cried until there was no one there to see her. He knew this. He kissed her. Brid was blubbering. Outside in the yard, he got on the pony's back bellywise and then straight, and took the reins. They had tied two sacks neck to neck and put them on the pony's back in front of him. And then Dualta led the pony out. Dominic swayed with the motion, his eyes shut.

When he opened them, he saw the remains of the house. It was getting light. It hadn't taken long to burn. The roof had fallen in when the heavy rafters had collapsed. Just two stark gable-ends, their edges standing up dirtily. And the stink of burning straw.

And behind the house Ned and the children and his wife were clearing out the cow's stable. There was a lantern hanging in there. Ned came and put his hand on his knee.

'Go home,' said Dominic. 'My mother wants you all. Go home to her.'

'No, bygob,' said Ned. 'Here we were born, boy, and here we stay. Tomorrow I will go into the big wood and cut new rafters. On your way, Poric! Be off with you. Here is Dominic. Never fear, Dominic, we'll whip them yet, you'll see.' He forgot himself. The hand became a fist that pounded Dominic's knee. Then he went away from him. 'What are ye doing? Have ye no wits? Is no one able to do a hand's turn but my son Sean and my son Poric that has to go on his holidays? On with ye. Blow the bugle.'

Remembered that, he did, they like ants clearing out a stable for their own use. 'Well,' shouted Mairéad, 'better people than us came out of stables.'

Dualta left them at the cross where the road, if you could call it a road, more of a sheep track, led off towards the distant hills.

'I'll have it arranged,' he said. 'Take it easy. Poric knows where to go. I'll have a doctor there too.'

He stood and looked after them until the great expanses of the plain of bog and rock swallowed them from his sight, two battered men. His good hand was clenched until it hurt him.

But looking after the slouched figures, he felt no despair. Nor listening to the roaring voice of Ned, getting dung scraped out of a stable. How else can you get to know the quality of a people, he wondered, except when things like this happen to them?

And then he went home, his mind coldly making plans.

13

THEY WERE sheltering in this dry-walled thatched hut near the gap in the hills that looked down on the big lake. It was a calm evening. Sometimes there were showers, completely unexpected since they seemed to come from a clear sky. But this was the way of the September weather. You could see the bog plains on all sides, broken by the sheen of the many lakes. The sedge was turning to a golden-brown colour. There was no sign of life except for an odd mountain sheep with a black face, who came on them unexpectedly, started with fright and then ran away. Once, for twenty minutes, they watched a hawk hovering over the bogs as if he was suspended from the sky with an invisible wire. To the right of them, in complete contrast to the stretching bog plains, there was a rock-strewn valley littered with stones, like the quarry of a giant who had aimlessly taken to breaking and scattering the great boulders.

'There's something coming now,' said Poric. He had been

leaning against the lintel of the doorway looking down into the lake valley. Dominic got to his feet. It was very painful. He had to hold his breath, helping himself up by grasping the stones of the wall. He stood for a moment and then went into the open. He looked down. He could see the open car, like a toy, making dust on the dirt road. There hadn't been enough rain to settle the dust.

'We'll go away from here,' he said. He walked away from the little shelter. They went over two folds and then fell full length with their eyes peering between tufts of heather. They saw the car appear over the rise in the road in about fifteen minutes. It held only one man, the driver. He was a tall man. He was crouching over the wheel. They didn't move. He stopped the car near the shelter. He got out. He stood on the road, looking around him. He was wearing a soft hat and a dust coat. He wore a moustache, turning grey. He saw the pony Saili then, trailing the reins, disgusted with the poor feeding of the dying sedge. He went towards the pony. She looked at him, shied and ran away for a few yards. He put his hands on his hips and looked around.

'Go around behind,' said Dominic, 'and see if there is anything following him on the road.'

Poric pulled back and, when he was out of sight of the man, went to peer over the hill down into the valley. He turned and shook his head, so Dominic rose and walked towards the man with his hands in the pockets of his coat. He had to walk very slowly. The man saw him, turned towards him and waited. How long will we have to spend our lives like this now, Dominic wondered?

He stood near the man. He was about forty, with a strong face and long arms.

'Are you the patient?' he asked.

'I don't know,' said Dominic.

'I was told there would be two of you,' he said.

'There's the other,' said Dominic as Poric came over the rise.

'He would make two with his size,' said the man, looking at Poric. 'I'll get my bag.' He went towards his car.

'Don't you want to ask any questions?' Dominic asked.

The man stopped and looked back at him. Suddenly he smiled.

'It's many a time a person's mouth broke his nose,' he said in Irish, to their surprise. They laughed and closed on him. 'Show me, now,' he said turning to look at them.

'Take the big fellow,' said Dominic. There were crude bandages wrapped around Poric's arms, bits of shirts and things. He took these off efficiently, not very kindly. He examined the arms.

'Some of these will have to be stitched,' he said. 'It will be sore on you. Have you more?'

Poric struggled out of his shirt, and turned his back and sides. The man looked at them, probing them with his fingers.

'Not too bad,' he said. 'Clean cuts, not too deep. You will have to come home with me. Don't put back your shirt. I'll dress them. Let's see you,' he said then to Dominic.

Dominic let him examine his head and face.

'You should be examined for fractures,' he said, pressing with his fingers. 'Hairline fractures are hard to detect. You mightn't have any. On the other hand you might. No stitches. The big cuts under your hair will heal. How do you feel?'

'My brain feels addled,' said Dominic, 'but then I think it was always that way.'

He saw the eyes of the doctor twinkling, laughter creases forming around them.

'You won't die,' he said. 'It's only the people who are sorry for themselves who die. Anything else?'

Dominic sat down and started to remove his boots. He had to go very cautiously with them. The doctor squatted in front of him and helped. He took his feet in his hands then. They were tri-coloured, black and red and blue. The doctor probed them with his fingers, looking now and again into Dominic's face as he did so. Sometimes he couldn't help wincing.

'I don't think there are bones broken,' he said. 'The side of a mountain is not the best place to diagnose, but I don't think so. I'll treat the burns. You'll have to put them up for a few days.'

Dominic laughed.

The doctor went to his bag then. He got out bottles and cotton wool. They were to remember this place in the mountain. When he wanted water, he got it from a clean-looking little river that had been scoured by the stones and the gravel, but when he was finished they felt soothed.

'I have to go into the village there,' he said. 'There's a baby due. I don't know how long I will be. When I come back it will be dark. You can come down with me. I'll take the big fellow home and you go to the house you were told of. Will that suit?'

'You are very kind,' said Dominic.

'I'd like to think so,' said the doctor. 'Today, you. To-morrow, a purgative to constipated policemen. You see, it's all one.'

Dominic knew it wasn't. They'd take him very fast if they knew he was helping the running men.

'Here's some cigarettes,' he said, giving him a packet. Then he took his bag and set off walking. There were many villages in the folds of the hills. You'd never know they were there if you hadn't to avoid them as they had done.

'Hey,' Dominic called after him. 'Take the pony.'

He paused. 'Good idea,' he said. Dominic was going to get to his bandaged feet to help him, but the doctor walked to-wards the pony saying: 'Pshough. Pshough. Pshough.' Dominic was waiting for the pony to run from him, but oddly enough she didn't. She extended her nostrils a bit, and backed a bit, but she let him catch the trailing reins and her mane, and then in a smooth flowing movement he was on her back and settling himself. 'The bitch wouldn't let me do that,' said Dominic. 'The females don't favour you,' said Poric laughing.

'Leave her at the village,' shouted Dominic, 'they'll get her home.'

The doctor nodded, and set off. In two minutes he was over the hill.

'Maybe it's good these things happen,' said Poric. 'If they make you meet good people.'

'If people are what they seem,' said Dominic doubtfully.

133

'You have to trust somebody,' said Poric indignantly. 'He's a great man.'

'I won't trust anybody,' said Dominic. 'Not any more. Lowry trusted somebody and look what happened to him.'

'I'm going to trust everybody,' said Poric forcefully.

'You'll be sorry,' said Dominic. 'Didn't what happened to you put a crust around your nature?'

Poric thought over this.

'No,' he said. 'Why should you blame other people for these ones. They are not normal. They are only a portion of their own people.'

'Well, they put a crust around me,' said Dominic grimly. 'It's an inch thick. You have seen a dog approaching a friendly-looking man with his tail wagging. And the man raises a stick and beats him. The dog will always be wary, ever again. He won't wag his tail. I won't wag mine any more.'

He believed this.

Later, in the darkness, he stood in the lane and looked at the house. It was a long thatched cottage, with smooth white-washed walls and a new thatch. There was enough light from the stars to see this. The windows had dark blinds on them, so there was not much light to be seen from inside, the gleams of light shone through the imperfections in the door, long streaks that ran across the gravel yard. He looked back towards the main road which was several hundred yards away. There was no movement on it. It was a clear starry night.

He approached the door walking as silently as he could. It was difficult on account of his sore feet. He stood in front of the door, hesitating. He might have to run, and he knew he was not capable of running very fast. He knocked. He could sense the hesitation inside, the imagined terror of people in those times. Knocks one time meant different things to now. In fact there was never any need to knock because doors were always open, lighting up the night in friendly invitation to enter friend, and chat and smoke and spit into the ashes of the fire.

The door opened only a few inches. This was contrary to

things too, this cautious opening of doors. He saw a portion of the man's face, like a sliced face, centre portion. What could you guess from it, a beaked nose under beetling eyebrows, thick lips and a firm chin split in the middle where he found it hard to shave?

'My name is Dominic,' he said.

The door was flung wide. The man held his arms wide. He was beaming. 'By the power of God, you made it,' he said. 'Come in. Maria, it's Dominic, he's here. Swing the kettle on the iron. Put half a dozen brown eggs in the saucepan. Come in, Dominic. We were praying for you.' He practically hauled him in. He was in his shirt, with red braces holding up his frieze trousers, a big man, with a welcome in his face, his smiling mouth, his bobbing Adam's apple.

Dominic was pleased. The woman came forward to shake his hand, wiping her hand first on a check apron. She had been mixing the dough for a cake on the kitchen table. 'We are glad to see you,' she said. 'We only heard an hour ago that you would be here. There was a man to be with you. What happened to him?'

'He is safe,' said Dominic. 'You are Boat Brady,' he said then to the man. 'You were at my father's requiem Mass. I didn't know it was to be you. I would have felt easier.'

'We didn't know it was to be you, either,' Boat said, pulling a wooden chair to the fire. 'Sit down. Man, it's good to see you. You had to run?'

'Yes,' said Dominic. He saw that his face had shocked them, but only for a moment. Now they were looking into his eyes, although one of his eyes was nearly closed by the swollen and puffed flesh.

'Two of mine are abroad,' said Boat laughing. 'It's all right. The harvest is nearly home, so I won't miss them. You are in a safe house here, Dominic. They raid us twice a week regular. They were here the night before last, so they're not due again for a few turns.'

'Your belly must be slack,' said Maria, vigorously poking at the turf fire, bringing it to a bright blaze under the black kettle. 'Are ye all well behind?'

135

'Yes,' said Dominic politely, 'we are all well. Dualta was home. I'm sure he's gone away again now.'

'That Dualta,' said Boat laughing. 'He nearly drove Uncle Marcus mad with the uniform. You remember that, Dominic.'

'Yes,' said Dominic, thinking it was ten years ago, it seemed.

'And your mother is well?' Maria asked.

He thought of his mother. Now, tonight, she would be feeling all that had happened.

'She is as well as can be expected with the two sons she has,' said Dominic. 'Would you mind if I took off my boots?' They were killing his feet. As long as he was moving it wasn't too bad, but not sitting here with the heat swelling them. He bent and took them off tenderly. They watched him with impassive faces, as he freed them and then stretched them in front of him with a relieved sigh.

Boat said grimly looking at them: 'Your day will come, eh, Dominic?'

'That's right,' said Dominic.

'You can't go fast on those,' said Boat then. 'If they come there is a quick dart into the back down the fields with a boat at the end to go across the lake. You can't do that. Maybe it's not safe for you to be here. I think I'll go to the neighbour up the road and get you in there. They are innocent people, too poor to be powerful, or to be raided. I'll do that now. You never know with those ones.'

He rose up and got his coat from the pegs behind the door. He put a worn and soiled hat on his head. 'I won't be long. Drink your tea and eat hearty.' Then he was gone.

'Where are the family?' Dominic asked her.

'The sons are away,' she said. 'Little Catherine is down with the measles. She got them in school. It's the devil and all to keep her in bed. She's asleep now. The other one . . .' she stood for a moment thinking. 'Ah, well,' she said. 'Now, here's the kettle boiling. Move over to the table.' She was very efficient. The table was laid in a flash, the strong tea being poured, and fresh cake-bread sliced and thickly buttered for him from a fresh print of butter. He was surprised to find that

136

he was hungry, and could eat, although his jaws were sore and he had to chew gently as the pressure of eating sent shots of pain all over his face and head.

Maria was uneasy with him, he knew. Because, he supposed, she thought of her own sons in his position, having things like this done to them. She would be saying aspirations probably now over and over. Please God, don't let them do things like that to my sons. He was trying to think of something else too, something important that was evading his memory, something he should know, when the door opened and Boat came in panting, and stood with his back to the door and said: 'We're too late. I saw the lights of the lorry a mile away. They mightn't be coming here, but we can't take chances. You can't run, so you must stay. But where the hell? Maria, clear the table. Hold on. I think, see.' He bent his head, closed his eyes. He hit his forehead with a loud slap. He bent and caught Dominic's boots and flung them into the loft over the bedroom door. He threw his coat up after the boots.

'There is only one place now,' he said, 'Wait for me!' As if Dominic was going anywhere. Dominic wasn't frightened. He felt almost indifferent. What did it matter? He was tired, of course, and his brain was addled as he had said. He watched as Maria cleared the table. She did it very efficiently and replaced it with the cake dough, and scattered a handful of flour on the table as well. Boat had thrown off his coat and gone into a room opposite the fireplace. He came out of that now. He had a little girl wrapped in a blanket. She would be about ten. Her face was flushed. She was spotted from the measles. She had a startled look in her eyes, woken from her sleep like this. Dominic felt a wave of tenderness for her helplessness. He was as helpless himself.

'Only one way,' said Boat. 'Only one bed big enough. Come with me, Dominic, and do what you are told and keep your head down. They might not come but I have a terrible feeling they will.'

He opened the door near the fire. The lamplight from the kitchen shone into the darkness of the room. Boat went in there

137

and Dominic followed him. There was a big double bed in this room.

'Go into the bed beside Finola,' said Boat. 'Finola! Finola! Here's a young man getting into bed with you, but he has all his clothes on.' Boat chuckling. At a time like this! Now he saw her raise her face. She had not been asleep. It was an indifferent face, cold and unmoving. She just turned on her side away from them. 'Go on for the love of God,' said Boat: 'Don't you see it's a feather mattress. It would hide a regiment of Lancers and their horses. In with you, Dominic. It will be only for a few minutes. Then I will release you.'

Dominic was amazed. He got into the bed. Sure enough his weight sank it.

'You mustn't cry now, Catherine,' Boat was saying to his little girl. 'This is a big adventure, see. Nothing like this ever happened to you before. This is your cousin Dominic. You must save him, Kate. Just close your eyes and go to sleep.'

Dominic felt the clothes pulled over his face. His weight was bringing the bodies of the big girl and the small girl on top of him. It had all happened before he had been aware of it. If he had been in his right senses he might have fought against it. But here he was, half smothered, lying in his clothes in a feather bed. He could feel the stiffness in the body of Finola. That was what he had been trying to recover in his mind, that Finola, Lowry's Finola, was the daughter of Boat Brady. What was she doing here now? She should be in the town teaching in the school where she had been appointed. This was crazy. He was about to struggle out of it when he heard the banging on the door outside. Despite himself, he shrank. He imagined he would always be like this when he heard banging on doors. He put up his hand to feel for an opening in the clothes covering his face. When he felt the air with his hand, he held the opening. He heard the voices. The same sort of voices, and Boat's voice. Boat genuinely didn't give a damn for them. He could hear that from the way he spoke. Not sneeringly. He wasn't that way. It was a lack of fear. He thought Boat genuinely felt superior to the voices.

'You should come more often,' he was saying. 'What would

138

we do without you? We just got in three machine guns and a couple of field guns. The machine guns are up there on the loft with me old boots. That's right. We have the cow tied to the field gun. We keep the dynamite up there in my room under my pillow. Not there? Where could it be gone. In there? You want to catch the measles? My little girl is in there with the measles. Did any of ye have the measles or were ye ever children? Or maybe ye never grew up. All right if you want to. I have two sick girls in there, but don't let that stop you.'

Dominic was aware of the extra light in the room. He felt the little girl's hand clutching and he took it into his own and squeezed it. It fluttered in his hand for a time and then held on tightly and confidently. He was angry now, not at his own position, but that this little sick girl should be put to this test.

'Are you satisfied? Don't mind them, Kate. They are just joking. Turn your face now and go to sleep again. Do you think the child is hiding a few hand grenades?'

Finola hadn't turned to them. So that look of indifference he thought he had seen on her face was true? She had looked sicker than Catherine.

The door closed. He didn't move for a moment. Then he pulled himself up a little. He put his hand on the hot face of the child. She snuggled her cheek into his palm. He listened. He heard the door being closed and bolted, the loud talk outside, and the sound of the feet and the sound of the lorry starting up and going off into the distance. Then he put his arms under the child and got out of bed holding her. When Boat opened the door, he walked into the kitchen with her.

Boat sat on a chair, his elbows on his knees. He was hardly able to speak now. He was rubbing sweat off his head and his face with a hand that had a tremble in it.

Dominic looked at the girl. She was looking gravely at him. Then she smiled. She was a small edition of her big sister, he thought. She had small pointed teeth.

'You are the bravest girl I ever met, Kate,' he said. 'Isn't this so?' he asked her father.

'If they were giving medals,' said her father, 'she'd be weighed down with them.'

'If you will marry me,' said Dominic, 'I'll wait until you grow up. Will you do this?'

She put her head on one side.

'I'll think of it, Dominic,' she said. It made them laugh, the three of them, a little hysterically, Dominic thought.

Then her father took her into his arms.

'Pure gold,' he said as he took her. 'Pure gold. Say good night to Dominic.'

'Good night Dominic,' she said.

Dominic bent and kissed her on the forehead.

'You'll get the measles,' she said.

'I don't give a damn,' said Dominic.

She laughed with glee.

'Then you'll have to stay,' she said.

'Forever,' said Dominic.

'Off we go now,' said her father and took her away.

'What's wrong with Finola?' Dominic asked.

Maria's forehead was creased.

'She is very sick,' said Maria. 'And we can do nothing with her.'

'I'm nearly a half-doctor,' said Dominic. 'Maybe I can do something with her.'

She shook her head.

'It's only the dead can help her,' said Maria with a sigh. 'Only the dead, and they don't come back.'

'We'll see,' said Dominic, looking at the door and thinking of the strange dead look on her face. 'We'll see.'

14

'TAKE THE lamp,' Dominic said to them. He was sorry for them. The father, such a decisive man about everything else, was so upset about his daughter.

'We only met Lowry once or twice,' Maria said. 'He would charm the birds off the trees. I don't wonder she is so sad. But she is making herself sick. And that's not good. She will pay no heed to you, I am afraid.'

'Come on, Maria,' Boat said, his arm on her shoulders. He had taken the paraffin lamp from the wall and was holding it in his hand. It lighted the planes of their faces, making them seem sad and worn. 'Dominic is of an age with her. Young people are a mystery to me. You only read about people dying from broken hearts. This mustn't be so with her. Life must be lived, eh, Dominic?'

'That's right,' said Dominic.

'People mustn't bend under burdens,' Boat said. 'Else how would the world survive at all? She comes from a good surviving stock. This is what makes me weary with her. But I have no power over her.'

'Go to bed,' said Dominic.

Boat went to say something, and then clamped his mouth shut. They went to the room door near the back, raised the latch and went in with the light. Dominic was in darkness, except for the flickering light of the turf fire that threw huge shadows of the chairs on the wall where the harness hung on the wooden pegs. He put his head back and closed his eyes. He would dearly love to go to bed and sleep. That was what he wanted to do most. He took the long tongs and fixed the fire. He pulled out the glowing coals and put fresh sods of turf at the back and the sides. The fire was dulled for a few moments and then it began to blaze. He squatted in front of it, feeling its warmth on his body, and then he rose and went over to her room. He threw the door open. He could see little from the reflected light of the fire.

'Finola,' he said. 'Would you come to the kitchen, I want to talk to you?'

He peered closely. All he could see was her tossed hair on the pillow. She could be asleep, but he doubted it. The way she was lying somehow he knew she was awake, turned away from the world. 'I haven't seen you since we met last,' he said. 'I want to talk to you now.'

He took a chance then. He went back and sat on the stool on the far side of the fireplace. He drew back until he was

141

shadowed from the fire and she would be able to see only the bulk of him. He didn't want her to see his face. There were enough complications as it was.

He listened. No sound came from the room. He thought she would come because so far as she knew he was the last one to speak to Lowry. But this mightn't be sufficient to bring her either.

The time passed. All he could hear was the loud tick of the pendulum clock hanging on the wall. The face of it was yellowed with age, and it beat the half hour and the hour with a sort of gasp like the breathing of a bronchial chest.

Then she was there, standing in the firelight. She wore a long white nightdress, that almost reached to the ground, and she had pulled on over that a dressing-gown that was too small for her, probably one she had used when she was away at school.

'Sit down,' he said softly. She obeyed him automatically. She sat on a stool in the light of the fire and he was shocked at her appearance. Her hair was in tangles and reflected no lights. There were very deep shadows around her eyes. Her face was very thin. This should have excited pity in him, but it didn't. He felt himself getting angry. He remembered her gleaming hair held back by a slide; the lively eyes, the soap fragrance that always surrounded her. It seemed to him that she was a caricature of what she had been. 'What's wrong with you?' he asked. She looked in his direction, but she made no answer. Her hands were held listlessly on her lap. One of them just twitched.

'If anyone had told me that you would react like this to the death of Lowry, I would have spit in his face,' he said. He waited to see what would happen now, and he was pleased when she made as if to rise and go. 'Don't go,' he said. She sat again, she dropped her head, looking at her hands.

'The last time we met,' he said, 'you and I talked. I remember things you said. You said that leader types were in a hurry, that they left ordinary people like us to sort things out afterwards. You asked me if I thought you were a feather-brain. I didn't think so then, but I am wondering now.'

142

He was watching her hands. They were clenching on one another.

'The three of us were together in the sunshine for a short while,' he said. 'You held Lowry's hand and you looked up into his face. Do you know what I thought then? Would you like to hear?'

She made no answer.

'I thought of a girl lighting a candle and looking up into the face of the statue of a saint,' said Dominic. 'That's what I thought. You came out to me now because you know that Lowry and I went away and left you looking after us. You came because what you want to know is what Lowry said when we were together? Will I tell you?'

He saw the hands clenched whitely, and a sort of a sound came out of her pale-lipped mouth.

'I remember the first time I saw you,' he went on. 'It was down at the grave of my father. And I never forgot you. After we left you I said to Lowry: She's a great girl. You know what Lowry said? He said: Maybe you better take this money and papers, Dominic. You are less noticeable. Lowry never even looked back at you. You know that? He never even looked back at you.'

He watched her hands come up to cover her face, coldly. He was amazed at his own anger.

'Lowry didn't love you, Finola. Lowry was in love with a dream. Lowry was incapable of human love until his dream was accomplished. Don't you know that? Lowry wasn't courting you, he was courting death. That was his dream. He didn't want to die for you. He wanted to die for unborn children. He was in love with a woman called Ireland, and not one called Finola. He had no time. And you know this is true, don't you? Don't you?'

'No! No!' she said, rising to her feet and turning to flee. He wouldn't let her. He went over to her and caught her shoulders in his hands. He had to squeeze tightly to hold her.

'This is true, and this is what is killing you,' he shouted. 'You weren't in love with a man either. You were in love with

143

a dream, an intangible saint, a plaster statue, the ideal of what all men should be in those times.'

'Let me go!' she said. 'Let me go!' her head averted from him, in loathing, he thought.

'If I am wrong,' he said, 'what is wrong with you? Is this the way Lowry would wish to see you, fading away like a rustic Ophelia, instead of being out bandaging wounds, comforting widows, visiting prisoners. This was the way you were. This was the way you should be. What are you doing now? Fading away in a welter of self-pity. Are you the only one who has lost a lover? Or are you pitying yourself because you never had him as a lover, and you knew it.'

She hit him then, right smack on the sore side of his face so that he had to release her and bend his head, holding it in agony.

'You weren't worthy to put polish on his shoes,' she was shouting. 'And you talk like that of him. Beside you he was a giant. Small man. Small man. Dragged to chariot wheels, afraid of every shadow. That was you. You weren't even fit to be with him. You weren't even fit for his shadow to cross yours and you say these things about him. Get out! Oh, get out!'

Then she started calling: 'Father! Father! That you should say things like that to me. About him. And he thought much of you. And he is dead! Dead! and you talk like this about him. Father! Father!'

Her father was there, with the lamp in his hand, coming towards her saying 'Easy! Easy! Finola, for the love of God. Finola!'

'Get him out of here,' she shouted at him. 'I don't want him in the house. Father. Get him away from me. I can't stay if he is here.'

'Right,' her father shouted. 'We'll throw him out. They are waiting for him but what does that matter? Let's throw him out so they can shoot the poor little bastard. Is that what you want?'

There was a big silence.

Dominic had straightened up. He was looking at her admiringly. For a girl who was half a ghost a short time before,

144

she was looking live enough now. Her eyes were flashing, her hands were clenched. And then he saw the look in her eyes changing as she became aware. She was looking at a very bruised and blackened face, one eye practically closed, cut and swollen lips. He was dark too and unshaven and this must have made him look worse.

'What happened to you?' she asked quietly. Her father looked at her in astonishment. He had to scratch his head.

'I tripped over a matchbox,' said Dominic.

She saw his grin, that was more a grimace. She saw the gaps where his teeth had been at the side of his mouth. Then she put her hands up to her mouth, held them there, and he saw tears starting from her eyes. She kept looking at him, and then she turned slowly and walked to her room. They watched the door closing. They listened. They heard her crying.

It was hard on her father. He kind of shuffled like a dog with his bare feet on the cement floor. Dominic heard this sound.

'What in the name of God did you say to her?' he asked.

'Terrible things,' said Dominic.

'It's the first time she cried,' said her father.

'You were a good half-doctor, Dominic,' Maria said then from her bedroom door.

'No,' said Dominic. ' A quack. I could have killed her.'

The three of them stood there in silence until they could hear no further sound from the room.

'Will she be all right now?' Maria asked.

'I don't know,' said Dominic. 'I'll say a few more words to her.'

'Will it set her off again?' Boat asked. 'That would be too much.'

'I'll have to,' said Dominic. He opened her door again and went in. He was glad of the darkness. Because he would have to tell lies.

'Finola,' he said softly. 'My sorrow for what I did to you. I only wanted to bring you back to what you are. It wasn't right for you to be grieving like that. I had to distract you. I know you loved Lowry. I know Lowry loved you. You will

145

have to forgive me for the things that I said to awaken you. But life must go on. What Lowry died for must go on. We cannot turn our backs on it because we are so sad.'

'They beat you,' she said.

'Not to death,' he said.

'I will be all right now,' she said.

That was all. As he stepped back to the door he thought: What kind of a man am I at all, or what kind of a half-man? Because I may as well face the truth. I'm jealous of a dead man, not of his greatness but of his personality. Alive he couldn't compete with him; and dead he thought he had even less chance of competing. But she would be all right now.

Sam was standing in the kitchen when he closed her door.

'Look who's here,' said Boat.

'He frightened the life out of me,' said Maria. 'He came like a ghost.'

'Hello, Sam,' said Dominic. 'Long time since I saw you.'

He thought Sam was looking thinner, if possible. He didn't seem to be able to fit his skimpy raincoat.

'I heard about you,' said Sam. He came over to him. 'Well, at least they improved your looks,' he said then.

Dominic laughed. He thought it was good that he was able to laugh.

'I said something funny again,' said Sam.

'Action, Sam,' said Dominic. 'We want action. Sick of being on the wrong end of the stick.'

'Right,' said Sam. 'We'll see what we can do to accommodate you.'

And Dominic felt good, and for the first time he felt ready to fight, just to fight and not to analyse.

'I'll get out a bottle,' said Boat. 'It's too cursed late to go to bed now anyhow.'

'We are going to have good times, Dominic,' said Sam. And he was grinning.

15

SAM HAD a weakness. He didn't understand the country people, and on account of this he was inclined to be afraid of them. He felt at home with terraces of houses at his back, the smell of coal fires from chimneys, thick traffic, concourses of people.

But he faced this gathering of men in the field near the Church after last Mass on a Sunday in October as if he was their father. They knew he was a stranger, since anyone who lived two miles outside the borders of their parish was a stranger to them and would remain so for centuries. They had left their carts and horses outside and their womenfolk and the children waited there patiently for them. To Sam their closed faces would look sinister. To Dominic they were readable as he could spot the types from knowing the people of his own village at the other side of the county. He could place the funster and the big farmer and the feckless one; he could recognize the one who was probably a shopkeeper from the one who was a cattle jobber. He could tell the sheep farmer from the tillage man. But to Sam these men with their big wrists and heavy clothes, some with moustaches and locks of hair growing high on their cheekbones, with their brass studs gleaming in the cold sun, and stout sticks in their hands, were as unpredictable as the behaviour of cattle on roads, or children on streets.

The OC of the local company stood behind him. He was a big simple man who suspected that some men of his company had put their land hunger before their patriotism in the events of the last week.

Dominic and Poric stood behind him. They kept their hands in their overcoat pockets and their faces were grim, on orders from Sam. Dominic supposed that they looked menacing. Poric was big and scowling. There were two scars on his face, which gave a completely false picture of his actual character.

147

'Everyone knows,' said Sam to them, in his thin raspy voice, 'that the people of this parish in East Galway suffered a lot from landlords over many years. So when the police were withdrawn from the area, you took matters into your own hands. You drove this man's cattle all over the country. You knocked his fences. You ploughed up many acres of his parkland. You divided over eighty acres among yourselves. That still leaves him many hundreds of acres, I agree. But would you have done this thing if the police hadn't been driven out for you? Who drove out the police? Was it yourselves, or the young men who are winning your freedom for you? Would you have done this if the police were still here?'

They didn't answer his questions. He might as well have been addressing the waters of a dark lake.

'This might have been excusable,' he went on. 'But you attack the house and you loot it. This is robbery with violence. The priest in there this morning already told you what he thinks about it. We have been sent from Headquarters to tell you what the leaders of the struggle think about it.'

At this point Sam looked over his shoulder, nervously, at Dominic and Poric. He had made them keep aloof from everybody since they came to the parish two days ago. They didn't speak. They just looked. When Sam was asked who they were, he just laughed, and said 'Executioners' and people laughed with him and kept looking at the hands which they kept in their pockets. All this was pure bluff because all they had in their pockets was their fists. Sam was a strategist.

'The powers that be,' Sam went on, 'want you to do those things. They want to say: See the anarchy that prevails as soon as our law is withdrawn from the countryside. They want you to do those things. And you bloody well oblige them, don't you?'

Dominic saw Sam's neck getting a bit red at the back.

'Sinn Fein Land Arbitration Courts have been set up,' said Sam. 'They fix up all these land questions. They work under difficulties. But their settlements have been fair. The landlords' agents have agreed with their findings, and disputed

148

land has been handed over to the hungry at a fair rate of compensation. The Arbitration Court is coming here and they will hear your case and they will do justice to your longings. But I'm damned if they will come here while you are branded as a pack of thieves and robbers.'

'You keep your mouth shut, Skinnymalink!' a man in the crowd suddenly shouted at him, waving a stick.

This seemed to spark Sam.

'There's nobody here that can shut it,' he shouted. 'You make me feel sick. Every day there are men dying for you. Did you know that? They are dying in ditches and jails and camps. Towns are being burned; houses are bonfires, and all you can think of is to go and loot a mansion. You are betraying the men who are dying for your liberty, you stupid bastards! That's all you are. What must they think, buried in quicklime graves? That this is what they died for, so that some fellow will steal a grandfather clock that wouldn't even fit in his house. Is this the symbol of freedom? Is this why men of your own blood are dying and suffering, and all you can think of is pinching piss-pots.'

Dominic had never seen Sam angry before. But he was now. His thin neck was shoved forward so you could see the strength of his jaw. His neck was red and his face was pale. The men he was addressing were angry, you could see that, but Sam didn't care.

'I have here a list of the stolen things,' he shouted. 'We are going up to that house. By six o'clock tonight I want every piece of the stolen goods to be returned to the house from which they were stolen. If they are not returned, you'll pay. I don't know how you'll pay. But you will. We'll make your name a shame in the length and breadth of Ireland. I promise you this. I know there are decent men among you who must be ashamed. I can understand that what happened was a sort of thing that men would do in a fever. What I am doing is giving you an opportunity to redeem yourselves. If all men can't be out on the hills with a gun, they can live at home with their conscience. This is the least that your country asks from you. She doesn't want your blood or your lives or your treasure.

149

All she wants from you is a clear conscience, and if you can't give her that, she'll spit you out of her mouth.'

And then he walked away abruptly.

Dominic thought if it was anyone else they might possibly have killed him. Because they were angry. He could see it from their eyes, and the clenching of their fists, and the moving of their heavy boots on the grass of the field.

But Sam was the leader type. He had this certain something; this lack of fear, and this dedication that carries conviction. He had thrown away the strategy. Dominic and Poric moved after him. He was walking past the tethered horses and carts with his head bent and his hands in his pockets. They strolled after him, making no effort to catch up with him. Sam believed, Dominic thought. Sam wouldn't know if they would eventually win or lose, but he believed, like the other leader types Dominic had met. Dominic knew why. Sam didn't care why. That was the difference in their feelings. Sam didn't care if they failed. There were other generations coming after them. It was a few men, like Sam, born in this time, that made the movement implacable, Dominic thought, thinking of some of them he had met. Men like himself and Poric would be simply the arms of service.

Half a mile down the road, they turned into the imposing gateway of the house. Beautifully curving railings, pillars and tall gates all done in wrought iron. The whole place was surrounded by high walls, which all men knew had been built with the sweat and blood of the starving during the famine times for fourpence a day, just enough to buy a meal for the starving families and leave themselves with slack bellies. Only God knew how many men and boys had died for the building of these high walls. But that was time past and this was the present and the struggling republic mustn't have its name tarnished. Sam would think like that although he would never say it.

The carriage drive wound beautifully between an avenue of beech trees, which had lost most of their leaves to the first heavy frosts of the year.

The door between the pillared porticos was open.

Sam stood there and pulled the bell.

A nervous maidservant, in a blue dress and a white apron and a white cap on her head, came to the door. She stood there plucking at her apron with her fingers. She made the gesture Come In, but Sam shook his head. He turned his back on the door. He saw Dominic and Poric getting close to him, but he seemed to be looking through them. This man came to the door. He was dressed in a tweed suit of knickerbockers. He was bald. Sam heard him and turned.

'I have spoken to the people,' he said. 'All the things removed from your house will be returned.'

The man didn't believe him.

'I have given you my word,' said Sam. 'We will wait here to see that it is.'

'Won't you come inside?' the man asked. 'Won't you come in and have some refreshment?'

'No, thank you,' said Sam. 'You know that we are in a dangerous position. All I ask is that no word about us be sent to the authorities.'

The man looked at him, his head on one side.

'You have my word that the authorities will not be informed,' he said.

'Thank you,' said Sam and walked away. He passed Dominic and Poric. He went a little way down the avenue, and then sat on the grass with his back against the great bole of a beech tree. The man retired and closed the door. Dominic could see the faces of ladies looking out of the glass of the big window that faced on to the lawn.

They went down to Sam. Dominic got on one knee. 'There is a telephone in the house,' he said. 'Wouldn't it be advisable to cut the wires?'

Sam looked up at him, thinking.

'It would be,' he said, 'but he won't. He gave his word. It should be as good as mine.'

'How good is yours?' asked Dominic sitting beside him.

'That remains to be seen,' said Sam grimly, looking down the avenue.

One hour, two hours, three hours they waited there, rising

151

now and again to stretch their legs. Poric had provided himself with a few slices of bread, being a big man. They shared these, but their stomachs were rumbling with the hunger.

About dusk, it started. A cart came into the avenue. It was an ass cart, and on the ass cart was a beautiful grandfather clock, looking out of place. The man driving the cart paid them no heed. He went past with his face straight in front, but when he had gone on a little and saw that Sam was not looking at him, he winked solemnly at Dominic.

Dominic wanted to laugh with glee, but didn't like to. He always thought of this as Sam's miracle, because nobody but himself believed in it. But it happened, as they stood there and watched the procession of carts pass by, with all the useless things that people had taken in a frenzy from the looted mansion.

It all came back, down to the last tool, the last spoon and the last bedroom utensil.

'They are great people,' said Sam to the OC. 'They are a great people. How can we lose?'

This was one of Sam's little victories that Dominic remembered.

The other one was odder.

A certain soldier from the barracks suddenly made a habit of coming late at night to a club where all sorts gathered to play cards, or billiards, or drink beer. When he had had a few he would become belligerent. He would open his tunic, adopt a fighting position and shout: 'If there's any effing Sinn Feiner here, I'll deal with him. Hear this. In here, on the street, around the jail, anywhere at all, I'll powder him!' Then he would sing a song:

'Never marry a soldier, a sailor or a marine,
But marry a bould Sinn Feiner with his — all painted
    green.
So right you are! Right you are!
Right you are me bould Sinn Feiner! Right you are!'

It was a men's club and they were used to bad language, but this fellow was a little fighting bantam of a man, butty and dangerous, so they would calm him down with free beer and when he was well drunk, eject him.

Sometimes he would start all these challenges before he went into the club at all, standing on the pavement and addressing all who passed by. 'Are you a Sinn Feiner, cock? If you are I can plaster you. And I can plaster your father! I'm Moriarty, the best fighting man of the Munsters. I can handle two of ye with one hand. Bring me your best Sinn Feiner and I'll batter him into a cocked hat.'

This particular Friday evening, it was raining. The street of the club was only dimly lighted. Moriarty came around the church corner and stood under the light, looked around for a passerby, and then roared at a thin young man hurrying home with a parcel under his arm.

'Are you a Sinn Feiner, Skinny? If you are, come here to me until I embrace you to death. Hear me!'

Suddenly a large hand was laid on his shoulder and he was spun around. He could only see a man's chest in front of him, for Poric was very tall. He had to bend back his head to look for his face.

'I'm a Sinn Feiner,' said Poric gently to him. 'And I want to fight you.'

'Oh, no,' said Moriarty.

Dominic had to laugh as they closed in on him. His dismay at the size of Poric was so obvious. He didn't get time to say any more. Poric swung his arm around his back and rushed him across the street. Dominic grabbed his free arm. Sam said to the skinny young man: 'A lunatic. We have to get him back to the barracks.' The young man said nothing, just turned the collar of his coat up around his neck and hurried away. The soldier couldn't say anything. If he started to shout, Poric put the pressure on his arm and he just gasped and went along with them. They got him down the narrow street between the tall store houses. Here they turned right and Sam went ahead of them and opened a wicket gate into a yard. They pushed him in here, in through another sagging doorway which was feebly lighted inside by one cobweb-covered bulb. It was an engineering workshop with a bench. Poric pushed him and he ended up with his back to the bench. He was rubbing his arm.

'Listen, soldier,' said Sam. 'You aren't even small potatoes. I don't know why we bother with you. Just that it's not good for morale to have you going around cursing and shouting your head off. So you can have your choice now. Fight the big fellow, or fight the small fellow there, or if you like, I'll fight you. We get this over and then you keep your big mouth shut. It will be a fair fight. We'll only half kill you.'

'I don't want to fight anyone,' Moriarty said plaintively.

'That's a quick change,' said Sam. 'For the last week you have been wanting to eat a Sinn Feiner.'

'How the hell else could I get in touch with ye?' Moriarty asked.

'You wanted to get in touch with us?' Sam asked.

'What the hell do you think I've been doing?' Moriarty asked. 'Why should I be making an eejit of myself else?'

Sam laughed. 'Oh, so that's it.'

'Ye'er not very bright, are ye?' Moriarty asked, still rubbing his arm.

'That's right,' said Sam. 'What do you want?'

'You want guns, don't you?' Moriarty asked. 'We have guns.'

'Who's we?' Sam asked.

'Me and some others,' said Moriarty. 'Listen, we had a bit of a rumble in the barracks with the Scots. We were blamed. Some damage done. What do they do then? They dock our pay. Listen, by the time we have paid for the damage they assessed on us, we'll be old men with whiskers, and we won't have the price of a packet of cigarettes for the next ten years.'

'So,' said Sam.

'So we raided their quarters, the Scots,' said Moriarty. 'And we lifted a few things, guns and such, and we'd like to flog them, but who'll buy them but Sinn Feiners, see? This way we get some of yeer money and the Scots get kicked in the ass for losing equipment. You see?'

'Yeh,' said Sam sadly. 'I see. You are an Irishman?'

'What's that got to do with it?' asked Moriarty.

'For a wild moment,' said Sam, 'I thought you might be motivated by patriotism.'

'What's that?' Moriarty asked.

'You wouldn't be trying to trap us, would you?' Sam asked.

'Get sane,' said Moriarty. 'What's it got to do with us. We want to get back at these Scots. Boy, will they be in a mess. Right up the kilts for them, this will be.'

'How can you deliver?' Sam asked.

'Can't deliver,' said Moriarty. 'That's too dangerous. You come and collect. Be in the farthest field from the barracks on Monday night and we'll make the deal. Right?'

Sam thought it over. 'Right,' he said. 'I wouldn't like to be you if anything out of the way happens.'

'Look,' said Moriarty. 'This is business. Right?'

'Right,' said Sam.

'I have my head screwed on,' said Moriarty, grinning. He had small pointed teeth.

'You know the way out,' said Sam. Moriarty waved at them and went.

The following Monday night, they waited inside the stone wall of the field and watched the iron gate. They had the place well staked out. Poric was out in front leaning over the far wall. He had a revolver. Sam and Dominic sat on a stone watching the gate. They were ready to jump over the wall and run. Across the road behind them on a small hill there were two men with rifles to cover them as they ran. They would have to run fast because the riflemen had only five rounds between them, but they would cause a diversion.

'Do you think they will come, Sam?' Dominic asked in a whisper.

'I have a feeling they will,' said Sam, sighing.

'What makes you sad about it, Sam?' he asked.

'I don't know,' said Sam. 'It's not logical. My feelings. You know the way many men have died to get arms. This doesn't seem right.'

'What's wrong with it?' Dominic asked.

'These men are soldiers,' said Sam.

'But they are Irishmen,' said Dominic.

155

'They shouldn't be doing things like this,' said Sam.

'That's not logical,' said Dominic.

'That's what I said,' said Sam.

'You're a queer mixture, Sam,' said Dominic. 'Have you a wife?'

'I have,' said Sam. 'She's a grand girl.'

'She mustn't see much of you,' said Dominic.

'She knows,' said Sam. 'I have two babies as well.'

'I'd never suspect that of you, Sam,' said Dominic.

This seemed funny to them. They both laughed.

Then they heard the sound of horse hooves on the road outside. They tensed themselves and pulled back into the shelter of the wall out of the moonlight. The horse stopped at the gate. They saw three soldiers with the horse. There were two canvas sacks on the horse's back. He was a white horse, a sturdy jumper, Dominic thought, trained for the stone walls. They could recognize the figure of Moriarty. He bent low to the ground and called: 'Are we here? Are we here?'

Sam rose and came into the light. Dominic stayed where he was.

'Here I am,' said Sam.

'Thought you mightn't come,' said Moriarty. 'Here are two friends no names no pack drill. Unload the loot, boys.'

They took the two sacks from the horse's back and emptied them on the grass.

'We have an auction, see,' said Moriarty. 'We are honest men. We take an oath not to sell arms to rebels. So this is what we do.' He bent down to the ground and took up a pair of boots with spurs on them. 'Here's a pair of officer's boots,' he shouted. 'What am I bid on them? If the price is right, as a free gift we throw in a Lee-Enfield rifle. What am I bid?'

'Two pounds,' said Sam.

'What? This beautiful pair of boots for two pounds. You wouldn't buy the cow that supplied the leather for that.'

'Three pounds then,' said Sam.

It was a bizarre scene, Dominic thought, as it went on. A bridle and a Lee-Enfield rifle. An officer's cap and a box of unprimed grenades. A swagger stick and another Lee-Enfield rifle. They were honest in this, they protested. They were just making presents of the arms and selling the goods. A saddle and two hundred rounds of ammunition. Dominic was tingling. He felt this couldn't be true; that it was the sort of thing a battalion quartermaster might be dreaming of in the unending search for arms; the cry rising to heaven from the poor battalions. A white horse and three ·45 revolvers.

'But we don't want a bloody horse,' Sam protested, 'with a regimental mark on him. What would we do with a horse?'

'Under a plough,' said Moriarty. 'That's where I'd put the bastard instead of a soft seat of a Scot.'

Thirty pounds.

Sam paid out, slowly, for money was scarce. He whistled and the men came from the other side of the road, and Poric from the field and they gathered up the stuff and put it back in the sacks. They tied the necks of the sacks and put them across the horse's back again.

'Bring the stuff to the dump,' Sam told the two men, 'and then let the horse loose somewhere back here. They'll think it strayed.'

They left and the gate was closed. Moriarty was dividing the money on the spot with the two men.

Then he said: 'Well, so long, ye bould Sinn Feiners. It was nice doing business with ye.'

'Come here, Moriarty,' said Sam. He came over to him. 'I'm worried about you.'

'No need,' said Moriarty. 'We won't spend the money all at once. Half a crown now, half a crown again. Real shrewd. They won't know. We'll be safe. But those bloody fellows will be in the soup, boy.'

'Not that,' said Sam.

'What else?' the soldier asked.

'You see nothing wrong in what you are doing?' Sam asked.

'Listen, are you a Sinn Feiner or a priest?' Moriarty asked.

'I mean, why?' Sam asked. 'Why do you do it? I mean you are an Irishman. Is that the why?'

'You mean this patriotism stuff?' Moriarty asked, puzzled.

'Sort of,' said Sam. 'Do you know why we are fighting?'

157

'Sure,' said Moriarty. 'The others have the cake. You want to get a cut of the cake. This is fine.'

'Do you want us to win?' Sam asked.

'You can't,' said Moriarty. 'No harm in trying. But you are up against heavy stuff. They'll grind you down. But get as much as you can while the going is good. Right, boy?'

'We are fighting for your freedom as much as anybody else's,' said Sam, desperately, Dominic thought.

'Not mine, boy,' said Moriarty. 'I'm free right now. There will always be top-dogs. You get in, these are the boys who will take most of everything. But the little fellows can get some too, by fiddling about. You see?'

'No,' said Sam. 'Feeling like that, wouldn't you be better dead? Don't you see any purpose in living?'

'As long as there is beer in a cask, or tobacco in a piece of paper, I'm alive, boy. We must go now. We'll be missed. Glad to have met you. Hope we don't meet in the field.'

'Would you shoot us if you were ordered?' Sam asked, pursuing him desperately.

'Sure,' said Moriarty. 'That's what soldiers are for. They say Shoot. So you shoot. Doesn't matter who you shoot. If you don't shoot, they'll shoot you. I knew a fellow down the South. They shot him because he wouldn't be a member of a firing party. He had fair hair, this boy. He wasn't even Irish. You see?'

'No,' said Sam, 'I don't see.'

'Then you never will,' said Moriarty. 'Thanks for the bean-feast.' And then he was gone.

Sam stood looking after him.

'Under the words,' said Sam, 'maybe he is a patriot. Goddamn it, under the words he must have feeling. He won't say it right out. But he must have.'

'Some people haven't, Sam,' said Dominic.

'But he must have,' said Sam. 'I tell you he must have.'

Now Dominic sighed.

'Come on, Sam,' he said, 'let's go,' thinking that they met interesting people and went interesting places since they became what was known as Sam's Squad.

But the next place Sam put them was far more dangerous.

16

ONE THING leads to another. If you set up land courts, you have to set up ordinary courts, and when those make decrees, they have to be enforced. So you have to have your own police to do this, since the police of the foreigners were busy rounding up rebels, and raiding, and shooting up houses and towns, and enforcing the curfew, and they paid no attention to normal criminal activities. The Sinn Fein police had to track those down and bring them to Sinn Fein courts where they were judged by ordinary men with common sense. It was the first time in history that judgements in courts weren't tied up and wrapped around with yards of impenetrable legal tape and jargon. If criminals were sentenced you had to have jails to put them in, but since all the jails were heavily overcrowded with patriots, sentenced criminals were put in charge of Sinn Fein police who took them away to serve their sentences at unknown destinations. The Sinn Fein police were not armed. People had decided this from the beginning. Their police would be the first unarmed force in the history of the country. So, when the other police captured them, they could put up no defence. They were taken away, received savage sentences, and the criminal they were holding was allowed to go free.

Dominic thought over these things as he sat on a flat rock in this island on Lough Corrib, one of his medical books open between his legs.

It was a beautiful day in January.

It was an almost circular island, rising uniformly all around about six feet from a rocky shore. This rise was a mass of tangled thorn trees, mountain ash, hazel bushes, ferns and briars, which even wtihout foliage provided good shelter for the interior of the island, which consisted of four fields of about ten acres divided by loose stone walls. Five black bullocks of the hardy Connemara breed inhabited the island with himself and Poric and the Tangler.

He rose to his feet at this thought, and went through a path in the bushes to look. Poric and the Tangler were hacking at a field which Paddy No wanted to put under potatoes next year. It was a fairly rocky field. The Tangler wasn't killing himself, Dominic saw. He looked incongruous with a pickaxe in his hand, and he wearing a bowler hat. His trousers were bagged around his boots, probably because they weren't his own trousers in the first place. His wrists were thin, and his face was scored with deep lines which made him look like a thinker or a philosopher. He was neither. He was a vicious little fellow, who having bought cattle from several farmers at fairs, followed single ones home, and having knocked them unconscious with a blow of a heavy stick, took what money they had on them.

He was sentenced to six months' hard labour. This was the third unknown destination they had taken him to. The others had been houses on the mainland. They had escaped from the last one by the skin of their teeth.

Poric had his coat off and his shirt sleeves rolled, even on this cold day, and was methodically digging into the rocky ground with a powerful thrust of his boot on the shoulder of the spade.

'Everything all right, Poric?' Dominic asked.

'Fine, Dominic, fine,' said Poric, smiling and leaning on the spade.

'Me back is sore,' said the Tangler. 'I have a pain in me oxter.'

'Don't make me cry,' said Dominic.

'I'll die out here,' said the Tangler, 'and what'll ye do then? That'll be murder. That'll fix ye!'

'We'll bury you with pleasure, Tangler,' said Dominic.

'I want a smoke,' said the Tangler. He had a whining voice.

'We have none left,' said Dominic. 'Paddy will be out today.'

'I wish he'd hurry up,' said the Tangler. 'I'm dying for a smoke.'

'Make up your mind what you are going to die from,' said Dominic.

'Taunt me,' said the Tangler. 'Go on, taunt me. It's not enough to make me suffer but you taunt me.'

'I'll do more than taunt you,' said Dominic, 'if you don't shut up. You have no idea how glad we will be to be free of you.'

'That's right, taunt me,' said the Tangler apathetically, raising the pickaxe.

Dominic noticed Poric smiling. He went over to him. 'I'll never make a policeman, Poric,' he said.

'Maybe after a bit of training,' said Poric. 'You have to have the training. But this is not being a policeman. It's being a warder. And that's different.'

'Well, I'd never be a warder so,' said Dominic. 'All I'd feel like doing all day is going around kicking fellows like the Tangler in the backside.'

'That wouldn't do,' said Poric gravely.

'As Sam would say,' said Dominic, 'it's not patriotic.'

He left Poric spitting on his huge hands and went over to the hut. It was a simple hut, of necessity. Paddy had brought over a lot of pointed pine stakes as though for building a cow shelter. These had been driven into the ground on a small height, trenched around and roofed with scraws and sedge thatch. There was a fireplace and a hole in the roof where the smoke sometimes went out. They could only light a fire at night, in case people would see smoke on the island and get the police to investigate. They could be potheen makers. They had put up a few shelves. Dominic had made a trip home at Christmas to get some of his medical books to catch up on his neglected studies. They had some primitive utensils, mostly tin. Paddy No came once a week with supplies of food and turf hidden under the bales of hay he brought in the boat for the cattle. They had plenty of blankets, and when they lighted the fire at night were cosy enough even in the cold weather. And the Tangler was a good cook, Dominic had to admit. On account of the wandering life he led, and much practice of ditch-cooking, he could do wonders in the pot oven they had.

He took a half cigarette from his pocket and lighted it, and smoked it carefully.

He came out of the hut then and went through the bushes and walked on the rocky shore. The waters of the lake were calm and still. The sky was blue, a cold steel-blue, with white clouds all around the horizon and low down. The hills all around the lake and the far-off mountains to the west and north were the colour of bilberry juice. He walked to the makeshift pier, just many loose boulders thrown together. He had to keep back near the bushes. There were other islands around them, one to the right inhabited. He could see the sun on the thatch of the cottage and smoke rising from the chimney. There wasn't much colour in the fields, as the frost had tainted the green grass, but they often looked over at the house on the island, or at night watched the light in the windows of the houses on the mainland about half a mile away, thinking with some nostalgia of the comfort of the people who lived in them.

He sighed and sat on the rock.

He peered at the shore of the faraway bay opposite him, and thought he detected Paddy's boat putting out from there. He had to wait quite a while before he was sure, because the boat was grey and the background was grey, but eventually he was positive, so he walked through the bushes and even though he couldn't see Poric, he shouted: 'Paddy is on the way!'

He sat down again to wait patiently.

Paddy was a tall rangy man. He always said No. If you said: It is a fine day, Paddy would say: No, there's rain on it. If you said: It will be a good harvest, Paddy would say: No, the oats is ruined, or the potatoes will rot in the pits. It was just that he was incapable of agreeing with anything anyone said, but he was a good man and kept his mouth shut and did everything that was asked of him without a murmur. Sam said of him, a silent soldier.

He saw the boat on the glassy water, making odd ripples in the calm as it came closer and closer with the steady pull of the oars. He saw the piled haybales that concealed their provisions and then he saw something else that startled him.

He got to his feet. He called: 'Poric! Poric!' He waited for him, heard the pounding of his running feet in the fields, and when he stood beside him said: 'Look, that's not Paddy

162

No.' This being January the arc of the sun was low and its shine on the waters was blinding. Poric shaded his eyes with his hands.

'That's not Paddy,' he agreed. 'But what danger can there be? We are enough to take care of one person.'

They squatted in the bushes, watching closely.

'That looks awful like a woman to me,' said Dominic.

'You have an eye for the girls,' said Poric. 'I believe you. Has Paddy got a wife?'

'How could he?' asked Dominic, 'when he can never say yes.' Poric laughed. 'In fact he doesn't like women. He says they are too positive about everything. That's a girl all right. For a slender one she is useful with the oars.'

You couldn't mistake her now, the slim waist, the woollen beret on her head, her hair. There was something familiar about her. He got a glimpse of this as she turned to have a quick look at the island behind her and altered her stroke to bring her into the pier.

'That's Finola Brady,' said Dominic, wondering. 'What's she doing out here? Doesn't she know it's dangerous?'

'She'd even row well in a currach,' said Poric admiringly.

'She shouldn't be doing things like this,' said Dominic. 'There are plenty of men in there if Paddy couldn't come.'

'Shout at her so and tell her to go away again,' Poric suggested. Dominic looked at him. Poric's face was bland.

'That would be a silly thing to do,' he said.

She was very efficient. She guided the boat until the keel grounded on the sand, then she jumped out lightly and pulled the boat up farther. She stood there then and looked towards them. They remained hidden. She started throwing the bales of hay on the shore. Then the bag of turf. She had trouble with this since it was heavy, but she managed. Then she took the flour bag of provisions and walked up towards them. When she was out of sight of the house on the other island, they came out of the bushes and confronted her.

She was startled for a minute. 'Oh,' she said, 'you frightened me. Hello.'

'Hello,' said Dominic. 'Where's Paddy?'

163

'Paddy has the 'flu,' said Finola.

'No!' said Dominic. They listened to the sound of this word and then the three of them laughed.

'Yes,' said Finola. 'Truly he has.'

'Could they get nobody else to come but you?' Dominic asked.

'I wanted to come,' she said. 'I thought I'd like to see you all.'

'You are looking well,' said Dominic. She was. She had colour in her face and the smudges under the eyes had gone. Her eyes were clear and there was a sparkle in her hair. He thought it was like getting an unexpected gift to see her. She was wearing silk stockings and light shoes, and a blue belted raincoat. He thought she looked very well. He felt the blood throbbing in his pulses. He looked at his wrist. He thought this feeling was strange and useless. He felt his face. He hadn't shaved for two days.

'You look like a pirate,' she said.

'Not Poric,' said Dominic. 'Look at him. Poric shaves every day. He's a real policeman.'

'I'll throw the hay to the cattle,' said Poric, 'and bring up the turf.'

'Do that,' said Dominic. 'We'll be around in the shelter near the hut. I don't want the Tangler to see her. I'll throw him some tobacco to keep him quiet.'

Poric went down to the boat. Dominic took the flour sack from her and felt for the box of tobacco. He took a plug from this. 'Go around by the shore,' he said. 'I'll connect up with you.' She smiled and walked away. She had to balance herself with her arms to help her walk on the rocks. He thought she did this gracefully.

He shouldered the sack, jumped the wall into the first field, and the next field. He came to the wall here. The Tangler wasn't killing himself. 'Here!' he called. 'Here's your tobacco.' He flung it. The Tangler caught it expertly. 'The blessings of God on you,' he said, meaning the opposite, Dominic supposed, and felt for a knife to cut it for his pipe, sitting cross-legged on the ground like a born tinker.

164

Dominic left him. He threw the sack into the hut and broke through into the north shore. She was standing there, looking back at the purple mountains. She heard him coming. 'If you have to be anywhere, this is a nice place to be,' she said.

'Over a thousand years ago the monks discovered that,' he said. 'They lived on the islands, but they could choose their company. They weren't warders of disreputable prisoners. Come in here.'

She went with him where the bushes had made a circle and the grass had been saved from the touch of the frost. It was shut off and the sun shone into it. They sat down. She loosened the buttons of the coat at her neck. 'It's quite hot in here,' she said. 'You'd think it was summer.'

'This morning,' he said, 'there was ice all around the shore. There was a little wind blowing. It stirred the ice, broke it up. It sounded like the singing of a million birds.'

'You haven't lost the romance,' she said, laughing. She was leaning on her elbow.

'Are you well?' he asked.

She looked directly at him.

'Yes,' she said. 'As well as can be expected. I am on holiday from the school. We have been very busy. Sam thinks everyone is like himself, that they can do without sleep. I'm glad to be home for a few days.'

'I hope you are being careful. I heard they cropped some girls in the town. I wouldn't like you to lose your hair.'

'Short hair is coming into fashion again,' she said. 'They are becoming more and more despicable.' The muscles on her jaws were suddenly tight.

'Listen,' said Dominic. 'Don't be doing anything rash. There are plenty besides you to take chances.'

'In these times,' she said, 'everybody has to take chances. It's by taking chances that we are surviving. We are not taking enough chances. There are too many people preaching caution. That will get us nowhere at all.'

'Listen, calm down,' said Dominic, putting out his hand and covering hers. This action stopped both of them. It was

165

the first time he had felt her skin. It was very soft. They both looked down at his hand covering hers, and then they looked into one another's eyes, and as if she had spoken, Dominic knew what she was thinking. Here was a man's hand, not big, with short fingers, and dark hair on the backs of them. She immediately thought of a narrow hand with long slender fingers. Lowry could play the piano very well. He always did so at parties or dances. He had music in his slender hands. He saw the stricken look in her eyes for a moment. He took away his hand and lay on his back with his arms over his eyes. Normally this sort of speaking without speaking would have meant something close; that they were thinking together, feeling together; but Dominic just felt a dark cloud in his breast. He felt that whatever way the real fight would go, this one was already lost.

She was silent too. He couldn't see her, but he knew that she was pulling at blades of grass. It would take me, he thought, to fall in love with a girl like this, and then with his thoughts, he proceeded to talk himself out of this notion.

Poric came to relieve the silence.

'The cattle are fed,' he said, sitting down beside them, 'the Tangler's pipe is filled, there's food in the hut, turf for the fire, and what more do we want of life, tell me?'

'Do you like living on an island, Poric?' she asked.

'It's all right,' said Poric. 'I will live anywhere at all as long as somebody orders me to go there. You see?'

'You are not that dumb,' she said.

'I'm dumb enough,' said Poric. 'I like being ordered about. Dominic is a better man than me. He hates being ordered about, but he does it.'

'I just don't like the Tangler,' said Dominic. 'If it wasn't for the Tangler, this would be a great life.'

'Tell us about the outside,' said Poric, lying back. 'Living on an island, the world does pass you by. What is happening?'

'I brought a few papers,' said Finola. 'Men are dying. Women too. These are accidents, they say. There are ambushes and hangings and shootings. And all the time the great

166

majority of people are going to races, and meetings, and the picture houses, just as if nothing at all was happening. At times this is frightening. But it has always been this way, if you read history. History shows that. Freedom has rarely been won by the people, but despite them, by the few men with dedication. Isn't this true?'

'It is,' said Dominic. 'Think of what George Washington had to go through. The people, when they took over in France, turned the dreams of the few into carnage, and that led to a dictatorship. Maybe it's as well that the majority go to the race meetings and the opera and the picture houses, and leave the right ones to carry on the war for them.'

They discussed this for some time.

It was warm in the shelter. It was really like a summer's day. You could be fooled. Dominic and Poric knew how cold it was in the hut at night on the faded bracken.

Finola thought how attracted she was by Dominic. A small man, well proportioned, badly needing a shave, with kind intelligent eyes. She would like to be his friend, a close friend. There was a sympathetic bond between them. She thought of the searing things he had said about her love for Lowry. He said afterwards he hadn't meant them. But she wasn't sure. Was Lowry to her like a statue to which she had lighted candles? She didn't think so. His face came before her mind now; the smiling eyes and the fair hair falling over a pale intelligent forehead, and she felt very bleak. She put out her hands and felt the grass under her fingers and clutched it. Would she always be like this, she wondered. Was Lowry for ever?

They must have been two hours lying in the sun in the shelter. As soon as the arc of the sun was low, the shelter suddenly became cold.

Poric sat up first.

'You see,' he said, 'the sun was only a deceiver.'

Dominic sat up. Suddenly, he was filled with panic. 'I haven't heard the Tangler for some time,' he said. 'Did you bring the oars away from the boat, Poric?'

Poric thought, his forehead furrowed.

'No,' he said then, and as soon as he said it they were both on their feet and running, madly, over the walls, across the fields to the pier on the other side.

There was no boat.

They looked closely and they could see that the boat was nearing the far shore.

Finola came up to them, panting.

'Amn't I the stupid amadaun?' said Poric.

'The foxy bastard,' said Dominic. 'It was my fault. I should have remembered.'

'If I hadn't come it wouldn't have happened,' said Finola.

'What will he do?' Poric asked. 'Will he just scuttle like a rat?'

'He'll scuttle like a rat to the nearest policeman,' said Dominic. 'And here we are. I can't swim half a mile. Can you, Finola? I know Poric can't. Poric comes from my own place, where they say why learn to swim? It will only take you longer to drown in the sea.'

'I can't swim that far,' said Finola.

'None of us could,' said Dominic. 'It's too cold.' Think now, he told himself. Try to be a leader for once. The thought of Finola taken on this island was too much. He couldn't bear the thought of it. What was the alternative? 'You know the shore, Finola,' he said. 'That nearest point there about five hundred yards, is it an island, or mainland?' It was a long stretch with scrub trees bent away wearily from the west wind and grazed by goats. They could see the goats.

'It's an island,' she said. 'It is only about two hundred yards from the mainland. The shore all around it is very shallow. If we got there we could wade to the land.'

'Come on,' said Dominic, 'we will have to move fast.' He ran away from them. They followed him. He ended at the hut. He looked at it for a few seconds. He counted the pine stakes that held it up. One at each corner and one each side of the makeshift doorway.

'Poric,' he said. 'Get out the stakes and we can make a raft. Right?'

'That's it,' said Poric, going inside and heaving.

'Finola,' he said, 'get all the pots and things, any sign of our habitation, and throw them far out into the lake.'

He liked her reaction. She didn't ask questions. She did what she was told. Dominic went into the hut and stuffed their belongings into the two rucksacks, threw them outside and then helped Poric to dislodge the fenceposts. It wasn't hard. They pulled two corner ones and the roof collapsed. It was then easy to get the other two and the two doorway posts.

Dominic knew he had to move fast. He knew he would have to have the raft launched before they had time to think. So they had six pine posts still with their bark, placed side by side on the grass. They still had the hammer that they had erected them with and the axe. They nailed them together with the timber they had used for the shelves and bits from the roof joists.

'Now, lift them,' said Dominic. 'Finola, you bring down the two rucksacks to the shore after us.'

They were heavy, joined together like this, but Poric was very strong and Dominic had strength himself. It was more awkward than anything else, really. They had to be careful crossing the rocky shore. They could have twisted their ankles and then they would be in a fine mess. He looked over to the far shore. He could see no sign of the Tangler and his boat, so he must already have scuttled away. It would now all depend on how long he was finding a policeman. Thinking of his vicious face, Dominic knew he would find one. They patrolled the lacework of dirt roads on that side very frequently.

The raft floated.

'Now, wait,' said Dominic. He went back to the place of the hut and he found two boards and the axe. He ran back with them. He used the axe to chop the bottoms of them into paddle shapes. 'Now, Finola,' he said. 'You get on first carefully. Take this rucksack and kneel on it.' She did this, cautiously. It was a good raft. It took her weight well. 'Now you, Poric, at the back, kneel on this one and use the paddles,' he said. Poric had to go into the water and free the raft from the bottom so that it floated and took his great weight too. There was about an inch of it over the water. Dominic went

169

into the water then and gave it a push and it wobbled away from the land.

'Here,' Poric shouted then. 'What are you up to?'

'Don't be a fool,' said Dominic, 'it won't take three. Paddle, Poric, when I tell you.'

'Dominic,' Finola called, 'what are you doing.' She tried to turn towards him, but the raft wobbled dangerously.

'Be careful, Finola,' he shouted. 'Keep facing to the front.'

'They'll catch you, Dominic,' she said. 'They'll catch you. I don't want them to catch you.'

'They won't,' said Dominic. 'When you reach the island, Poric can come back with the raft. You can go to the shore and get another boat. There's hundreds of them turned bottoms up there. Go on, Finola. I'll be all right. You'll see. Paddle, Poric. Paddle for the love of God!'

'You fooled me, Dominic,' said Poric plaintively, but he paddled as he was ordered to. 'You fooled me properly.'

'The faster you go, Poric, the sooner you'll be back,' said Dominic. 'I'll be waiting for you. Hurry, man, now, hurry! Give it all your strength.'

'Oh, Dominic,' Finola was wailing.

'Paddle, Finola, paddle,' Dominic called to her. They paddled.

He didn't stop to watch them. He ran back to the hut and he started to scatter everything. It was just a pile of old lumber and scraws and sedge. He couldn't wipe out the paths they made coming and going, but he ran to the field where the cattle were, threw down the stick at an opening in the walls and shushed them over to the hut. He took armfuls of the hay they had been cosily chewing and scattered it over the hut place. He thought they were very indignant with him, but they would trample down a lot of the signs. Then he ran back to the shore to look at the raft. They were making good progress, he saw. He also saw her face turning back to the shore and he heard her voice calling his name: 'Oh, Dominic.' He didn't let this trouble him. I can be decisive when I have to, he thought. Let her see that. He didn't want the police to get her. And if they got Poric into their hands again, they might even kill him.

There was a wind springing up from the north. He had been afraid of that. It was good for the raft as it was driving it, but it would be hard trying to get back. It was all a gamble. He sat on a stone and watched. The sun was low on the horizon. The clouds were beginning to be tinged with pink, the blue sky turning crab-apple green.

He saw them landing on the island, and he saw Finola running.

He saw Poric trying to launch the raft into the wind. He saw, even from here, that he was having a hard job. It was too blunt to face into the waves. Now it would depend on Finola. He couldn't see her, but he could picture her in the shallows, her stockings ruined, her shoes saving her feet from the sharp stones. He must remember to get her a pair of stockings sometime. The hem of her clothes would be wet.

He knew he had lost the game when he heard the sound of an inboard engine on the lake. There was only one body in charge of an inboard engine. They used it to hunt for potheen makers as well as Sinn Feiners.

He stood and waved at Poric. Go back! Go back! It was ridiculous. Poric couldn't see him at this distance. But he heard the engine. He could see that; see him standing straight and listening and then drawing away from the water, heaving at the raft, pulling it into the scrub. It was the only thing to do.

Dominic thought of himself. He could play hide and seek with them in the bushes for hours. But eventually they would get him. They would leave a guard on the boat, so he couldn't get away that way. He would not be taken from the bushes like a terrier taking a rabbit.

So he went to the nearest field and he sat in the middle of it. He lighted a cigarette, and smoked it.

He felt calm. He hadn't all that to lose.

The sun was sinking and the sky blazing when they came into the opening and saw him sitting in the field. There were two of them and a sergeant. They had rifles. The Tangler was with them.

'There he is! There he is!' the Tangler was almost dancing.

171

They came up to him. They looked at him.

'What's your name?' the sergeant asked.

'Joe Murphy,' said Dominic, smiling.

'Oh, he's a liar! He's a bloody liar!' the Tangler shouted.

'This man has made a serious charge against you,' said the sergeant. Dominic couldn't see their faces under the peaks of their caps. There was a strange light all about them. The two policemen were standing back with their rifles cocked. A dangerous animal. If they only knew, Dominic thought.

'I never saw this fellow in my life,' he said.

'What are you doing here so?' the sergeant asked.

'Studying botany,' said Dominic, which was partly true.

'Not a so-called Sinn Fein policeman?' the sergeant asked.

'What's that?' Dominic asked.

'You had better come with us,' said the sergeant.

'Oh, what a liar he is!' the Tangler was saying.

'Search the island,' the sergeant said to the others. 'Hold out your hands,' he said to Dominic, and handcuffs clicked on his wrists. It's the first time I have had those anyhow, he thought.

'Over there was the hut,' the Tangler was telling the policemen. 'And here was the field they had me slaving like a nigger. They nearly killed me. Do you see the stones they made me lift. I hope they hang you, hear? I hope they hang you.'

Dominic was on his way to the boat. There was a policeman guarding it. He had a rifle too.

Before he stepped into the boat, he looked across at the shore. He wondered if Finola was standing up there, with her small hands to her mouth, and tears in her eyes. He hoped not.

He felt indifferent about the future anyhow.

17

DOMINIC SAT at the door of the hut watching the rain until the sky became dark. There was discontent in the hut. 'Shut that bloody door,' a voice was shouting, 'or we'll die with the cold.'

He wasn't in jail. Someone said you couldn't get a sparrow into the jail, it was packed so tightly. You couldn't even buy your way in with money, they said. So this camp, staffed by the military, was set up on what men called the Island. Huts and barbed wire and mud and cold.

They slept in their clothes on the wooden floor with a blanket wrapped around them. The food was poor; bully beef and buckets of tea, milk and sugar in together. People who didn't like sugar in their tea hadn't much choice.

He closed the door and went to his place, wrapped the blanket around him and lay with his head against the cold iron. The atmosphere in the hut was fetid. All the smells that confined men make with no chance to wash properly or change clothes or socks. He knew none of them in his hut, just one man with prematurely grey hair and a strong jaw who had been put in during the afternoon. 'What's your name?' he asked. 'Joe Murphy,' said Dominic. 'Pleased to meet you, Joe,' he said. 'My name is Joe Murphy too. Isn't that a coincidence?' 'No,' said Dominic, 'threequarters of all the men in here are named Murphy.' 'We should form a club,' the man said, chuckling.

Dominic knew instinctively that you had to be careful. It was a screening camp. Men were rounded up and thrown in for being caught out after curfew, or for singing rebel songs. Disturbance of the peace covered a multitude of crimes. They were signed in and screened and signed out again. But it stood to reason that there would be one or two people in each hut who would be official listeners. So Dominic just kept to himself, never spoke except in grunts and monosyllables.

About four feet up, the sides of the hut were perforated with bullet holes. The police had the right of entry for interrogation purposes. The soldiers never interfered with those. They came and took away men, and they always returned bleeding.

Some evenings, he was told, they loosed off their guns at the huts, so it was better to be lying down after darkness.

He felt lonely and depressed. He thought of the island. He would even suffer the Tangler, he thought, for the freedom and the sweet smells of that island. His interest was aroused by nobody, except maybe the boy in the far corner who kept lying down with his face turned to the wall. His lips tightened when he thought of this boy. I must do something about that boy, he would think again and again, but he could never arouse himself sufficiently. He wondered at this apathy. He tried to throw it off, but he found it difficult. He hated being confined. It was the first time it had happened to him, so it took getting used to, he supposed.

He must have dozed off.

He was awakened by loud noises, the throbbing of the lorry engines, the shouts of men outside, and the shooting of guns. He knew by the tense silence in the hut that they were all awake now. It happened like this always when the black fellows came. They would all wake, and listen tensely for the door of the hut to be kicked open. Dominic had been here three nights and so far it hadn't happened to this hut.

He had just thought that, when it did happen, and the door was kicked open and blinding torch lights fastened on them, and they were shouted at: 'On your feet! On your feet!'

They got to their feet, blinking their eyes. Dominic kept his face half turned from the light and his eyes screwed up. Looking back he could see the men's faces. They were oldish men, some of them, and he could see the fright in their eyes. The jaws of the second Joe Murphy were tight and his eyes were angry. You want to watch it, Joe Murphy Two, he thought, get that look out of your eyes.

Then he felt the hard hand on his own jaw and his face being turned to the light.

'Well, well, well, Joe Murphy,' said a familiar voice. 'Remember me?' He could smell Mac's breath. It was loaded with whisky. 'Hey, Sergeant! Sergeant!' he called, 'come and see what I've found.'

Dominic saw Sergeant Nick's face coming into the light from outside. His face was hard. Sergeant Nick was getting thin, Dominic thought. He had shaved off his moustache. He was dressed in civilian clothes. 'Remember me, Joe?' Mac asked, still squeezing his jaw. Dominic shook his head. Mac freed him. 'Never saw you before,' said Dominic.

Mac laughed. 'A foolish thing to say, Joe,' he said, 'because it will be easy for us to refresh your memory.'

'Sergeant!' Nick called.

The army sergeant came from outside. The sergeant was always very neatly dressed. His boots always shone, his buttons were bright, his cap stiffened and worn mathematically on his head. Men said he wasn't too bad.

'You know this man?' Nick asked.

'Admitted three days ago,' said the sergeant. 'Charged with impersonating a policeman, holding a citizen against his will, name Joe Murphy.'

'Take him out,' said Nick.

'Out, Murphy,' said the sergeant.

Dominic went out. He couldn't make a break for it. The camp and the huts were surrounded by barbed wire. It was patrolled by a platoon of soldiers. The sergeant guided him to the administration hut. It was pleasant to get in there. It held bunks for the sergeant and a corporal, but it also held a fat-bellied stove, giving off a lively heat. The sergeant went to a table where many documents were placed in neat piles. He went through those until he found a form and handed it to Nick. He took it and looked at it.

'I know more about him myself,' he said. Then he turned to Dominic. 'You know a lot of things, Dominic, if only you would talk. You know certain men in this town, and you must have a good idea of the whereabouts of your brother. We would exchange you for your brother any day.'

'A poor swop,' said Dominic.

'Joe,' said Mac, 'don't be insolent. You know what happened the last time you were insolent.'

Mac was drunk, Dominic saw. He had a close look at his eyes from the naked bulbs hanging from the ceiling. They were bloodshot.

'And you remember Skin?' Mac said, pulling Skin forward. His face was very pale. He too was drunk, Dominic saw, holding himself straight with an effort.

''Lo, Joe,' he said. 'Pleased to meet you again.' He held out his hand. Dominic took it. Skin's hand was moist. 'Let's go and play a game of snooker, Joe,' he said.

'Will you tell us a few things we want to know?' Nick insisted. 'Has anyone ever told you about the rewards there are for doing your duty to your country? Before it's too late, Dominic. We have them on the run. You know that. It's only a matter of time until all this foolish business is over. Do you understand? I don't want anything more to happen to you. Believe me, Dominic.'

'You took the wrong side, Nick,' said Dominic. 'You used to know me better.'

'All right,' said Nick. 'Take him out. Don't forget you asked for this, Dominic. We gave you every chance.'

'Here, where are you going?' the sergeant asked. 'This prisoner is in my charge.'

'He'll be returned to you,' said Nick. 'The police have full rights of interrogation in this camp.'

Dominic thought the sergeant might intervene. Mac went up to the sergeant and put his face close to his. 'You heard what the man said, Soldier,' he said. 'Or are you hard of hearing?'

'You'll be responsible,' said the sergeant, 'if this man escapes from custody.'

Dominic could have laughed. It was a poor appeal. There were about seven of the police there, with holsters strapped to their thighs, as well as Nick in his civvies. Dominic thought that despite the civvies he still looked like a policeman.

'All right, bring him out,' Nick said.

Two of them took his arms. They went into the night, down the steps into the mud of the paths and over to the gate in the barbed wire fence where a soldier stood on guard under the feeble light. It was raining. Dominic could feel the rain soaking his hair, running down his neck. It was cold rain too.

'Open it,' they said to the soldier. He hesitated a moment but then he pulled back the big bolt. The lorries were outside, their engines running, to provide light, he supposed. But they didn't go into the lorries. They walked to the left by the high wall, and walked stumbling on the grass, heading down where the place gave way to the boathouse and the water from the river was tapped to fill into the canal.

Dominic wondered if he was to be killed. They went out of another gate here and walking by the light of their torches they came to the bank of the river. It was a very dark night.

'Dominic,' said Nick. 'We don't want to do this. You are a nice decent young fellow. There is nobody here but ourselves. Nobody will even know that you told us anything. For God's sake have sense. What does this bunch of lunatics mean to you? You should be back at College studying for your examinations. All we want to do is to lay our hands on them and take them out of circulation.'

Dominic said nothing. He knew it would be no use saying anything. How could you say anything to Nick? He had taken his stand and he was going to stick to it until he died. Dominic hoped that his death would be soon.

Mac's arm was around his shoulders. 'Listen, Joe, I didn't like hitting you before. On my oath, you're a nice chap. Skin and me are sorry for you. We like you. Tell the bastard a thing or two and we'll all go and have a drink.'

Dominic felt the handcuffs on his wrists and somebody at his feet tying them with a rope.

'Would you, Mac?' he asked, thinking he was fond of Mac in a twisted sort of way. He felt the fumbling at the back of him and then the kick and he was in the river. He had swallowed water because he had gasped at the coldness of the stuff enveloping his body. Then he shut his mouth and started counting. He was completely helpless, his feet tied. They had tied a rope to the manacles and they were playing him like a fish. They were keeping him down with a stick or an oar or

177

something pressed into the small of his back. He thought his lungs were going to burst, when he came up again, and feeling the freedom drew air into his lungs. They pulled him to the bank. A hand caught him by the hair and turned his face around. He saw Nick's face in the light.

'We can keep this up all night, Dominic,' he said.

Dominic didn't answer him. He felt as if his body was encased in ice. Then there was pressure on his back again and he was forced under the water.

It's the indignity, he thought. This is what hurts a man's soul. He is entitled to dignity. He thought, to console himself, that there is indignity in having a man pull your teeth in a dentist's chair; there is indignity in a doctor examining your body, but that is an indignity to which you submit voluntarily. What was happening to him, after all, was only the repetition of the centuries. All down the years people like himself had to suffer indignity, and this is a thing that all human beings will revolt against eventually. They will say: We have had enough! We cannot suffer any more indignity.

His face was free again. He heard the gasping of his own throat as he sucked the precious air into his lungs.

'Well, Dominic,' Nick's face said to him: 'Have you changed your mind?'

He couldn't answer him. He had no wind or words and his limbs were petrified. He felt himself being pushed under again, and this time there was terror in his stomach because he knew he mightn't survive. He hadn't the strength to hold his breath. He felt the water slipping silkily into his mouth. He thought: so this is the end of me, and then he was on the bank gasping like a fish, burping.

He could see just legs all around him as he lay there trying to get the sickness out of his stomach.

Then he heard Nick's voice beside his ear.

'That's only a taste, Dominic,' he heard him saying. 'You think it over. We will be back again and again, and sometime you will talk. Think it over, Dominic. Save yourself a lot of suffering. I will kill you or get your brother. Do you hear?'

Then he was lifted to his feet. He felt himself stumbling

along, supported by arms, all the time trying to draw wind and water from his stomach, feeling as if all his body was numbed by the cold. Thinking of his brown tweed suit, almost new, and what his poor mother would say if she knew the state it was in now. Feeling his clothes sticking to him. It was like being wrapped in icicles.

He remembered hearing the drawing of the bolt of the gate at the entrance to the camp, and being pushed, and stumbling and falling flat on the mud inside the gate, and also hearing something so astonishing that he thought it was a nightmare or a wish fulfilled, a voice saying into his ear as he fell: 'Sam says don't shave.' This was just crazy. It could only have come from one of the police. They were all the English type of police, or were there some of the Irish police among them? But this was a crazy thing: 'Sam says don't shave.' It was so crazy that he laughed feebly into the mud of the path.

There were legs beside him again, khaki ones this time.

'All right, up, up. Leave down the bloody gun, Tom, and lift him up.'

This was the voice of the sergeant.

He felt himself being half dragged, half carried into the most beautiful heat he would ever feel again in his life. He just stood there listening to the chattering of his own teeth, taking a long time to realize what the sound was. He felt their arms at his clothes. He was sitting on a chair and his boots and socks were taken from his feet. Then he was stood up and his clothes were dragged from him.

'Here, move,' he heard the sergeant say. 'Rub yourself with this or you'll die, Paddy. Here! Rub yourself with this.'

He felt a coarse towel in his hand, and started slowly to rub himself. As his strength slowly returned his rubbing became a bit more vigorous. He rubbed himself back into consciousness, until he became aware of the brightly lighted hut, and the stove that was almost red hot, feeling the warmth of it seeping into his bones, and the cold shake leaving his limbs.

'Here, drink this,' the sergeant said. He held out his hand for the enamel mug. It was red hot. It was filled with cocoa.

179

He felt the sergeant throwing a blanket around his shoulders. The hot liquid went slowly down into his stomach. It tasted wonderful.

He looked at the sergeant.

The sergeant was spreading his sodden clothes on chair backs the other side of the stove.

Here is something wonderful, Dominic thought: one side of them half kills you and the other side tries to save you. This is a paradox.

'The bloody black bar-buggers!' the sergeant said savagely.

Dominic noticed that the sergeant wasn't wearing his cap. It was the first time he had seen him without. He had brown hair stuck closely to his skull with oil. Very neat. A skating rink for flies. Wasn't that what they used to say about the oiled-hair boys?

'That's alliteration, sergeant,' he said, half tittering and thinking: I'm not apathetic any more.

18

HE AWOKE and felt suffocated. For a moment he was afraid, his heart beating very fast. Then he found that his mouth was covered by the blanket. He raised his arm to throw it off and nearly died with the agony of the pain in his shoulder and upper arm. He lay with clenched teeth until the pain passed. Then he raised his arm very cautiously. He found that both his arms were strained – that he could hardly lift them.

He looked around him. The hut was deserted except for the boy in the corner sitting with his back to the wall and staring straight in front of him. There was a pale shaft of sunlight coming in through the windows. He saw that his clothes were lying beside his head. They were dried but very creased and crumpled from the wetting, and the smell of the tweed was pronounced. He sat up and, bit by bit, slowly and cautiously, dressed himself. The leather of his boots was hard and stiff and whitened from the water and the drying. They hurt his feet when he stood up in them.

He looked out the door of the hut. He saw men walking or squatting in the shelter of the huts, absorbing the winter sunshine. He wondered how he felt. He decided he didn't feel good. He wondered how he would feel if they gave him another session in the river tonight. This thought made his arms ache.

He went over to the boy. He squatted in front of him. The boy's eyes met his indifferently and then turned away from him. His mouth was a mess. They had used him as a hostage on one of the lorries. This was their latest stunt. If the lorry was ambushed the hostage was to be killed. They hadn't killed this boy, but one of them had put him on the ground and kicked his teeth in with an army boot. Dominic wondered at the mentality of any human being who could do a thing like this to a boy of seventeen. His lips were cut and bruised. It takes a long time for a crack on your lip to heal. He tried to visualize how painful his mouth must be. He remembered the pain in his own jaws and gums when two of his teeth were knocked out.

'Gums don't take that long to heal,' he said. 'They harden in a few weeks and you will be able to crack nuts with them.'

He was a good-looking boy before this treatment, he had thought. He had brown curly hair, fine eyes and a straight nose.

'Are you afraid?' he asked. The boy didn't answer him, just held his head turned from him. He was getting angry with him. This apathy could be contagious, he thought. I could sink into a state like this very easily myself, not worrying what came next or caring.

'You'll have to shake yourself out of it,' he said. 'You saw the one who did it. You know him. You will tell his name and he will be taken care of. He will get the same treatment that he meted out to you. But you'll have to wake out of this apathy. You hear?'

'Leave him alone,' said the man who came up the steps

181

and into the hut. He was the grey-haired one with the strong jaw, Joe Two. 'You don't have to take out your tantrums on this boy. He has had enough of tantrums.' He was carrying a mug of tea and two slices of bread. 'Here, take this. I brought them for you. They might ease your feelings.'

Dominic got up, wincing as he put down a hand on the floor to help himself up. He had to stay that way for a little before he could rise. He took the tea from him and left the boy. 'Thanks,' he said. 'It is just that it makes you mad to see him. If you could get your hands on the fellow who did this; the things you would do to him.'

'No, you wouldn't,' said Joe Two. 'It's not in your nature. Pat there doesn't want anything but his mother. She hasn't seen him since he was taken away two weeks ago. For all she knows they might have killed him. That's what's worrying Pat, not getting back at the fellow who dusted him. Eh, Pat?'

The boy turned his head to him, and nodded.

'Well, she'll know first time a man gets out of here, who-ever he is, don't worry, boy. I'm only beginning to get this camp organized.' He sat down beside Dominic, and lighted a cigarette. 'You were late in last night, Joe,' he said to Dominic. 'Did you have a date?'

'Yes,' said Dominic shortly.

'Must have been with the water babies,' said Joe Two. 'Are you afraid? You told the boy he was.'

Dominic thought over this as he chewed the bread. It was stale bread and the butter was tainted, but he was eating it. If you were in a jail and sentenced to a certain amount of years in a jail, you would feel safe. Warders could be cruel or kind or indifferent, he imagined, but they would stay more or less with the rules even if you were a political prisoner. But this camp frightened him. It had no rules, where these fellows could take anyone out of it at night and do what they liked to him. There were no inquests to worry about; no coroner sitting over your corpse. He thought of them coming back again tonight and taking him out and doing the same thing with him, and his stomach was like water.

'Yes,' he said.

'Listen,' said Joe Two, 'I have been in many jails since this thing started. There are three kinds of prisoners, Sinn Feiners and IRA men and stool pigeons. That is, politicians, fighting men, and rats. I'm not a rat and I'm not a politician. So you can talk to me, see.'

'I'm afraid they will make me talk,' said Dominic.

'I see,' said Joe Two. 'Well, every man has a breaking point. But the strange thing is that it is only a small minority who break. This is a proved fact already. They cannot break a man whose mind is made up to die first. You don't look the kind of man to me who would break under torture. Is this a consolation to you?'

'No,' said Dominic, laughing in spite of himself, 'because it implies a lot of agony.'

'Pain is in the mind,' said Joe Two, 'beforehand. I have experienced some of it myself. You know the one about cowards die many times before their deaths, the valiant taste of death but once. This is tripe. I think the valiant in that case is just a stupid moron who cannot appreciate pain. The thing to do is to imagine the worst pain they can cause you, suffer it a little beforehand, and then you find that the actual thing is not as bad as you imagined it to be. And there's something else!'

'What's that?' Dominic asked.

'There's always the last minute,' said Joe Two. 'You never know until the last minute. You hope until the last minute, right up to it, that something is going to happen to save you from this pain. If it doesn't, then you think, well, the next time, before the last minute, something will happen to save me from it. You see, this is the virtue of hope, and it is often rewarded. And besides, these poor creatures who oppress us are not worth talking about. Just let them carry on with their inferior games and say poo to them.'

Dominic laughed.

'That reduces it to simplicity,' he said.

'Now, we'll get Pat to write a letter to his mother,' said Joe Two, 'and we will become filled with hope that it will be delivered.' He got an old cigarette packet, and took out the interior of it so that it formed a squat blunt cross, one side glossy and the other side rough. He took a stub of pencil from his pocket and went up to the boy. He sat beside him.

'Now, Pat,' he said, 'write as many words to your mother as this piece of cardboard will hold.' Pat took the piece and the pencil, and thought, and started to write. Dominic left down his mug and went up and sat opposite them.

'I'm trying to place you,' he said to Joe Two. 'Not a farmer. Not a schoolteacher, not Government. Were you a soldier?'

'I was,' said Joe Two. 'And a sailor, and a tailor. I was lots of things. It doesn't matter what you are, it's what you want. One day I stood idly listening to a political speech from a platform and suddenly there were police there batoning all around them. I got a thump on the skull. I thought this should not be; that people should be entitled to listen to speeches, good or bad, without getting clonked on the skull. That was my first term in jail. I took the baton from the policeman, you see, and sent him to hospital. So it was a fair exchange. So you see in me not a patriot whose breast is burning to free Caitlin ni Houlihaun, but just a bystander who got a blow on the sconce and decided to do something about it.'

'Will this do?' asked Pat.

Joe Two took the cardboard from him. He read: '*Dear Mammy, I am very well and safe and you are not to worry. Your son, Pat.*' He read it out aloud. He paused for a few moments. 'It's a good letter,' he said then judiciously. 'It's a filial letter, filled with lies, but containing great comfort.'

To Dominic's surprise, Pat laughed. His bruised mouth opened, so that Dominic could see the mess his gums were in. Dominic couldn't laugh. He dropped his eyes.

'Now, Pat,' said Joe Two, 'on the other side write the name and address of your mother, and she'll have it in her hands, please God, within twenty-four hours, or as soon as our friend here is delivered, whichever the sooner. That is the virtue of hope.'

Delivered! thought Dominic.

But he was, and in a strange way.

Just before darkness fell there was confusion at the main

gate. A police tender drove up and two Irish police forcibly ejected a character from the tender and pushed him in the gate. The sergeant came out of the hut and took a look at him and said: 'Listen, get that fellow out of here. What do you want to do, chum, dirty up my nice camp?' He had cause for complaint. The new prisoner was one of the most tattered individuals anyone had ever seen. He was wearing about four coats, all in a bad state, but serving their purpose in that where there were holes in one there were no holes in the one over it, so that he was adequately covered. His hair was growing through an old felt hat pulled down on his head. There was a rope tying his four coats, and attached to this was a tin mug and an old billy can. He wore several bulky trousers caught up in old boots that were untied and captured the ends of the trousers. He was very black and unshaven and he was protesting vigorously.

'I tell ye I never said it!' he was roaring. 'I'm damned if I ever said it. Will ye listen to me?'

'He was down the main street disturbing the peace,' the tall policeman said.

'I claim to God yeer lying,' he was roaring. His roaring was bringing men from the huts to stand and listen and grin. It was easy to divert them.

'Why the hell did you bring him here?' the sergeant was asking indignantly.

'His offence was political,' said the policeman gravely. 'He was cursing His Majesty. We all heard you, Fourcoats. It was terrible.'

'It's a lie,' roared Fourcoats. 'It was the fella in the pub. He was telling me the terrible things that happened to him during the war outside. Listen, can't ye. He said, "Drink a pint, Fourcoats, and shout to hell with the King of the Egyptians." Not the other one, may his name be praised and glorified.' He raised the battered hat from his thatch of black hair.

The policeman was trying to hold in his laughing.

'It could have led to a breach of the peace. This is no time to be on the public street roaring To Hell with the King.'

185

'Listen,' the sergeant was saying, 'get him out of here! He stinks!'

'Ye know me well,' shouted Fourcoats. 'Don't I clean all the lavatory bowls of the sergeant in Shrule? Can't you talk to him. He knows me. Talk to him. I wasn't meself. I was talking about the King of the bloody Egyptians.'

'The Egyptians have no king, have they?' said the policeman.

'Then I was deceived,' said Fourcoats. 'Can't ye listen to me? This fella told me the King of the Egyptians was going to castrate him and make him a thingamabob in the harem with all those girls. Wasn't that a terrible thing to do to a Christian? On me oath. This was why I was cursing him. It was nothing to do with the other one at all, may his name be praised. Listen, don't keep me. Let me go! I'll be on me way. Can't you talk to the sergeant in Shrule. He'll vouch for me, you'll find.'

'Can't you throw him into the barracks below?' the sergeant asked reasonably.

'No room,' said the policeman. 'We're full up. He's on the charge sheet. Let him out in the morning. Here's an order.'

'You can't do that!' the sergeant said. 'Haven't I enough on my plate as it is?'

'You have Fourcoats on your plate now,' said the policeman, 'and you can do what you like with him.'

'Listen here,' said the sergeant, but it was no use. The policeman was gone and the tender had revved up and departed. The sergeant was furious. He turned back on Fourcoats. 'Now look what you've done to me!' he shouted at him. 'What am I going to do with you?'

'Let me go, sergeant,' suggested Fourcoats. 'I'll be gone like a whisper. I do hate to be shut up. I'll take to the road. Throw me out like a good man, and be done with me.'

'An order is an order,' said the sergeant, waving the paper in his face. 'I have to put up with you, but where am I going to put you?'

He looked at the huts and the men at the doors watching

and grinning. He wasn't looking at them long, because as soon as his eyes rested on them they all hurriedly retreated and closed their hut doors with a bang.

The men of Dominic's hut tried to do the same thing, but oddly enough they were prevented by Joe Two. He stuck his foot in the door and stopped them. They were going to object, but he was a big man and he just looked at them, and they protested no further.

'Sergeant,' he said, 'as an act of great charity, we are willing to let the man come in here. Any man who cleaned the lavatory bowls of the barracks in Shrule deserves to rest his head in our hut.'

'I don't want to rest me head anywhere,' Fourcoats protested. 'I want to get on the road.'

'Get in there,' said the sergeant, 'before I kick you in. If I had my way you'd sleep in the river and get a little of the hum off you. All right, in with you!' He pushed him, and then rubbed his hands.

Fourcoats stumbled into the hut, talking away. 'Is this justice?' he was asking. 'When I was only cursing the King of the Egyptians? What do I want in with a bunch of bloody Shinners. I love me King of England. I'm not afraid of ye to say it! Ye hear that?'

'All right,' said Joe Two, 'get over in that corner there and keep your mouth shut.'

'Wait'll I lay me hands on the fella that led me wrong,' said Fourcoats, going to the indicated corner which was hurriedly cleared for him. 'I believed him, so I did. The things the King of the Egyptians did to him! And I believed him. Am I an eejit?'

'Yes,' said Joe Two, 'and shut up. We have enough troubles without listening to you. Hear that? Keep your mouth shut or we'll shut it for you!'

Fourcoats looked up at him, his eyeballs startlingly white in his black and hairy face. Then he hunched himself in a kind of ball, shoved his hands in one of his four sleeves and subsided muttering. There was a distinct additional smell in the hut.

'Oh, my God, the smell,' someone groaned.

'Why did you do that?' Dominic asked Joe Two.

'How do you feel?' Joe asked him.

'I have been thinking,' said Dominic. 'If they come, I will fight. I'm not going to walk out of here like last night. They can beat me unconscious first.'

Joe thought over this. 'That's not a bad idea,' he said. 'They might just do that. They are very impatient. Did you notice something strange about our friend Fourcoats?'

'Just the smell,' said Dominic.

'You are very unobservant,' said Joe. 'Come on outside and we'll watch the stars appearing.' He rose and went out of the hut. He stood outside leaning against the wall. It was very cold. 'I smell a fine hand at work,' he said when Dominic was standing beside him. 'That business about the King of Egypt was good. Don't you notice that Fourcoats is approximately your size?'

'What?' ejaculated Dominic.

'He's your size,' said Joe Two, 'and he's black-haired, and for some reason you haven't shaved, so you look very like him too. Have you thought that if you were dressed in his clothes how much alike you would be?'

Dominic had his hand up feeling his beard. 'Sam says don't shave,' he said.

'What's that?' Joe asked.

'I thought I was dreaming,' said Dominic. 'I thought I just imagined I heard these words last night, but they must have been spoken.'

'You said Sam?' Joe asked. 'Would this be a man known as Sam Browne?'

'Maybe,' said Dominic.

Joe Two laughed. 'What a character,' he said, slapping his thigh. 'All very subtle, but we might have missed it. What did I tell you about hope? Before morning we just jump Fourcoats and you go out instead of him. This is the most beautiful and masterly plan of escape I have ever heard of. And the beauty of it is that Fourcoats doesn't know. Sam has a friend in the police, eh?'

188

'Sam seems to have friends everywhere,' said Dominic. 'You mean we strip Fourcoats and I wear his clothes.'

'Yes,' said Joe Two, 'it's a daunting thought. Maybe torture would be better, eh, or all those things about pain we were discussing?'

'No,' said Dominic, feeling a tingling in his pulses. 'This is the way. If they don't come. Or if they do come and I am still able to move when they have done with me.'

'If they are not here by two,' said Joe. 'They won't be here at all until the next time. And let's hope it will be too late by then.'

They hunched down at the wall of the hut and waited for the light to die.

Later they sat in the hut, and watched the darkness, waiting for the sound of the lorries to turn into the camp.

It was nerve-racking. Dominic was sweating, even though it was extremely cold in the hut.

19

THE SERGEANT helped. He threw open the door of the hut almost before dawn and shouted through the fug over the blanket-clad bodies: 'Fourcoats! Out! Hear this, you latrine survivor, out of my camp. I was told to keep you until the morning and it's morning.' He watched the bundled body rising from the far corner where he had been isolated, muttering and scratching. He came towards the sergeant grumbling and rubbing his eyes with his fists.

'Out with you!' the sergeant said, pushing him, 'and don't come back. Do you hear?'

The rumpled scratching man said: 'Breakfast.'

'Go to the police,' the sergeant said. 'They are the boys for you. Let them give you breakfast. They put you in here. Off with you. And don't come back.'

They were outside now and approaching the barbed wire

gate. 'You see this fellow,' the sergeant said to the sentry. 'If he comes back give him a bullet in the breadbasket. That way he won't have to eat breakfast any more.' He winked at the sentry. The sentry gave him a tip of the rifle butt on the backside as he passed through the gate. The sergeant paused a few seconds to look after him, his boots slobbering on the gravel, his elbows working furiously scratching around his waist. He was glad to see the back of him, and went contentedly into his hut for breakfast. The fellow had been on his mind all night. The sergeant hated anything untidy. Now that Fourcoats was gone he felt better and in better appetite.

Dominic had to force himself not to hurry his walk. There were about a hundred yards to walk before he could come out on the road near the canal bridge. Every yard of it seemed four miles long. He had no difficulty about the scratching. His whole body seemed to be crawling in the filthy clothes he was wearing. He wondered how much was imagination and how much reality. He had got into the clothes in the dark. That wasn't too bad, until he had sat crouching for two hours waiting for the dawn, terrified of falling asleep, hating the aroma of the clothes that rose from his body.

He had tackled Fourcoats himself in order not to implicate anybody else. He had gagged him with his handkerchief, tied his hands with his tie, put his own boots on him and tied the laces, and then waited for the dawn. He wondered how much time he had and wanted to break into a run. He had until the breakfast came. Some of the others in the hut must have known what went on. The language when Fourcoats was discovered would be choice; the comedy high class. He hoped the sergeant wouldn't get into trouble, but he couldn't afford to worry about him.

All the time he expected the hue and cry to burst out behind him. When he reached the road, he leant against the wall near the bridge and found that he was breathing fast and there were spots in front of his eyes. He wasn't as fit as he normally was. He recovered himself and crossed the bridge. There were very few people up and about at this hour. If a walker came towards him he lowered his head and muttered

190

away into his black beard. He just saw the feet of the passer-by and noticed that they gave him a wide berth the nearer they came to him. He was convincing to them anyhow.

Around by the jail there was further danger. The main gate there was sandbagged and patrolled. He kept his head averted from it, crossed the bridge over the river, went down by the waterside and then cut over to the houses on the far side. He knew where he was going. Nobody had told him, but it was the one place he could think of. He walked down the front of the houses which opened on to the path. He noticed the different coloured chalk crosses on the doors. These were the results of the raids. The colours of the chalk indicated what the raiders thought of the household. Green chalk was the most dangerous and the people in that house would always get a thorough rumbling.

The chalk mark on the house he was heading for was green. There was good cause for this because it was the house of Lowry's people. He walked past the houses without looking at them at all. Farther down he turned off the road and went around by the back. Here there were narrow littered lanes, containing overflowing dustbins, bags, tins and throw-outs. He carefully counted, although he recognized the wooden gates that led into the yards at the back of the houses. They had latches. He tried this but found that the bolt was shot on the inside. He wondered if he would climb the eight-foot high wall, or if he would be too conspicuous. He decided to knock, although the yard gate was a good way from the house. He knocked three times with a pause between each knock. He expected to have to do this for a long time until he might get attention, but to his surprise after the third knock the gate opened, he went in and found himself looking at Finola. She had her back against the gate, closing it and bolting it while she still looked at him, then she did a strange thing, she threw her arms around his neck, and put her face to his and hugged him.

'No, no!' said Dominic, pushing her away. 'Look at me!'

'What's wrong with you?' she asked. She was joyful.

'How did you know me?' he asked.

'We were expecting you,' she said. 'I have been waiting here since the dawn, praying it would work. Didn't it work? Didn't it work well? Isn't Sam a genius?'

'Yes,' said Dominic.

'What's wrong with you?' she asked anxiously. 'Are you tired? Are you hungry?'

'Yes,' said Dominic. He was watching her animated face, noticing where his rough beard had reddened the side of her cheek.

'Come on in,' she said.

'No,' said Dominic. 'I'll stay in the shed. I won't go in with these clothes on. Will you favour me? Get me some clothes and a basin to wash in. Do this, Finola. I'm going mad with the itch. You were foolhardy to come close to me.'

She took a good look at him then, standing back from him. She put one hand up to her mouth to cover her laughter.

'Forgive me,' she said. 'I wish we could have a photograph of you for posterity, so that we could show them to your grandchildren and say: This was your grandfather in the war in his uniform.'

'They should have a photograph of Fourcoats too,' said Dominic bitterly. 'He is wearing my good suit.'

'I'll bring you back the stuff,' she said. He watched her running up the short cement path of the yard to the back door and then he went into the shed. It held coal, a bicycle, cardboard boxes filled with old newspapers. He started shedding his coats here and throwing them into the yard. He had retained his own vest because Fourcoats didn't wear a shirt and he had been afraid to chance it. He was relieved to be freed from the clothes, although he thought he should be very pleased with them, as they had given him his freedom.

She came back with a big glazed basin and a large ewer of hot water, with towel and soap and trousers and shirt and socks. She gave them to him. 'Can I be talking to you from outside,' she asked, 'while you are changing? Here's the razor. You look handsome with a black beard. The clothes belong to Lowry. I hope they fit you.' She went outside. She kept talking. She really seemed pleased to see me, Dominic thought wonderingly. The box with the razor had a small mirror in the back. He propped this on one of the wooden shed supports and started to shave.

'How did you get away?' she asked. 'Were you afraid?' She didn't give him time to answer. 'You know, on the island, when you made Poric and me go, you know what I thought afterwards?'

'What?' Dominic asked, his head strained back.

'You were like a wild duck protecting its young,' he heard her say. 'The mother duck. She flaps around as if she had a wounded wing, attracting the notice of the hunters so that the young ones can get away. I cannot tell you how I felt when I saw them in the boat and you going away in it. I felt like a traitor because I was free. Poric was raging with you. He'll probably have a row with you when he sees you.'

'Poric never fights with anybody,' said Dominic. 'I just tricked the pair of you, that was all.' It was such a pleasure to dip a piece of the towel in the water, soap it and rub his body clean. 'There should have been another way to outwit them, but I couldn't think of it. What happened was the difference between leadership and cunning. I'm cunning, that's all.'

'That's not true,' he heard her say. 'Why are you always running yourself down?'

'All egotists possess a mock modesty,' he answered her. 'When I talk poorly of myself, I'm thinking the opposite.'

'That's not true either,' she said. 'I enjoyed that few hours on the island, even if it meant I was responsible for them catching you. Did they do anything bad to you in the camp?'

His arms were still aching, his shoulders were sore.

'No,' he said. 'They didn't have time, owing to the great planning ye did out here.'

'It was Sam,' she said. 'Sam thought of it all, because he saw Fourcoats in town. I hope they don't do anything to poor Fourcoats.'

'Fourcoats could talk himself out of the grave,' said Dominic. 'He'll talk so much they will give him an escort to get rid of him.'

He came out now to her. He looked at the discarded clothes. 'Will someone get rid of those?' he asked.

'Maybe it would be better to fumigate them,' she said. 'And they could be used again for something. Nobody would ever know you in them. Not even your own mother.'

'You did,' he said, rubbing his wet hair with the towel. She looked at him, then dropped her eyes. 'That's different,' she said. 'After all, I was expecting you.'

'That's right,' he said.

'Come in and eat,' she said. 'We couldn't find shoes to fit you. You can try yourself.'

'It's hard to find shoes to fit,' he said, sorry he had said it, knowing that Lowry's shoes wouldn't fit him anyhow, 'or clothes.' He had to pull Lowry's trousers well up on his waist, and still the ends of them were rubbing the ground. Not a big enough man to fit Lowry's clothes, or to wear Lowry's shoes.

'Why do you say hurtful things?' she asked, puzzled.

'I said nothing hurtful,' he answered curtly. 'You imagine things that are not there.'

They walked silently up to the door. She was frowning. The joy had gone out of her. He wondered if he had blown it out himself.

Lowry's mother and sister were in the kitchen. There was great heat in the kitchen from the black range. Lowry's mother was a grey-haired woman. Bobbed hair, she had, and always a cigarette in the corner of her mouth. She had a strong face.

She got up from the table and came over to him and put her arms around him. 'By God, but we're pleased to see you, Dominic,' she said. 'You are as welcome as fine weather.' Lowry's sister caught his arm and pressed it. 'It's marvellous, Dominic,' she said. 'Just marvellous. We never thought it would work out.'

Dominic was always startled when he saw Lowry's sister. She was dressed in black and had long fair hair tied with a ribbon at the back. If Lowry had been born a girl he would have looked just like her. 'Sit,' said Lowry's mother, 'and have your tea.' She pulled a chair for him at the kitchen table. The tea was poured. He sat there. At the other end of the table there were many letters. 'You see what we are at,' she said. 'Steaming open letters. I know we are doing it for our country and it's necessary, but do you know I never get over a feeling of guilt at opening other people's letters, even if they are the police.'

He laughed.

'That's the Irish all over,' he said. 'They go into agonies over things.'

Lowry's sister was over at the steaming kettle. She would bring the letter. Lowry's mother would open it, scan it, and then hand it to Finola, who was taking notes in a book.

'Not that we don't get lots of surprising information,' she said. 'Some of it is grim. You would be surprised at the people who write to policemen; and what they write about. What they say about their neighbours. Times like these bring out the best in people, but it also brings out the worst in them too. We have a surprise upstairs for you when you finish eating.'

'You have?' said Dominic. 'I hope it is pleasant.'

'I hope so too,' she said, smiling, carefully resealing a letter. 'It's your brother Dualta,' she said. 'He came last night. So did the raiders, so he had to go out the skylight and spend half the night clinging to the roof. We let him sleep.'

'Dualta,' said Dominic, feeling pleasure. He hurriedly finished his tea.

'Don't choke yourself,' she said. 'He won't fly away.' This amused her. She coughed through the cigarette smoke.

'Ah, I want to see him anyhow,' he said, rising.

'He's in the first room on the right up the stairs,' she said.

Dominic went to the door. He paused there to look back at them. They were intent on their work. He knew the postman left the letters early, picked them up again afterwards for the afternoon delivery. Imagine women engaged on work like this. It was dangerous. She had already lost a son. She was a widow. There was a picture of her husband on the mantelpiece. He was holding a round football. He had loved all things Irish, but principally Irish football. He was wearing a jersey with horizontal stripes, and long black togs. He had a black moustache. He died of pneumonia many years ago, probably

195

from all the wettings he had got playing football all over the county in improvised fields with no pavilion. He was a fighter against the imposition of a foreign culture. You must play Irish, talk Irish, to be Irish, he used to say, as Lowry often told him. If he was here now he would probably be dying or dead or in prison or on the run. Dominic thought tiredly that he was well off where he was.

He was suddenly depressed. Finola didn't look at him. He went up the narrow stairs. He opened the door softly and went in. The blind was down but it was a yellow one, and a muted light fell on the sleeping body of his brother. He was lying on his back. Dominic sat on a chair and watched him. He was sleeping deeply, his hands outside the clothes. There was a revolver on the pillow beside him. If he turned his face, it would be staring at him in the eyes. He saw lines on his brother's face that had never been there before, and he noticed that there were a few grey hairs at the sides of his head. You had to look closely to find them on account of the fair hair, but they were there. He looked at the scar tissue around his wounded eye, and the mutilated hand, and he wondered, what kind of times are we living in at all? Where are we going? Are we getting anywhere at all? What is it about? It was as vague as religion. Religion was not sensible. It was just something that despite all reason was true. It was faith. You knew that Christ rose from the dead. This was the anchor, and in the same way you believed deep down, despite all the evidence to the contrary, that what you were doing would bring freedom to your country. Faith was necessary.

He put his head in his hands.

'What's the problem, Dominic?' he heard his brother's voice.

'Lowry's mother, Lowry's sister, Lowry's girl. Lowry's clothes,' said Dominic.

'You are obsessed with Lowry,' said Dualta.

Dominic looked at him.

'I'm so pleased to see you,' he said. He grasped his brother's arm. He felt very warm towards him. He could see the same warmth that he felt in Dualta's eyes. 'You never knew Lowry,' he said.

196

'No,' said Dualta. 'It's past, all that. We are living. We carry on the best way we can. I was upset to hear about them getting you.'

'That didn't bring you,' said Dominic.

Dualta laughed.

'No, in these times what happens to your brother is not important,' said Dualta. 'But humanly speaking, I don't like what happens to you. Did they do anything to you.'

Dominic thought of the suffocating water.

'Not much,' he said. 'But it was as well I was freed. I might have talked.'

'You wouldn't,' said Dualta. 'You would be so busy thinking of how weak you are that you'd be dead before you got around to it.' He laughed, and got out of the bed. 'I know you, boy.'

'You always wake up straight away,' said Dominic aggrievedly, 'and wide awake. It takes me half an hour.'

'Didn't you hear?' Dualta asked. 'All brothers are different.'

'When we are away I miss you,' said Dominic, 'but when we are together, I know that we will have a row in the end.'

'Hello, Sam,' said Dualta. Dominic turned quickly. Sam was standing in the doorway. He hardly recognized him in his neat brown suit, hard collar and tie, with a tiepin, and a rolled fedora hat.

'You made it, Dominic,' said Sam.

'I nearly didn't,' said Dominic. 'I hardly took the hint. It was a fellow called Joe Murphy who is not Joe Murphy who took the hint. Not me. I haven't enough brains for hints.'

'What Joe Murphy?' Sam asked. Dominic described him.

'Oh, him,' said Sam. 'He's a dangerous fish if they only knew. He's all right. He'll get out of there with the power of his mouth.'

'He spotted Fourcoats,' said Dominic.

Sam laughed. He had an odd way of laughing. He closed his teeth and blew air through them.

'The poor old bastard,' said Sam. 'You should have seen him in the street cursing the King.'

'How about it?' Dualta asked abruptly. 'Is it fixed?'

197

'Yes,' said Sam. 'There are three or four of them for you. They should do.'

'Good,' said Dualta.

'What's up?' Dominic asked.

'We are going to take care of Mac,' said Dualta grimly. 'You remember Mac, don't you?'

'Yes,' said Dominic. 'I remember Mac.'

'Well,' said Dualta. 'I can tell you that Mac will remember us. Mac has got away with too much.'

Dominic thought of Mac, and his heart started a slow pound.

'Mac isn't the worst of them,' he said.

'They are all good when they are dead,' said Dualta. 'Right, Sam?'

'Right, Dualta,' said Sam.

20

'YOU UNDERSTAND what you have to do?' Dualta asked him in a whisper.

'I do,' said Dominic.

'Don't forget,' said Dualta. 'If he comes out on his own he will have no gun. If there is a civilian with him, he will have a gun. If so, leave it. If something goes wrong and he has a gun, shoot him. I prefer it the other way, to make him suffer a little to see what stuff he is made of. All right?'

'All right,' said Dominic.

'I will be out the front to head him off,' said Dualta, and then he left him, walking down the dimly lit flagged passage silently, because they were wearing socks over their shoes. They had done a lot of running and dodging around back alleys and dimly lit streets after curfew to get where they were now. It was a strange place. Long ago these back streets of tall houses had been the homes of the city merchants. Now they were nearly all in a state of utter decay. A few of the rooms here and there that still had roofs over them were occupied by families. They were the most appalling slums that Dominic had ever seen or smelt. He had seen one lighted room with a mother and a father and eight children, very badly dressed, huddled around a fireplace where some sticks burned. He had often seen the children, raggedy and bare-footed, collecting fallen branches in rackety prams from the trees at Taylor's Hill or the Barna woods. As far as he could see they had no beds, and their bedclothes were made up of rags.

He was standing in one of these rooms off the passage. If he looked up he could see the stars. He was standing on a heap of rubble. Part of the original door was still attached to the sagging door frame. In the passage there was one guttering gaslight attached to the ceiling. From the right he could hear the loud voices of the drinking men in the pub, and if he peeped out he could see the rectangle of light from the door of the pub and tobacco smoke swirling in the light like motes in a sunbeam. There was no toilet in the bar, so men had to come back to this passage and relieve themselves where they would in its long length. So it smelled evil enough.

Beyond the bar there was a big hall where they showed films. These were over now. He had heard the playing of the piano which accompanied the action of the film. He could have told from the music what type of film it was. There were a lot of sad haunting bits now and again broken up by action music and ending with the soft paeans of love and happy ending. After that the hundreds of feet on the passage, the loud voices. The sound of the men drinking in the pub remained the same all the time.

He tensed and got to his feet, taking the gun from his pocket when he heard the feet coming down the passage. He looked through a crack in the door. It wasn't Mac. It was a soldier; his tunic collar was open, his cap on the back of his head. He staggered a bit. He was humming a song. He went past the door. His feet didn't stop, on and on he went the whole length of the passage. He was obviously leaving by the back door which was about thirty yards away.

Dominic relaxed again. He could smell the terrible dampness on the plaster walls, which if you saw them in the daylight he was sure would be covered in green moss and fungus. He thought of the people living in the tenements. Was that a reason to fight, so that they could be free of the vile dirt and complete poverty? It was as good a cause as any. You had to translate the idealism of revolt into something practical, like better living, more opportunity, the end of bigotry.

He knew Mac had come out of the pub by the sound of his voice. He knew Mac's voice well by now. His heart thudded dully as he put his eye to the crack. He saw him, taking both sides of the passage, a huge man, and he was alone. He was laughing to himself at some joke that had probably been flung after him as he was leaving.

Dominic pulled back, let him pass the doorway and then stepped softly into the passage. He walked a little until the light was at his back and illuminating Mac. He had the gun in his hand. He could easily have shot at the broad back ahead of him. Did he want to, he wondered? Would he if he had to? He thought he would. He thought he wasn't the same young man he had been, even a year ago.

'Stand still, Mac,' he said, 'and don't open your mouth.' He saw the pause for his words to make sense in the fuddled brain and then Mac stood still. 'Walk nice and slowly along the passage,' he said. 'We are going out the back way. Now, walk!' He didn't have to put any menace in his voice. He meant it all. Mac started to walk stiff-legged, and then did exactly what Dualta thought he would do. When he got around a sharp bend in the passage, he suddenly started to run. 'Stop!' Dominic called, and it acted as a spur. Mac ran faster.

He burst out of the shabby doorway, jumped the two stone steps, turned to run left and found a man standing in the middle of the roadway with a gun in his hand. It was a dark street shut off by the tall warehouses. All he could see was this man in a coat and what little light there was glinting off the gun. He turned, swivelled his body and ran away from the man.

Dominic came out of the doorway and saw him running

right. Dualta, who had headed him off, nodded and they ran after him, not very fast, just jogging. The street was very badly lighted. There was nearly as much light from the stars.

There was another street turning up to the right. Mac ran into this, and saw another man in the middle of that road, waiting for him. He swerved again and went back on his tracks and ran ahead. He would have run towards the river, but he was stopped here again by another man, so he turned left and ran towards the docks. Dominic felt sorry for him. Mac hadn't the stuff of heroes, he knew. He didn't have to see him in panic-stricken flight to know that. He must be suffering, he thought. He was like a hare running from coursing dogs.

There were two further street openings, and these were also blocked by men standing in the middle of the road. So Mac had no place to go except towards the docks, and he ran now in that direction saying: 'Ah! Ah!' They closed in on him, running. Dominic knew that all this time Mac was expecting to feel a bullet in his back.

They trapped him between two huge baulks of timber near a gaslight, right on the edge of the docks. He had nowhere to go from there except into the greasy water below him. On the far right a huge bulk of a tramp ship loomed, high out of the water because it was relieved of its cargo of timber. There were two dim lights shining on the vessel. Mac looked over towards those desperately. But he couldn't run towards them any more. He was shut in on all sides. They could see the whites of his eyes in the light of the gas lamp. He was breathing heavily, the great chest rising and falling. He hadn't much of a belly for such a big man, but he wasn't fit. The fear of death was naked in his eyes.

Dualta walked towards him.

'You wanted to meet me, Mac,' he said. 'I'm Joe's brother. You remember Joe?'

'Listen,' he said, finding it hard to talk. 'I didn't mean, you know that. Here, Joe, tell him, what did I do, only a few clouts on the ear, mate. You tell him, Joe.'

'Shut up,' said Dualta. He tapped him on the chest with the barrel of his revolver. 'You make me sick, Mac. Don't

201

you know how to die?' He pulled back the trigger until it clicked into place. Now all he had to do was pull it.

'No, listen,' said Mac, holding out his hand as if it would hold back the bullet. 'I didn't mean. I didn't know. Lots of things, see, I didn't know. Hey, Joe there, Joe, listen to me.'

'You bastard!' said Dualta, suddenly angry. Dominic was surprised at his anger. 'We have come up with some of your comrades in the streets of Dublin. Cornered like you, and what did they say? They punched their hands over their hearts and they said: Here, Paddy, you bastard. Give it to me here, here, here! And they took it here, hating the sight of the man behind the gun. They died defiantly, you hear, Mac, not like rats; like men, not like rabbits, like men. You do too, Mac. Gather your courage. You're big, Mac, when you are clobbering boys, or smacking down girls. Be big now, Mac. Stand up to it. Thump your hand over your heart and say: Give it to me here, Paddy! Go on, Mac! Go on, Mac! Say it! Say give it to me here, Paddy!'

Dominic found himself clutching his own gun so hard that his hand was hurting. He was sure Dualta was going to kill Mac. He was waiting for the sight of the bullet disturbing the front of his tunic. A man is born to die sometime. This is true. His end is inevitable. But when a man decides to kill a man, is he interfering with the providence of God, or is he being an instrument? He thought of this; self-defence, a just war, or the execution of a criminal. Mac would come under two headings. They made their own laws, appointed themselves their own judges, so he could hardly object to being judged by the men who had to suffer under their self-created laws. Telling himself all this, tensed, for the shot that would blot out poor Mac forever.

Mac got on his knees. Dominic felt terrible about this, but he did. Maybe it was the strong drink, and the running, but he got on his knees and said, 'No, listen, listen,' so that Dualta would have to shoot him in the head.

Dualta didn't. He bent down to him, the gun at his forehead and he said, biting out the words: 'You're not worth it, Mac. You're not worth it,' and then he straightened, and

202

putting his shoe against his chest heaved at him and sent him sprawling backwards into the water of the dock. They waited to hear the splash, and then Dualta said angrily: 'Come on, for God's sake, let's get away. Thanks, lads,' he said to the silent men around him. 'Better vanish. We'll be seeing you.'

They melted away into the baulks of timber. Dominic felt limp. He knew Mac would be all right. There were steps near where he was kicked in.

'Blubber,' said Dualta, anger still in his voice. 'You saw him. Big strong man of straw. Was a fellow like that worth a bullet, was he?'

'No,' said Dominic.

'You thought I meant to shoot him?' Dualta asked.

'Yes,' said Dominic.

'I had no intention,' said Dualta. 'Men like him are over here for loot and liquor and a pound a day. No cause beyond that. No patriotism, just another soft war, fighting amateurs. Why should I kill a one like that?'

'I don't know,' said Dominic, a little bewildered.

'By God, but we frightened him,' said Dualta. 'Did you see him? He'll carry a gun in future, I bet you, and he'll watch his step. We better split. I'll see you back at the Lowrys'.' He stood up. He was grinning at Dominic. 'Did you think I had become a killer, Dominic? Shoot everyone at the drop of a hat?'

'No,' said Dominic. 'I know you can kill easier than I can. But I didn't want you to kill Mac.'

'Why?' Dualta asked.

'I don't know,' said Dominic.

'You are still a sentimentalist,' said Dualta, and turned and walked away from him, into a dark black street.

Dominic waited for a while until he could see him no more and then followed after him. He liked Mac. This was a terrible admission. How could he like a fellow who had done those things to him and to other people as well? But he thought of him a little fondly. I must be sick, he thought then, but he was determined on one thing: to get out of the town into the country air. He was terrified, cooped up in narrow streets. He was afraid of the long way he would have to go now, dodging the patrols of soldiers; the Crossley tenders of the auxiliaries. Out in the open you could see them, the dust rising for miles behind their vehicles. They could never come on you unawares, and you had the wide land to hide in.

He was to discover the dangers of the countryside too.

21

DOWN IN the South they had evolved the flying column. Men were withdrawn from companies and battalions, supplied with the few arms that the battalions possessed, trained for a week or more and then sent into an attack, to strike hard and vanish quickly. This column might be disbanded and another formed, so that eventually every man in a battalion would have been trained and would have seen action.

As they went through the small fields on this soft April morning, Dominic thought that they had seen plenty of training but little action. It wasn't the fault of their OC, he thought, looking to the right where he walked fields, climbed walls slowly and carefully. He was a man with a big broad face, a slow way of speech, and enormous hands. It requires big hands to use a ·45 revolver with accuracy, and this was Michael John's favourite weapon.

Dominic thought he had brains. He didn't seem to have, from his slow speech and bright blue eyes and constant laughter. He just didn't have luck. They had waited three nights in succession for a pair of lorries that always travelled a certain road at a certain time. They had their mines laid, with eighteen men in good positions, and the lorries never came. When they lifted the mines and went away, the lorries came. 'The people are afraid,' said Michael John, who knew that someone was getting into the town to warn them. 'You can't blame them. You know all the burning they do after an ambush. These people don't want it to happen to their village. You can't blame them, but if I could only get the one that's telling, what I wouldn't do to him.' Over three hundred small towns had been burned and looted, innumerable houses.

But Michael John had this leader quality, whatever it was. He didn't give orders but made suggestions. This was his nature. But the men did what he suggested because they wanted to please him.

There were just six of them now, coming up from the lower lake where they had been manoeuvring, heading south. There were six more men about two miles away to their left and another six a mile on their right. Their rendezvous was a hazel wood on high ground about half a mile across the public road, that wandered a bit, and then ran straight as an arrow towards Mayo.

Dominic looked to his left where Poric had taken the easy way and was walking in a narrow lane. He could see his head and shoulders over the top of the bushes. Beyond him was another man. Michael John was in the centre, with three men spread out to his right.

There was no danger. They could see the road on each side of them and it was free of traffic. On the right they had as a landmark an old square-built ruined castle standing on a height, with a lake behind it leading to the high ground of the hazels.

Dominic thought that at least they were fit. He noticed this because they had been climbing walls, jumping into lanes, crossing fields, some clean but some a wilderness of thorn bushes, for three hours, and he was still not short of breath, and could still vault a wall with ease. He did this now and saw Poric grinning at him. He laughed at him and waved his hand. They had established a very warm relationship, himself and Poric. They could almost conduct conversations without talking, reminding him of accounts you read in the sagas of their own Fenian and Cuchullainn epics of the friendship that grew up between warriors.

Not that they were real warriors yet. Warriors without a decent battle to prove themselves, like iron not tested by fire. Burning mansions was a poor way to be a warrior, he thought, frowning. He was reminded of this by the thin column of smoke that rose into the windless sky ahead of him. Probably some farmer burning gorse or refuse. Two mornings ago, they had burned a mansion over in the east of the county. The orders came from the top; for every cottage that is burned by the enemy, a Unionist mansion is to be burned in reply. This would soon stop the burning of poor men's cottages, since princes' palaces are much more expensive, and princes scream louder than peasants.

He hadn't liked doing it.

It was a Georgian mansion with two nice wings. It was well proportioned. The windows were slender with sort of Grecian arches over them. It looked very nice sitting in the sun in the green parkland when they drove up in the commandeered lorry with the big tins of paraffin.

The owner couldn't believe they would do such a thing. Dominic didn't blame him. There was his wife, a nice lady whose hair was white, a son and a daughter. The order to them was unintelligible. They had nothing to do with the burning of the thatched cottage of Jimmy Mahoney on the previous Friday. Michael John was hard-faced and inflexible. How much time had they? Why, they would have as much time as Jimmy Mahoney, five minutes to get their most precious possessions out of there.

The man was going to appeal, but as he looked at Michael John he knew there would be no answer to his appeal, and as the paraffin was emptied into milk cans and the men started to spread all over the house scattering it, they and their servants began a frantic running match.

As he scattered the oil on the carpet in the living-room, on the fine furniture with the delicate legs, on the leather-bound books in the library after they smashed in the glass, Dominic knew that they were vandals. You had to tell yourself that these people deserved no pity, since for centuries they had separated themselves from the people and oppressed them with their exactions and fines, or complete indifference. They themselves had chosen the way and were undoubtedly heart and soul, in prayer and practice, on the side of the foreigner;

they were bringing this destruction on their own heads. A mansion was worth say, six thousand pounds, a cottage four hundred, so each mansion was worth at least fifteen cottages. He knew that when a few of them were burned that the other burning would stop abruptly.

All the same it was sad, to see much beauty transformed into dirty black ugliness. He had tried to keep remembering Poric's father setting up house in the stable when they burned him out. He would forever hate the disgusting smell of paraffin. He didn't know if others felt the same way he did. Their faces were closed. They just set about burning the mansion with cold-blooded efficiency. Certainly they didn't do it with joy, that he could see. They just did it, and they waited outside until the flames had really caught hold and they were sure it would be reduced to blackened walls, gutted stones, before they left and went away, for the most part silent.

Thinking of these things now he saw they had come close to the road. They paused and looked. On the straight length at the left, nothing. At the curves on the right, nothing. The decayed castle was a gloomy grey rectangle. It reminded him of the mansion. Man was always destroying things, and beautiful things. At the time they wouldn't seem beautiful. It was only afterwards that men felt pity for the things their hands had destroyed.

They were on a height here, a sort of a quarry that had been used for supplying gravel for the road.

Dominic went left and jumped on to the road. He saw Poric and the other man doing the same. He saw Michael John on the height, looking right, presumably at the two men there who would cross the road and head for the hazel.

They were caught flatfooted.

There was a lorry drawn up under the height where Michael John stood. There was a mixture of police and soldiers. They were out of the lorry, sitting on stones, chatting and drinking out of mugs. Fortunately they hadn't their weapons in their hands, but Dominic just had time to see the startled look on their faces and their hands reaching for their weapons when he ran for the loose stone wall on the far side of the road and threw himself over it. As he dived he heard a bullet singing in the air.

His inclination was to run for the cover of the hazels, but he knew that would mean death. He didn't know how many of them there were, about eight, he thought. He turned and crept back to the stone wall. He looked for a suitable opening, and pushed through the barrel of the rifle, his fingers automatically having freed the safety catch. He could see nothing but legs. He fired. The butt hit his shoulder hard because it was held loosely, so he tightened himself up to it and took aim at kneeling khaki legs. He thought the legs collapsed. He wasn't sure. It had all happened so suddenly. Bullets were flying, ricocheting off rocks. Michael John had been caught out. There should have been scouts sent out ahead of them. The others had been surprised too, but all they had to do was charge the wall and it would be over.

He heard Michael John's voice then: 'Number Two Company. Enfilade!' and he heard the sound amidst all the sounds of Michael John's revolver seeming to come from different directions. It was a bluff. The other two parties were miles away and couldn't possibly come in time to save them. It mightn't have worked, but from the hazels suddenly there came the cracking of a rifle firing fast, as quickly as the man there could pull the trigger. It was far away, but Dominic heard the tinkling of glass, which could only come from the lorry, and the sound of the bullets hitting the steel of the lorry.

He heard more firing. He fired away himself, trying desperately to get something into his sights through the narrow opening. He heard shouting and the sound of the lorry engine, and as the firing slackened he raised his head over the stones and saw the lorry racing away around the bend towards the town, with the men clinging to it. He jumped on to the road and got on one knee and got in a snap shot at the retreating lorry, and then it was out of sight around the Castle Hill.

A silence descended on the road. There was the sound of two shots, as the men farther out sent bullets after the lorry.

Michael John stood up on the height over the road. The revolver was drooping in his hand, and he was wiping the sweat off his face with his cap. He is a leader all right, Dominic thought. If he failed one way he succeeded in another. Then he noticed the soldier lying on the ground. He tightened his grip on the rifle and went close to him. He was stretched back, still clutching his rifle.

'Get up!' said Dominic, not knowing if he was alive or dead.

'Can't,' he said. Dominic approached closer and looked at him. His eyes were very frightened. He was only a boy in his teens, hardly starting to shave. Dominic leaned down and took the rifle from him. It was slack in his hand. Then he saw the blood on his right trouser leg.

His instincts made him put down his own rifle and bend over the young soldier's leg. He took out a knife and sliced the trouser leg over the blood and saw that his leg was a mess He could see pieces of white bone.

Michael John was beside him. 'Is he bad?' he asked.

'His thigh bone is shattered,' said Dominic.

'What shall we do with him?' Michael John asked.

'Shoot him,' said one of the men. Dominic looked up at him. He was a burly man. His face was white. The hands on the gun were trembling. Dominic noticed that his own limbs were shaking. This was the shock of the whole affair.

'They shoot all our wounded,' the man said. 'I'll shoot him,' clicking back the bolt on the rifle. Dominic noticed the eyes of the young soldier. He didn't want to die. Dominic waited for Michael John to speak. There was an appreciable pause. Then he said: 'We are not like them. Put down your rifle.' He squatted down beside Dominic. 'What will we do with him?' he asked.

'Are you a professional soldier?' Dominic asked. 'You hear me?'

'No,' said the young man swallowing. 'I'm a conscript.'

'I'll dress it as well as I can,' said Dominic, 'and then we'll leave him. They will be back very shortly.' He took bandages and iodine from his pouch, which was all he had. He saw that there was no artery cut in the leg. It should be splinted. Would they have time for splinting it?

'Gather up,' Michael John was saying. 'We'll go to the hazels, and meet the others and get out of here fast. It will only take them fifteen minutes to be back with reinforcements. Where's Poric?'

Dominic heard this and his heart stopped. He remembered running across the road, jumping the wall, with the impression that Poric had been on his left doing exactly the same thing. He stood up. They were looking at one another. None of them moved, so Dominic crossed the road and looked over the wall. He didn't want to look over. He saw the great bulk of Poric lying there with his face buried in the grass. He jumped the wall and went over to him. He could see the blood soaking the back of his trenchcoat. He turned him over on his back gently. The bullet had come out in front. His chest was soaked with blood. He was alive, but he was unconscious. He pulled away his coat and undercoat and opened his shirt front. The ragged wound was on the right side of his chest. He was alive, but how much alive was he? Had the bullet hit a lung?

'Well?' asked Michael John.

'Bad,' said Dominic. 'Where will we get a doctor? How will we get a doctor?' He was stripping the clothes off him. A man got on his knees to help him.

'Listen, Michael John,' a man shouted at him. 'Here's the fellow that was firing the rifle.'

Dominic heard only the voices. He was too intent on Poric's life, wondering if it was ebbing away, wishing him to open his eyes. An old voice talking: 'I was up in the hazels cutting the scallops when I saw them. Like a picture. You coming up behind and them in front not knowing you were coming up behind. How could I warn ye? I knew my son kept a gun for safety in a dyke near the wood. Sure I went for it. I got it that time. Never fired a rifle in me life but I can snagg a snipe left and right.'

'You saved our lives,' said Michael John.

'It was only instinct,' said the old voice.

'You're a hero,' said Michael John. 'Somebody should write a song about you and they will. Have you the horse and cart with you?'

'Loaded and ready for the town,' said the old voice.

Michael John was back beside Dominic.

'Only one way,' he said. 'Put him under the scallops and bring him into the town. You'll find a doctor somehow. The safest thing to do is to do the dangerous thing. You can go with him.'

'How, in the name of God?' asked Dominic. His hands were covered with Poric's blood.

'This way,' said Michael John. 'Hey, Finn, where would Jack the Post be now?'

'Near enough at this hour,' said the voice of Finn. 'He'd be on his way back.'

'Look for him,' said Michael John, 'and bring him here. If you are not here in five minutes don't bother.'

He was beside Dominic now, helping him, dabbing softly at the wound with a piece of bloodied bandage.

'I never got farther than that,' said Dominic, 'just how to put on a bandage,' winding it around the great chest again and again, tightly.

'Nobody notices a postman,' Michael John was saying. 'Put on the postman's jacket and hat and wheel his bicycle and you could go into an army canteen. This is the best I can think of, Dominic.'

Dominic paused to look at him.

'Your best is very good,' he said. 'We could carry him and hide in one of the caves near the river, but we might kill him. It will have to be this way or nothing. How about the soldier? Will he see? Will he tell?'

'It might have been wise to shoot him,' said Michael John. 'Marney, go over to the soldier. Squat in front of him and give him a cigarette. Keep him in chat. Come on, the rest of you. We'll carry Poric by the wall to the gap. Where's your horse and cart, man?'

'Around the bend,' said the old man. 'I'll go and ready him.'

Poric wasn't light weight and they had to be careful. They used his overcoat as a stretcher. It seemed a long way. They were conscious of the passing of time, of how close they were to the town.

The old man emptied tied bundles of scallops out of the cart. Dominic made a rough bed on the bottom of the cart with his overcoat and his short coat and they put him in and covered him with his own clothes. There was blood on his lips. His breathing was raspy. Then they carefully covered him again with the bundles of scallops so that they wouldn't lean too heavily on him.

Finn captured the postman. He was a cheerful one with a red face. He was very plump. Nobody could reason out why he was plump when he cycled so many miles a day. He handed over his tunic and his hat. He knew a house where he could pass the evening until his clothes were returned to him. He pointed out the house. Dominic memorized its position as he pulled on the tunic. Then the old man got the horse going and Dominic walked beside him, wheeling the heavy bicycle.

Michael John walked a few paces with him.

'I'm sorry, Dominic,' he said. 'I made a mistake. It nearly got us all killed.'

'You recovered,' said Dominic. 'If ever I am out again with a column I want to be with yours.'

He felt the weight of Michael John's hand on his shoulder.

'Poric will live,' he said. 'I feel it in my bones. Come back to me. You have the making of a good soldier.'

Then he was gone. Dominic looked back to see them. They were all standing. They waved at him and then they jumped over the wall and he saw them running towards the hazels.

The old man was nearly dancing at the horse's head.

'It was good,' he said. 'You should have seen me. I remembered the son and his training. Pull the bolt and the bullet pops. And it did. I had the feeling of power when I felt the gun alive. I made stars of the glass of the lorry. Did you know that?'

'I heard it,' said Dominic.

It all happened in such short a time. How long? Maybe ten minutes. Just like that. A few seconds was all it took to die. He didn't want to think of Poric now, for the moment. If he backed a little he could hear the rasping of his breath.

They were halfway to the town when the six lorries came out of it making great columns of dust.

212

He tensed himself as they approached.

The old man pulled the cart to the side of the road and held the horse by the nostrils. They stood there.

One by one the lorries passed, covering them with dust. They were packed with soldiers, holding rifles. The middle lorry had a mounted machine gun. Not one of them stopped. Run, run, run, Michael John, he said as he looked after them. Michael John was a good man. They would never catch him like that again. They wouldn't catch him now.

He started to wonder how in the name of God he would get a doctor for Poric, and where would he go with him? What would he do with him? He hadn't the fast brain in an emergency of a Michael John.

All he had was hope.

22

HE STOOD under one of the trees and looked down at slow moving water. It was a cut-off from the river that was taken to drive the turbines of the electric company farther down. It was very clear water. He could see many things down there, kitchen utensils that had been dumped, old rags and things, weeds and a slim trout holding his body to the flow of the water with a slight flick of his tail. He was aware of the soft sun and the leaves bursting newly in the branches over his head, but he was more conscious of Poric and what was happening to him, and of his inevitable end if he didn't get help soon.

He didn't turn around but he rejoiced when he heard the voices of the children behind him released from the school. It reminded him of the pleasure he had felt himself when he was finally free of the camp and all it had meant. This he felt was something that had been re-enacted since the beginning of time; children freed from school and bursting into the fresh air like human bombs. He listened to their chatter and their arguments as they passed behind him in a body; he even smelled their incarceration from them as the gentle wind wafted the waves of their bodies to his nostrils. Then there was quiet again as their voices faded into the distance. He felt sad. They knew so little of what was happening and they didn't care. These things were for grown-up people, although he had seen little tattered boys chased by the police up back alleys for singing 'Kevin Barry'.

He listened closely now again. In the distance he could hear the water of the river thundering over the weir, a continuous unending rumble of sound, that had gone on since the river was created and would continue while it was there, and he reflected that it was almost as indifferent to the happenings of men as the little children.

Then he heard the door opening and closing and the sound of the light footsteps on the pavement, so he cautiously turned his head and saw Finola coming out and walking away, her head a little bent, a frown on her forehead and a bunch of copybooks under her arm. He said nothing, willing her to look in his direction, but why should she look at the figure of a young postman leaning on a wall, looking into a flowing stream?

He coughed, and after a second she turned her head towards him. All she saw was a young postman, fairly handsome, looking at her. She didn't even meet his eyes, but turned her head away again. She was used to drawing the glances of young men, but then something clicked in her head as she thought, and she turned and walked quickly across to him. 'I nearly passed you,' she said.

He turned from her and leaned on the wall. He was so pleased to see her. He was beginning to doubt if he would ever contact anybody he knew. Also the sight of her nearly drove the thought of Poric out of his mind, and he felt mean about this. 'What's wrong?' she asked him, leaning on the wall beside him.

'Poric is bad,' he said. 'Where can I find Sam?'

He heard her drawing in her breath.

'You can't find Sam,' she said. 'Sergeant Nick is on to him. Sam left the town two nights ago.'

214

Dominic groaned, lifting the postman's cap on his head. 'Without Sam we are lost,' he said.

'Where is Poric?' she asked.

He thought of this, of the old man driving his horse and cart to the back places of a long row of houses in the west part of the town, where a cousin of his had married a woman, and lived there until he was killed in the war. She was a widow with three children and she took lodgers. She made no fuss about taking a dying man into her house and putting him on a bed in a room behind the kitchen. Even if there were chalk marks on the doors and another raid due any night.

'He's in a house,' he said. 'But they might raid it again tonight. If he doesn't get a doctor soon he will die.' She saw sweat breaking out on his face. She put her hand on his arm.

'We'll do something,' she said.

'How about the Union hospital?' he asked. 'The doctors there?'

'They are watching that too closely now,' she said. 'They are even looking under the bandages. All the doctors I know had to leave town. The ones that are left dare not treat bullet wounds and not report them. Is Poric very bad?'

Dominic groaned. 'Poric might be dead by now,' he said.

'I will go out to him,' she said.

'You are not a surgeon,' he said. 'He needs a surgeon.'

'What will we do?' she asked.

Dominic leaned his head on his arms and thought. This is where a leader would say: Such a thing and such a thing.

'Can you get me a change of clothes?' he asked then. 'People are beginning to look oddly at me in this. They know their own postmen here and wonder at a strange face. If we do that, then you must come with me. We will have to take a big chance. It may not even work.'

'I'll do whatever you want me to do,' she said. 'I'm glad you came looking for me.'

'I thought you'd never come out the door,' he said.

'Follow me down to Lowry's place,' she said. 'It's the only house I can think of, even if it is dangerous. There are bound to be some clothes there with so many men coming and going.'

'Right,' he said. 'Fast, fast, or it might be too late.'

She looked at him, and then walked away. He allowed her a few minutes and then followed after her. He was becoming conscious of the uniform. This was a small town. Most people knew other people, and postmen were known to all of them, and despite what people said he had seen many eyes looking at his face although they weren't supposed to look at anything but a uniform.

Half an hour later, they walked down the street towards the canal bridge. He was walking arm in arm with her. He was wearing a raincoat and a cap pulled down a bit over his eyes, but as they came nearer to the bridge he saw that they were too late. There was a house near the bridge where they were stopping people and searching them.

He stopped. They stood there, a casual couple talking.

'They must have got a tip,' he said. 'If they are searching at this bridge, they will be at the others too. You go back. I have to go on. It is unlikely that there will be any of them here who know my face.'

'No,' she said, smiling for onlookers. 'I'm going with you.'

'You can't,' he said. 'You got me the clothes. Please go back. You would be no good to anybody in prison.'

'You have a poor opinion of me, Dominic,' she said.

'Oh, no,' said Dominic.

'Oh, yes,' she said. 'You don't know me at all. You say Finola thinks such a thing. Therefore because I think that she thinks this, it is right. The end.'

'This is not so,' said Dominic.

'It is,' she said. 'I resent it very much, if you must know. You don't know me at all, or what I am thinking. You are always telling me what to do on the assumption that you understand the intimate working of my mind. Well, you don't.'

'Don't let's have an argument in the middle of the street at a time like this,' he said.

'Why not?' she asked. 'As far as I am concerned your mind is full of cobwebs.'

'I never claimed to have a great brain,' he protested.

'You don't have to,' she said. 'It's obviously addled.'

216

What's happened to us now, he wondered?

'Listen,' he said. 'Every second counts, for Poric. Can't you please leave me, and we can have arguments again.'

'Is it because you have a gun in your pocket you are afraid for me?' she asked.

'How did you know that?' he asked.

'Please, Dominic,' she said disdainfully. She was really angry with him.

'After the camp,' he said, 'I decided I would never go back in again. That is why I have a gun and why I intend to use it if I am recognized. So, will you leave me alone?'

'And how are you going to be searched and they not to find the gun?' she asked.

'It is a small gun,' he said. 'I will hold it in my hand when I have to raise my arms to be searched. If they see it I will use it and run.'

She looked at him. She saw that he meant it. His jaw was hard and his eyebrows pulled down. She thought that Dominic looked old. His face was drawn. She remembered the boyish bewildered face of him that time near his father's grave. She reflected that he had changed a lot since that time. She thought it was sad that young boys had to become young men very fast; that they would never know what happened to the years they had lost.

'I'm going with you,' she said. 'And nothing can stop me. I know Poric too. I am fond of Poric. I want to help him. Will we stay arguing here now or will we go on?'

He glared at her. She thought he was going to say something biting, but he shut it off, buried his hands in his pockets and turned away. She had to run a few paces after him, and hold his rigid arm to her side until it became less rigid. Finally he had to look at her. She smiled at him and was immensely pleased to see his eyebrows raising themselves from his eyes.

'You are not at war with me,' she said.

'If you only knew,' said Dominic.

There was a jam of ass carts and horse carts and delivery carts at the bridge. They had to line up behind a block of indignant people and wait. He thought how lucky it was that

217

the cart of scallops had crossed the bridge before they started the searching. Most people were silent. It is not a pleasant thing to have your person violated by hands you hate. He stood on his toes to look at the faces of the police. He could not see a face he recognized and he hoped that none of them would recognize him.

They were ruffling shopping baskets and patting bodies under held-up arms. He noticed that they put their hands into some men's pockets. He felt the gun in his pocket and eased the butt of it into the sleeve of his coat, holding the barrel with the tips of his fingers. He was determined to use it. He knew this. He would then run across the wooden bridge and run right in the hope of getting up by the canal and into the maze of backyards up there.

They shuffled more closely to their examiner. He had a clipped black moustache and his face was completely indifferent. He wore a holstered gun strapped to his thigh and carried a carbine across his back. Dominic wondered again at the sweat of fear that came over him. He felt beads of it on his upper lip, but couldn't free a hand to wipe them off.

The man didn't leer as he patted the pockets of Finola's coat. He just glanced idly at her face before he turned his attention to Dominic. He didn't look at him either, which was fortunate, on account of the sweat. Dominic wondered what he was thinking as he went through this performance. Was he thinking of his dinner or his wife or of drink or his home somewhere in England? Whatever he was thinking didn't show. He was thorough with Dominic, putting his hands into the pockets of his raincoat, and patting his trousers pockets. The up-held hand with the gun in it was pointing towards the wall of a building. Anyone across the bridge looking in this direction could have seen it, but there was no one watching from there.

When the policeman made a gesture with his thumb, Dominic let the gun slip down fully into his sleeve, grasped the end of the sleeve and slowly lowered his arm. Finola caught his other arm, pressing it closely to her, and they walked slowly across the bridge.

He was waiting to hear a shout after them, but none came.

Slowly they walked the few yards separating them from the bridge and the turn of the street. When they reached it, he had to pause and draw air into his lungs. He found that his legs were shaking and he was glad of the support of Finola's arms.

They opened the wrought-iron gate and walked up to the door of the house.

It had seemed different the last time Dominic had been here, when they had raided the man for his beautiful shotguns, but he was the only person Dominic could think of.

'He is an Irishman,' Dominic said. 'I know he may call the police and hand us over, if we wait to be handed over. But we have to take a chance on him. There are only about one in a hundred people in the whole country engaged in this struggle. I have a feeling that there are not more, simply because nobody ever asked them. I am going to ask this man, because there is nothing else I can do. Dammit, men gamble on horses, so why shouldn't I gamble on a human being. I know one thing, most people are good.'

'They are not all like you,' she said.

'We have to do something,' he said, 'when Sam isn't around to guide us. You haven't seen Poric. I'm tortured by the thought of him.'

He didn't know if it was the same girl who opened the door. She looked at the young couple on the steps and smiled and made a gesture with her hand. They walked into the hall and into a room on the right. The blinds were half drawn. It was a shaded room, smelling faintly of disinfectant. The furniture was severe, polished table and leather-covered chairs, and it felt a room apart from a home, where nobody lived. There were no other patients. They sat on two chairs and looked at one another. Dominic's face was very determined, she saw. She thought that she was very fond of Dominic. She wondered if this was something to do with the animal nature of man. Is it possible to love a person with your body at the time that you are loving another person with your mind; a faraway cry in the spring evening, a laugh on the wind on an April morning?

Dominic's hand was clenched into a tight white-knuckled fist on his knee. She bent forward and placed her own hand over his fist, and it slowly relaxed into a hand again, and he smiled at her.

The doctor saw this when he came into the room and jumped to the wrong conclusions. He was well used to young couples coming to him, with their mixture of embarrassment and joy and diffidence.

'Ah,' he said rubbing his hands, 'and when do you expect the blessed event?'

It took a moment for his remark to percolate, and then he saw the face of the young man turning red, and the girl looking at this result, and laughing out loud at the look on the young man's face, a slightly familiar face the doctor thought, frowning in an effort to remember.

'No,' she said. 'We want to see you about something else.'

'Oh,' he said. 'What is it?'

'Do you love your country, Doctor?' the intense young man asked.

This intrigued the doctor. He sat down on another chair. He wasn't old, they saw, but his hair was white. He wore a neat dark suit and a high collar with a striped tie.

'What is my country?' he asked.

'If you don't know,' said Dominic, 'I can't tell you. I have a sick friend. I cannot take him to the hospital.'

'Why?' the doctor asked.

'He is wounded,' said Dominic.

'Oh,' said the doctor.

'If you gave us a note, maybe they would take him into the hospital,' said Dominic.

'Is he bad?' the doctor asked.

'He might be dead by now,' said Dominic.

'Where is he?' the doctor asked.

'He is about ten minutes away,' said Dominic.

'When was he, eh, taken ill?' he asked.

'This morning,' said Dominic.

'Oh,' said he. 'Where is he wounded?'

'In the chest,' said Dominic. 'He has been unconscious

220

since. If we can't get him seen to, he will die. We don't know where to turn.'

'What made you think of me?' the doctor asked.

'I thought of you,' said Dominic, 'because one night we came and took guns away from you.'

The doctor stood up abruptly.

'My Greener gun!' he said. 'You are the one. I was wondering why you looked familiar. By God, young man, you have the nerve of the devil.'

'No,' said Dominic. 'Only desperation.'

'I hate you,' said the doctor, 'for what you stand for, for what violence is doing to this country which you ask me if I love. I hate your politics, and the other side equally. I dislike violent men, and the results of their violence. I see no future in what you are doing. Does this answer your questions?'

'No,' said Dominic. 'My friend is sick. He may be dying.'

'Am I the reason for that?' the doctor asked angrily.

'Maybe you are,' said Dominic. 'If more men took sides there could be only one result to this struggle. If too many men remain on the stile it can go on forever.'

'It's not the duty of a doctor to take sides,' he said. 'It is the duty of a doctor to heal, not destroy. Would you shoot me if I sent word to the police? I suppose you would, eh?'

'No,' said Dominic. 'If you send word to the police it is I who would be shot for taking a gamble on you.'

'A man is dying and you sit there talking,' the doctor said. 'How will you get him here?'

Dominic was standing.

'Do you want some of your house painted?' he asked.

The doctor's jaw dropped.

'No,' he said, 'certainly not.'

'There is a man with a painter's handcart,' said Dominic. 'He and I could come to your back door with the handcart, buckets, ladders, canvas, paint, brushes, and we could come in the back way and paint some of the house for you.'

'Before curfew?' the doctor asked.

'We could just get here before curfew,' said Dominic.

'You better hurry,' the doctor said. 'Nobody has ever come near this house. There is a top room that is never used. Can your girl friend there do any nursing?'

'I can,' said Finola.

'Well, go,' he said. 'Hurry. A man is dying. But never again,' he shouted at them as he ushered them towards the back part of the house. 'You hear that? It's purely for humanity. It's nothing to do with filthy politics. You are all wrong. You'll blow up the world before you are finished. You'll blow up God Almighty.'

He banged the back door on them. The little maid was looking at him with her mouth open.

Dominic held Finola's hand hard as they ran up the back way towards the gate that led into the lane.

Dominic knelt on the floor with the Rosary beads in his hand. Poric was lying on the iron bedstead, covered by a white quilt. His face was bloodless. His big hands were lying across his stomach. It was strange to see them devoid of colour. You could hardly detect his breathing. The voice of the priest had just stopped intoning the prayers for the dying. He was an oldish man with long white hair and an ascetic face. Dominic looked over at him now. His eyes were closed. He was praying. Dominic was saying the Hail Marys of the Rosary and the words were meaningless. Poric had received Extreme Unction. The doctor had come two minutes ago and felt his pulse, looked Dominic straight in the eyes and shook his head. He had left again, closing the door of the attic softly after him.

He didn't want to look at Finola who was kneeling across the bed from him. Poric's head was framed by two brass candlesticks on tables each side. They could be waking him. There were hollows in his temples. The candles flickered now and again.

Dominic raised his head to the skylight. He could see a small rectangle of stars.

Everything is essentially people, he thought. Generals thought of divisions, colonels thought of battalions, captains thought of companies, but all these consisted of men, individual men made up of souls and bodies, who were completely important to themselves.

This wasn't a war in the proper sense. It was an uprising in which a few determined men gathered together a few thousand other men and awoke them to the idea of liberty, and then with inadequate arms went out to fight a superbly-equipped Empire from ditches and stone walls, in city streets and back alleys. The casualties would not be great, but in their own small way they would be momentous. In this, because they were so few, men were important, each one of them a great loss.

He remembered Poric since they were boys together, riding donkeys on the strand, fishing for pollack from the rocks, learning awkwardly to dance sixteen-hand reels in the schoolhouse; listening to story tellers at the hoolies, watching the Aran men dancing jigs and reels in their pampooties, the early giggling and courting of girls at the gable-ends, while the girls still wore pinafores and admired their bare feet. His whole life had been bound up with Poric.

Poric wanted nothing from life except to be a policeman. It seemed an awful simple ambition, and look where it had led him – to death in the attic of the house of a courageous doctor, who abominated his reason for dying.

Dominic had never admitted, not even to himself, that Poric was going to die. He wouldn't admit it now. He thought only of the time when Poric would be well. The others knew he was wounded and that he must be in the town. A fly could hardly get in or out of it now. He had listened from the landing as Sergeant Nick had questioned the doctor. They hadn't searched the house, since the doctor had the reputation of being on the right side. He had given an exact description of Poric and his record of being a renegade policeman.

From then Dominic thought only of getting Poric away when he was no longer in danger of dying. He had travelled the Claddagh quays at the night time, searching for a fisherman who would use his pucaun to get Poric over to Clare or back to the coast where some of his own people might be able to hide him.

Years afterwards men and women would be reminded of these times by the sound of a revving Crossley tender, or a heavy knock on their doors in the night time, or the sound of an English accent. Dominic would always remember it, if he survived, by the sound of army boots on pavements. They seemed to him to have a peculiarly deadly and foreboding sound. But down in the Claddagh they were more sinister, because for the first time down there he noticed that the black fellows were wearing rubber soles. He was two hours playing tigg with them, as they searched silently; once hanging over the quay holding to a rope that tied a boat, another time hiding in the third boat out, while they searched the other two. One time he had escaped without fighting, only because he had felt the hand of a woman on his wrist, saying 'Shush! Shush,' almost startling the life out of him, but he followed her in the pitch darkness and she guided him into the village of thatched cottages, over the stones of the yards, into a candle-lighted house where he saw that she was blind.

'But it's different now, Poric,' he said, out loud. 'Sam is working on it. I saw Sam. Sam's plan will be foolproof, you'll see, Poric. He'll get us out of here as easy as a poc fada.'

Startled, Finola looked up at him. She felt a great pity for Dominic. She thought that his loyalty to Poric was almost frightening. You cannot will a person back from death, she wanted to tell him. You cannot do this. She thought that when Dominic loved a person, then Dominic loved that person forever, without change. It could prove to be very hard on him, all his life; it could plague him.

Dominic had spoken in Irish.

Poric answered in Irish.

'What did you say about Sam, Dominic?' he asked.

Dominic had been addressing the stars in the skylight. Now he looked, thinking his hearing might not have been right. Poric was looking at him. Poric's eyes were open. Finola saw that Dominic reacted to this just as if he had been expecting it all along. He put out his hand and caught the pale hand of his friend and pressed it.

'He has a beautiful idea, Poric,' he said, 'for getting us out of town. It would take him to think of it. Wait'll you see!'

'Sam is a great trickster,' said Poric. 'Where are we now, Dominic? What am I doing here? Was that Finola that went out the door?'

For she had risen and gone down the stairs for the doctor.

The priest had risen too and come to the side of the bed. He put out his thin hand and rested it on Poric's forehead.

'We are pleased to see you awake, Poric,' the priest said.

'My thanks to you, Father,' said Poric. 'I was bad then with yourself here?'

'You weren't too strong,' said the priest.

'I don't feel strong now,' said Poric. 'Do you think I am going to die?'

'You are not,' said Dominic, almost shouting.

The doctor came in then with unbelief in his eyes. He went over to the bed as the priest made way for him, and took Poric's wrist into his hand. They all waited while he did this. There was fear in Poric's face. Fear, Finola thought, which means that he is thinking and feeling, or how could he feel fear?

The doctor left his hand free then.

'I don't understand it,' he said. 'But he's not out of the wood yet, you know.'

'You saved his life, Doctor,' said Dominic. 'I knew you would.'

'Do you think so?' the doctor asked. 'He's not saved yet. He shouldn't be improved at all. If it continues, I don't think I can quite claim to be the one that saved his life.'

'What happened to me?' Poric asked. 'Tell me what happened to me.'

'I'll tell you, Poric,' he said, sitting on the bed, his face shining. 'I feel as tall as the stars.'

23

YOU HAD to have a permit to drive a car or own one. The doctor of course had a permit. So Poric was lying on the car floor in the back and Dominic was crouching over him as they went through the town. It was Saturday, and the carts with their potatoes and vegetables and bonhams and eggs and prints of butter were heading into the market-place. The country people were talking loudly in Irish and Dominic thought he could even recognize some of the voices. He wanted to pop his head through one of the side screens and address them by name.

They weren't searching the carts much at the bridges going into the town since they were more interested in what they might contain going out. He knew that the doctor's car wasn't held up at all because they knew him and his profession.

'Isn't it lovely to hear the Irish?' Poric whispered as they passed over the wooden bridge into the comparative safety of the street. Dominic nodded at him. Poric looked like somebody who had been pulled through the barrel of a gun. His face was pale and there were purple circles around his eyes, and his neck was thin for his collar. But he was alive and that was the main thing and he would continue to be alive. He had a wonderful strong frame and he would soon fill it up again.

Their progress through the crowded streets was slow, he thought. The doctor blew his horn a lot and muttered to himself. They hadn't wanted him to do this at all. They would have found another way. But he insisted on it. The sad thing was that it was not nationalism that was making him do this thing, but a feeling of humanity. Where did one begin and the other end? He had attended Poric as if he was getting a hundred guineas for the job, sheltered and fed them, risking his life, or at least persecution, all, as he insisted, for the purposes of humanity, since this was his job and his profession. And getting Poric away from the town he regarded as part of all that.

226

Dominic traced their passage up the two long streets and their turning left towards the other market-place near the river quays. Here there was a further confusion of carts and cries and the doctor must have nearly paralysed his hand pressing the rubber bulb of the horn. After some time the car came to a stop. The doctor was looking around him.

'The timing was good,' he said then. 'The quays are clear.'

'Will we get out so?' Dominic asked.

'I see no danger,' said the doctor, leaning back and opening the door of the car. Dominic backed out and stood and looked. The quays were clear of boats. He could see the tops of some white sails way up the bend of the river. Then he looked to his right. The slender mast of the yacht was to be seen over the wall. Then a face came up from there and looked angrily at him. The man was wearing an old yachting cap; steel-framed spectacles. He had a very thin face and a mouth like a rat-trap.

'Ye are late,' he called. 'Am I to be arsing around here all day?'

'Come on, Poric,' said Dominic. He stood watching him getting out of his awkward position on the floor. He didn't help him. Poric managed by pulling himself along with his hands and letting himself sit on the dust of the roadway and then using the open door of the car to help himself to his feet. 'Good man,' said Dominic. 'Don't do too much too fast,' said the doctor. 'Hurry up!' said the face over the wall. Poric made his way towards the face, slowly and haltingly.

Dominic stood beside the car.

'We cannot repay you,' he said. 'There is only one thing I can think of. I don't know where it is now, or where it will be in the future, but when all this is over, I will get you back your Greener gun.'

The tired face of the doctor suddenly brightened. 'Do that,' he said. 'A good gun is like a good suit. It fits you everywhere. It was my size, this gun. I could get a left and a right with snipe. For yourself, go home to your mother and settle down to your medicine and leave all this work to the gunmen. Life is short.'

Before Dominic could say any more he put in the pedal and made a most dangerous turn on the quay, a full turn that nearly brought himself and his car to a watery grave, and then he was gone and Dominic felt that he hadn't thanked him enough.

'Well?' the voice said behind him. Sam should have told him that this Matt fellow was as crusty as a sick sow.

He went to the quayside and down the abrupt steps where the slender yacht was resting. Poric was lying down on the floor of the yacht, his head and shoulders pushed into the locker in front and his big legs stretched one each side of the centreboard. 'Are you all right, Poric?' Dominic asked. Poric nodded. He couldn't talk, Dominic saw, he was breathing so fast from his efforts.

'Do you know anything about sailing?' Matt asked. He was on the quayside coiling the rope that had tied them to the bollard.

'No,' said Dominic, cheerfully, 'not a cursed thing.'

'Am I a genius?' Matt asked, coming into the boat, 'and is Sam a son of a bitch? Put on that jersey and the cap, and look like something that knows something about boats. Keep out of my way.' He was pulling on a rope and the white sail rose and caught the south-east wind, all this while Dominic was pulling on a blue jersey. Dominic, trying to keep his feet, thought it was all done very smoothly. The sail was tied off, he was at the rudder, holding the guiding rope of the boom, and the small boat hissing its way in a wide circle with the railway bridge looming over their heads, dodging, it seemed to Dominic by a miracle, the massive stone pillar holding the bridge and heading up river, all in a breathtakingly short time.

'I am not a genius,' said Matt. 'And Sam is a son of a bitch. I always knew it, but now I really know it. Sit on the gunwale and hook your feet under the rope loops, and lean back to balance her.' Dominic did these things as if he had been doing them all his life. 'I'm the best sailing man, possibly, in the British Isles. All these amateur yachtsmen up there today haven't a chance with me, if I get a fair wind and an opportunity. There are navy men up there too. Did you know that?'

'No,' said Dominic breathlessly, his head and shoulders out over the water, suddenly realizing it was a beautiful day, that the sky was blue, the May sun was warm, the breeze was fresh, and he was in the open air for almost the first time in many weeks. He breathed it into his lungs.

'There's a warship in the bay,' said Matt. 'So there's a couple of naval people racing. In given circumstances I could sail the blue breeches off them. You understand that?'

'Perfectly,' said Dominic, who didn't give a damn.

'If I had an assistant who understood even the rudiments of sailing, and wasn't carrying about two ton of man in the boat – what weight is that fellow lying down?'

'He doesn't weigh two feathers now,' said Dominic, 'to what he used to weigh. So you are lucky. You might as well have a chicken in the boat.'

'Don't tell me that,' said Matt. 'I saw the size of him. I'd be as well off with two bullocks aboard. That fellow must weigh as much as a cock of hay.'

Dominic heard Poric laughing and he was pleased.

'If you agree to do a thing,' he said, 'do it with a good heart, you sad bastard.'

'It was blackmail,' said Matt. 'If I had any power in this town, I'd have that Sam fellow locked up. On my solemn oath I would.'

'No such thing as having a soft heart, or being an Irishman, or trying to help your neighbour?' asked Dominic.

'Horse manure,' said Matt eloquently, clearing his mouth and spitting into the water. 'I suppose all you fellows think you are heroes. Ye are off cavorting in the hills courting the lassies, no doubt, and eating cabbage and bacon, while the rest of us have to carry on at our jobs. I like winning races. Do you understand that?'

'No,' said Dominic. 'Why?'

They had to tack as they turned a bend.

'Shift!' Matt shouted. Dominic ducked in time as he pulled in or he would have been decapitated by the boom, which swung across. He got to the other side and wiped his forehead.

'The next time you do that, would you give us a word of warning?' he asked.

Matt chuckled. 'Good training for you,' he said. 'You scuttled like a rabbit that time. You would make a fairly decent yachtsman if I had time to train you. We are late. These gentry up there won't wait for Matt. They don't want Matt, because Matt can sail them into the water. So if I am a minute late they cross me out. You understand this. Hold this tiller and rope. I want to put up the foresail. Quick, now, we haven't all day, and watch where you are guiding her. Keep in the middle of the river.'

It was his precise orders that Dominic wondered at. He was back holding the tiller with one arm and the sail rope wound around his other arm, while the thin figure of Matt was scrambling up to the poop. He stood on top of this and fixed the small white sail. Before he came back Dominic enjoyed the smooth power of the little boat. It gave one great pleasure to feel her under one's hands. Then Matt came back and again he tacked and turned up the Cut towards the wide open spaces of the lower lake. They went up here fast, as they had all the force of the wind in their sails.

'When we get to the mouth,' said Matt, 'keep your head turned from the boats where their lordships will be, quaffing rum and smoking cigars. They know I always have another one with me. You don't look unlike him from the back but don't let them see your face. My assistant is a handsome fellow and we don't want to shock them.'

Dominic laughed.

'Your mother might disagree with me,' said Matt, 'but she'd be the only one. They won't inspect the boat, but if the pinnace is coming over to us throw those bits of canvas over your man's legs.'

It was a lovely feeling speeding past the rustling rushes of the banks. The smell of the air was so clean, laden with the scent of the rushes and the wild thyme and the mint on the shores. Even the birds didn't seem too disturbed at their passing. The bog larks were high in the air and singing. Dominic suddenly realized how little he had seen the daylight and the

good things since the time they were on the island so ineffec-
tually guarding the Tangler.

'Here they come now,' said Matt. 'Loosen that rope and
let down the sail to take the wind out of her.'

Dominic did this correctly. He had noted the right one in
the seeming confusion of all the other ropes. He looked for
praise to Matt, but he didn't get any.

'Turn your back on them,' said Matt.

Before he turned, Dominic could see a big white motor
boat anchored at the mouth of the Cut. There were many men
and ladies sitting on the deck of this. The clothes of the ladies
were colourful in the sunshine. This fat fellow shouting
through a megaphone. There were many small boats and
bigger motor boats anchored and tossing gently in the waves.
Out on the wide section of the lake, the blue water was
decorated with the white yachts making towards the right hand
shore.

'You're late, Matt?' the megaphone man shouted. 'We will
have to disqualify you, old chap.'

'Look at that!' Matt shouted, pulling a large turnip watch
from under his jersey and flourishing it. 'Three minutes before time. You want to get yourself a timekeeper. Are you
afraid of Matt or what?'

Dominic heard laughter from the boat.

'All right,' he heard the magnified voice, 'Go on the gun.
You have lost time.'

'Sail up,' said Matt, and Dominic raised it, having antici-
pated this call, but now, grinning, he knew he would get no
praise. He had been under a little tension for a while. He had
seen soldiers' uniforms and police uniforms on the boat as well
as the others.

'You know what I have to do?' Matt asked.

'What?' Dominic asked.

'I have to lose a race deliberately,' said Matt. 'Can you
have any notion what this means to me?'

'Maybe,' said Dominic.

'You never could,' said Matt. 'It's a matter of time, and I
can't make the time because I am carrying extra weight. I

231

will have to account for this. So I have now to do something I never did in my life before. I have to sail badly. You see those islands way over on the left?'

'Yes,' said Dominic.

'We have to get in there,' said Matt. 'The fellows, the stewards, have a boat, a motor boat, and when they see me sailing badly they will chase us up to see what is wrong. If they catch us, you know your goose is cooked. There's nowhere to go out here. But that is not the thing that worries me; it's the bad sailing I have to do.'

Dominic didn't understand him, but he looked around him and he spotted the motor boat, doing wide circles in the middle of the lake, white water at its bow all the time as it moved in the inner ring of the sailing yachts that were stretched now over this wide area.

The boat which had been sailing so sweetly suddenly started to sail badly.

Dominic didn't know how Matt was doing this, but it was no longer smooth and easy. Its action became broken. The mainsail was inclined to flap, and then belly again. He heard Matt groaning. Then he gave her her head again and she sped along as if making up for the loss. The nearest yacht ahead of them was about half a mile away and it seemed to Dominic that they were hauling up on her when the speed of the yacht became erratic again.

'Great God!' Matt shouted. 'I would prefer to hit my own mother, God rest her, than to be doing this. You see the burden of guilt you have put on me? You see now why I hate Sam?'

'To hell with Sam,' said Dominic. 'I think the motor boat is getting curious.'

'We'll give her another good sail, so,' said Matt. 'We'll have to keep them off until we tack over near the islands. There are shallows there. When I shout, lift the centreboard.'

'What's that?' Dominic asked.

Matt swore. He even took off his cap to do this and addressed the sky.

'Between your man's legs,' he said, 'you'll see an iron

232

handle. Just pull on it until it comes up full and then lock it into place. If I had to do these awful things, why didn't I get somebody with brains.'

'Oh, I see it now,' said Dominic, bending over.

'Great! Wonderful! You should be a Professor of Mathematics,' said Matt. 'Are they still coming up after us?'

Dominic looked. 'No,' he said. 'They are sheering off again.'

'With the centreboard up they won't be able to follow us in the shallow places,' said Matt. 'But it must look like an accident. We'll have to time it very closely.'

He staggered the yacht forward for another mile. Dominic could see the yellow marker where they would have to turn. The motor boat was watching them. When they staggered it turned its nose towards them. Dominic could see the sun glinting off binoculars. As soon as they went smoothly again the boat turned its bow from them.

'Once we get to the marker,' said Matt. 'It will have to be a straight race between them and us, and I don't know who is going to win it. You understand this. I am not trying to betray you.'

'Just tell me what to do,' said Dominic, wondering what poor Poric was thinking of all this, sorry that he could not at least see the sky and have his face in the fresh air.

'Now!' Matt shouted, as they closed on the marker and tacked. Dominic was prepared this time and the action was very smooth. 'Keep your eye on that cursed motor boat. In five minutes I'm going off course, so you can start praying then.'

Dominic kept watching the steward's boat. It was obviously watching them. He could hear them saying: What the hell is happening to old Matt. I never saw him sailing like that before. In five minutes Matt turned right off course and he saw the boat waiting, pausing, and then heading for them in a surge of white water.

'Here they come now, Matt,' said Dominic, leaning out over the water as the wind filled the sails.

'Right,' said Matt. 'This is going to be the worst fifteen

minutes of your life, my boy. That'll teach you to come sailing with a man that has to betray his lovely boat and his dead generations of sailing people, and all the people who have confidence in him and have even put down money that he can win this cup. And I won't win it. How am I to explain? What do I say to my friends? Won't they fry me for the rest of my life over this despicable action. Why did I ever hear of that Sam? Wherever he is at this moment I hope he is suffering. I hope they hang him.'

Dominic kept one eye on the motor boat and the other eye on the islands ahead of them. He had his hand on the handle of the centreboard, and as the boat closed on them his heart seemed to him to be beating faster and faster.

It seemed a whole lifetime to him until he heard Matt shout: 'Now!' and he pulled and it seemed to him that the boat was running on rocks. They were everywhere about them, pockmarked yellow rocks lurking evilly under the water. Now he didn't know what to fear; the motor boat or the rocks.

They heard calling behind them. Then they had passed the tree-clad island and were racing towards another one. The whole place was a mass of shallows, but Matt weaved through them like a fish. They came up on another island and rounded it and the sail started flapping. Matt shouted 'Tack!' and they tacked. In another few minutes he shouted 'Lower the sail!' and Dominic lowered the sail, and they were then in deep water again and heading unerringly for a small cove, a sandy one, with heaped rocks on either side making a small pier. The yacht grounded and turned on its side.

'Out!' Matt shouted and Dominic bent for Poric.

'Are you all right, Poric?' he asked.

Poric was too busy painfully trying to get to his feet to answer him. This time Dominic had to help him out of the boat, and at the same time several men with rifles came running out of the bushes. Dominic could hardly believe his eyes when he saw one of them was Dualta.

'You made it! You made it!' he shouted, throwing his arms around Dominic, hurting his back with the gun. 'Poric!' he said then. 'Poric,' squeezing his hands.

Matt shouting: 'Get off the bloody jersey. Give it to me, man.' A small fellow facing Dominic, taking off his jacket as Dominic peeled the jersey over his head.

'I came by bicycle,' the little fellow was saying. 'I'd prefer the yacht. Me backside is sore.'

'You fellows,' Matt was shouting. 'Help with the rope. Get some rocks. I'll cut it and you fray the ends as if it had broken.' Two of the men with Dualta proceeded to do this.

'It's great to see you,' Dualta kept saying. 'We didn't know if you could make it.'

'Why are you here?' Dominic asked him.

'They sent Sergeant Nick to Dublin in plain clothes to see if he could recognize faces. He recognized me. He was too well guarded. We couldn't get at him. So I decided to take a holiday. You know Morgan? We are going back to Morgan for a while. Have a rest in the country. Eh, Poric? Feed you up.'

'Right, that's enough!' Matt shouted. 'Let ye get out of here. These fellows will land and come across by the shore.'

'Goodbye, Matt,' said Dominic. 'I'm sorry you had to lose. On my oath I am. You know that.'

'Maybe I didn't lose,' said Matt sourly. 'Maybe I won something. Go away. If they see your ugly face, we are lost.' Then he cupped his hands around his mouth and started shouting: 'Ahoy! Help! I broke my rope. Come to me! I broke me rope!'

And the rest of them went into the hazel bushes, Poric's arms resting on the shoulders of Dualta and Dominic.

'You see the blue mountains,' said Dualta. 'That's where we are going; back to the blue mountains for our holidays.'

They laughed with him, but suspected that they would get more than holidays.

24

IT TOOK them three days to get into the valley.
Their final journey was made in a turf boat. It was a pucaun, and it looked incongruous on the sparkling waters of the great lake. They were more used to pucauns sailing on the sea. The man who sailed the boat was called Bigmouth, presumably because he rarely opened it except to take a clay pipe from his mouth and spit. He was a slow careful man with everything he did; listened to their conversations with folded arms, and then would grunt or spit in acknowledgement.

'Anyhow,' Dualta said, 'it's unlikely that the police will get any information out of him afterwards since even we can't knock a word out of him.'

They laughed at this.

They were not inclined to talk.

The boat was empty on their journey. He was travelling by way of the lake up almost into the valley ahead of them, where he would fill her with turf which he was bringing back to the other side for sale. Poric lay on the ballast in the bottom stretched full length, soaking up the sun. Because it was a period of bright sunny weather. Dualta remarked on this that it was bad ambush weather, because the prolonged dry spell was making ground hard where it had never been hard and it would allow the searching soldiers to take vehicles on to ground which had been forbidden to them before.

The breeze was good but not fresh. It bellied the tarred sail. The boat was black and broad-bosomed, a good solid boat that went its way like a work-horse, uncomplaining, except now and again for the creaking of the big mast and the slight groaning of the blocks.

They were coming into the part where the mountains were rearing all around them. The lower parts were tilled and the green grass was turning into the hay of June. The potato stalks were young and green and the shooting oats just a whisper behind the stone walls. They felt safe.

'Isn't it strange the safe feeling that mountains give you?' Dualta asked as they passed one on their left that reared itself to the sky.

Dominic had been thinking this same thing, oddly enough.

'They have been here as long as the world,' he said. 'I am terrified in the towns.'

'Towns have great bolt-holes,' said Dualta.

'So have rats,' said Dominic.

Dualta laughed.

'This was a great thing I found in Dublin,' he said. 'If you were stuck you could knock on any door at all.'

'They would need an army to search one of those mountains,' said Dominic. 'They have a million folds in them to shelter you. I have a very odd feeling about all this. I have the feeling that I have been here before.'

'You say that?' said Dualta, surprised. 'It's something that has been at the back of my own mind, a sort of a tingle of familiarity.'

'Strange,' said Dominic, 'since I haven't been here before.'

'Our people came from around here,' said Dualta. 'Maybe that's the reason.'

Slowly the boat turned right, having to tack. This was done slowly and ponderously, and Dominic had to smile, thinking of the tacking of Matt and his little yacht.

On their right a ruined castle loomed up. It was built on an island out from the mainland.

'You know,' said Dualta, 'that the Elizabethans fought against us here, and later the Cromwellians. It's not easy to think of them in these green valleys.'

'Why is it not easy?' Dominic asked. 'Nothing has changed but the clothes and the weapons.'

'Have you any romance in you?' asked Dualta lazily.

'Too much,' said Dominic, 'but it is pounded out of me now.'

The sun was warm on their faces. He noted with pleasure that Poric was getting colour in his face and that his big hands which he held across his belly were reddened a little too.

Bigmouth grunted a signal to them and they came to their feet. On their left a sort of pier had been built out into the water on wooden piles where the lake narrowed into a river bounded by acres of rushes. Bigmouth lowered the sail and the boat glided smoothly into the pier and they stopped her by holding on to the baulks of rough timber. She was soon tied up.

Bigmouth then took Dualta's arm and pointed the way he wanted him to go. 'Cross a road,' he said, 'then deep into the valley to the end of the river. Cross there and go north. Another road. Cross this when you see the cut in the hills. In there.'

It all seemed most unclear to Dominic, but Dualta shouldered his rifle and said: 'Thanks. We are grateful to you. Is there anything we can do for you?'

Bigmouth looked at him, lifted his cap, put it back again, took out his pipe and spat on the shore.

'Thanks anyhow,' said Dualta and set off.

Dominic waited to see how Poric was managing. He seemed to be doing better. A narrow track led up from the boat to a low hill and when they topped that they could see the valley opening out before them; a sort of green and brown gigantic maw.

Dualta waited for them.

'Did you know Bigmouth spoke more than four words?' he asked. 'It must be a good omen, like when the oracle at Delphi spoke.' He laughed. 'It's a long walk ahead of us. Are you fit, Poric?'

They watched Poric as he considered. He smiled, showing his big teeth.

'If ye can do it,' he said. 'I can do it.'

'Right,' said Dualta, and set off across the bogs. Dominic let Poric travel first and followed after him.

It was too fine a day to think of death or destruction, although they knew that houses in the pockets of these mountains had been burned and blood had been spilt in the valley.

238

The ground had hardened under their feet from the dry spell. Normally they would have had to choose their steps with care, but now they could walk confidently. It was hard to think of things like that as the valley smiled now in the sun, with the whitewashed cottages on the hills and the many sheep grazing the steep mountains looking in the distance like so many balls of wool. There was just the one main road coming in from the left in a cleft in the hills, and then over a bridge where the river flowed into the lake, and parting there to swing right around the lake and left down into the valley. They paused before they put a foot on the first road. It was easy to see that it was empty, so they went straight down into the valley. They avoided groups of houses, or even single houses, although they were aware that eyes were watching them, and their movements would be as well known and discussed as if they were described in *Old Moore's Almanack*.

It was a three-hour walk under the hot sun. They had to loosen their collars. They stopped ten minutes in every hour and sat down and smoked cigarettes. Poric was sticking it well. He had to halt now and again on account of his breathing being short, but the other two knew instinctively that they couldn't offer assistance. This was Poric's battle with his own body.

They went far down into the valley before they came to where one river ended and, farther ahead, another one began, to run down into the sea on the other side.

They rested here and drank water and shared the bread and butter and cold bacon that Dominic was carrying. It tasted very good. They were in a secluded hollow, where the river had piled up yellow gravel. They could have been alone in the world except for the curious cattle who put their heads over the green bank to look down at them.

They made a more cautious approach to the road that went down the valley to the sea. Several times as they approached it they went to ground as the sound of a motor vehicle came to their ears. Only one was dangerous, they saw, a police tender with six men in it that went up the road towards the lake when the sun was getting low.

They crossed the road in a rush and ran for the cleft in the hills on the other side. They rested when they had got out of sight from the road here. The road was very bad. It was littered with rocks and even big boulders that the floods had brought down, so it was unlikely that any motor could even dare to travel on it.

They relaxed their caution and that was their undoing.

Suddenly, two armed men, as if they had been born from the ground, confronted them with their legs spread and guns in their hands.

Dualta cursed and swung up the rifle.

'No, no, Dualta,' one of the men said. 'You're dead.'

'My God, Morgan,' said Dualta, 'you frightened the bloody life out of me.'

'You have gone soft, Dualta,' said Morgan, coming over to them. 'The city has dulled your reflexes.'

He wasn't a demonstrative man, as Dominic knew, but Morgan squeezed their hands and pounded their backs. All the time Dominic was looking at the other man with a puzzled frown.

'It's you!' he shouted then. 'It's Joe Two!'

Joe Two was grinning at him.

'I wondered how long it would take you,' he said, coming forward and shaking hands. He was wearing brown leggings and riding breeches and a trench coat, with a bandoleer of bullets around his chest.

'How did you get away?' Dominic asked.

'I talked so much they had to let me go,' he said. 'If they knew I had anything to do with Morgan I wouldn't be here. Ah, no, it's poor Fourcoats I'm sorry for. It was the worst day of his life to find himself dressed in respectable clothes, your suit.'

They laughed.

'I'm so pleased to see you,' said Dominic. 'I didn't know you were part of Morgan's lot.'

'Poric,' Morgan said. 'How are you? We are pleased to see you. It was bad luck what happened to you.'

'No,' said Poric, 'it wasn't bad luck, but good luck in a way.

240

You find out things about people maybe you would never know.'

'True,' said Morgan. 'We better get on. I don't know how you timed it, Dualta, but you might be in good time for a good scrap.'

'Why did you think I brought a rifle?' Dualta asked.

'Let us go, in the name of God,' said Morgan. 'We must try to get to the place before dark. It's good to see ye, even if ye are Connemara men.'

Morgan went ahead with Dualta. They had plenty to talk about, Dominic surmised, about the politics of the fight and the way things were going.

'Tell me more about the camp, and Fourcoats, Joe Two,' he said. 'It's like meeting an old chum who shared the same school.'

'Oh, that Fourcoats,' said Joe, and kept them entertained for some time, so that the brutal climbing seemed less hard than it was in the twilight.

By nightfall they found themselves billeted in this village in a small sheltered valley in the mountains. There were about ten houses in the valley and they were roughly two men to a house, although since one house contained a young woman who was pregnant all refused to be billeted on her because the people insisted that the men they were sheltering should occupy their own beds while they sat up by the fire. It was only for one night, they said. The men needed sleep more than they did, they insisted. They would have the rest of their lives for sleeping. They had killed a couple of sheep and boiled the flesh in great three-legged pots, with stones of potatoes and hot sweet tea.

Later, while Morgan and Dualta and the company captain talked politics, the rest of them gathered in a carthouse belonging to one of the houses. They had seen Poric in bed. He had embraced the feather mattress of this bed with profound relief, Dominic saw.

Here Dominic got to know some of the men of the column as they sat around on hay in the fitful gleam of a storm lantern that hung from a cross-beam.

They were loading cartridges with buckshot, or else carefully

241

taking a cartridge of plain shot and cutting it around about the charge and just below the wad. In this way the half cartridge would leave the barrel of the gun in a compact charge like a bullet and was good for almost fifty to a hundred yards range. For the rest they had about fourteen rifles of the Lee-Enfield type, a few Martini rifles that had to be loaded bullet by bullet at the breech, shotguns, some revolvers and a few grenades.

They were hopeful of an engagement the next day. Morgan's plan was simple. Several of the men had left the hills and gone down by dark to the road below. Here they would blow a bridge and come away. It was the custom of the police in these cases to drive out in strength from the market town near the sea, collect as many local people as they could, and make them rebuild bridges or fill in trenches or cut away trees that had been blocking the road.

Morgan's information was good, he told them. He thought this time, knowing his enemy, that they would come out. When they had passed, he would swoop from the hills and be waiting for them as they came back.

The men hoped this would happen.

They had been in engagements that were not successful. They had lost many men. They were bitter about the forces in the town, who had maltreated the bodies of the dead in the last engagement.

Dominic examined their faces in the light of the lantern. They were mostly in their early twenties. Some of them were townsmen and some of them farmers' sons. In the main they were big men, or if they were not big they were strong. Several of them had fought through the Great War with the British Forces. Most of them had been on the run for a year now, and they had become hardened to the existence. They explained that they were not like the flying columns of the South, with different men coming together, training, striking and leaving to make way for new men to be trained. Force of circumstances had made them into a permanent column, using the hills as home. Dominic thought their constant hardships had made them into a formidable force.

'Hardship my eye,' one said. There was a bottle passing the rounds very carefully. It wasn't a big bottle, but it held the innocent watery-looking potheen. 'For God's sake don't let Morgan see it or we'll all be kilt.' The bottle passed the rounds, each man wiping the neck with his palm before passing it on. There was only a mouthful for each, keeping a sup for the three sentries who were out. Morgan was a cautious man, they told him. You were liable to be shot personally by him if you snoozed on the sentry duty. Yet he felt they were fond of him.

'If we win this war and get rid of the bastards for good, you know who is the real hero?' a man asked. He was the eldest of them. He had a broad lined face, with humorous eyes, and a slight American accent. By some chance he had fought with the American Army, missing most of the fun, he said dryly, before coming home and being caught up in this one. 'You tell us,' he was urged.

'The ordinary people,' he said. 'Gentlemen, you are passing through the greatest period of our history and you don't stop to think about it. How many in the whole of the country are at this moment in the same position as we are?'

'Not enough,' said some voice bitterly.

'Say three thousand. Since one Irishman can bate ten Englishmen, that's about the odds.' They laughed. 'Well, three thousand men take a lot of feeding, and a lot of sheltering, judging by the way you fellows can scoff food. Look what happened to two living sheep. There they were this morning and now there's not a trace of them except the fleece.'

'Make your point,' he was told.

'There is hardly a house in the country where you can't knock on the door and ask for food and shelter, even though they know the terrible consequences, and many have paid them. This is the greatest period in history because the people are great. Right? If it wasn't for them, where would we be? We'd be like hares on the hills, eating heather.'

'Do hares eat heather?' someone asked.

'Well, you know what I mean,' said the man.

'I heard from a fellow,' said Joe Two, 'where they sought

shelter from an unmarried woman. She was very prissy about her house. You could eat off the floor. They were very dirty and very wet, but she took them in with joy, and she didn't even wince when she saw their dirty boots, or their sweaty bodies lying on her beds. All flounces and furbelows, you understand. She gave them all the food she had and sent them to their beds. They had to leave all their equipment in the kitchen. She was going to clean it and dry it at the fire. Well, she did this. She didn't go to sleep at all. When they came down in the morning, their boots were shining, their trench coats dried, their leggings polished, their rifles hanging in a neat row by the fireplace, and something else that nearly petrified them with fear.'

'Well, what was that?' Dominic asked obligingly.

'She had a clothes line stretched across the kitchen, and hanging up there caught with clothes pegs were six hand grenades, hanging by the rings.'

Somebody sensitive drew breath in through his teeth.

'He said you should have seen them getting her gently out of the house, and then approaching this line on their feet, softly, softly, and reaching up gently, gently, and releasing the grenades from the clothes pegs. He said he looked in a mirror afterwards and that his hair had turned white in five minutes.'

They laughed at Joe Two's careful exaggeration.

'They are great people all right,' some man said. 'They were never as good, but are we as good as all the fighting generations that have gone before us?'

They thought over this.

'That's a question,' said Joe, 'that our children will have to answer.'

'Well, you'd better hurry up and make some children,' said a voice, 'or we'll never know.'

They laughed at this, Joe Two as heartily as any of them.

It was very odd, Dominic thought, sitting like this in a carthouse, on the eve of a battle. It was a calm night. There was no moon, but the stars were bright and unclouded. You could hear a dog barking now and again.

Then Morgan stood outside.

'Ye should be in bed,' he said. 'This is not the time to be wide awake. Tomorrow is the time to be wide awake. Right?'

They started to get to their feet, then from way below on their left they heard the distinct sound of a muffled explosion. It seemed to hang on the air for a moment and then travel from hill top to hill top.

'That's that,' said Morgan. 'Now it is up to us to take care of the rest.' They filed past him and went two by two to their welcoming billets.

25

DOMINIC FELT somebody shaking his shoulder. He awoke and saw Joe Two smiling at him. 'You must have an easy conscience,' he said in a whisper. 'It's time to get up.'

Dominic swung his legs out of the big bed. Three of them had been sleeping in it with most of their clothes on in case of an alarm during the night. It was barely dawn, he saw. There was white mist pressing against the small window panes.

He looked at Poric. His eyes were open. 'There is no need to go easy,' said Poric. 'I am not bed-sick.'

Dominic thought what a fine big bed it was that three of them could find sleep in it.

'You should rest awhile,' Dominic said. 'Yesterday would kill a horse.' He felt stiff himself.

'No,' said Poric, getting out of bed. 'I'll see ye off.'

Dominic went down to the kitchen with Joe Two. The lady of the house had a bright fire going and the iron kettle steaming. She was in her bare feet and was wearing a canvas apron.

'I'll fill the basin for your wash,' she said.

'The Connemara men are fierce lazy,' said Joe Two. 'Look at me. Washed and shaved and breakfast in my belly.'

'Thank God the childer didn't wake up,' said the lady. 'They would have the life tortured in us.'

Dominic shaved and washed himself while Joe Two sat at

245

the fire and talked to the woman. Did she like living here and wouldn't she prefer to be in the town? God help his head. One felt sorry for those poor town creatures, what sad lives they must lead. They debated this in soft voices, an argument that has gone on since men built the first towns for themselves. The Irish were never dwellers in town, she taught him. They went from place to place and left towns to foreigners.

Dominic liked the hot tea with cream in it and sugar, and the hot home-made cake with the freshly churned butter. He didn't feel like talking. He felt a sense of excitement, like he had often felt at school when there was a free day coming up, or when he was called out of class because his mother and father were waiting for him in the parlour. This was a ridiculous comparison, he thought.

They went out with their gear to the sound of the whistle, having searched to make sure they were leaving nothing incriminating after them. Because, if all went well, they knew the village would be raided.

He stood for a few moments with Poric at the door.

'We will catch you up in a day or so,' he said. Poric was being shifted to another house over the mountains, farther north. 'I am like Dualta's tail the way he is wagging me. He seems to be on a tour of the commands.'

'I will be watching for you,' said Poric. 'Be cautious. I would like to see you again.'

Dominic laughed and punched his shoulder.

The column gathered together in the street of the village. It was a bit weird. They were all enveloped in a white mist. It was due to the fine weather. Men seemed much bigger looming out of the fog. Morgan walked by the column.

'This mist is a gift,' he said. 'We will be able to get near the road if it lasts for another few hours. Keep in touch with the man ahead of you until we get down. Let us go.'

It was an easier march than yesterday when they had been climbing all the time. Now Dominic was carrying a loaded shotgun and a linen cartridge pouch over his shoulder as well as his few belongings in a haversack on his back.

The road down the mountain was not good. The floods of

the wet days had raddled the track. It was filled with loose stones and enormous pot-holes that had been dried by the June sun. Sometimes they could walk on the grass verge or the thums of heather, but visibility was about three yards in this, and if you didn't keep in touch you could be wandering around in circles for ever. Dominic had been lost like this once when he had gone after the wild geese, and it wasn't a pleasant feeling.

They were travelling for an hour, when the mist magically vanished. It seemed like magic. One moment they were enveloped in it and the next moment it was gone and the sun was shining from behind them over their left shoulder and the land below was as if it was suddenly illuminated by a giant torch, a coloured one. They were still fairly high in the hills and they could see the ocean with all the islands, still clinging to some of the mist, growing out of it, and the sea was as calm as a pond. They could see part of the winding road below them. It was bare of traffic. It would be about six o'clock in the morning.

They travelled for another half hour, and then found all the men resting in the heather, while Morgan and Dualta and other officers lay full length on the top of the hillock, looking through binoculars.

Dominic was glad to rest. The muscles of his legs were aching from yesterday's climbing.

He thought they were an incongruous-looking bunch of men lying there in the heather. It was difficult to see in them an army. Some wore leggings and boots and riding breeches, with trenchcoats and leather bandoleers holding their ammunition. Others wore no coats or no caps, just like working men about to start the day, except for the ammunition they wore and the carefully tended rifles. Some of them wore caps with the peaks of them turned to the backs of their heads. Most of them were browned from the sun. Their bellies were flat and they looked very fit, and he noticed that there was no urge to talk on any of their parts. They had been through many mornings like this, gathering information and waiting and waiting, only to find another abortion.

Then suddenly all of them stiffened to attention, rising on their elbows or, those resting their heads on their hands, pushing up their heads, as they heard the growling of the engines of the lorries. It was a far-off sound, but it was unmistakable. Dominic looked up the hill where Morgan had flattened himself. He turned on his back and slithered down a bit, before he came to his feet. They watched him. He wasn't a tall man. His face was calm and pale, because he had the sort of complexion that never turned brown from the sun. Sun hurt him, so he always wore a wide-brimmed hat to keep it off his face.

'They're gone back,' he said. 'The hope is that sometime during the day they will return. They must be about the same number as ourselves, eighteen to twenty. They have a Lewis gun in the second lorry. So it's man for man, except the machine gun. There is a very good ambush position farther west, classic, with a wood and winding road and two bridges. That is where they would expect it, so we will hit them here at this straight stretch of the road. It's dangerous, but if we can get there without being seen, we will have the first shock in store for them. You must get there without being seen. Follow the officers. They know where each man will be. We know most of those fellows in the lorries and what they have done. This time we might have a chance to pay back.' He lifted his head and listened. The sound of the lorries became fainter and fainter, until he had to strain to hear them.

'Right,' he said. 'Now you must not be seen. Maybe now you will appreciate all the crawling on the bellies there was so much groaning about. We'll go.'

They rose to their feet. They broke up into four groups, that went off at five-minute intervals. Dominic was the last to go. He was with Dualta and Joe Two and the man they called Yank on account of his accent.

It wasn't too hard. The ground looked level as it fell away from the hills but it was filled with folds. In all they had to crawl only a few hundred yards between the folds, but the ground was dry and they could avoid wet spots.

At one stage they were joined by Morgan.

248

'I have a thought, Dominic,' he said, smiling.

'What's this?' Dominic asked.

'A few hundred years ago,' he said, 'we would have all been cutting one another's throats, the O'Flahertys and the O'Malleys and the Joyces and the rest of the clans. It took an awful long time for us all to get together.'

'History at a time like this,' said Dualta, jeering.

Morgan patted Dominic's shoulder and then he was gone.

Dominic was dismayed when they got near enough to see the position.

'Morgan is mad,' he whispered to Dualta.

'Morgan knows what he is doing,' said Dualta.

'Isn't it awful open ground for a machine gun?' Dominic asked.

'Just keep your head down,' said Dualta. 'Come on!' They had to rise to their feet and follow Joe Two, who was running in a crouch. There was a loose stone wall ahead of them. The four of them lay there while Joe Two peered through the stones. Then he was up and off again and they followed him. They could see the road clearly now. It ran as straight as an arrow for half a mile.

Two more runs and they were only ten yards from the road, which was on their right. It wasn't a bad position. There was a sort of a dyke in which they could stand and a two-foot stone wall over this. If the weather was bad they would have been standing in two foot of water and muck, but as it was the mud barely covered their boots. They were spread out ten yards from each other and if they bent a little they could not be seen. Dominic looked through the openings in the stones. Straight ahead of him was a rising hill covered with a few straggling hazel bushes that deserved credit for surviving the strong west winds that must blow in on them. There were riflemen in here and as they settled and dug themselves in it was very difficult to see them. Because he was on rising ground he could see beyond them another batch of riflemen pouring into a dyke he never would have expected to be there. It had been built up over a long period of years by the farmer who drained it and piled the decayed rushes and weeds higher

249

and higher. Then he saw the other men crossing the road below in a rush to the shelter of a roofless house, with only the gable-ends standing and the walls, and behind it a gnarled thorn tree silhouetted against the sky. There were no windows or doorways in the house. He saw the men go in and then vanish. As hard as he looked he couldn't see even the tip of a rifle barrel.

So there they were set. Dominic and the men with him were to be the last resort if the lorries got through the other fire.

He found with surprise that his mouth was dry and he had to wet his lips with his tongue.

They would have a long wait. The others mightn't even come back this road.

A boy was on the road now. He was walking beside a donkey that had two panniers of turf on his back. The boy was whistling. He was in his bare feet and the backside of his short trousers was well patched with different coloured materials. Sometimes he would bend down and take a stone from the road and fire it aimlessly into the water of the river on the far side, once disturbing a snipe with a shout of glee. He was sure that all of them watched the boy and the donkey passing the long length of the road and thought of their own youth.

Then they were left to the empty road again, and the blue sky, from which the sun was shining and becoming very hot.

He remembered reading about the Normans coming to Ireland and a few hundred of them routing thousands, all because the Irish disdained to use armour, and tried in their proud way to fight the rivers of iron opposed to them with their naked bodies and leather shields. It took them a long time to learn to fight iron from the shelter of a ditch or a stone wall.

The others were aggrieved at this. Come out from behind the walls and fight fair they called, like the children in the Bible who cried: We pipe and you will not dance.

He supposed you would have to work up a hate in order to be able to kill, or would this interfere with your aim? What had happened around his own area gave cause for hatred. The volunteer shot nine times in the belly at the docks, and not dying until he had crawled home and they sent for a priest. It would have been so easy to shoot him in the brain instead. The young fair-haired priest taken out and shot and buried in a bog. The man taken from the side of his wife and shot. The two young men over whom they had poured petrol and set them alight and then dragged them behind a lorry until the battering mercifully killed them and stopped their screaming. The pregnant woman sitting on the wall in the November sunshine who had been shot in the belly. Houses on fire, towns on fire, lootings, beatings, there was indeed plenty of cause for a hate.

But that wasn't the point. They were merely mercenaries without a cause, who had been given licence to do what they had done. He thought now that their defeat was inevitable, however long it took, because they were without a cause.

The sun rose higher and became hotter. Waves of heat were dancing on the road. Joe Two came with a water bottle and he drank some from it, enough to wash out his mouth. The water was lukewarm and had the tang of the bottle on it.

The waiting was deadly. First he was thirsty and then he was hungry, but he knew that if somebody offered him food he would not be able to swallow it.

The sun traversed the sky and started to decline on the right. In all that time nobody passed on the road except the boy and the donkey and one drunken man wheeling a bicycle. He was singing. He was happy. He probably didn't know that he was taking both sides of the road. His singing was unintelligible. He was barely gone by when in the distance Dominic heard the sound of the lorries.

He wiped off his sweating hands on his coat, checked the gun to see if it was loaded, and emptied out the cartridges so that they lay on a grassy ledge in front of him, twenty in all plus the two in the gun, cut cartridges and buckshot cartridges. Joe Two had a rifle and Dualta had one and Yank had another shotgun.

Even with the noise he didn't really believe that the lorries would come. It seemed to be another one of those practices, like long ago with that mock ambush. He felt that if the lorries did come that everyone would just stay quiet and let them go their way in peace.

But he was looking down the road, and as it came around a bend he saw the snub nose of the lorry. As it turned into the straight he saw the sun flashing on its armoured sides. He could see the black uniforms standing up in it, some of them sitting on the sides. Another twenty yards behind, the other lorry came after it.

He felt his heart thumping. His heart always thumped when he stalked a rabbit and raised the gun, or turned on his back to fire at the patiently-waited-for wild geese, but this wasn't the same, this wasn't the same at all.

He watched the lorry coming up the road at a fast clip. Shoot! Shoot! Shoot! he was ready to scream, when the air was split with shooting.

Morgan's marksmen didn't miss. He saw the glass shattering, the driver slumping and the lorry careering over to the left, slewing and stopping, and the flashes from the rifles as the men in it dropped to the floor and started firing.

The second lorry stopped too. He saw the driver ducking down, not shot. But the lorry stopped and the guns from it started blazing. It was slightly oblique. He saw the two men jumping down and reaching and he saw the machine gun being handed down. He saw them bending and travelling with it to the side of the road where there was a low ditch, and he saw one man getting down and sitting behind the gun and sighting it and the other flat on the ground, feeding it from a box.

He raised his gun to fire. It was ridiculous. He was too far away. They hadn't enough ammunition to waste it. In a fever of impatience he heard the chatter of the gun and saw it lacing the low hazel bushes and then saw the man firing it just turn on his side, slowly and wearily, and lie there. Where the machine gun pointed, the top of the ditch was being cut by bullets, lowering it with lead to reveal more of the machine gun. He saw the feeder pull away the body from behind the gun, and get behind it himself, while another came down from the lorry and crawled on his belly to the box. The machine gun started to fire again, but almost at once the gunner arched

252

his back and slumped on top of the gun. The men in the ruined house were firing from there. The third man pulled away this body and he went to turn the gun to aim it at the house but he died as he tried to lift it. He fell over the gun and then toppled off it.

From the first lorry there came the swoosh of the rifle grenades then. You could see them rising and arching and falling and exploding, Dominic saw with wonder. And the fire was accurate enough. He saw the clods and bushes rising in the air. But bullets were screaming and ricocheting off the armoured sides of the lorry. One rifleman higher up was getting the bullets inside the lorry, and then Dominic saw one of the men rising from the hazel bushes and running and zig-zagging, his arm flashing as he fell, and the grenade falling into the body of the lorry and exploding.

He couldn't see any more, because the driver in the second lorry, with his body hidden, had raised an arm to the wheel and suddenly the lorry was moving. It passed the first lorry, from which there appeared to be no shooting now, and came straight up the road, swinging wildly from side to side but gathering speed.

Dominic rested the gun on the wall and sighted. He knew the others were doing the same.

The driver thought he was clear.

He came towards them, raising himself and looking behind, and their combined fire hit him. The glass shattered, the lorry turned left and hit a mound and stopped.

The four of them were about to rise from their hiding place when bullets started singing all around them and they ducked again, but not before he had seen seven men jumping from the lorry and, firing as they ran, veer to the left and throw themselves into a sheep shelter of loose stones that had been erected to save the sheep from the worst blasts of the winter. It was soon bristling with guns firing, and Dominic found that they were enfiladed. He instinctively crouched and turned right and got on his knees in the mud and crawled back to where the ditch wound round to the right. His back was exposed. Every moment he expected to feel the impact of a bullet.

253

He got around the turn. The other three were crouching there and firing.

There was a white cloth waving from the first lorry.

Some of the men rose from their shelter.

'Get down! Get down!' they heard Morgan shouting, and they got down fast. They had worked this trick down the South. Held up their arms in surrender and then as soon as four men appeared shot them dead. They had paid for it, but it was a lesson learned now.

Morgan himself made his way to the road, squirming and turning and dodging with a revolver in his hand. He had only one dangerous moment until he gained the shelter of the back of the lorry. He raised himself and looked in. He saw that it was indeed a surrender. There was no one in it fit to fight.

He raised his arm in a signal, and two of his own men made the same trip towards him.

'They're out,' he said. 'One stay to guard them. Get our friend on the gun.'

Dominic and the others were firing at the sheepcote. It was hard to see if they were having any effect, but they were loosening some of the stones.

How long? He didn't know, but soon the sheepcote was surrounded with twenty guns, and in another five minutes a machine gun was added to it. They had all left their positions to close on the sheepcote, taking chances, running and diving.

Once Dominic was beside a panting man. His teeth were clenched. 'Don't let them surrender!' he said. 'Don't let them surrender!'

But they did.

There was nothing else for them to do, because the machine gun was ripping away their hiding place, handled by a man who knew its paces, tapping and sighting like a professional.

It was a white piece of shirt they held up.

The firing stopped.

'Throw out your guns!' Morgan called. Men waited, still hidden. The guns were thrown out. They counted them. Seven guns.

'Come out with your hands up,' shouted Morgan.

They did this, one by one, and as they came the men rose from their shelter and circled them, their guns pointing.

For a moment Dominic thought that they would kill them.

Morgan was watching them too. He didn't interfere. When they were within five yards of them, they stopped, and looked at Morgan. The tension died out of their faces. Two of the black fellows were wounded, one in the shoulder and the other in the leg.

Dominic felt drained. He looked about him at the others. Some of them were lighting cigarettes with shaking hands.

He felt his own limbs shaking.

They laid seven bodies side by side on the road. Two of them had been mutilated in the face by the grenade. Others of them looked as if they were sleeping.

There were four walking wounded, and two who couldn't. They carried these over to the old house and left them there. They gave them water to drink from the canteens, and cigarettes.

The unwounded ones expected to be killed. Dominic watched their faces. Some of them were not afraid. One or two of them were afraid. They had cause to be.

'We are not going to kill you,' said Morgan. 'Some of you deserve killing, but I tell you this, and you are to bring this message into the town. If there are any reprisals on anybody in the town or neighbourhood, I tell you now that we will follow each one of you and kill you, wherever you go. You know this is no empty threat.'

A man had been killed in New York City. He fell thirty storeys down a lift shaft. A man had been killed between a ship and the pier in Cairo.

The lorries were burning.

The column formed on the road between the burning lorries.

Dominic watched them. They lined up, stamping out the cigarette butts they were smoking. He saw that some of them were pale under the sunburn.

He thought: if you have never killed, it is a shock to kill. Normal decent people, not professional soldiers, it must be a

255

shock to kill. They didn't look exhilarated. They had won a victory. They were loaded down with rifles and ammunition and equipment and a working Lewis gun. They marched up the road and turned right to the hills. Even then they weren't talking. Two columns of smoke were rising straight in the air.

They parted with them and Morgan farther up. They were going to double back on the road farther down, cross it and get over to the other hills on the right.

But Dualta and Dominic were going the other way.

Morgan was pensive.

'I'm glad you were here, Dualta,' he said.

Morgan didn't look exalted. He was pale and his straight body was slouching.

'So was I,' said Dualta.

'Now you can tell them we are worthy of assistance,' said Morgan. 'Now we are really ready to fight. But we want more ammunition, more, much more. If the fight today had lasted another half hour we would have had to back away. Don't have us backing away any more, Dualta, eh?'

'I promise,' said Dualta. 'Now I can tell them you have the men and the men have a leader. You'll get your supplies.'

'Come and see us again, Dominic,' said Morgan, turning away and following the men.

Dominic tried to think back to the Morgan he had first met at his father's requiem Mass. This was a different man. The same and yet much different.

'Times make the men,' he said to Dualta.

'If there were twenty more like him,' said Dualta, 'this would have been finished and done with long ago. Come on, brother, we don't want them to get us in the bag.'

He set out for the mountains, and Dominic, following him, felt infinitely weary.

The sun was a huge globe in the sky behind them.

256

26

THERE WERE three bridges over the river and four over the canal. They had pickets on the canal bridges, since they were the most westerly. It was impossible to get out of the town without being searched at one of the bridges. Some days they were meticulous, other days they were not so careful. It was not safe to count on their moods. Dualta and himself had talked about it, listened to reports and decided to try and get out of the town openly by the bridge near the Earl's Island camp. This always had a picket of soldiers near it, but away from it, and the military were not nearly as security-minded as the others.

So Dominic walked slowly towards the bridge on this July evening, just before curfew, with his hands in his pockets. One of them was holding a gun.

There were very few people abroad. It was raining, a soft rain with no bite in it, but very wetting. This was good because he thought it might keep the soldiers in shelter.

He saw a woman coming towards him from the opposite side. She was wearing a shawl. She was not stopped. There was a young man walking in front of him with his head down against the wind. Dominic kept some yards behind him.

He found that his hands were trembling and his legs seemed weak. He supposed he was bound to be nervous after more than a month of travelling the hills of the province. The fine weather had been a curse. As they had foreseen, the ground had hardened and there had been widespread military searches. They had netted few, because there were no guides available for them and every person was a potential spy for the columns who moved ahead of the searchers or broke through them in the dark by paths well known to them. But it had been very harassing. They had had to sleep many nights in sheep shelters, or abandoned houses, or under large boulders. They had blown many bridges ahead of the searchers, but the river beds were so dry that their vehicles could by-pass them.

Then he and Dualta, who was about to make his way back to Dublin, had spent a wakeful week in the town. On two nights they had barely got away before raids.

Dualta had said to him: Get across the bridge and into the College and wait inside the wall in the bushes.

What he longed most for in all the world at the present moment was the bed at home in his own house; the lamps lighted in the evening, the front door opened to reflect a rectangle of light into the night, and the knowledge that you could go to bed and sleep and sleep until the kind face of your mother awoke you in the morning. These simple needs seemed completely unattainable.

The young man crossed the bridge, his shoes knocking a hollow sound out of the wood.

Dominic kept following him, waiting every moment for a soldier to emerge from the shadows to challenge him. No one came and he followed after the young man, his head down. He heard his heels on the bridge, and as he passed, out of the corner of his eye, he saw the two sentries in a hut. They had no intention of challenging the rain, he saw, and walked past, thinking of the nerve-racking and smelly time he had come out of that place wearing Fourcoats' rags. Farther on, he had to stop and lean against the wall. He thought his nerves were going to hell. How much longer, he wondered, would he be able to stand up to all this? He felt depressed.

He cut into the gate and went straight, edging into the bushes under the trees. Everything was dripping wet. He went along here and pushed through until his back was resting against the wall. He turned up the collar of his coat; turned the peak of the cap he was wearing around so that the rain would run on to his coat and not down his neck, and he waited.

Since his mind was filled with blackness, he tried not to think of anything at all. When he thought of the days he had spent at the College, of the lectures and the old carefree life, he felt as if it was a thousand years ago. Also it made him think of Lowry, and the young men now scattered in jails and

258

camps all over the country, and that didn't help, so he tried to make his mind a blank.

Not for long.

Two shots scattered the stillness of the closing night and brought him awake, his palms flat against the stones. They were revolver shots. It could only be Dualta. The odd closed-down rain seemed to enhance all the sounds. He heard boots on pavements and then he heard the quick crackle of rifle shots. He stayed where he was. Dualta would have to come to him. He moved farther out until he was clear of the bushes and looked back at the drive. He saw the running figure cross-ing it and waited.

Dualta was hardly panting, he noticed. That's what all the exercise on the hills was doing for them both.

'I'm here,' he said.

'Up to the top and over the wall,' said Dualta. 'Fast. We have no time. Across the roads into the fields and run like hell.'

He was gone already. He still had the gun in his hand.

They ran to where the wall curved, and jumped and scrambled to the top of it. Dualta took a look and said 'Go!' They got over the wall and jumped to the pavement. There were no people he could see or vehicles. But they could hear those army boots on the pavements and the sound of a lorry. They ran across the road and jumped the wall there. They were in a field. They ran across the grass. They cleared an-other wall and ran across another field and as they cleared this Dualta shouted 'Down' and they lay full length the other side of it. Lights swept over their heads. They could hear the sound of several lorries now and voices and the boots.

'Now,' said Dualta again, and they got up and ran. They ran for three more fields until they came to the culvert of the light railway that ran into the quarry on their left.

They stopped here. There was a lorry on the right and there were soldiers with rifles walking the railbed. There were four of them following one behind another. They let them pass and then they crawled as silently as they could across and down the other side. There were many briars on the other side.

Dominic felt them searing his hands. They gave the soldiers more time and then they climbed a wall and were in another field. They ran crouching here. Their feet made no sound on the cropped grass. They could see the lights of a lorry to their left and to their right, their headlights approaching each other. They lay supine beneath another stone wall until the lorries had met, stopped and then passed one another, and as they passed they crossed behind them and dropped flat inside a wall. Then they ran again. They ran almost beside the lorry on their left inside the field and then, as it turned towards Rahoon, they crossed the road in its wake, into a field with trees over another wall, and Dominic found himself stumbling and falling on old battered headstones.

'Over here,' he heard Dualta whispering. He saw the bulk of him and went towards him and as he did so, Dualta seemed to disappear. He stood there a bit bewildered. 'Down here!' he heard Dualta say and he stopped and reached and found his hand and climbed down into the tomb. He stood there in the dark, and heard the oiled slab closing behind him.

He was breathless now, his lungs bursting, and sweat soaking his whole body. He threw off the cap and flattened his sweat-soaked hair to his head with his hand.

A match scratched, and flared. He saw Dualta's face, looking thin and aged in the matchlight, and then they were enveloped in the light of the candle.

He didn't know what to expect. What do you expect to find in a tomb? There was a bench each side and a butter box between where the candle was lighted standing in a bottle.

Dominic sat down on the bench.

'Am I sitting on a coffin?' he asked.

'No,' said Dualta. 'They mouldered away long ago. The bones are buried outside.'

'Oh God,' said Dominic, 'this is the lowest we have come yet.'

'And the safest,' said Dualta. 'That was a near miss.' He raised his legs and stretched himself on the bench. He closed his eyes.

'What happened?' Dominic asked.

'I killed Sergeant Nick,' said Dualta.

Just that. A statement of fact. Dominic could say nothing. He pulled himself up on the bench and clasped his knees with his arms.

'I shot Sergeant Nick. He was responsible for quite a few deaths,' said Dualta. He wasn't excusing himself, Dominic thought. 'He was always very well guarded. He slipped up tonight. He was alone.' He held his left hand out into the light of the candle. 'See that?' he said. Dominic looked at his hand. There was a livid scar across the back of it. 'He fired. I fired. I was lucky.'

'Did you know he might be at the bridge?' Dominic asked.

'I thought he might,' said Dualta.

'Was he lured to the bridge?' Dominic asked.

'What's wrong with you?' Dualta asked, sitting up.

'I don't know,' said Dualta. 'I just think of him as a young policeman long ago. There didn't seem much harm in him, just a bit officious.'

'There's no harm at all in him now,' said Dualta, lying back. 'We were lucky to get away.'

'Is there any air getting in here?' Dominic asked, pulling at the collar of his shirt.

'There are holes bored up over your head,' said Dualta. 'We won't suffocate.'

'How long will we be here?' Dominic asked.

'I don't know,' said Dualta. 'They are going to search like they never searched before. Maybe we will be here until Judgement Day.' He laughed.

Dominic thought: He can laugh after all that. He took off his wet coat and put it under his head. He could lie back on it if he didn't stretch out his legs. He could see the massive stone of the tomb over his head. Part of the walls of the tomb had lichen and moss growing where the rain had penetrated.

Dualta said: 'Dominic, are you not well? Don't you feel well?'

Dominic said: 'Dualta, I feel very tired.'

'If you are that tired,' said Dualta. 'You'd even sleep in a tomb.'

And Dominic did just that.

He had been in worse places. It seemed to him now that he was back in them again: the dug-out by the river which he had shared with the rats and a wounded man. You couldn't keep the rats, big water rats, out of the place. They hung the cooking tins up on the rafters supporting the earthen roof, but they got up there somehow and they rattled the cans. He awoke shouting once when a rat fell and ran across his face.

He went through the beatings he had got. They seemed monstrous, and he seemed to be screaming with terror; huge distorted faces screaming at him; enormous fists rising and falling on him.

He saw himself seeing clearly how hopeless it was. What were they all doing, the young hanged men and the young shot men, and the thousands of men and women doing penal servitude in prisons and dirty unorganized internment camps? He saw decent men shooting, shooting with distaste, or avid for death, the black guns red in their huge hands.

He saw himself arguing with Dualta. What use is this, sleeping in a tomb? How is this contributing to liberty? What have I done? What is it all about?

Dualta was shouting at him: We can never lose and we can never win. It will go on for ever. This is the total tenor of life.

He was shouting back at Dualta: It won't do. I won't go on. It is better to be a dead hero. See, you are shot and you are dead and you are a hero, and you are not alive, living with the rats and the bones of dead men in your nostrils.

Dualta suddenly seemed to him to grow enormously. He was dressed in a trench coat and he had a bandoleer around his chest, and his legs were spread and his lips were drawn back on his teeth and he was shouting at him through them: You are a coward, Dominic! You were always a coward! You are a traitor to your country. I will not let you surrender.

There was a gun in his hand, and blood dripping from the back of his hand, and his eyes were filled with hatred, and suddenly there were red spurts of fire from the gun, and he felt them going into his belly, and his whole body was seared with the agony of them, and he held out his bloodstained hands, and said pleadingly: No, Dualta, no, don't shoot me, Dualta. I am your brother. Dualta, don't shoot me; I am your brother.

Dualta's shouting voice awoke him.

'Dominic! Dominic! For the love of Christ, Dominic!'

He saw Dualta's face above him. It was not filled with hatred but anxiety. He felt his hand on his forehead.

'You are awake. Thanks be to the great God for that! How do you feel, Dominic. I had to hold you down.'

Dominic thought over this. He felt weak, and spun out. His tongue seemed to be swollen, his mouth chalk-dry.

'What's up?' he asked.

'How do you feel?' Dualta asked. 'I don't know what's wrong with you. You have been nearly two days in a fever. How do you feel?'

'I'd love a drink,' said Dominic.

Dualta bent, and brought up a bottle. It was filled with milk.

'Try this,' he said.

Dominic sat up. He took the bottle and put it to his lips. It tasted very good.

'I went out last night,' said Dualta. 'I went to a house. I got the milk and some bread and butter. Would you be able to eat?'

Dominic stopped gulping the milk. He sat up. He tested his feet on the earth. He was sound.

'I had terrible dreams,' he said. 'I dreamt you were going to shoot me. I thought you had shot me.'

'Oh, Dominic,' said Dualta, putting his hand on the side of his face. 'What made you dream of a thing like that? How are you now?'

'I feel fine now,' said Dominic. 'Maybe it was just that I needed a long sleep, even if it was packed with evil dreams.'

'I was thinking of trying to get a doctor somehow,' said Dualta. 'If you weren't better I would have got one somehow, tonight.'

'How long have we been here?' Dominic asked.

'Tonight will be the third night,' said Dualta. 'It's even getting me depressed.'

263

Dominic could see from the cracks in the tomb that it was daylight outside. 'You got little sleep with me carrying on like that,' he said.

'We'll sleep enough in the grave,' said Dualta, grinning. 'Are you sure you are all right?'

'I am,' said Dominic. 'My head feels clear. I must have been sweating.'

'Buckets,' said Dualta. 'I thought you were going to sweat away your life. The body they say is ninety per cent. water. You must have lost sixty per cent. of yours. Are you sure you are all right?'

Dominic had to laugh at the care for him in his brother's face.

'I'm fine, Dualta, fine. It was only a spasm. As soon as I can smell the air outside again, I will be as good as new.'

There was a stone pounding on their tombstone and a voice was shouting: 'Come out! Come out!'

They were clutching one another's shoulders. Dominic saw Dualta's face turning pale. He supposed he must be the same himself. Dualta had a gun in his hand. He could see that he had wrapped a piece of a white shirt around the hand with the burn.

A boot was kicking at the front slab.

The voice was shouting, 'Dualta! Dominic! Come out! It's me! It's Sam! Open up, Dualta!'

They looked at one another in disbelief.

Then Dualta loosened the catch of the slab and it swung out and they saw Sam's thin face looking in at them. Sam was actually smiling. His face was lighted up.

'Come out!' he said. 'It's over! They signed a truce. Come on into the open air, you poor creatures!'

They must have stood there staring at him for minutes with their mouths open.

'Don't you believe me?' Sam asked. 'The Truce has been in force since twelve o'clock yesterday.'

This stirred Dualta.

He climbed out of there fast.

'Yesterday!' he was shouting. 'And why did you leave us

here all this time. A whole day. Sam, why did you do that to us?'

'I didn't know where ye were,' Sam was shouting. 'I searched every bolt-hole in the county looking for ye. This was the last place I was trying. And here ye were. By God, Dominic, you look like death coming out of that tomb. But I'm so glad to see you.' He threw his arms around him and embraced him.

'Isn't it great?' he asked. 'I don't know how long it will last but it's great for a breather.'

Dominic was looking at the sky. It was a blue sky with white clouds in it. And then he saw somebody waving at him from over the wall and calling his name. For a moment he thought it was part of the dreams. That looks like Finola, he thought, waving at me over the wall and calling my name, and then he was running and stumbling over broken headstones, long grass, forgetful of everything, finding that he had more strength than he had thought as he vaulted the wall, stumbled at the unexpected height on the roadside, and reached for her.

She smelled of clean soap, and every scent that was desirable. She was the farthest imaginable thing you could think of that was in no way connected with a tomb. He kissed her, forgetful of the bristles on his face; held her as if he would never let her go, and when he looked into her eyes, he knew she felt the same as he did, knew it from the brightness of her eyes and the trembling of her body against his own.

'You are spring water,' he said, 'and birds in the sky and new mown hay and the singing boglark.'

She just looked at him, saying nothing, raising a hand to touch the side of his face. He was pale under the sunburn, there were black bristles on his face, his eyes were bloodshot, his clothes smelled stale, but she knew that it was what was inside him that made him important for her.

'Enough!' Sam was shouting. 'Will we be here all day? No time to waste on stuff like that. Eh, Dominic?' laughing. 'I even have a car. I don't know if it's against the terms of the Truce, but I have one. Come on! In with ye. If two men ever wanted a wash it's ye!'

265

Dominic remembered getting into the back of the open car. The leather was hot from the sun. But he just held on to her as if he would never let her go. He was barely conscious of their progress.

'I'm going by backways,' said Sam. 'Some of the black fellows are still Shinner hunting. It might be too soon to taunt them.'

'What are the terms of the Truce?' Dualta asked.

'We don't attack them,' said Sam. 'They don't attack us. No provocation on either side. Envoys to go to London to discuss a settlement.'

'I must get to Dublin today,' said Dualta.

'All right,' said Sam. 'Will you chance the train?'

'We'll go a few stations out maybe,' said Dualta.

Dominic came out of his feelings for a few moments.

'Won't you come back and see mother first?' he asked.

'No,' said Dualta, back over his shoulder. 'Too much to do. I should have been in Dublin days ago. Man, there will be things to be done. Are the others keeping the Truce?' he asked Sam.

'Sort of,' said Sam. 'There are a few of them who won't. But we'll try and keep the lid on the pot.'

'Was it bad, Dominic?' Finola was asking him.

'That was terrible,' said Dominic. 'That tomb. Never again.'

There were some bonfires on the hills last night,' she said. 'Everybody was at the doors of their houses, walking on the streets. Nobody could believe it. We searched and searched for you and we couldn't find you.'

'You have me now,' said Dominic. 'For ever, or until the end of the Truce. You look very beautiful in the daylight.'

He felt that he was sitting on a cushion of air.

He should have been cautious. Surely life had taught him enough by now.

They went into Lowry's house.

Lowry's mother was a strong woman, with great strength of character. But when she saw Dualta and Dominic coming into that kitchen the strength left her. Dominic could see this in her face; that she had been expecting Lowry to come in that door too, and of course he couldn't, and she broke. It is just as terrible a thing to see a strong woman breaking as to see a strong man breaking.

Finola's hand was in his and he tried desperately to hold on to her, but she broke his grip and went over to Lowry's mother and put her arms around her, and the eyes she turned on Dominic seemed to him to be stricken with guilt, so he ran away from there and went into the streets and ignored their voices calling after him.

All he could see was the road home and his mother at the end of it and clean sheets and the scouring sea.

27

THE SQUARE was crowded. For a change it wasn't crowded with politics but with cattle for the October fair. Dominic leaned one arm on the side of the ass cart, and with the other hand fondled the curly head of the black and white calf that was tied with a rope to the wheel. The calf kept trying to catch his fingers with his mouth to suck them. There was squealing coming from the cart, where a piece of sacking tied across it kept four young bonhams from jumping out. But it didn't stop them squealing and grunting, and now and again Poric, who was on the other side, would give them a belt with his big hand and quieten them for a while.

Nothing could be more normal than a fair, Dominic thought, even if the whole country was in a state of suspended animation while a settlement was being discussed in London.

None of the people here seemed to be worried. There was a great noise rising in the cold air, and little noise from the ground, which was thickly covered in cow dung and drowned the sound of hobnail boots. There were bargaining men roaring at one another, some of them in Irish, which he thought, grinning, had more colourful curses than the English tongue.

Raising of hats to heaven, and banging of sticks in the dung, and there were many stall holders selling old clothes and new clothes, and hawkers with holy medals and doo-dahs, and tinkers squabbling and a strong man being tied with chains in order to break them, and away on the left three-card-trick men had set up their little tables. There were Claddagh women with their shawls and the round flat baskets of fish on their heads, crying their wares of fresh herrings. They were easily excited to anger and free with the language of abuse. Horses were whinnying, mares trying to get from under their carts at the call of the stallions on the Bohermore.

The police were discreet. They didn't move through the fair, he noticed, just walked here and there in twos, or leaned against the walls of the shops, their eyes keen under their helmets. It was taking time, he thought, to get accustomed to walking in the streets without fear. There were many men in Volunteer uniforms in from the country. The pubs around about were crowded, and so packed with drinking men that most of them had come on to the pavements with glasses of porter in their hands.

Suddenly he felt something hard poked into his back and a voice said menacingly: 'Don't move!' and even though he recognized Sam's voice he couldn't stop his body from jumping in alarm.

'You are sensitive,' said Sam.

'You shouldn't do that to a humble farmer,' said Dominic.

'Hello, Poric,' Sam shouted, 'are you well?'

Poric pushed out his chest and hit it with his hands. 'Look at that!' he said. He was dressed in a bainin and a blue knitted gansey, with a cap worn on the side of his head. He looked well. 'I could beat any man in Ireland.'

'It would be easy to find somebody to fight you today,' said Sam. 'How are you, Dominic? You look like a farmer. You smell like a farmer.' He was looking at Dominic's boots. He had pushed the ends of his trousers inside the heavy home-knit socks. His boots were heavy with dung. He had a little switch in his left hand.

'Wouldn't you like to buy a few bonhams or a calf, Sam?' Dominic asked.

'Where the hell would I put them?' Sam asked.

'In your stomach,' said Poric.

'When the Republic is established,' said Sam, 'the first thing we will have to press for is to have fairs taken off the streets.'

'God forgive you,' said Dominic. 'The pubkeepers would lynch you. So there is going to be a Republic, Sam?'

Sam was silent. He put his hands in his pockets a\d leaned against the wheel.

'You remember the day long ago that you were at the meeting, Dominic?' he asked.

'The time you wanted to know if I could shoot a policeman?' Dominic asked.

'Aye,' said Sam. 'We have come a long way since then, eh? What are you doing at home?'

'Making hay,' said Dominic, 'cutting oats, bringing home the turf, lying on the sand, doing nothing, except drilling all the young fellows who have grown up. They are mad for guns and drilling. We have no guns, so I leave the drilling to Poric. He's a good drill master, a hard man. Eh, Poric?'

'I'll make men of them,' said Poric.

'It's funny,' said Sam. 'After the Truce we got enough volunteers to win four wars. Where were they all before that?'

'Growing up, maybe,' said Dominic. 'It surprised me to see how the young ones had grown up.'

'The ones I mean were grown already,' said Sam. 'I saw fellows in uniform I never even knew were in the Volunteers. So many of them that we could have beaten the Russian Army. I asked some of them what they were doing and they looked at me with great mystery and said they were in Intelligence. With all of them we must have been very intelligent. We were more intelligent than we knew. So many of them seemed to come out from under the stones. Like your man over there.'

This was a man in Volunteer uniform outside the pub. He was quite drunk. He was squaring up to a civilian. He was hardly able to articulate. His words were blurred. All he was

269

saying was: 'Where were you? Where were you?' He was pounding the civilian on the shoulder each time he said it. His face was red. The civilian was becoming alarmed. The two policemen farther up were looking but had no intention of doing anything.

Then a big man suddenly came from the far side. He pushed the civilian away, and grasped the volunteer by the lapels and literally raised him off the ground. They couldn't hear what he said to him, but they saw his face blanching, and a little sobriety coming into his eyes. He said: 'All right, Michael John! That's all right, Michael John.' The big man let him down and gave him a slight push. The volunteer pulled down the jacket of the uniform, made a sort of shamefaced salute, turned his back and went away. It hadn't taken long. Michael John turned towards them. They saw his eyes were hard and the muscles on his big jaws standing out. Then his eyes rested on them, anger left his face and he came over to them.

'Dominic!' he said, almost crushing Dominic's hand to jelly, 'and the brave Poric.' He shook hands with Poric. 'How are you? You are looking well. I knew a good thing couldn't be killed.'

'I'm strong enough now to fight you, Michael John,' said Poric.

'I won't ask ye in for a drink,' said Michael John. 'There is too much drinking. It's good to see you. Eh, Sam, nice to see them. At least we know these fellows, and where they were.'

'Is all well with you, Michael John?' Dominic asked.

'What is well?' asked Michael John. 'A truce is a good thing, but if it goes on too long it's a bad thing. It's hard to hold men together. They begin to think it's all over. And by God, it isn't all over. The longer the cursed thing goes on, the less people are willing to fight. Is this true, Sam?'

'It's dangerous,' said Sam, 'when people let down their defences. But there is a worse thing.'

'What's this?' Michael John asked.

'Men are beginning to walk on opposite sides of the road,' said Sam.

270

They considered this. Dominic felt a shiver going down his spine. Sam was serious.

'No,' said Michael John. 'This is not so. I won't listen to you. This can never happen. We only have one enemy, and we should be fighting him now. The Truce has gone on too long, you hear. That is all. But when the people are faced with it again, they will rise to it again, you'll see. The people are great, Sam.'

'They were,' said Sam, 'as long as the soldiers don't start walking on opposite sides of the street.'

Michael John suddenly clapped him on the back, making him stumble. 'You worrier,' he shouted. 'Away with you. Come with me. I want you to meet some men. They'll straighten your spine for you. Dominic, will ye be here long? We must meet again before Poric and yourself go home.'

'We'll be here for a few hours more,' said Dominic.

'We'll see you so,' said Michael John. 'It's good to know where we can lay our hands on two reliable men.'

'Where's Dualta, Dominic?' Sam suddenly asked, as he was going. For some reason this question upset Dominic.

'In Dublin, I think,' he said. 'He hasn't been home at all. He writes and says he will be home next week, and then he doesn't come. He must be tied up in politics.'

'God spare us from those,' said Sam. 'We will see you.' He waved a hand and went away with Michael John. Dominic kept looking after them as they made their way between the throngs of people.

'What does he mean, opposite sides of the street, Dominic?' Poric asked him.

Dominic looked at him.

Poric was honestly puzzled, he saw, his forehead creased with thought.

'Leave it, Poric,' he said. 'It's a bit complicated.'

'Does he mean us or them?' Poric asked. 'Sometimes I don't understand what Sam does be saying.'

'Forget it,' said Dominic. 'I'll leave you for a while. I want to wander around. You know what to sell the calf for if anyone is interested.'

271

'I'll do that,' said Poric. 'I'll get a better price than you. You are too soft.'

Dominic laughed and left him.

He pushed his way through the crowds of animals, and men, and carts, and dogs, and children who should have been at school, barefooted boys making nothing of walking in the muck which was squeezing up between their toes. They were very raggedy, he saw, with torn jerseys and patched and frayed pants, cut down from elder brothers' or fathers'. Was it worth all the fighting, he wondered, so that every little poorly dressed boy should have a new gansey in the Republic? And would they?

He got clear of the Square. The crowd had eased. He turned to the right and crossed the road so that he wouldn't have to walk on the side of the barracks. He still got an uneasy feeling from it. The red brick, so out of place in this town of grey limestone and green trees, seemed alien and menacing. He kept his eyes averted from it as he passed.

Then he heard the English voice shouting across the street at him: 'Hey, Joe! Joe Murphy! How are you, Joe Murphy?'

He looked. He didn't stop walking. Skin was standing on the pavement across from him. His legs were spread, his hands on his hips. He was grinning, the black tapes on his cap were being blown by the wind that swept in gusts down the street.

'Hello, Skin,' Dominic said.

'Like to fight, Joe?' Skin asked.

'There's a truce, Skin,' said Dominic. 'Didn't you hear?'

'Oh, that,' said Skin. 'Fight you when it's over, Joe, or maybe have a drink, eh?'

'One or the other, Skin,' said Dominic. 'One or the other.'

He was embarrassed. He was sorry he had come this way. Some of Skin's comrades were lounging there, people passing by with baskets and shopping looking curiously at this exchange, pretending they hadn't heard it.

Dominic found that his hands were clenched; that he had to relax his muscles. It was hard to forget. He beat at his coat with the switch. It seemed to him that Skin would have liked to stop and talk with him. He was not unfriendly. How could this be? You cannot go through what they had gone through and have friendly chats about the weather.

He went down to the riverside. He walked down a ramp there and shuffled his boots around in the clear water to get the dung off them. He used the point of the switch to clean out the welts. He kept his mind very intent on this task. He didn't want to think of how much Sam had disturbed him. Then he heard her.

'I called you,' she said, 'and you didn't even hear me. So I had to run after you.'

He was immensely pleased to see her. Her face was flushed from the running. She had copybooks under her arm.

'I don't know how I missed hearing your voice,' he said. 'Maybe it's because I'm always hearing it and then find you are not there.'

This stopped her. She dropped her eyes.

He came up from the ramp.

'Sit down and talk to me for a while,' he said. There was a tree near them. Somebody had put stones for a seat under the tree looking out over the weir and the river. They had to sit close together, their hips touching. This made Dominic very conscious of her.

'You haven't been to see us, since,' she said.

'I have been too busy doing nothing,' he said.

'I don't believe that,' she said.

'It's true,' he said. 'It took me nearly a month to wake up in the morning and find I wasn't in that tomb. So I did all the normal things about the place, hay and oats and turf, and hooleys, and weddings, and wakes. They always go on.'

'Do you dance at the weddings?' she asked.

'You should see me doing a jig,' said Dominic.

'There are many pretty girls out there,' she said.

'Thousands,' said Dominic. 'I'm having an awful job picking one.'

'You didn't come back to the University,' she said.

'A man can only do one job at a time,' he said. 'The one I started in on is not over yet. So there is no time for medicine.'

'Will it be over soon?' she asked.

'No,' said Dominic. 'I don't think the Truce will last. I

273

don't think any delegation can accept the terms they will be offered. I think we will have to start all over. What way will we be then? This is the problem. What kind of new fighting will we have to do. This is something the leaders must work out, not people like ourselves. Just to be ready. No time for medicine, so, no time for love.'

'Don't you court the girls at the gable-end?' she asked.

'Sure,' said Dominic. 'Lips as soft as rose petals, sweet breath like dew, harvest moons on the sea. It's all no good, though. You know that. There is only one girl for me.'

There was silence between them then. He knew she was feeling the same as he was himself, but he didn't know, only vaguely, why there should be such a barrier between them.

'Why did you walk away that night?' she asked.

'I saw your eyes when you held Lowry's mother in your arms,' he said. 'I knew it was no use staying.'

'You still assume that you know everything other people are thinking,' she said angrily. 'How do you know what I was thinking?'

'You were thinking of Lowry,' he said. 'You were thinking you were unfaithful to Lowry because you and I had kissed and felt deeply. You felt you were a traitor. The dead hold all the aces.'

'You are very bitter,' she said. 'I loved Lowry. I woke up every morning thinking of him. I went to sleep every night dreaming of him. I thought I would die when he died, but I didn't.'

'I understand this,' he said. 'Only too well.'

'You don't,' she said. 'I might think of Dominic in the morning, but I don't dream of him at night. I like to be kissed by Dominic. I like to be near Dominic. I would like to be married to Dominic and have children with Dominic, but is this love? I was in love. I loved Lowry. How can I turn about and say I love Dominic? Freedom cannot be divided. Love cannot be divided. It's one and forever, like freedom. How can I say I love Lowry forever, and that I love Dominic forever? Please tell me this?'

'I cannot tell you,' he said. 'I can only tell you about how I feel myself, and I don't care about living or dead, just that.'

274

'You weren't quite right about what I was thinking,' she said.

'You are like the state our poor country is in at the moment,' he said. 'A state of suspended animation. Nobody breathing hard. I cannot help you. You must solve this for yourself. In my own heart I don't even know if I want you to solve it. I like the notion of being in love forever with a man who is dead. It is almost like loving your country, or God. It is invisible, intangible.'

'Dominic,' she said, almost groaning. 'I don't want to be fickle. I just don't want to be fickle. Don't you understand? I might destroy you if I was only fickle.'

He put his hand on hers.

'You will never be that, no more than myself,' he said. 'It is only the future can solve it, whatever it will be like.'

A train from Connemara thundered suddenly over the bridge that spanned the river. As it crossed the boards it made a booming sound like the noise of distant guns firing. There were black clouds creeping up into the sky behind it. He hoped it wasn't an omen.

Finola was holding his hand hard and her head was bent.

28

DOMINIC THOUGHT that the welcome for the prisoners off the six o'clock train on this January evening was a bit hysterical.

There were bands, and bullrush torches soaked in paraffin, and tricolours floating everywhere.

There were drays waiting to parade the prisoners and a few cars.

Dominic was standing near the steps of the station, and he had to keep his elbows pushed out from his body or his ribs would have been crushed.

He thought they were hysterical because they wanted to put

off thinking about the future. They had waited nearly six months for the news of the Treaty. They were shocked when it was signed. People hoped that it would not be ratified in the Dáil, but it was ratified, 64 to 57.

There was suddenly a great shout and deafening cheering as the first of the prisoners came from the station and stood on the steps, with packages under their arms, standing, a bit bewildered, he thought, blinking, making an effort to raise their hands in a sort of salute to the volume of noise that welcomed them. He thought they didn't look well. Their clothes, he thought, were shabby and their faces pinched. Some of them had been in jails or dirty camps for years. They were unused to freedom; they were unused to being able to dictate the course of events that had passed them by faster than the train that had brought them from their incarceration.

He didn't feel like cheering as he looked. He felt like crying. He was waiting for a sight of Peter O'Flaherty.

The first lot of prisoners were enveloped in the welcome. Anyone who thought of making a speech had no chance. The crowd surrounded them and raised them on their shoulders and carried them to the sidecars that were waiting farther down, with tall tricolours stuck in poles in the lampholders.

He wanted to shout at the people: Why are you so stupid? Don't you know that it's not over? Why can't you use your heads?

He remembered himself and his mother in the kitchen when they had got hold of the newspaper with the great headlines:

TERMS OF THE PEACE TREATY
FREE STATE OF IRELAND
ARTICLES OF HISTORIC AGREEMENT
A RELATIONSHIP THE SAME AS WITH CANADA
'ULSTER' GETS A MONTH TO SAY
IF SHE WILL STAY IN
IRISH PROVISIONAL GOVERNMENT AT ONCE

It was only when you read on that you realized the Irish Republic was lost in the small print. He remembered feeling sick, incredulous and utterly bewildered that they all assumed now everything was all right, very good, terrific agreement, solid future, friends forever. Couldn't they see?

So he and his mother thought: It will be all right. The Dáil will never ratify this Treaty. They couldn't possibly. But they did.

So he wondered if this hysterical welcome was to blind their minds to the future; whistling passing a graveyard; telling fairy tales to brighten the hardship of reality; holding a great wake to forget the actuality of death.

The prisoners came in a stream. They were welcomed, jostled, clapped on the back, and carried to the drays and the sidecars and the motor cars, and the cavalcade set off towards the Square and the parade of the main streets.

The crowds around Dominic thinned, as most of them followed after the cars, shouting and singing the songs that the Rising had given birth to; not listening to the words, he thought, or they would have seen the mockery of the situation.

He was almost alone when he saw the figure of Peter come out of the station and stand on the steps, a cardboard package under his arm. Dominic paused for a moment, searching his face. It was thin, and his body didn't fill out his clothes. Dominic thought he looked sad.

He ran lightly up the steps and faced him. Peter's tired eyes turned to him. Dominic drew himself up and made a very good salute and said: 'Welcome home, Captain!' They looked at one another for a moment, and then he put his arm around him and squeezed his shoulder.

'You dodged the parade, Captain?' he said.

'It should be hearses,' said Peter. 'What have they done to us, Dominic?'

Dominic knew that Peter was as bewildered as he was himself.

'I have a hired car down the road,' he said. 'Your mother is waiting at home for you. We spent days and days whitewashing the place for you.'

'Can you whitewash a country?' Peter asked.

'Can't you be a bit happy?' Dominic asked. 'Can't these things wait for a night and a day until we go home and all the

277

neighbours welcome you and we get drunk and eat roast goose and currant cake?'

Peter smiled.

'All right,' he said. 'Sure, we can't disappoint the neighbours. And it's good to see you, Dominic. Weren't you lucky to stay out of their hands?'

'I was,' said Dominic, after a pause. 'Come now. We better go straight home. They will have your coming timed to the minute. I will give you an account of my stewardship tomorrow.'

'They didn't find the dump?' Peter asked as they went down the steps.

'No,' said Dominic.

'Good,' said Peter. 'We'll need them.' He was grim.

'Smile, Peter,' said Dominic. 'Look, you are home. Weren't you always the one with the quip and the joke? Whatever we have to face, let us face it with our teeth if we can't put our hearts into it.'

'That's it,' said Peter. 'We'll go home and we'll get drunk for a night and a day.'

But they didn't get home just then.

There were two men waiting at the turn out from the station. They came against them. Dominic recognized one of them who had been with Michael John the time Poric was wounded.

'Hello, Pakey,' he said, holding out his hand.

Pakey shook it. 'Michael John would like to see you both,' he said.

Peter and Dominic looked at one another.

'All right,' said Peter, 'we'll go and see Michael John.'

The two men led the way. They followed after them, thinking: Michael John, what way would Michael John jump? This uncertainty. Dominic had been wondering if he was alone with his thoughts and his sickness. Not now, because he knew that Peter felt the same. But what about men like Michael John? He thought of Sam saying: Men are walking on opposite sides of the street.

In the distance behind them as they turned to the right they

278

could hear the great volume of sound thrown up by the narrow streets, and once when he turned to look he could see the reflection of the thousands of torches on the low-lying clouds.

They went in a passage that was dark, and a door opened, and they went along a dimly lighted hallway. He could hear a lot of voices on his left, and the clink of glasses and the smell of porter. Then they followed Pakey into this room. It held no glasses, no porter, just some wooden chairs and a plain table, and sitting at the table was Michael John, and Morgan.

They both rose. 'Morgan!' Dominic said, most pleased to see him. His face was calm and pale, and his mouth with its thin lips twisted into an attractive smile as he shook Dominic's hand. Michael John was welcoming Peter with abandon, nearly lifting him off his feet.

They sat down at the table. There was only the four of them now. Morgan's face was sober.

'Tell us something, Dominic,' he said. 'How do you feel?'

Dominic thought over it. 'This is something,' he said, 'that every man must settle for himself. It is the same as making up your mind about the existence of God.'

'It doesn't have to be thought over,' said Peter.

'Let him go on,' said Morgan.

'Well,' said Dominic. 'My brother always talked of me as the reluctant revolutionary. This was true. I had to reason my way to it. But when I did, I took an oath and this is the oath I took. *"I do solemnly swear that I do not and shall not yield a voluntary support to any pretended Government, authority, or power within Ireland hostile and inimical thereto, and I do further swear that to the best of my knowledge and ability I will support and defend the Irish Republic and the Government of the Irish Republic, which is Dáil Éireann, against all enemies, foreign and domestic, and I will bear true obedience and allegiance to the same, and that I take this obligation freely without any mental reservation or purpose of evasion, so help me God."'*

There was silence in the room as he said this, thinking over it, and pronouncing it.

'The Free State is not the Republic,' he said. 'This Provisional Government is not Dáil Éireann.'

Morgan let the breath out of his mouth, and put his arms on the table.

'Your brother Dualta doesn't feel like that,' he said, looking quizzically at Dominic. He saw the frown on Dominic's forehead.

'Do you know this for sure?' he asked.

'I do,' said Morgan. Dominic thought over this, his heart sinking.

'Peter and myself are going home to a reception committee,' he said. 'You know where we stand?'

'I do,' said Morgan. 'We must count heads. They will be hard days ahead. We have to know. Now we know about Peter and you and we know where to find you.'

'And soon,' said Peter, hitting the table with his hand. 'Soon, Morgan. Don't let them build barricades.'

'Right,' said Morgan. 'You go home and count your heads, Peter. And be sure of them. Persuasion can only come from strength, not weakness.'

The parade had cleared the town as they drove home.

One thing they saw at the barracks near the canal bridge. The doors of the barracks were opened and many women and children were going in and coming out of the place. They were looting the barracks of various things, furniture and satchels and bric-a-brac, and the strange thing was that they were doing all this under the smiles of the policemen, who were joking with them. They had to stop the car for a time before they found a space to drive on. The kids were screaming. Shouting: 'Hey, Joe, look what I got!' waving a patent-leather satchel, or an odd black boot.

It seemed to Dominic a mean way for their foes to leave, because they were leaving. There was no grace or dignity about an evacuation like this, organized looting under their sardonic gaze.

They didn't talk much on the way home. It was all right for Dominic to advise laughter and good humour, but he felt none of it himself, nor any elation at the sight of the hated policemen and their auxiliaries finally packing.

They cheered up at the sight of the first bonfire, and from then on they had no time for gloom even if they wanted to be gloomy.

The people took Peter from the car and carried him on their shoulders up that long long road to the place of Eamon of the Shop where Pierce and Poc Murray and the remnants of his company were waiting to welcome him, and it was a good hour before they delivered him to his mother, promising to retrieve him again in an hour for the real festivities. By that time Peter was half drunk. Dominic himself wasn't quite sober, but he managed to drive the car to his own house.

When he went in Poric was talking to his mother in the kitchen.

He seemed a bit embarrassed, Dominic thought.

'Poric,' he said, 'you weren't at the welcome. What came over you?'

'I wasn't,' said Poric, grinning. 'I'm going down later on. I wanted to tell you my news first.'

'What news is this?' Dominic asked.

'It's great news,' said Poric. 'Sean Ned has been made a lieutenant in the new army and I am being called up to the new police, the Civic Guard. Isn't this great news, Dominic?'

Dominic sat on a chair and shook his head to clear it of the fumes.

'Tell me that again, Poric,' he said. 'You are going off to join the new police and Sean Ned is in the new army. Do you mean that bunch of bastards out at Beggars Bush?'

'What's up, Dominic?' Poric asked. He was genuinely puzzled, Dominic saw.

'You stupid bullock, Poric,' he said. 'Can't you read the signs of the times. You cannot go and join this bunch. They have sold the Republic. Don't you read a paper? Where have you been?'

'But they are our own Government,' said Poric. 'Isn't this what it was all about? Now we have our own Government, we fight for them. Isn't this the way it is?'

'It is not,' said Dominic. 'They are no Government. They are a crowd of opportunists who have come together to bury

281

the Republic. You cannot have anything to do with them, Poric. Use your head.'

'Look,' said Poric. 'I want to be a policeman. I was in the other police and then I was in the Republican Police. Now they write and say I am to be in the new police, the Civic Guard.'

'Who writes to you, who writes to you?' Dominic asked.

'Why, Dualta,' said Poric. 'He arranged it all. I'm going off tomorrow.'

'Look, Poric,' said Dominic. 'These are not new police. They are not Republican Police. They are going to be a force of oppression, to put down people who disagree with this provisional Government. You can't do this, Poric. You just can't do it.'

Poric stood up. Dominic, in complete disbelief, noticed that his mouth was tight.

'The way I see it, Dominic,' he said, 'this is the Government, and they have the right to form a new army and a new police, and I am asked to be one of their policemen and I'm going to be one. My brother Sean Ned thinks the same as I do.'

Dominic said: 'Poric, I wouldn't believe it of you. After all we have been through together, I wouldn't believe it of you. You can't do this.'

'I'm sorry, Dominic,' said Poric. 'But I am going to do it.'

'Get to hell out of here,' said Dominic.

'Dominic!' said his mother.

'Go on!' said Dominic. 'Get to hell out of here. If you can throw our friendship out of the window for the sake of these people, there's very little friendship between us. Go on, now, Poric!'

He walked away from him and stood looking out the window into the dark night.

Poric moved towards the door. He was puzzled and hurt, Dominic's mother saw, like a big child who had offered a gift to a grown-up and had been rebuffed.

'I didn't think you'd feel like this, Dominic,' he said. 'I was great with joy. I thought everything was fine. They signed the Treaty and we have peace and our own Government and our own army and our own police. I thought like this. I didn't know you felt against it.'

'Well, you know now,' said Dominic, turning towards him. 'You big slob. You have no brains. You don't know what's happening. Do this thing and you'll always regret it.'

'It's the way I think, Dominic,' said Poric pleadingly.

'If that's the way you think,' shouted Dominic, 'you should never have left the old police. You were well suited to them. You didn't have to go through all that you went through just to go back to them again, because that's what you are doing. You will probably be sharing a bunk with the bastard that belted you with a buckle. But you can't see this!'

Poric was bewildered at the anger in Dominic's eyes. He was looking at Poric as if he hated him.

'Every man is entitled to his opinion,' he said. 'That's all that's in it, Dominic. This is the way I think.'

'If that's the way, then I'm sorry for you,' said Dominic. 'And all I want to do is to see the back of you.'

He walked over to the fire and kicked at the smouldering sods of turf.

He knew Poric was standing there looking at him. He could imagine the look on his face. But he didn't care. This was bigger than friendship. He heard the door closing.

'Is he gone?' he asked.

'He is gone,' said his mother sadly.

Suddenly, Dominic felt sad. He sat on the stool with his head in his hands.

'This is bigger than friendship, Mother,' he said. 'You see that?'

'I don't know,' his mother said. 'Friendship is a big thing too.'

'And Dualta!' said Dominic. 'Dualta! What's wrong with Dualta? Where did he get twisted?'

'Dominic,' she said, her voice tired. 'You cannot take it all on your own back. All men don't see the same things the same way.'

'Then they are looking at it with blinded eyes,' said Dominic. 'If only I could see Dualta, and talk with him!'

He was to get the opportunity.

29

IT WAS a July morning when Sam came up the dusty road on his bicycle. He left his bicycle leaning against the wall outside the gate. He stood for some time looking at the house before he sighed and came in. Another time he would have gone round the back way into the yard. He would have joked with Brid or Poc if he was in the yard and then gone into the kitchen, where Dominic's mother would have immediately hung the kettle on the crook to make tea.

Now he went to the door and knocked formally, taking off his hat and holding it in his hand.

There was a delay before it opened. Dominic's mother stood there wiping her hands on her apron. Her eyes lighted up when she saw who was at the door. He was pleased to see this.

'Sam!' she said, 'it is so long since we saw you. Come on in! I'll just put the kettle on the fire.'

'No, not now, ma'am,' said Sam, but she did it anyhow and he followed her in.

'Isn't the weather very good?' she said.

'Yes,' said Sam. 'The weather is indeed good. Is Dominic around?'

She straightened herself from the fire. He thought she was growing old. Her hair, as thick as ever, tied in heavy plaits around her head, was almost completely white. She had a fine sensitive face, and her eyes were clear, but she looked sorrowful.

'Yes,' she said, 'Dominic is here. He is back in his father's room. You are lucky to catch him. He is rarely here now. I might as well have no sons.'

'Well,' said Sam. 'That's what I'm here about. Dualta is coming.'

Her hand went up to her heart as if it had suddenly started beating too fast.

'How do you know?' she asked.

'He came to me,' said Sam. 'I am a person now, ma'am,

284

that all men spit out of their mouths. I'm a neutral. So he came to me and asked me if I would come out and see you and tell you he was coming and to tell you he was coming, whether or which, and he didn't care if Dominic was here or if he wasn't here. This is the bald message.'

She sat down on a chair feeling for the back of it with her hand. 'I haven't seen Dualta for over a year,' she said. 'Of course he has written letters, but letters are not very satisfactory, are they?'

'No, ma'am,' said Sam, who had got into the habit of believing that there should never be anything in writing.

He heard the room door opening. Dominic came into the kitchen. He stood there and looked at Sam. Sam looked back at him boldly. Sam wasn't afraid of anyone, really. He had taken up a position and he was sticking to it, however much it was breaking his heart. He waited to see what Dominic's reaction would be. This Dominic, he thought, has become a man in a shorter time than anyone I remember. But who wouldn't in these times? Sam often looked at the young men like Dominic and could cry for them because they had lost their youth too fast.

Dominic came to shake hands with him. He was smiling. Sam noticed that when he smiled there were definite creases in his face.

'I'm glad to see you, Sam,' he said. His handclasp was firm.

'You don't think those who are not with you are against you?' Sam asked.

'Not you, Sam,' said Dominic. 'We know where your heart is, even if your hand won't follow it.' He sat on a chair sideways, his arm encircling the back of it.

'You heard what he said,' his mother said. 'Dualta is coming.'

'He can only come the coast road,' said Dominic. 'It's the only small slice left they can travel on.'

'Will you wait?' she asked. 'Will you quarrel? If you think you will, I don't want you to wait.'

Dominic thought over this. He felt anger rising in him, but he suppressed it.

'I will wait,' he said. 'I hope we won't quarrel. You look very respectable, Sam.'

Sam did. He was wearing a brown suit. His boots were dusty from the road. He wore a stiff butterfly collar around his thin neck and a neat tie with a pin in it.

'I am respectable,' said Sam. 'I go to my job from nine-thirty until five-thirty. I'm trying to make up for all the lost hours I owe the job.'

'Are you bored, Sam?' Dominic asked. 'Have you no niggling desire to be at the middle of things, finding out in your mysterious ways all that is going on?'

'No,' said Sam. 'Not much. It's easy to see now what's going on, isn't it? The first shots have been fired, haven't they? The first brothers have died, haven't they? Oh, yes, Dominic, I know what is going on.'

'I'm making the tea,' his mother said. 'Turn into the table.'

Sam had made no effect on Dominic. His eyes were hard all the time he was speaking. Sam was used to this look now, the impatient moving of the body. He thought sometimes that they were becoming petrified inside themselves, so that sometime they would end up not men of blood and flesh at all, but men of stone.

'Poor Sam,' said Dominic. 'Why did Dualta use you as an advance scout?'

'Don't say that,' said Sam. 'I am nobody's scout. You know that.'

'Sorry, Sam,' said Dominic, reaching for a piece of bread and buttering it, just to be doing something. He wanted to be nice to Sam. Sam was all right, but there was no halfway in these things. There was no time to wait for explanations. There was no use talking of past friendships; of the men who had gone one way and the men who had gone another. 'Who are you neutral against?' he asked. He couldn't help himself. 'Sorry again, Sam,' he said. His shirt sleeves were rolled. His arms were muscular and hairy and sunburned, Sam saw. He was all the time moving, his legs, or his hands, or his arms, or his eyes. He wasn't calm any more.

They had finished one cup of tea when they heard the

distant sound of the lorries. They looked at one another and listened.

'What's the difference?' Dominic asked sardonically. 'It's just the same sound, because they are the same lorries.'

'One lorry, one car,' said Sam. 'You couldn't expect him to come on his own with things the way they are?'

'If he had the courage of his convictions he would have come on his own,' said Dominic.

'Dominic,' said his mother. 'Dualta is my son. He has his convictions. You have yours. If you think there will be trouble between you and him, in the name of God, I ask you to go, now.'

She saw the tenseness flowing out of him. He came over to her. He put his hands on her shoulders and his cheek against her hair.

'No row, Mother,' he said. 'I promise you. I will be calm.'

They heard the sound of the car coming to a stop outside the gate and the engine throbbing. They heard the sound of the lorry close to it. Then the engine sounds died. They heard the squeak of the gate and the heavy footsteps on the gravel. The door was open so that he could come in, and he came in and looked at them.

He was dressed in the uniform of a Free State Captain, dark green, with polished leather straps from his shoulders supporting the broad belt at his waist, from which a holstered revolver was hanging.

'Mother,' said Dualta, holding out his arms and coming over to her. Dominic walked to the window. The sight of the uniform filled him with revulsion. He wanted to say: Khaki became you better, brother, but he managed to bite it back. He looked blindly out the window, then saw that the car held two Free State soldiers in front and the lorry held about ten of them. They had their rifles in their hands, pointing outwards.

Dualta thought his mother hesitated before she came into his arms. This somehow was like a blow in the heart to him. But he squeezed her and held her out from him to look at her. She obliterated the first thought then, by raising her hands to his face, and pressing his cheeks.

'I am glad to see you, Dualta. It is so long. You are well?'

'Fine,' he said. 'Fine. I couldn't come any sooner. And now I have only come to say Hello and Goodbye.'

'You will have tea,' she said. 'It is in the pot.'

'I will have tea,' he said. He sat on a chair and threw his cap on the table. Sam looked at the cap badge, a double F with radiations in bronze.

'You are a hot man on a bicycle, Sam,' said Dualta. 'You made it in the time you said you would.'

'I have good lasting wind,' said Sam. Dualta was drumming his fingers on the table, or rather one thumb and a finger, Sam saw. There was something wrong with the rhythm on that account. It made him sad.

'Hello, brother,' said Dualta, looking towards the window.

'Hello,' said Dominic, turning and coming down, standing with his back to the fire. Their faces were like closed books in hard covers, Sam thought.

'Good weather for the hay,' said Dualta.

'Good weather for everything,' said Dominic.

'Here's your tea, Dualta,' said his mother.

'Thank you, Mother,' he said. He put in sugar and started to stir it. Dominic sat down. His mother sat down. He looks very well in that uniform, his mother was thinking. Dualta always made a good-looking soldier. His fair hair was thick, but there were many lines on his face, she noticed, too soon, too soon, and why do they have to grow up so soon? The feeling between them was almost tangible. How did this happen?

'Brid is well?' Dualta asked. He mentioned other names of the neighbours. It was very forced. There was absolutely no way out of their dilemma. So Dualta burst it.

'Can I talk to you, Dominic?' he asked, remarking how hard he found it to pronounce the name of his brother.

'Yes,' said Dominic. 'We can go up to the room.'

'Do one thing for me,' said their mother, her hands clenched.

'What is it?' Dualta asked.

'Let Sam be with you,' she said.

'That's fine,' said Dominic, relieved. 'It's an ideal position for Sam to be in.' He walked over to the room door and went in.

'Dualta,' his mother said. 'Please go easy. Let you both go easy. Thank you, Sam.'

'I'm only trying to save him, Mother,' said Dualta. 'I have nothing against him.' This must be a lie, he thought, when I find it hard to pronounce his name. 'Come on, Sam. You can be chairman.'

Sam found himself sweating at the thought, but at the pleading look in the woman's eye he rose and followed Dualta into the room. He closed the door behind him. Dominic was standing at the window, his hands clenched behind his back.

'We better sit down,' Sam said. He would prefer to be any place else in the world, even in jail.

He sat on the old man's chair. The table was covered with a green cloth. The room remained unchanged. It was a history of the Irish nation in pictures and ballads. Poor Ireland, Sam thought. Dualta was frowning as he looked at three rifles that leaned against the wall near the fireplace. He suddenly turned and sat. Dominic sat on the opposite side from him.

'I'm here for one reason,' said Dualta. 'I want to save your life, because you are my brother, and if you continue on the road you are going you will lose it.'

'Or you,' said Dominic. 'Is it too late to ask you to come back to the Republic?'

Dualta indicated his uniform.

'I am the Republic,' he said, his lips tight.

'You represent,' said Dominic, 'not the Republic, but a country you have created whose name sounds like a spit.'

Dualta put his head in his hands. Then he dropped them on the table.

'I'm not going to let you make me mad,' he said.

'Listen, Dualta,' said Dominic. 'Please don't treat me any more as if I was a young brother in short pants without a mind of his own. We are on level terms now. Just don't do big brother for me or I'll get up and walk out of here.'

'All right,' said Dualta. 'You are grown up. Look, we accepted the Treaty because it was the best terms we could get at the time. We regard the Treaty as a stepping stone, the freedom to achieve freedom.'

'You signed an ignoble document,' said Dominic. 'You betrayed your oath to the Republic.'

'If the Treaty was not signed,' said Dualta patiently, 'we would have been faced with an immediate and terrible war. These were their words.'

'What had they been doing up to that, playing tiddly-winks?' Dominic asked.

'In comparison,' said Dualta. 'We didn't defeat them. We made it impossible for them to rule.'

'If they had a pill box every five yards of the country,' said Dominic, 'we would have found ways to beat them. We were all one, people and volunteers, and you destroyed that with your pens.'

'Listen,' said Dualta. 'I know it's nearly impossible to make you see. The people were tired of war. They wanted peace. The very people that voted for peace were the ones that nurtured us in their houses on the hillsides. These were the ones. They were tired and they wanted peace and you won't give it to them.'

'Not all of them,' said Dominic. 'Not all of them, brother. You had the slanted Press and the power of the pulpit behind you, and voting registers from which not even the men who fought them to a truce could put their names to a vote. You bound no fighting man to you, Dualta, only opportunists and people mad for power and all the tradesmen and sycophants who would have as cheerfully voted for the Union Jack.'

'All right,' said Dualta. 'Your mind is set. Now you can listen to the talk of power. You will be crushed, because we have the power.'

'Even so,' said Dominic, 'what will it prove? Will your conscience always be easy? If you grind the last one of us into a blob of blood, do you think you will have won anything?'

Dualta persisted.

'We tried everything with them. You know that. Pacts and promises, coalitions.'

'You reneged on every one,' said Dominic.

'God dammit,' said Dualta. 'Somebody has to rule.'

'With borrowed guns,' said Dominic, 'like you used on the Four Courts and in the Dublin streets?'

'Just tell me, just tell me,' said Dualta, 'what makes you think that you have all the right on your side? Just tell me. Try and persuade me.'

'Nobody can persuade you,' said Dominic. 'When you threw away your oath to the Republic and spat on the graves of the men who had died for it, you went on past persuasion. There is nothing left to you but the cannon of our enemy and a paid professional army filled with the disbanded members of British regiments. You will be sorry, Dualta, believe me. You will be sorry.'

'Listen, you poor simpleton,' said Dualta. 'Your head is filled with dreams, and romantic notions that have nothing to do with reality. Listen, you won't be fighting them, but us, and we know you. You are our brothers. We know how you think and how you feel. We know where you keep your dumps and your hideouts, and we'll winkle you out of every one of them. We'll sweep the jails and fill them with your leaders. We'll bring you to your senses.'

'Now you are talking,' said Dominic. 'Now you are out in the open.'

'For God's sake, Dominic, can't you listen to reason!' Dualta shouted. 'I don't want you to die. I don't want you to end up in jail. You are my brother. There can be only one end to it all. Can you listen to me, for the love of God!'

'I've listened long enough to you,' said Dominic, standing. 'You have said all you came to say. Now if you don't want to stay, you can go.'

'I tried,' said Dualta, standing. 'Nobody can say that I didn't try.'

He went out of the room, fast. He went down to the kitchen. His mother was standing near the fire. He put his hands on her shoulders.

'Mother,' he said. 'Mother, where do you stand? Just tell me, where do you stand?'

'Dualta,' she said. 'Are you asking me to choose between my two sons?'

'For his sake, that stupid stubborn fool,' he said.

'Your father was called a stupid stubborn fool too,' she said.

'All right,' he said. 'Just tell me.'

'You cannot partition freedom,' she said. 'You cannot divide liberty.' He dropped his hands from her shoulders. He groaned.

'What hope is there for him when even you feel that way,' he said. He turned from her and walked to the door, taking his cap from the table and pulling it down over his eyes. He turned at the door. 'Mother,' he said, pointing at her, knowing Dominic was standing in the room door. 'Talk him out of it. Get him away from it, if you love him. There can be only one end for him, I tell you, only one end. And you are his mother.'

'Oh, Dualta,' she said. 'Please sit down and drink tea and we can talk of times long ago, not now, and the way you are feeling. Dualta, please come back and we will sit and talk.'

'It's too late,' he said and went away. His angry boots were heavy on the gravel.

She just stood there, and she was crying. Dominic didn't feel good. He came over to her. He put his arms around her shoulders. He was upset, because she was always one to cry in the night time.

'Don't, Mother,' he said. 'It will be all right. Everything will be all right,' knowing of course that it wouldn't and that he hated the sight of his brother. Maybe if he was out of that uniform. But all he had to do was to conjure up the sight of him and he felt real hatred, so that he could tackle him with his bare hands and kill him and feel no remorse. His limbs were trembling.

Sam was putting on his hat going out the door.

He looked back at them and his face was stricken.

'Oh, my poor country,' said Sam, and went out as the lorry and the car roared into reverse and set off back towards the town.

Dualta, sitting in the back of the open car, was glad of the breeze on his hot face. He was sweating under his clothes. He was trembling. It was all so clear to him, every move that had happened from the beginning of the Truce – until now. Nobody could foresee that the others would be so stubborn in their false faith. You could understand the desire to share in power, but the sublimation of romanticism and Celtic twilight to this degree was terrible.

Five miles on he saw the sudden movement on the bridge ahead of him and came awake from his feelings. He stood, tapping the driver on the shoulder and shouting 'Fast! Fast!'. He saw the men on the bridge ahead of them. He pulled out his revolver and fired in their direction. He had no hope of hitting them. But they looked up and they ran, jumping the stone wall at the side and into the heather. 'Fast! Fast!' he said to the driver, and they roared over the bridge. He had turned and waved at the lorry behind. It had picked up speed. When they crossed the bridge themselves he looked behind at the lorry. Some of the men were firing at the figures scattering up the hillside. It would do little good. You can't be accurate from a moving vehicle, but they crossed the bridge and had no sooner crossed it than it went up in a flame and then a plume of black smoke. 'Keep going!' he shouted at the driver. 'Just keep going! We'll be back for them soon.'

Then he sat down in the seat.

Later he stood on the roof of the Free State headquarters in the town and watched the barracks in Renmore burning. It was like a scene out of the Inferno. The flames were reaching a hundred feet into the air and the looters were coming back with their spoils, chairs and tables and iron bedsteads and blankets and food.

The officer who was with him said, 'Well, we squeezed them out of there anyhow, even if they burned it. They are great arsonists, these Republicans.'

'Not Republicans,' said Dualta. 'After all, we are the Republicans. They are irregulars. You must remember that.'

'My apologies,' said the officer.

'Somebody must put out the fire.' said Dualta.

'If there is anything left,' said the officer. 'We Irish are a wonderful people. Aren't we?'

'We are,' said Dualta. 'We are.'

Suddenly he thought of Dominic and himself sitting by a haycock near the sea, and he felt very sad, but he knew that this was merely sentimentality.

30

IT WAS October. The night was pitch black. There was a strong south-east wind blowing in from the sea. Dominic was leaning against the bank, waiting, like all the rest of them. He thought he could taste the salt from the sea on his lips. He could see the men in front of him and a few of the men behind him and the bulk of their few vehicles drawn into the side under the bank. They had been walking for eight hours. They had been waiting now for twenty minutes and he could feel the wind cold on his face and ears.

He tensed when he heard the sounds in front of him. He left his shelter and cautiously went up the road where Morgan and the others were gathered.

He heard the sound of their voices, cut short by the wind.

The scouts were back. Morgan and Joe Two and Peter were there with other leaders.

Morgan said: 'So they got careless. You hear that? We will go in as we planned. They have no pickets out, only the sentries in front of the barracks. Start the column moving. Stop at the Cross. We'll split up there. Right.'

Dominic went back. He said to his men: 'Move on' and then set off himself, taking his rifle from his back and carrying it in the crook of his arm like a shotgun. God be with the days of stalking the wild geese, he thought. You went through just as much hardship as this but for a different reason.

The strong wind was good. It muffled the sounds of their moving; of the boots of the men and the chug-chug of the engines of their transport. You just had to keep your mind blank, he thought, holding your breath the same as the stalking of the birds, not to think, just to carry out your part.

Morgan was at the Cross with Peter.

Peter said: 'We'll cut left here now, Dominic. You have your watch.'

'I have,' said Dominic.

'If you hear shooting,' said Peter, 'start your operations right away. Otherwise, wait on the watch.' He set off to the left, with his men following after him. If it was daylight you would have been surprised to see some of the men following him wearing Free State uniforms. They were men who had come over to them with their arms and they would be used as a war trick if possible. He thought of the round trip Peter would have to make, up the hills and circling the small town by the sea, and coming in from the back.

Morgan said: 'Are you right now, Dominic?'

'Yes,' said Dominic.

'We'll wait for you to start it. Start it whatever happens. If we are not in place it will be our own fault.'

'Something I remember, Morgan,' said Dominic.

'What is it?' Morgan asked.

'Remember that time back, that good ambush against the others? You said something to me then before it began. You said all the tribes were together at last, the O'Flahertys and Joyces and O'Malleys. A few hundred years ago we would have been killing one another.'

He could barely see Morgan, just the outline of him and the soft hat he wore that shaded his face.

He felt Morgan's hand on him, squeezing his shoulder.

'That's the birth pangs of a nation, Dominic,' he said. 'We have to ride the wind.' Dominic thought his voice was hard, but somehow sad in its hardness.

'Good luck, Morgan,' he said.

'Collect the women,' said Morgan, 'and bring them in with you. The cellar should be prepared if all has gone well. With no pickets out there should be no danger, but walk easy.' He turned away on the road to the right.

Dominic went back. 'Are you all right, Poc?' he asked.

'Rarin',' said Poc. He had with him five other men, Reardons and Conroys.

Dominic walked back. He stopped at the first car.

'All right, Finola,' he said. 'You and the other girls come with us. Stay close. If I tell you to scatter, scatter. Get back here to the car.'

He saw them coming out, gathering up their bags of bandages and supplies. There had to be women in war, but he regretted it. If they were at home they would be in jail.

When he saw that they were ready, he set off. The three girls were behind him, followed by the men.

They started down the road into the town. They had to take this town. They were being squeezed to death by two arms. The others had landed from the sea farther up the coast, and taken a sea town there. They had had to abandon that, burning the barracks after them. It was the same strategy in the South. Landing from the sea, pregnant with more and more power and arms supplied to them by their former enemies. Cork was gone and the towns of the South, and the fighting was being squeezed into the hills, the old guerrilla fighting all over again. So they had to break the arm of this town. It was filled with supplies and guns and ammunition which they badly needed.

The leaves were scattered at the edges of the road and the wind took them and sent them playing along, making a tapping noise on the ground. This was a good sound, as it camouflaged the noise they were making themselves.

They came to the street of the town, down the hill. He could barely see the houses on the opposite side of the street. He had to bend down to see their bulk against the sky. There weren't many stars to be seen. There were black clouds scudding across the sky. There will be rain later, his mind recorded. He counted from the end house in the row until he came to the one he wanted. It was easy enough to pick out since it was a storey higher than the others.

'Now,' he whispered. 'Go fast, and go easy if you can. If you see anyone, drop flat and hope for the best.'

He took a long breath and then ran across the road. He was accompanied by hundreds of leaves, laughing, he thought, but they covered their move very well. He waited crouched in a doorway until he was sure they were all behind him. Then he moved on, counting. When he came to the door he paused, then pushed it with his hand and it opened. 'Down the cellar,' he whispered. He followed them in and closed the door. He felt for the big bolt and shot it home. Then he shuffled in the hall until he felt the steps on the right under the stairs. He went down those, cautiously. They were wooden steps and steep. As he got near the end of them he noticed a light coming on below.

It was a big cellar. The windows were boarded off. Somebody had lighted a candle and then another one. They were thick Christmas candles and their butts were set into turnips cut in half. There was an iron fireplace with a fire burning in it and two big kettles were steaming.

'We could be at home,' said Poc. 'Girls, ye ought to make a cup of tea.'

The others laughed.

'Shush,' said Dominic. He went to the boarded window on the right which was facing towards the barracks. He could see nothing. 'There is a sentry across the road,' he said. That quietened them. He went over to Finola. She was taking stuff out of her bag, bandages and bottles, very efficiently. He thought her face looked thin in the light of the candle. He supposed all their faces looked thin, and maybe drawn. He thought they had not laughed much for a long time. When they laughed, it was a bit hysterical, like long ago when the prisoners came home.

'You are all right, Finola?' he asked.

She looked at him, and smiled. 'I am all right, Dominic,' she said.

'It's a change from teaching little girls,' he said.

He thought her eyes were wistful.

'It is a change,' she said.

'Right, we'll go upstairs,' he said to the others.

'We'll be back for breakfast, girls,' said Poc. 'Turn my eggs and make the tea strong.'

Dominic looked at Finola again. She met his eyes. He thought how nice it would be to sit down and talk to her for a few hours if things were different. But things weren't different.

'If anything goes wrong,' he said, 'get into the streets and into some house. Don't let them take you.'

'All right,' she said, and he left her.

He divided them up. Two men at two windows in the top room, three in the second, and himself and Poc in the lower room. There was no need for them to break glass, since there was no glass in the windows. There had been a fight here in August when the others had invaded from the sea. He sat on the floor and rested the barrel of his rifle on the window frame. He thought there was a faint streak in the sky. He took the watch from his top pocket, disconnected it from the strap and placed it on the window sill. He could hardly see its face. The wind was blowing in through the open windows and exploring the room. It had blown some leaves in here too and was moving them around like scratching fingers.

He waited.

It was a good plan, like all Morgan's. The others were in two barracks. Morgan would take care of the other one, which was the stronger. The one they were attacking was merely a requisitioned house that had been strengthened with sandbags and barbed wire. They didn't quite know how many soldiers were in there. He listened now. Over the noise of the wind he thought he could hear the boots of the sentry on the pavement. He would be the first man to die.

He hadn't shot at a Free Stater yet. He thought now of Sam's sardonic question about could he shoot a policeman. In these times was this the total value of a man's worth? He thought of his brother Dualta. He had been right in a lot of respects. Dualta was a pragmatist, he thought. Dualta would use power ruthlessly, like they were using it. The dusted prisons were filling nicely again like the skin of a blood pudding. The internment camps were open for custom. Military courts were set up. The penalty for being caught carrying arms was now execution. Nobody had any doubts that there would be executions. So you were better off to be caught dead than caught alive. There was military censorship, all the privileges of power. And they were trapping the leaders. They knew too much about movements of men, and dumps of arms. Why? Because the glorious unity of the people had been shattered. It was pitiful the way the propaganda was working. Brave men were captured and you read in the papers that all and each one of them shouted with their hands up: Don't shoot! Please don't shoot! I am not armed! When you knew these men and their courage and bravery, it made you sick to read this schoolboy propaganda; wondering if people would believe it, afraid they would. He thought of wide areas of the country laid waste; with burning barracks, blown bridges, toppled telephone poles.

He stopped thinking and peered out the window. He gripped his rifle. Because the dawn was here. The sentry across the road was standing now. Dominic could see his figure but not his face; the spread legs in the brown leggings and the shape of the rifle.

He let the tip of his rifle peep over the sill and took aim at the face of the soldier and waited for the light.

He hadn't killed anyone yet. All he had been engaged in was the detail of the evacuation of a town, the burning of their quarters so the others couldn't use them, the payment of traders, one or two long-distance skirmishes in the hills, firing at long range. But this was different.

He watched and saw the face of the soldier appear, his chin resting on the foresight of his rifle.

Slowly, slowly his face came into view.

It was a very young face, he saw, as Irish as an Arran Banner potato. He was moving his face from side to side, trying to keep awake. His eyes would close and his head droop a little, then he would come alive again with a jerk. Several times he put his free hand up and rubbed his eyes. As the light got brighter, Dominic saw that he was very young. He could only be seventeen. He could nearly see the down on his face.

He looked at his watch. It was only a minute off the time. Now everybody should be in place; Peter and his men would be around the back of the barracks.

He took a better sight of the young face. He looked at his

299

watch. He could imagine the bullet going into the forehead under the peak of the cap. He took the first pressure on the trigger and at the last moment raised the sights and saw the bullet hitting the masonry over the boy's head. Move now, his mind shouted at him, or I'll have to kill you. The boy moved. He went in through the sandbagged door like a rabbit. Dominic started firing at the windows of the house. All around him the firing started. He saw flashes coming their way from the windows as the soldiers woke from their sleep. Up on his right he could hear the sound of the guns, cackling he thought, cackling like an old crone, or the laughter of their enemies.

He heard the bullets that came in through his own window, hitting the soft plastered walls behind him and travelling on. Now and again a bullet hit the stonework of the window and whined away into the dawn. The shooting, he noticed, had outsounded the wind.

He watched the two men crawling along under the windows of the house opposite him. They were below the rifle fire. The soldiers could not look out, of course, so the men had an easy time, as Morgan predicted – if it is easy to be handling a home-made mine, pre-set, that might go off at any minute.

He fired a clip and reloaded and fired again. He had done this several times when the men ran away after crawling, and Dominic himself ducked under the sill. The blast that came shook the house and the floor he was lying on. He peered again. There was a pall of smoke around the doorway, but gradually, as the wind dispersed it, he saw that there was a black gaping hole where the door had been. This was the point where Peter would attack at the back, and they would have them between two fires. They could surrender or they could come running.

'Stay there!' he shouted at Poc. Poc nodded.

Out on the landing he shouted up the stairs: 'Now! Now!' He waited until he knew they heard him and he turned out and ran to the door that faced the barracks. It was bolted. He went on his knees and opened the bolt and drew in the door a few inches to him. He could see the soldiers coming out of the house. Some of them had only trousers and vests on them.

He saw their mouths open as they shouted. They lowered themselves from the windows and dropped, picking up their rifles. They were spewing out of the place. Some of them had their hands in the air, shouting. He waited until the last of them had come, followed by Peter who had a revolver in his hand. He was shouting too.

'Now!' Dominc shouted, flinging the door open and running out, going left, dropping on his knee, firing, getting up, going into a doorway, sighting, firing. Now more of Peter's men should be coming from the bottom of the street, so that the soldiers would be bottled up. On both sides of the street they moved fast. Into a doorway, sight, fire. The soldiers would have to give up. They had only what ammunition they took with them in their rifles.

But suddenly a strange thing happened.

An open car came from the end of the street. This couldn't be Peter's men. They had no car down there.

There was an officer in the car standing up and shooting from it. There were three soldiers with him. They got out of the car, and the officer stood up firing and rallying the soldiers from the house to him. 'To me! To me!' he was shouting and they were racing towards him, slanting across to find shelter behind the car and under the commands of an officer.

For a few moments it looked as if it would work, but then the sound of shots came from behind them and Dominic saw several of the soldiers fall as they went towards the car.

So he shouted: 'Now! Now!' and all his men came from their doorways and converged on the soldiers, shouting and calling, and firing their rifles, hardly aiming.

And then they were in among the soldiers, not firing now, using the butts.

It seemed to take so short a time.

Dominic saw a young soldier on the ground. His arms were raised over his head. There was awful fear in his face, half squatting, half leaning on the dusty ground.

One of the men raised a rifle butt to kill him, but Dominic lurched sideways against him saying: 'No! No!' falling himself on the ground and looking up to see the madness dying from the other man's face. He said gruffly to the young soldier, 'On your feet! On your feet!' and a strange thing, he noticed that this was the young soldier whose life he himself had spared a short time before. How lucky you are, he thought, how lucky you are, you don't know. He bent for his own rifle that was lying on the ground.

Now he could only hear the sound of the wind, and the firing still going on from far up the town. Here it was very peaceful. As he straightened with his rifle he found himself looking at a face. He saw this face. It was the face belonging to the officer, and he thought, I recognize that face. The head of the officer had been holding the cap on his head but now it rolled off, and the head turned until the cheek was in the dust and he was looking at the fair hair of his brother.

He couldn't believe this.

He thought it was just a hallucination, so he went over and he raised the officer by the shoulders and he rested his head on his knee. He found himself whimpering: 'Dualta! Dualta!' as if by calling his brother's name he would somehow make it a hallucination. But he didn't succeed. He put his hand on the cheek. It was quite warm to his touch. 'Dualta!' he said. 'Oh, Dualta! Wake up! It's me! It's Dominic!'

Dualta didn't answer him.

'Listen, Dualta,' he said. 'Listen, Dualta.'

Dualta didn't answer him, although his eyes were open and staring at the stormy sky.

Dominic raised him higher, until his head was resting on his shoulder. He could even see the small hole just at the bridge of his nose, which could be a bullet hole. He didn't know that his clothes were being soaked with blood from the hole in the back of Dualta's head.

He said again 'Dualta! Dualta! Listen, Dualta!' Patting his cheek. Dualta wanted a shave.

'This is not true,' he said. 'Listen, Dualta.'

He was conscious of a great silence, just the howling of the wind.

He heard her voice.

'Dominic! Dominic! It's no use, he's dead.'

302

He looked across at her. Her face was near his.

'It's my brother, Finola,' he said. 'It's Dualta.' He wanted to say, I don't mind that he is in this uniform. It doesn't matter, see. This is Dualta.

'He's dead, Dominic,' Finola said. 'Can't you listen? He's dead.'

His mouth was open. He was breathing hard as if he had been running a long way.

'Oh, Finola!' he said, and he dropped his head until his own face was resting on the face of his dead brother.

For how long?

He raised his head, and looked around. He could see he was surrounded by feet with boots and legs with leggings; different kinds of leggings, laced ones and strapped ones, and rifle butts resting on the ground. He looked at Finola. She was crying, he saw. But girls are always crying.

He was conscious of another sound as well as the wind, the sound of the engine of a car. They hadn't stopped the engine of Dualta's car.

He got on his knees now and he put his hands under his brother's body and he got to his feet holding him in his arms.

He looked around him.

Morgan stood looking at him, and Peter and the others. In silence. The shooting was over.

He looked at Morgan.

'He is my brother Dualta, Morgan,' he said.

'I know, Dominic,' said Morgan.

'I must take him home,' he said.

Morgan didn't answer him.

'He must go home,' said Dominic. 'I have to bring him to my mother.'

Morgan said nothing.

Dominic walked to the car. It had no doors. He gently put his brother into the back seat, straightened him up, his head resting against the high back. He took his hands and put them on his lap, pausing over the one with the missing fingers. He looked at his face. He reached and closed his eyes with his fingers. Now he looked as if he was sleeping.

He backed out, still looking at him.

Then he turned back to Morgan.

'You see,' he said, struggling for the words, 'it can become too much for the individual. Like this. Just little men, with love, and brothers. You see, men with brothers.'

He held out his hand, as if he was pleading. Morgan's jaws were tight, but his eyes were soft. He stood there with his legs spread, a revolver held loosely in his hand, a soft hat shading his face, a Sam Browne belt around his trench coat.

You make a bronze statue of a man like that, on a plinth with a rough sky behind him, 'lover of the lost cause that is never lost', carved on the pedestal.

Dominic got into the seat of the car behind the wheel and set it going and made a wide circle towards the edge of the town where it petered out along the coast road by the sea.

He was conscious of the circle of silent men he was leaving behind him. My friends, my dear comrades, forgive me, but this is my brother Dualta and he is dead and I may be the one that killed him.

He heard her shouting then.

'Dominic! Wait! Wait!'

He eased the speed of the car and she came to the side and she sat in beside him.

'You don't have to do this,' he said. 'Finola, you know you don't have to do this.'

'I must, Dominic,' she said. 'This has resolved it.'

He drove towards the coast road, driving by instinct, driving carefully, conscious of the burden he carried in the back seat and in his own heart, and when he started to cry she put out her hand and rested it on his. He was conscious of this.

The clouds broke over their heads and the threatened rain fell, and before them she could see the sea, and if she looked behind her she would see the smoke rising from the captured town.

But she didn't look behind her.

She kept looking ahead of her.